...**Art**... ...chieve-
...t Awa... ...inated
in the Best Contemporary Paranormal category of the
Romantic Times Reviewers' Choice Awards. She's a
dessert and function cook by trade, and lives in
Melbourne, Australia.

Visit her online:
www.keriarthur.com
www.facebook.com/AuthorKeriArthur
www.twitter.com/@kezarthur

Praise for Keri Arthur:

'Keri Arthur's imagination and energy infuse
everything she writes with zest'
Charlaine Harris, bestselling author of *Dead Until Dark*

'Keri Arthur is one of the best
supernatural romance writers in the world'
Harriet Klausner

his series is phenomenal! It keeps you spellbound
d mesmerized on every page. Absolutely perfect!'
FreshFiction.com

By Keri Arthur

DARKNESS UNMASKED

A Dark Angels Novel

KERI ARTHUR

piatkus

PIATKUS

First published in the US in 2013 by Signet Select an imprint of
New American Library
a division of Penguin Group (USA) Inc.
First published in Great Britain in 2013 by Piatkus

A CIP catalogue record for this book
is available from the British Library.

ISBN 978-0-7499-5721-6

Printed and bound by CPI (UK) Ltd, Croydon, CR0 4YY

Papers used by Piatkus are from well-managed forests
and other responsible sources.

MIX
Paper from
responsible sources
FSC® C104740

Piatkus
An imprint of
Little, Brown Book Group
100 Victoria Embankment
London EC4Y 0DY

An Hachette UK Company
www.hachette.co.uk

www.piatkus.co.uk

I'd like to thank the following people:

my editor, Danielle Perez; copy editor Penina Lopez; and the man responsible for the fabulous cover, Tony Mauro.

A special thanks to:

my fabulous agent, Miriam Kriss; my talented and funny crit buddies—Mel, Robyn, Chris, Carolyn, and Freya; and finally, my lovely daughter, Kasey.

DARKNESS
UNMASKED

Chapter 1

The office phone rang with a sharpness that jolted me instantly awake. I jerked upright, peeled a wayward bit of paper from my nose, and stared at the phone blankly. Then the caller ID registered and I groaned. The call was coming from Madeline Hunter, the bitch who was not only in charge of the Directorate of Other Races, but was a leading member of the high vampire council, too. She was also the very last person in this world—or the next—who I wanted to hear from right now.

Unfortunately, given that she was now my boss, she was not someone I could—or should—ignore.

I hit the vid-phone's ANSWER button and said in a less-than-polite voice, "What?"

She paused, and something flashed in the green of her eyes. A darkness that spoke of anger. But all she said was, "I have a task for you."

A curse rose in my throat, but I somehow managed to leash it. "What sort of task?"

But even as I asked the question, I knew. There was only one reason for her to be ringing me, and that was to track down an escapee from hell. She had not only the Directorate at her command, but a stableful of Cazadors—the high council's elite killing force—and they dealt with all manner of murderers and madmen on an everyday basis.

I even had one following me around astrally, reporting my every move back to Hunter. Trust was not high on her list of good traits.

Not that I think she had all that many good traits.

"A close friend of mine was murdered last night." Her voice held very little emotion, and she was scarier because of it. "I want you to investigate."

Hunter had friends. Imagine that. I scrubbed a hand across my eyes and said somewhat wearily, "Look, as much as I absolutely adore working for you, the reality is the Directorate is far better equipped to handle *this* sort of murderer."

"The Directorate hasn't your experience with the denizens of hell," she snapped. "Nor do they have a reaper at their beck and call."

So I'd been right—it *was* an escapee from hell. Not great news, but I guess it *was* my fault that these things were about in the world. It might have become my task to find the three lost keys that controlled the gates to heaven and hell, but the only one I'd managed to find so far had almost immediately been stolen from me. As a result, the first gate to hell had been permanently opened by person or persons unknown, and the stronger demons were now coming through. Not in great numbers—not yet—but that was thanks only to the fact that the remaining gates were still shut.

Of course, given the choice, I'd rather *not* find the other keys. After all, if no one knew where they were, then they couldn't be used to either permanently open or close the gates. But it wasn't like I had a choice, not anymore. It was either find them or die. Or, when it came to the choice given to me by my father—who was one of the Raziq, the rogue Aedh priests who'd helped create the keys, and also the man responsible for having them stolen—watch my friends die.

"Azriel isn't at my beck and call," I said, unable to hide the annoyance in my voice. "He just wants the keys, the same as you and the council."

Not to mention the Raziq and my goddamn father.

"*This* takes priority over finding the keys."

I snorted. "Since when?"

That darkness in her eyes got stronger. "Since I walked into my lover's house and discovered his corpse."

I stared at her for a moment, seeing little in the way of true emotion in either her expression or her voice. And yet her need for revenge, to rend and tear, was so strong that even through the vid-phone I could almost taste it. That sort of fury, I thought with a shiver, was not something I ever wanted aimed my way.

Yet, despite knowing it wasn't sensible, I couldn't help saying, "I'm betting the rest of the council wouldn't actually agree with that assessment."

I think if she could have jumped down the phone line and throttled me, she would have. As it was, she bared her teeth, her canines elongating just a little, and said in a soft voice, "You should not be worried about what the rest of the council is thinking right now."

The only time I'd stop worrying about the rest of the council was when she achieved her goal of supreme control over the lot of them. Until then, they were as big a threat to me as she was.

But I wasn't stupid enough to actually come out and say *that* to her. "Hunting for your friend's killer is going to steal precious time away from the search for—"

"And," she cut in coolly, "just where, exactly, is your search for the keys?"

Nowhere, that was where. My father might have given me clues for the next key's location, but deciphering *those* was another matter entirely. We figured it was somewhere in the middle of Victoria's famous golden triangle, but given *that* particular region encompassed more than nine thousand square kilometers of land, that left us with a vast area to explore. It was fucking frustrating, but all Azriel and I could do was keep on searching and hope that sooner or later fate gave us a goddamn break.

"It's probably in the same place as your search for my mother's killer."

The minute the words left my mouth, I regretted them. Hunter really *wasn't* someone I needed to antagonize, and yet it was her damn promise to help find my mother's killer that had made me agree to work for her and the council in the first place. And while I'd kept my end of the bargain, she hadn't.

For several very long seconds, she didn't reply.

She simply stared at me, her expression remote and her eyes colder than the Antarctic. Then she said, voice so soft it was barely audible, "Tread warily, Risa dearest."

I gulped. I couldn't help it. Death glared at me through the phone's screen, and she scared the hell out of me.

I took a slow, deep breath, but it really didn't help ease the sense of dread or the sudden desire to just give it all the fuck away. To let fate deal her cards and accept whatever might come my way—be that death at Hunter's hand or someone else's.

I was sick of it. Sick of the threats, sick of the fighting, sick of a search that seemed to have no end and no possibility of our winning.

Death is not a solution of any *kind,* Azriel said, his mind voice sharp.

I looked up from the phone's screen. He appeared in front of my desk, the heat of his presence playing gently through my being, a sensation as intimate as the caress of fingers against skin. Longing shivered through me.

Reapers, like the Aedh, weren't actually flesh beings—although they could certainly attain that form whenever they wished—but rather beings made of energy who lived on the gray fields, the area that divided earth from heaven and hell. Or the light and dark portals, as they preferred to call them.

Although I had no idea whether his reaper form would be considered handsome—or even how reapers defined handsome—his human form certainly was. His face was chiseled, almost classical in its beauty, but possessed the hard edge of a man who'd fought many battles. His body held a similar hardness, though his build was more that of an athlete than a weight lifter. Distinctive black tats that resembled the left half of a wing swept around his ribs from underneath his arm, the tips brushing across the left side of his neck.

Only it wasn't a tat. It was a Dušan—a darker, more stylized brother to the lilac one that resided on my left arm—and had been designed to protect us when we walked the gray fields. We had no idea who'd sent them to us, but Azriel suspected it was my father. He was apparently one of the few left in this world—or the next—who had the power to make them.

Of course, Azriel wasn't *just* a reaper, but something far more. He was one of the Mijai, the dark angels who hunted and killed the things that broke free from hell. And they had more than their fair share of work now that the first gate had been opened.

If you ask me, death is looking more and more the perfect solution when it comes to the keys. My mental voice sounded as weary as my physical one. I wasn't actually telepathic, but that didn't matter when it came to my reaper. He could hear my thoughts as clearly as the spoken word.

Unfortunately, it wasn't always a two-way street. Most of the time I heard his thoughts only when it was a deliberate act on his part. *If I'm not here to find the damn things, then the world and my friends remain safe.*

He crossed his arms, an action that only emphasized the muscles in his arms and shoulders. *Death is no solution. Not for you. Not now.*

And what the hell is that supposed to mean?

His gaze met mine, his blue eyes—one as vivid and bright as a sapphire, the other as dark as a storm-driven sea—giving little away. *It means exactly what it says.*

Great. More riddles. Another thing I really needed right now. I returned my attention to Hunter's death-like stare. "How did your friend die?"

"He was restrained, then drained."

"Drained? As in, a vampire-style, all-the-blood-from-the-body draining, or something else?"

She hesitated, and just for a second I saw something close to grief in her eyes. Whoever her friend was, they'd been a lot closer than mere lovers.

"Have you ever seen the husk of a fly after a spider has finished with it?" she said. "That's what he looked like. There was nothing left but the dried remains of outer skin. *Everything* else had been sucked away."

I stared at her for a moment, wondering whether I'd heard her right, then swallowed heavily and said, "Everything? As in, blood, bone—"

"Blood, bone, muscle, intestines, brain. *Everything.*" Her voice was suddenly fierce. "As I said, *all* that remained was the shell of hardened outer skin."

A shudder ran through me. I did *not* want to meet, let alone chase, something that could do *that* to a body.

"How can human skin be hardened into a shell?

Or the entire innards of a body be sucked away? It had to be one *hell* of a wound."

"On the contrary, the wound was quite small— two slashes on either side of his abdomen." She hesitated. "He did not appear to die in agony. Quite the opposite, in fact."

"I guess that's some comfort—"

"He's *dead*," she cut in harshly. "How is that ever going to be a comfort?"

I should have known I'd get my head bitten off if I tried sympathy on the bitch. "Where is his body? And is the Directorate being called in on this?"

If they were, it could get tricky. Uncle Rhoan worked for them—he was, in fact, second in charge of the guardian division these days—but he had no idea I was working for Hunter and the council. And I wanted to keep it that way, because the shit would really hit the fan if he and Aunt Riley ever found out. They'd always considered me one of their pack, but that protectiveness had increased when Mom had died. They'd kill me if they knew I'd agreed to work with Hunter—although I now suspected I couldn't have actually *refused* to work with her—and once they'd dealt with me, they'd track her down and confront her. And *that* was a situation that could *never* end nicely.

I'd already endangered the lives of too many people I cared about by dragging them into this mad quest for the keys—I didn't want to make the situation worse in any way.

"Yes, they are," she said. "But Jack has been

made aware of my wishes in this and will ensure you get first bite at the crime scene."

Amusement briefly ran through me, although I doubted her pun had been intentional. "That really doesn't help with the problem—"

"Rhoan Jenson will not get in the way of this. You are a consultant, nothing more, as far as he is concerned."

I snorted. "A consultant you're using to hunt and kill."

"Yes. And you would do well to remember that you remain alive only as long as the council and I agree on your usefulness."

"And," Azriel said, suddenly standing behind me. His closeness had desire stirring, even though I had little enough energy to spare. "You would do well to remember that *any* attempt to harm her would be met with even more deadly force."

Hunter smiled, but there was nothing pleasant about it. "We both know you cannot take a life without just cause, reaper, so do not make your meaningless threats to me."

"What I have done once, I can do again," he said, his voice stony. "And in this case, as in the last, I would revel in a death taken before its time."

Azriel, stop poking the bear. I've already antagonized her enough.

That is a somewhat absurd statement, given she is clearly vampire, not bear.

Amusement slithered through me again, as he'd no doubt intended. He'd grown something of a sense of humor of late—which was, according to him, a consequence of spending far too much time in flesh form. Whether that was true or not, I had no idea, but I certainly preferred this more "human" version to the remote starchiness that had been present when he'd first appeared. *You know what I mean.*

Surprisingly, I do. He touched my shoulder, the contact light but somehow possessive. *But her threats grow tedious. She must be made aware it gains her nothing.*

Hunter laughed. The sound was harsh and cold, and sent another round of chills down my spine. "Reaper, you amuse me. One of these days, when I'm tired of this life, I might just be tempted to take you on."

And she was crazy enough to do it, too.

"However," she continued, "that time is *not* now. I will send you my friend's address, Risa. The Directorate will arrive at his home at four. Please be finished with your initial investigation before then, and report your impressions immediately."

I glanced at my watch. She'd given me a whole hour. Whoop-de-do. "Where does he live, and what sort of security system has he got in place?"

"I've just sent you all his details."

My cell phone beeped almost immediately. I picked it up and glanced at the message. Hunter's friend—who went by the very German-sounding name of Wolfgang Schmidt—lived in Brighton, a very upmarket suburb near the beach. No surprise there, I guess—I certainly couldn't imagine her slumming it with the regular folk in places like Broad-meadows or Dandenong.

I read the rest of the text, then looked up at the main phone's screen again. "Is the security system just key coded?"

"Yes. Wolfgang is—*was*—a very old-fashioned vampire. He saw no need for anything more than a basic system."

And maybe, just maybe, that had gotten him killed. While there was no electronic security system on earth that would actually *stop* a demon, it wasn't beyond the realms of possibility that something other than a demon had killed her vampire friend.

I mean, no one could ever be one hundred percent right all the time. Not even Hunter—although I'm sure *she'd* claim otherwise. And really, what sane person would argue the point with her when she wasn't?

Certainly not me.

And yet you do, Azriel commented, a trace of amusement in his mental tone.

I think we've already established I'm not always sane. To Hunter, I added, "You're not going to be there?"

"No."

I frowned. "Why not?"

"Because I have"—she hesitated, and an almost predatory gleam touched her gaze—"a meeting that needs to be attended."

If that gleam was any indication, the so-called

meeting involved bloodshed of some kind. After all, the council—and Hunter—considered it perfectly acceptable to punish those who broke the rules by allowing them to be ripped to shreds by younger vampires.

Still, it seemed odd that she wasn't hanging around to garner my impressions, especially if she cared for the dead man as much as I suspected.

Like many who have lived for centuries, she has strayed from the path of humanity, Azriel commented. *For her, emotions are fleeting, tenuous things.*

But not all those who live so long find that fate. Uncle Quinn's not far off Hunter in age, and he's as emotional as anyone. Although he could also be as stoic and cold as any of them when the urge took him.

He is one of the few exceptions. It is very rare to live so long and hang on to humanity.

I glanced at him. *Does that apply to reapers as well?*

Reapers are not human, so we can hardly hang on to what we do not have.

But you are capable of emotions.

Again a smile touched his thoughts, and it shimmered through me like a warm summer breeze. *Yes, we are, especially if we are foolish enough to remain in flesh too long.*

In other words, I wasn't to read too much into what he said or did while he wore flesh, because when all this was over, we'd both go our separate ways and life would return to normal.

I wanted that. I really did.

But at the same time, it was becoming harder and harder to imagine life without Azriel in it.

He made no comment on that particular thought, and I returned my attention to Hunter. "Once I've checked out the crime scene, what then? Are you going to tell me more about him, or am I expected to work on this case completely blind?"

"Impressions first," she said, and hung up.

"Fuck you and the broom you rode in on," I muttered, then leaned back in my chair. "Well, this totally sucks."

"An unfortunate consequence of agreeing to work with someone like Hunter is being at her beck and call." He spun my chair around, then squatted in front of me and took my hands in his. His fingers were warm against mine, his touch comforting. "But there is little we can do until your mother's killer is caught."

I snorted softly. "Even if we *do* find her killer, do you really think she's going to let me go?"

"We both know the answer to that. But once the killer is caught, we will be in a better position to deny her."

"Maybe." And maybe not. After all, Hunter wouldn't have any qualms about threatening the lives of my friends if it meant securing long-term obedience.

"It does not pay to worry about things that may never happen."

"No." I leaned forward and rested my forehead

against his as I closed my eyes. "I guess we'd better get moving. I want to be out of that house before the Directorate gets there."

"Do you wish me to transport us there?"

His breath washed across my lips and left them tingling. Half of me wanted to kiss him, and the other half just wanted him to wrap his arms around me and hold me like he never intended to let go. Unfortunately, neither was particularly practical right now.

And it was a sad statement about my life when desire gave way to practicality.

"It'll be faster if you do." While I could shift into my Aedh form and travel there under my own steam, my energy levels were still low and I really didn't want to push it. Not yet, not for something like this.

He rose, dragging me up with him, then wrapped his arms around me.

"Wait." I broke from his grasp and moved around the desk, striding out of my office and down to the storeroom at the other end of the hall. We kept all of RYT's—which was the name of the café I owned with two of my best friends, Ilianna and Tao—nonperishable items up here, which meant not only things like spare plates, cutlery, and serviettes, but also serving gloves. It was the latter I needed, simply because the last thing I wanted was to be leaving fingerprints around Wolfgang's house for the Directorate and Uncle Rhoan to find. I tore open a box, shoved a couple of the clear latex gloves into the pocket of my jeans, then headed back into the office. I grabbed my cell phone from the desk and let myself be wrapped in the warmth of Azriel's arms again. "Okay, go for it."

The words had barely left my mouth when his power surged through me, running along every muscle, every fiber, until my whole body sang to its tune. Until it felt like there was no me and no him, just the sum of us—energy beings with no flesh to hold us in place.

All too quickly, my office was replaced by the gray fields. Once upon a time the fields had been little more than thick veils and shadows—a zone where things not sighted on the living plane gained substance. But the more time I spent in Azriel's company, the more "real" the fields became. This time, the ethereal, beautiful structures that filled this place somehow seemed more solid, and instead of the reapers being little more than wispy, luminous shapes, I could now pick out faces. They glowed with life and energy, reminding me of the drawings of angels so often seen in scriptures—beautiful and yet somehow alien.

Then the fields were gone, and we regained substance. And though it involved no effort on my part, it still left my head spinning.

"You," he said, expression concerned, "are not recovering as quickly as you should."

"It's been a hard few weeks." I stepped back to study the building in front of us, even though all I really wanted to do was remain in his arms. That, however, was not an option. Not now and certainly not in the future. Not on any long-term, forever-type basis, anyway.

Which, if I was being at all honest with myself, totally sucked. But then, I had a very long history of falling for inappropriate men. Take my former Aedh lover, Lucian, for instance.

"Let's not," Azriel said, voice grim as he touched my back and then lightly waved me forward.

Amusement teased my lips. "He's out of my life, Azriel, and no longer a threat to whatever plans you—"

"It is not the threat to *me* I worry about," he cut in, voice irritated.

I raised my eyebrows. "Well, he can hardly threaten *me*, given he and everyone else wants the damn keys."

"His need for the keys did not stop his attempt to strangle you."

Well, no, it hadn't. But I suspected Lucian's actions had been little more than a momentary lapse of control—one he would have snapped out of before he'd actually killed me. Although, to be honest, I hadn't actually been so certain of that when his hands had been around my neck.

I opened the ornate metal gate and walked up the brick pathway toward the front door. Wolf-gang's house was one of the increasingly rare red-brick Edwardian houses that used to take pride of place in the leafy bayside suburb. The front garden was small but meticulously tended, as was the house itself. I pulled out the gloves as I walked up the brick pathway toward the ornate front door, then said, "Lucian is no longer our problem."

"If you think that, you are a fool."

And I wasn't a fool. Not really. I just kept hoping that if I believed something hard enough, it might actually come true. I slipped the gloves on and switched the discussion back to my health. It was far safer ground.

"You can't expect me to recover instantly, Azriel. I'm flesh and blood, not—"

"You are half Aedh," he cut in again. His voice was still testy. But then, he always did sound that way after a discussion about Lucian, whom he hated with a surprising amount of passion for someone who claimed it was only his flesh form that gave him emotions. "More so, given what Malin did to you."

Malin was the woman in charge of the Raziq, my father's former lover, and a woman scorned. My father had not only betrayed her trust by stealing the keys from under her nose, but he had also refused to give her the child she'd wanted. Instead, for reasons known only to himself, he'd gone to my mother and produced me.

"Meaning what?" My voice was perhaps sharper than it should have been. "You never *actually* explained what she did."

And I certainly couldn't remember—she'd made sure of that.

He hesitated, his expression giving little away. "No. And I have already said more than I should."

Because of my father. Because whatever Malin did had somehow altered me—and not *just* by altering the device the Raziq had previously woven into the fabric of my heart, which had been designed to notify them when I was in my father's presence.

My sigh was one of frustration, but I knew better than to argue with Azriel—at least when he had *that* face on. "It doesn't alter the fact that a body—even one that is half energy—can run on empty for only so long."

A fact he knew well enough—his own lack of energy was the reason he'd been unable to heal me lately. Of course, reapers didn't "recharge" by eating or sleeping or any of the other things humans did, but rather by mingling energies—which was the reaper version of sex—with those who possessed a harmonious frequency. Unfortunately for them, such compatibility wasn't widespread, and Azriel's recharge companion had been killed long ago while escorting a soul through the dark portals. The good news was that he *could* apparently recharge through me—though *why* he could do this when I wasn't a full-energy being, but rather half werewolf, he refused to say. Just as he'd so far refused to recharge. Up until very recently, he'd been more worried about the threat of assimilation—which was when a reaper became so tuned to a human, their life forces merged and they became as one—than the lowering of his ability to heal me.

All that had changed when I'd almost died after a fight on the astral plane. Because, as I'd already noted, without me, no one could find the keys. My father's blood had been used in the creation of the keys, and only someone of his blood could find them.

Of course, making the decision to recharge and actually doing it were two entirely different things. Especially when I barely had enough energy to function, let alone have sex.

Which was another sad statement about the state of my life.

I punched the security code into the discreet system sitting to the left of the doorframe. The device beeped, and the light flicked from red to green. I opened the door but didn't immediately enter, instead letting the scents within the house flow over me.

The most obvious was the smell of death, although it wasn't particularly strong and it certainly didn't hold the decayed-meat aroma that sometimes accompanied the dead. Underneath that rode less-definable scents. The strongest of these was almost musky but had an edge that somehow seemed . . . alien? It was certainly no smell that I'd ever encountered before, although musk was a common enough scent among shifters.

Was that what we were dealing with, rather than a demon? I had to hope so, if only because I then had more of a chance of diverting the search to the Directorate.

The hallway that stretched before us was surprisingly bright and airy and ran the entire length of the house. Several doorways led off it from either side and, down at the very end, double glass sliding doors led out into a rear yard that contained a pool.

Like the front yard, both the hallway and the rear yard were meticulous—there didn't appear to be a leaf out of place, and there certainly wasn't even the slightest hint of dust on the richly colored floorboards. Whoever looked after this place—be it Wolfgang or hired help—was one hell of a housekeeper.

I took a cautious step inside, then stopped again, flaring my nostrils to define where the death scent was strongest.

"The body lies in the living area down at the far end of this hall," Azriel said. He was standing so close that his breath tickled the hairs at the nape of my neck.

I eyed the far end of the hall warily. Why, I had no idea. It wasn't like Wolfgang's husked remains would provide any threat. It was just that smell— the oddness of it. "Does his soul remain?"

"No. The death was an ordained one."

This meant that a reaper had been here to escort him to whichever gate he'd been destined for. It probably would have been comforting news to anyone but Hunter. "Does that also mean whatever did this isn't a demon? If this death was meant to be, then surely it can't be an escapee from hell?"

He touched my back and gently propelled me forward. My footsteps echoed on the polished boards, the sound like gunshots in the silence. Azriel was ghostlike.

"Whether this death was the result of an attack from a demon has no bearing on it being ordained or not. If death is meant to find you, there is no avoiding it."

"Which doesn't actually answer the question of whether or not a demon did this."

"It could be either a malevolent spirit or some kind of demon, thanks to the first portal being open."

And *it* was only open thanks to me.

"*That* thanks belongs to us all," he corrected softly. "It is a blame that lies with everyone who was involved in that first quest."

But in particular, with one.

He might not have said the words, but they hung in the air regardless. And while it was now very obvious that Lucian had an agenda all his own when it came to the keys, I didn't think he was responsible for snatching the first one. He'd been as furious as we'd been over its loss.

Of course, I'd also been sure that he'd never harm me, and his strangulation attempt had certainly proven that wrong. Yet I still believed he didn't want me dead. Not until the keys were found, anyway.

I frowned. "I thought you said malevolent spirits were of this world rather than from hell?"

"They are."

"Then why would the opening of the first gate affect them in any way?"

"Because the dark path is a place filled with dark emotions and, with the first gate open, these emotions have begun to filter into this reality."

"Meaning what?"

I slowed as I neared the living area and trepidation flared, though I still had no idea what I feared. Maybe it was simply death itself. Or maybe it was just a hangover from the hell of the last few weeks. Between escapee demons, malevolent spirits, and psycho astral travelers, I'd certainly been kept on my toes.

Or flat on my back, bleeding all over the pavement, as was generally the case.

"Meaning," Azriel said softly, "that it feeds the darker souls, be they human or spirit."

"So, basically, it's the beginning of hell on earth?" Two steps and I'd be in the living room. My stomach began twisting into knots. I flexed my fingers and forced reluctant feet forward.

"Basically, yes."

"Great." As if the weight on my shoulders wasn't already enough, I now had the sanity of the masses to worry about.

I entered the living room and saw the body.

Or rather, the body-shaped parcel.

Because Hunter had left out one very important fact when she'd described Wolfgang's death.

Not only had he been sucked as dry as a fly caught by a spider, but he'd been entangled in the biggest damn spiderweb I'd ever seen.

Chapter 2

"Oh god," I said, and immediately backed away. Unfortunately, I couldn't retreat far, because Azriel was right behind me. I might as well have backed into a concrete wall. "She could have mentioned some kind of spider got him. I *hate* spiders."

"Whatever was responsible for this death was something more than just a spider," he commented, a slight trace of amusement in his voice.

I scowled up at him. "You *think*?"

He obviously didn't catch the sarcasm, because he added, "Either that, or this was the work of a multitude of spiders, and the pristine nature of this house precludes that possibility."

A multitude of spiders ... A shudder went through me at the thought. I rubbed my arms and forced my feet forward again. Wolfgang had died lounging comfortably on the well-padded leather sofa that wrapped around the corner of the room. He was fully clothed, though his shirt was undone to his belly button, and his tie and shoes lay on the floor near the coffee table. His feet were crossed at the ankles, and there was a dreamy, relaxed expression frozen on the remains of his face. He'd obviously died totally unaware that anything untoward was happening.

The web that encased him was anchored to the floor near his feet, then spun up his legs and along the entire length of his torso, enclosing his arms and his body in a fine, transparent filament. Two tears on either side of his belly button indicated the puncture site and, if the size of those wounds was anything to go by, we were dealing with a *damn* big spider.

Another shudder ran through me. I took a deep breath that did little to ease the growing sense of horror, then stopped near his feet and flared my nostrils, drawing in the air and sorting through the scents. That odd, alien aroma was stronger here, but it didn't appear to be coming from the body itself but rather the surrounding air. It was as if the scent of the creature had so heavily perfumed the room that it lingered long after it had gone.

I hesitated, then tentatively prodded the silvery casing with a stiffened finger. It wasn't sticky as I'd expected, and felt a little like plastic—almost as if it had hardened in the air. I leaned a little closer to inspect the wounds. Other than a slight discoloring around the edges of the punctures, there was little blood, but the wounds themselves suggested the creature's fangs were at least as thick as my fist.

It was going to take more than one can of fly spray to get rid of *this* damn spider.

I closed my eyes, took another deep, shuddering breath, then said, "What do you know about spider-like spirits or demons?"

"I believe there is a spirit known as the Jorōgumo, but I know nothing about them." Azriel moved around the coffee table, then stopped opposite me, his eyes slightly narrowed as he studied Wolfgang's remains. Power shimmered through the air, sharp and almost bitter in the stillness. It died just as quickly, and his gaze met mine. "There is no brain left in this body, so I cannot read what memories might have remained."

"Hunter did say everything had been sucked away." My gaze rose to Wolfgang's face, which was free of the transparent net. "Is there any way you can find out more about Jorōgumos? I mean, I can Google them, but I can't imagine Google being a reliable source of information when it comes to facts about spirits."

"I can ask, but Mijai fight demons, not spirits."

Meaning I'd probably have to rely on earth-bound resources. Perhaps the Brindle witches could help. I frowned. "Why hasn't his body collapsed in on itself?"

"I cannot say. I am not an expert on spirits, let alone spiders."

"And when it comes to spiders, my knowledge stops at either avoiding them, or killing the fuckers on sight."

I glanced at my watch. Ten minutes gone and, so far, we'd discovered nothing Hunter hadn't already known. I looked around the room, hoping there was something that jumped up and screamed clue. As usual, fate wasn't being overly helpful.

I spotted his jacket flung over one of the kitchen

chairs and walked over to pick it up. His keys were in the left front pocket, and his wallet was in one of the inside ones. Opening the latter revealed his driver's license, several platinum credit cards, and at least five hundred dollars in cash. Robbery obviously wasn't a motive—which was an odd thought when related to spiders or spirits, but perhaps not if we were dealing with some sort of shifter.

Frowning, I put his wallet back and went through the rest of his pockets. The only other thing to be found was a business card for some place called Dark Soul. I flicked it over, but the back was empty. God, I thought, this had better not be another fucking blood whore club. I'd had more than enough of them lately to last a lifetime. I placed the card back where I'd found it, then did a search of the rest of the house. As I expected, I found absolutely nothing.

This was useless—and I told Hunter as much when I went outside to call her back.

"I do not care what you think in regards to the viability of this task," she snapped. The vid-screen had been turned off at her end, and I couldn't help but be a little thankful for that. I had the distinct impression her expression would not have been pleasant. "I merely want your impressions of the kill."

I couldn't see the point of that, either, given my impressions were unlikely to be any different from hers, but I took a deep breath and said, "He was killed by something that appears to have spiderlike tendencies. There's a musky scent in the air that is not dissimilar to the musk of shifters, but if it *is* a

shifter, then it's one I've not come across before."
My voice was as sharp as hers, which probably
wasn't wise given all the shit I'd said earlier, but
then, she *was* on the other end of the phone rather
than in person, so she could hardly smack me down.
Not immediately, anyway. "I didn't find anything
that hinted at who or what else might have been
here, but Azriel said there are spider spirits known
as Jorōgumos, so it's possible we're dealing with
one of those. I did find a business card for some-
place called Dark Soul."

"That is—*was*—one of his favorite music venues.
He'd been planning to go there last night."

"Why was he carrying one of their business cards
if he went there regularly?"

"I don't know."

Color me shocked, I wanted to snap, but wisely
resisted the urge. "So he might have picked up his
killer there?"

"Possibly. Dark Soul is not a vampire venue. It
caters to all races who enjoy alternative music."

"Well, it wasn't a human who killed him." Not
unless Spider-Man was fact rather than fiction.

"Of course not," she said coolly. "Wolfgang was
a powerful vampire. He would not have been taken
easily by anyone—or any race."

And yet he'd sat there and allowed himself to be
bound by a web and then sucked dry. I rubbed my
arms against the chill that stole across my skin.
How could anyone—powerful or not—allow something like that?

"Which means either he was drugged, or there

was some form of magic involved." And if it was the former, was there enough of him left to find a trace of it?

"Yes." Hunter's voice still held little emotion, yet it hinted at a fury so deep it scared the hell out of me. "Which is why I wanted you to investigate. Whatever did this was *not* of this world. I'm sure of it. I want you to hunt it down, but do *not* kill it. *That* pleasure I reserve for myself."

Well, I wasn't about to argue over *that* particular order. "If we can find this thing, it's all yours."

"Oh, you had better find it, trust me." She paused, as if waiting for a comment, but what the hell was I supposed to say to a threat like that? After a moment, she continued. "I will arrange for you to talk to Dark Soul's owner and view their security tapes. Perhaps we can identify who—if anyone—he was there with."

"They're hardly likely to talk to me, given I'm not anything official—"

"That will be fixed," she cut in. "Keep me informed."

She hung up again. My fingers clenched the phone so tightly, my knuckles went white, and it was all I could do not to throw the damn thing and then stomp all over it in frustration.

Azriel plucked it from my fingers. "Temper tantrums, as I believe you would call such an action, will do no good. And it may well destroy a perfectly usable device."

I raised an eyebrow. "Have you ever had a good temper tantrum?"

Amusement lurked in the rich depths of his mismatched blue eyes. "No. But I do believe that the longer I reside in your presence, the more it becomes a possibility."

I snorted softly. "You could be right. And for future reference, a well-timed temper tantrum is a very good form of stress release."

"Meaning, I'm wrong in believing there might be more pleasing alternatives than throwing a tantrum?"

I arched an eyebrow and stepped a little closer, but any reply I might have made was cut short as my phone rang. A quick look showed that it was Stane— Tao's cousin, and a black marketer who just happened to be able to hack into any computer system ever created. It was an ability I'd made full use of when it came to Hunter's cases as well as the search for the keys. I half thought about ignoring the call just to continue the gently teasing conversation with Azriel, but I knew Stane wouldn't be ringing unless he'd uncovered something important.

"Hey," I said, by way of greeting. "What's the latest?"

"Well, let's see," he said, the rich tones of his voice more gravelly than usual. He'd obviously been hitting the online gaming hard again. "My mother is insisting I meet the daughter of her best friend and has in fact arranged a double date for this evening. And I believe I have found that storage locker you were looking for."

I blinked at the dual information and decided to tackle the juicier one first. "A double date?"

"Yeah, the mothers are coming. Won't that be fun?"

His voice was dry, and I chuckled softly. "Oh come on, she might actually be *nice*."

"She's taking her mother on a *date*. What does that say about her?"

"Hey, your mother will be there, too, remember."

"Yeah, but my mother has become a conniving witch who plots incessantly to get me married."

"What makes you think her mother isn't?"

"Because," he grumbled, "it was apparently her idea, not her mother's. Besides, the word from the pack is that she doesn't approve of wolf clubs. Hates what they represent."

"She's a werewolf, isn't she? How the hell can she disapprove of the clubs?"

"Who the fuck knows? Maybe she's a prude."

Was it even possible to be a werewolf *and* a prude? It certainly wasn't a likely combination. "If you think it's going to be that bad, don't go."

He snorted. "My mother will make my life hell if I don't go. Trust me."

I grinned. Stane was afraid of his mother. Imagine that. "And the storage container?"

"Oh. Yeah." There was a brief whoosh of sound, and I had the mental image of him scooting from one screen of his massive computer "bridge" to the other. "I couldn't find anything listed under John Nadler's name, but I did find one under Genevieve Sands."

Who was one of Nadler's heirs, according to the information I'd gotten from a ghost. Nadler was the man behind the consortium that had been buying up the land all around Stane's shop. Not that he wanted the land, per se; he just wanted to control what lay underneath it—a major ley-line intersection. Such intersections were places of great power and could be used to manipulate time, reality, or fate. But they could also be used to create a rift between this world and the next, and we very much suspected that whoever had stolen the first key had used the power of the intersection to access the gray fields and find the gates.

Which, in turn, meant that John Nadler was either involved with the sorcerer, or was the sorcerer himself. Unfortunately, he was also a face-shifter, and it was damnably hard to track someone who could alter their facial features at will. Of course, I was *also* a face-shifter, but that didn't make it any easier for me to spot others of my kind.

This particular face-shifter had assumed the identity of the real John Nadler after he'd killed him—a fact we were sure of only because the body of the real Nadler had turned up just as we were getting closer to pinning down the fake. We suspected that at least one of the three people named in Nadler's will was in fact the face-shifter, but so far we'd yet to track any of them down.

"You want to send me the address?" I said. "I might go check it out."

"Just sent you that. I've also hacked into their security cams so we can screen who might be coming and going. But is there anything else you need done?"

I couldn't help smiling at the hint of desperation in his voice. "Haven't we already given you enough?"

"No. I mean, I have a double date I need to get out of, remember."

I chuckled softly. "Think of your mother's wrath, and—as they say in the classics—suck it up, princess."

"Some help you are," he muttered. "The rates are going up next time you want me to do something."

"You'd be bored to death inside a week if we weren't bugging you."

"That," he said grimly, "is undoubtedly true. Think of me suffering while you're off enjoying yourself somewhere tonight."

"Tell you what—I'll send a bottle of Bollinger for you to drown your after-date sorrows in."

"At least *that* would give me something to look forward to." His sigh was overly dramatic. "Chat to you later."

He hung up. Two seconds later, my phone beeped, an indication that Stane's information had arrived. The storage locker was located in Clifton Hill and wasn't all that far away from Stane's shop. I shoved the phone back into my pocket, then locked the front door of Wolfgang's house and met Azriel's gaze. "Can you take us there now?"

He stepped close again and wrapped his arms around my waist. I resisted the temptation to snuggle deeper into his arms, and a heartbeat later we were zipping back through the gray fields.

We reappeared near the intersection of Hoddle Street and the Eastern Freeway exit. The self-storage premises couldn't be missed—it was a three-story brick building that had been painted in orange and blue stripes, with a huge white lock on the front of it.

"How do you plan to access this locker?" Azriel said.

I scanned the building and noted the cameras placed strategically around the perimeter. Undoubtedly, it would be a similar story inside, and that meant it might be wise to indulge in a little face-shifting. If Genevieve Sands *was* connected to Nadler, then they might be keeping an eye on who went near their storage locker. It wouldn't be hard to do—anyone with the right sort of knowledge would be able to hack into the security system. The last thing I wanted was for them to see how close we were. We didn't need another possible lead closing down before it led to anything—or anyone.

"I guess how we approach it depends on who is at the desk," I said eventually. "If it's male, I'll flirt. If it's female, you flirt."

He raised his eyebrows. "The last time we did something like that, you stomped out in what I believe you would call a snit."

"It wasn't a snit," I replied, amused. "It was mere annoyance. You were flirting with a stranger at a time you were refusing to do *anything* with me."

"I am still not doing anything with you."

"That's true." I gave a mock sigh. "God, it's been so long, I can hardly even remember what a kiss is, let alone sex."

"Then perhaps," he said, and stepped closer, "I should remind you."

His lips met mine, and though the kiss was little

more than a tease, it was also the sweetest damn thing I'd ever experienced. It made me feel higher than a kite and warmer than the sun, cherished and oddly alive all in one quicksilver moment. And I sighed in frustration when he pulled back.

"Damn it, Azriel—"

He pressed a finger against my lips, silencing my protest. "What you desire and what your body is capable of are two very different things right now." He gave me a lopsided smile that was oddly endearing. "I want what you want, believe me, but I am not willing to tax your strength any more than necessary. And, right now, that's what we would be doing."

"The whole point of sex *is* to be taxed," I replied, exasperated. "If you're not boneless and replete afterward, then you haven't put enough effort into it."

"What effort can you put into it when you are all but exhausted?" He raised an eyebrow, expression amused. "Trust me, given the risks involved, I want nothing more than your maximum."

I laughed softly, then rose on tiptoes and dropped another quick kiss on his lips. "Believe me, when you give in—and you will give in, reaper—I'll give you one hundred percent, exhausted or not."

"A promise I will hold you to."

"As long as you *do* hold me, I don't care." I reluctantly returned my attention to the building in front of us. "Can't you just pull the information about the storage locker from the mind of whoever is manning the reception desk?"

"I could, but our sorcerer appears to have telepathic abilities, remember, and while it is unlikely he would sense any psychic intrusion on my part, it is a risk we should not take, given he is most certainly aware of my presence on this quest."

I frowned. "Does that mean clouding her perception is out?"

"No. Clouding is more a sensory intrusion than a mental one, and therefore it is safer."

"Then I guess you'd better make whoever is inside think we're cops."

"That I can do." He placed his fingers under my elbow and lightly guided me across to the thick shrubs that lined one side of the nearby parking lot. "If you wish to alter your facial shape, you will not be seen here by either the cameras or those driving by."

"Good idea." While Azriel might be able to stop people from noticing his comings and goings, the last thing we needed was some poor driver spotting what I was doing and having a freak-out. While humanity was as aware of shape-shifters as they were vamps and werewolves, very few knew of the existence of us face-shifters.

I flexed my fingers, then closed my eyes and pictured my own face—from the silver of my hair, the lilac of my eyes, the slight uptilt of my nose and defined cheekbones, to the fullness of my lips. Then I replaced it with more rounded features, thinner lips, and very short black hair. A black so rich it shone blue in the sunlight.

Once that image was frozen in my mind, I reached for the magic. It exploded around me, thick and fierce, as if it had been contained for far too long. It swept through me like a gale, making my muscles tremble and the image waver. I frowned, holding the image fiercely against the storm. Power began to pulsate, burn, and change me. My skin rippled as my features altered, and my hair suddenly felt shorter and somehow finer. As the magic faded, my knees buckled, my legs suddenly weak.

Azriel gripped my arm and saved me from falling.

"Damn," I muttered, leaning against him briefly. "That never seems to get any easier."

"Given you continue to function barely above exhaustion, it is unlikely to."

"It's not like I can do a whole lot about that," I muttered, and forced my knees to lock. "What I need is for the bad guys to stop creating havoc for a month or so."

"A situation that is unlikely. I am actually amazed that your father has let the lack of progress on finding the second key slide for as long as he has."

"He could hardly force me to look when I was all but dead in the hospital. Even he isn't that callous."

"I would not be so sure of that."

Actually, I wasn't. My father had shown a decided lack of parental care up until this point, and I had no doubt that lack would continue.

"Ready to go?" Azriel added.

I took another of those deep, steadying breaths that really didn't help all that much, then nodded. He touched a hand to my back again and guided me toward the front door, his fingers spearing warmth into my spine despite the thickness of my sweater.

A deeper, more resonant energy swirled as we entered the building—Azriel, touching the receptionist's mind to alter her perception.

So what will she see us as?

Police, as you wished.

Good. There were no cameras in this particular area, so the lie wouldn't immediately be uncovered.

The receptionist gave us a cheerful smile. "And what can I do for you both on this rather chilly autumn morning?"

"I'm afraid we're here on official business." Azriel stopped in front of the desk and gave her a warm smile.

Her smile grew. So much for him not flirting. "And what business would that be?"

"We need to know if there's a Genevieve Sands renting a storage unit here."

"Just a moment, and I'll check." She glanced down at her computer, quickly typing, then said, "Yes, she is. It's one of the larger ground-floor units."

"Would we be able to look at it?"

She frowned. "I'm afraid I can't let you in without a search warrant—"

"That's okay," I said, noting with amusement—and perhaps a touch of annoyance—that she barely even glanced at me. "We just want to inspect its location for the moment."

"I can't see the harm in that." She half shrugged. "It's unit G-18. I'll buzz you through the security door; then follow the corridor down and around to your right."

"Thanks, Maggie." Azriel gave her the sort of smile that would have melted the iciest heart. This poor woman had no hope whatsoever, and practically puddled on the seat. "It's appreciated."

"You're very welcome," she all but stammered.

Amusement glittered in Azriel's bright eyes as he turned away. I followed, knowing I probably could have danced around naked and she wouldn't have even noticed. I shook my head in amusement. *You, reaper, are incorrigible.*

He glanced at me, one eyebrow raised, and the laughter I'd caught earlier was now richer in the depths of his eyes. *And why would you say that?*

Because every time you have to cloud the mind of a pretty woman, you flirt.

On the contrary, I am merely polite.

I snorted softly. *Polite doesn't come in the form of a high-wattage, sexy-as-hell smile.*

His amusement deepened, and it shimmered inside me, warm and enticing. *So you think my smile is sexy?*

I rolled my eyes and nudged him with my shoulder. *Fishing for compliments, are we?*

No. I merely ask a logical question. The security door buzzed as we neared it. He caught it with his fingertips, opening it and then ushering me through. *It is the resonance of energy that attracts reapers rather than anything as fleeting as an expression.*

I followed the receptionist's directions, making a mental note of the regularly spaced security cameras, then glanced at him with raised eyebrows and said, *Does that mean you don't think my physical form is attractive?*

Who is fishing for compliments now?

I grinned. *Hey, it's not like you throw them around with great abandon.*

No, he agreed, and touched my back again, his palm still light against my spine yet somehow oddly possessive. Or maybe that was merely wishful thinking on my behalf. *And yes, I find your physical form attractive. But it is the being within that flesh, the timbre and music of all that you are, that is the most dangerous to someone like me.*

Because of the threat of assimilation. It was a sobering reminder of the risk we were taking, and I had to wonder whether it was actually worth it.

But how could I be around him and not want him? That seemed as impossible to me now as it would be to stop breathing.

"Indeed," he agreed softly. Almost grimly. Then he motioned with his free hand. "The locker we seek is just ahead."

I slowed as we neared it. It looked like every other unit in this area in that it was fronted by a double-sized roller door that was padlocked at either edge. I'm not sure why I'd been expecting something else—but maybe it was simply the fact that Nadler didn't seem to do *anything* that could be considered ordinary.

Of course, Genevieve Sands might *not* be connected to him in any way—but I seriously doubted that was the case.

"There is magic here."

Azriel stopped in front of the unit and crossed his arms. His expression gave little away, but blue fire flickered down the sides of his sword, radiating an energy that was oddly tense. Valdis—the name of the demon trapped within the sword, giving the steel a life and energy of its own—was as ready for action as her master.

I had a similar sword strapped to my back, but Amaya was shadow-wreathed and invisible. The only time anyone was truly aware of her presence was when I slid her dark blade into their flesh—although she did have a tendency to scream for bloodshed, and generally at the most inappropriate times.

"But what sort of magic? Good or bad?" I stopped beside him and eyed the roller door dubiously. I couldn't feel anything, but then, I wasn't always sensitive to magic.

"Neither. In fact, it is almost Aedh-like in construction."

I frowned. "The only Aedh we know who play around with magic are the Raziq, and I seriously doubt they'd be involved on *any* level with Nadler."

"There is Lucian."

I frowned. "Yeah, but he isn't capable of magic."

"That we know of."

True. But surely to god *he* wasn't linked to Nadler. Surely to god I hadn't been *that* gullible.

Azriel, perhaps wisely, made no comment about that particular thought.

I studied the innocuous-looking door for several seconds, then carefully raised a hand. As my fingertips neared the metal, energy began to flow across them. As Azriel had said, it didn't feel evil or dark, just wrong. It was also oddly similar to the magic in the circle of stones that had formed a protective barrier around the gateway Jak—my ex, and a reporter who was helping us—and I had discovered underground when we'd been searching for Nadler's base of operations in West Street. And that certainly suggested I'd been right in suspecting a link between Genevieve Sands and Nadler himself. According to Ilianna—who wasn't only my best friend but an extremely powerful witch—every spell was as individual as the person creating it. Two spells having the same sort of feel could only mean the same person was behind both.

"We need to get in there," I said. "We need to uncover what they might be hiding."

"I do not think that would be a wise move."

I frowned. "Why?"

"For one, the magic involved prevents me from entering, and two, I would think crossing the threshold would notify Sands, or Nadler, or whoever else might be the true owner of this container."

My frown deepened. "So is the spell reaper specific, or is it more generally aimed at energy beings?" Because if it were the latter, it would also prevent me from entering.

He hesitated, and his energy slithered around me as he carefully tested the boundaries of the magic. "Reaper specific, by the feel of it."

"Meaning whoever is behind this is more than a little familiar with your presence?"

"Yes." He glanced at me. "Lucian."

"You can't blame him for every bit of evil we come across just because you don't like or trust him," I said, irritated.

"He is Aedh, he was your father's *chrání*, he spelled you, and he is sexually involved with a dark sorceress. Why would he not be a suspect?"

Chrání was the Aedh word for a student or protégé, and it meant that even if Lucian hadn't been involved with the making of the keys, he most certainly knew a whole lot more about them than he'd ever let on. And while he'd been using me to keep track of everything we did to locate the keys—had, in fact, placed a *geas* on me that had made it next to impossible for me to resist him sexually, which was important given he could read my mind only during sex—my father had been keeping track of *him* through me. Blood called to blood, and that apparently meant he not only knew where I was at any given time, but he could read my thoughts from a distance.

"Look, I'm not denying he's involved. I just don't think he's responsible for this." I waved a hand at the door and, as I did so, my fingers brushed the unseen magic. Light danced across them, warm and almost welcoming. Which was decidedly odd. "It seems to react to touch, too."

"That is only logical. If whoever owns this had been hiding the real Nadler's body in a freezer within, then he or she would not wish to risk anyone breaking in."

"So why not ward against Aedh as well?"

"I do not know."

Neither did I, and it piqued my interest. "I've got to get in there. This could be the break we've been looking for."

"I do not think—"

"I know," I cut in. "And I'm going to try regardless."

Irritation swirled down the link between us, thick and sharp. I might not be able to catch his thoughts and feelings unless he wished it, but every now and again emotion got the better of his control. And while that could be a dual-edged sword—especially when it generally happened only when he was really angry over something I'd said or done—I wasn't about to wish it away. I actually liked getting glimpses of what was going on in my generally stoic reaper's mind.

I glanced toward the end of the hallway and studied the security camera. If I was going to get into the storage locker, I'd have to do it in Aedh form—and the last thing I needed was the transformation being caught on tape. "Can you do something about those things?"

"A well-placed blow from Valdis would do a good job of destroying them."

"I was hoping for something a little more discreet than that."

He contemplated the camera for a moment, then said, "Perhaps the woman at the desk can be convinced to turn them off temporarily."

"I'm sure you could sweet-talk the sun out of the sky if it suited you, reaper."

He frowned, though amusement creased the corners of his bright eyes. "That is an illogical statement."

"Which doesn't mean it's not true." I waved a hand. "Go sweet-talk. I'll wait here."

He turned and left. I contemplated the battered roller door for several seconds, then turned my attention to the doors on either side. Would it be worth breaking into them on the off chance there was some form of ventilation between the two rooms? In Aedh form I was little more than mist, so even the smallest of cracks would give access. With any sort of luck, the magic that protected Genevieve's locker was concentrated at the entrance rather than being all-encompassing. A long shot, granted, but surely some sort of luck *had* to fall our way eventually.

I contemplated the door for a few more seconds, then retreated to the other side of the hall to wait. Azriel returned a few minutes later. "The cameras at either end of this hall have been turned off."

I pushed away from the wall and handed him my phone. "I'm going to try entry from one of the other lockers. Hopefully, whoever set the spell might not have considered that eventuality."

"Unlikely. The magic feels encompassing."

"Meaning floor and ceiling, as well as walls?"

He hesitated. "Oddly, not the floor."

"Then maybe that will play in our favor."

"And maybe you just waste your time."

"Maybe. I'm still going to try."

"Of course you are."

He said it with resigned acceptance, and I couldn't help smiling. Then I took a deep breath, releasing it slowly as I called to the Aedh within me. Despite the sheer level of fatigue that still assailed me, she answered swiftly, and with such force, I gasped. It tore through me, a whirlwind of magic that rendered flesh and muscle and bone apart, until I was little more than particles of energy amassed in the air—a being who could see and hear, but not speak. I turned and headed for the locker to the right of the one registered to Genevieve Sands, sliding in through the small gap between the concrete and in the roller door. The area beyond was dark and crammed full of all sorts of boxes and antique-looking furniture. I swung around, scanning the wall that divided this locker from the other, but couldn't see anything that might give me access. But if there was going to be a gap, then it would more than likely be where the wall met the floor or roof, not in the actual wall. I rose up but couldn't see any access points along the joint between the wall and ceiling. Maybe Azriel was right—maybe this *was* a waste of time. But that didn't mean I was about to give up—not before I'd checked all options, anyway.

I made my way back down, slipping between a couple of the old boxes that were crammed along the base of the wall. Dust, cobwebs, and god knows what else fell around me, the bits clinging annoyingly to the particles that were my body. It meant that, at best, I'd be as itchy as hell when I re-formed and, at worst, I'd be brushing bits of debris from my skin for days.

There were lots of skeletal bits of spiders and bugs along the joint between wall and floor, as well as flashes of living things that skittered away as I approached them. I'd always thought being in Aedh form meant I was invisible to things that weren't either energy beings or in some way connected to them, such as the Razan, who were the human slaves of the Raziq. Obviously, I was wrong.

I slipped through another gap between the boxes, but drifted a little too high and caught the edge of the spell protecting the locker on the other side. Energy ran through my particles, a touch of lightning that didn't actually hurt. But it was warning enough that the spell, while it might not be Aedh specific, would certainly react to my presence if I got too close.

I moved on. As I neared the junction of the inner and outer walls, I finally spotted what I was looking for—a slight crack between the concrete of the wall and the floor. I slithered in.

And found emptiness.

Well, almost.

There was magic here—it rippled through me like a mild summer storm—electric, yet not threatening. But that wasn't all there was.

Standing in the middle of the room were two upright stones. I'd seen their like once before—in the tunnels Jak and I had found underneath West Street. Those stones had turned out to be a gateway, though it wasn't one we'd been able to use, so we still had no idea where it went. Maybe these stones were the same.

I approached them cautiously. Warm yellow

light—similar in feel to the light that had danced across my fingertips when I'd touched the magic guarding the door—flared between the two pillars, shimmering and swirling softly in the darkness.

When I retreated, the light faded. I studied the stones for a moment longer, then dropped closer to the floor. The magic that protected the walls and ceiling wasn't evident here. After a moment's hesitation, I called to the Aedh and changed back to human form.

I was already low to the ground, so the drop onto all fours was a little more elegant than usual. I stayed there for several seconds, breathing deep, waiting for the quivering in my muscles and the fierce ache in my head to ease off. Both were the inevitable result of becoming Aedh—I wasn't a full blood, and therefore paid a price that few Aedh did. This time, though, the aftereffect was nowhere near as strong or fierce as it usually was. Maybe constant use was making me more adept.

I pushed carefully to my feet, and a cloud of fibers and dust swirled around me. Another casualty of the Aedh shift was my clothes. They disintegrated just fine, but re-forming them was trickier, as the magic didn't always delineate between bits of me and other particles. And—like the dirt that clung to my atoms when in Aedh form—I often ended up with a dustlike sheen covering my skin rather than fully formed pieces of clothing.

I do not think this course of action wise, Azriel said. His disapproval spun down the mental lines between us, sharp but holding a hint of frustration.

You're probably right, but we need answers, Azriel, and we're not going to get them without taking chances.

You take too many chances as it is.

Maybe, but what other choice did I have? It wasn't like fate—or anyone else—was running around dropping clues at our feet. I drew my sword and stepped close to the gateway again. Fire flickered across Amaya's dark blade, spearing lilac light across the pillars and sparking the quartz within the stone to life. They stood about six feet tall and, like the ones we'd discovered underground, were covered in writing and symbols that resembled cuneiform. It was ancient, that writing—and *powerful*.

I swept Amaya in an arc around the floor, using her light to check if there was any sort of protection circle present. She was unusually quiet, which meant she detected no immediate threat. It should have been comforting, but it wasn't. Not when Azriel's tension flowed through me like a distant storm.

These pillars have no protection circle. The others did.

Maybe Nadler—or whoever else rents this storage locker—thinks the magic encompassing the perimeter was enough.

I frowned at the stones. *I wonder if these stones are a means of transport like the first ones we found were.*

That, he said, voice sharper, *is not something you should be discovering. Not when you have no idea of the type of magic involved or where it actually goes.*

Yeah, but as I've said, we're not likely to discover our answers by sitting here staring at the fucking things.

Risa—

I know. I know. I'm doing it anyway.

He didn't reply, but then, he didn't need to. His anger came through so thick and fast, it damn near suffocated me.

I gripped Amaya tighter. She began to hiss, the sound soft but fierce, filled with expectation. I continued to stare at the stones and hoped like hell I was making the right decision.

Then, before my courage gave way to common sense, I forced my feet forward and stepped in between the two stones.

Chapter 3

Nothing happened.

No light flare, no caress of magic, nothing. The stones were silent. Inert.

I raised a hand and tentatively brushed the stone's surface. Life pulsed under my fingertips. It was almost as if the rock had life and heart. The magic was there and ready to react. It just hadn't. Yet it had before . . .

I closed my eyes as the realization of what that meant sunk in. I'd been Aedh when they'd reacted, which meant these stones had been attuned to *that* form rather than human.

And there was only one being—one man—who had one, if not both, of those forms and who was also involved in the search for the keys.

Lucian.

Fuck! He really *had* taken me for a ride, and in more ways than one. The bastard had told me—constantly—that he couldn't take Aedh form, that the ability had been stripped from him by the Raziq when they'd tortured him for information. It seemed that might be yet another lie in a growing list of them.

He was not lying about being tortured, Azriel said. *Your father all but confirmed that.*

I raised my eyebrows. *You're actually defending him?*

In this, yes. And it grieves me greatly.

Amusement spun through me. *What about the whole "stripped of his powers" spiel? How much truth was there in that?*

I think it was skillfully mixed with untruths. I do not, however, believe he can attain full Aedh form.

So these stones might not be for his use? And did that mean we had another Aedh—someone we didn't know about—lurking in the background?

Azriel hesitated. *I am no expert in magic, but I suspect that if Lucian does use these stones, then they would be attuned to a full Aedh, in whatever form they might be in.*

Which might explain why they didn't react when I was in human form, but not why they did when I was in Aedh.

As I said, I am no expert in magic, but there would be little difference between you and a full Aedh when you take on Aedh form.

I grunted and sheathed Amaya. There was really only one thing I could do now—

Don't. Azriel's voice was as fierce as I'd ever heard it. *The risk is unnecessary. We can keep watch on this place and uncover whether Lucian—*

But even if we do confirm he's using these things, that won't tell us where these pillars take him. We need to know, Azriel. We need to start taking the advantage for ourselves.

But this—

Has to be done.

I cannot follow you when you are in Aedh form. The words practically stabbed into my brain. *No matter where those stones deposit you, until you take human shape again, I will not be able to help you.*

I know. But if I do get stuck, or I'm forced to change shape, I can use Amaya until you get there. She's more than capable of handling most things. I'd barely even finished the thought when Amaya's pleased hum began to run through the outer reaches of my mind. I shook my head in amusement. Trust me to get a sword that not only had a bloodthirsty bent, but also *liked* being complimented.

I am aware of that. I still think this is an unnecessary risk.

It undoubtedly was, but if we really wanted to get ahead of these bastards, we needed to do the unexpected.

I stepped out of the stones and called to the Aedh again. She came, changing me almost instantly, a storm of power whose force seemed even stronger than moments before. It shook me, and I couldn't help but wonder if it had anything to do with whatever Malin had done.

Then I thrust the thought away and drifted closer to the pillars. Once again they came to life, the light pulsing with the same beat I'd sensed when I touched the stone. Meaning I'd been right—they *were* primed to react to Aedh energy.

How they'd react to me actually entering them

was now the question to be answered—and I wasn't going to get that answer by hovering here staring at the damn things.

I forced myself forward, into the heart of the magic.

Just for a moment, there was no reaction.

Then power surged, tearing through my atoms, a sensation that was similar to and yet different from becoming an Aedh. It encompassed the particles of my being, then swept me into a bright orb of energy—where I hung, motionless, for several seconds.

Then the energy surged again, and I was suddenly back between two stones. But not the same two, I realized. These stones were smaller, darker, and stood in a square, windowless room rather than a storage locker.

Excitement and trepidation surged in equal amounts. I carefully moved from between the two stones, then slowly turned around. The room was small—maybe ten feet square—with white walls and coffee-colored carpet that had seen better days. There was nothing else besides the stones, although the carpet still bore the impressions of furniture that had once been present.

I turned fully around and found the door. It was closed and, on closer inspection, locked. Not that that was a problem in this form. I squeezed through the gap between the base of the door and the carpet, and found myself in a long, wide hall. Light flooded in from the ceiling-high, almost industrial-looking window to my right and, beyond it, there was a decent-sized courtyard. To my left were four more closed doors and, down at the far end, what looked to be a kitchen.

Other than the soft ticking of a distant clock, the house was silent. If someone was here, they were deathly quiet. I hesitated, then cautiously moved to the left. I wasn't about to take any chances, even though there was little chance of anyone seeing me in this form.

Anyone human, that was.

Which didn't mean I was safe. Whoever owned this place was, at the very least, involved with a magician. At worst, they were working with either Nadler or Lucian, or both. Either way, they were likely to be more knowledgeable about all things non-human than the average human.

The first door led into a small but neat bathroom, and the next two were bedrooms—both empty. I looked around for some clue as to who might be using them, but other than the fact they were male, I didn't find much.

The fourth door led to another bedroom, but this time, it wasn't empty.

I froze near the door and studied the man sprawled on the bed. The blankets were twisted around his legs, leaving part of his butt and his back uncovered. He was muscular and thickset—the body of a wrestler rather than a sprinter—and his skin lightly tanned. He had two tattoos on the upper part of his shoulders—one of a dragon with two swords crossed above it and the other a ring of barbed wire.

My stomach—or whatever the equivalent was in this form—sank.

We'd seen tats like these several times now, and not only on the man who'd unleashed the hell hounds on Jak and me when we were in the tunnel, but on the misshapen shifters who'd attacked me in a parking lot *and* on the man my father used to his deliver notes to a human courier.

Was this Razan the one from the tunnel? I really couldn't say because I hadn't taken all that much notice of what he'd looked like. But if he wasn't, why was he wearing the same branding as all the others? And why were there Razan involved with the machinations of a dark sorcerer in the first place?

I refused to believe my father was—in any way—involved with a sorcerer. Not when the magic he could command was stronger than anything a mere human—light or dark—could command. And given that he wanted the keys for his own quest of domination, it was hard to believe he'd be in cahoots with Nadler and his schemes. And yet his Razan appeared to have the same branding as this man and the others …

Then the reason clicked. Anger surged, so fierce and bright, and the man on the bed stirred.

God, I thought, I'm an *idiot*.

Lucian was the connection. He had to be. He'd been my father's *chrání*, so it was more than possible his Razan bore the same markings as my father's. And he was also involved with a woman who was a dark sorceress. She might not be the one we were after, but the odds were that she at least knew him. After all, how many damn dark sorcerers could there be in Melbourne?

The man on the bed rolled over onto his back and flung his arms wide. I waited for him to settle again, then drifted forward. It was a risk, because Razan were sensitive to the presence of Aedh. There was every chance my being in his room would tug at his awareness and subsequently wake him. But it was a risk I was willing to take, if only to confirm my suspicions about Lucian.

Not that they really *needed* confirming, but there was still some tiny, ever-hopeful part of me that wanted to believe I'd read the connections wrong, that I really *hadn't* been as big a fool as it was beginning to appear.

This room, unlike the previous one, was an utter mess. There were clothes strewn all over the carpet, shoes kicked into haphazard mounds, and piles of men's magazines opened to revealing images scattered everywhere. None of which told me much about the man's identity. But there was also a stack of change on the bedside table, and beside it were his wallet and watch. Unfortunately, the wallet was closed, and in this form I couldn't exactly change that situation.

Or could I?

If, as a half-breed Aedh in human form, I could reach inside a man's body, wrap my fingers around his heart, and squeeze the life from him, why couldn't I extract a driver's license from a wallet in *this* form? Or at least use the energy that was inherent in this form to open said wallet to get a better view of the contents?

It was certainly worth a shot.

I stared at the wallet and imagined the thing opening. Energy rippled along the length of my particles, then spun into a thin rope that glistened like lilac-tinted sunshine in the semidark confines of the room. I envisaged it wrapping around the wallet and, after a moment, the wormlike slither moved forward and did just that.

Pain ran through me, a sharp reminder that I wasn't anywhere near full strength and probably shouldn't be trying this if I wanted to function afterward. As ever, I ignored the warning and imagined the wallet flipping open. After a slight pause, the energy again reacted. The wallet flipped into the air, did a three-sixty, and dropped with a splat on the exact same side it had started on.

It certainly *didn't* open.

The man on the bed stirred, muttering something under his breath. I froze, ready to flee should he show the slightest hint of actually waking.

He reached down his body with one hand, roughly hauled the blankets over himself, then settled back to sleep. If I could have sighed in relief, I would have.

I glanced at the wallet again and tried opening just one side. All I achieved was flipping it completely over—but it was then I finally noticed the sturdy little press stud holding the wallet closed. Until that was undone, I didn't have much hope. As hot lances began to stab through my particles, I concentrated the energy on the press stud and somehow managed to undo it. I quickly flicked the wallet open—and none too soon, because the hot lances exploded into agony, and it was all I could do to maintain Aedh form.

I remained where I was, not moving, not doing anything, until the pain receded to a more comfortable ache, then carefully inched forward. The driver's license—visible through a somewhat grimy plastic window—said the Razan's name was Henry Mack. I might not remember what the Razan in the tunnel had looked like, but I remembered the name. It was a fake—one of two this man was using. His real name—which was part of the information Uncle Quinn had pulled from his mind—was Mark Jackson, and he lived in a Brunswick West warehouse rather than in Broadmeadows as his license stated.

I quickly checked out the rest of the place, but didn't find anything else. I hovered in the kitchen for a moment, staring out the window, wondering if I should risk using the stones to get back to the storage place or simply get there under my own steam. Or, given the lancelike flashes of pain that were beginning to stab through my particles, get as far as I could under my own steam.

Then I actually focused on what I'd been staring at rather blindly and realized it was two more stones. They were less than half the size of the ones in the small box room and formed part of the water feature that dominated one corner of the courtyard. But even from here I could see the cuneiform etched into the glistening stone, which in itself suggested they were at least created by the same hand as the others.

Curious, I headed out to investigate. The stones stood on a small rock island that had been built in the middle of the lily-filled pond. Water spurted from the top of each, then ran down their cuneiform-etched sides before trickling back into the pond.

As I approached the stones, they began to pulse with energy. This time, it was darker, more threatening. I hesitated, then mentally shrugged. I'd come this far—why stop now?

I entered the stones. Again the energy encaged my particles, then swept me not into brightness, but utter darkness. A darkness that was cold, devoid of sensation, and as frightening as hell. Then the energy surged, and I found myself in a very different garden. One that was lush and exotic, filled with plants and the happy calls of birds.

Where the hell was I? The air was hot and moist, and clung uncomfortably to my particles. Somewhere in the distance water bubbled, a soothing accompaniment to all the birdcalls. Yet no birds fluttered through all the greenery, and I soon realized why— the calls were being piped in from somewhere nearby. Then I saw the glass wall. I was in a greenhouse of some sort.

I moved in to the plant life. I had no sense that anything—living or otherwise—was close, but that didn't mean caution wasn't required.

After a few seconds I found a second glass wall, but this one looked out onto a backyard that ran down to sand and then sea. A sea that was blue and bright and vast and was nothing like Melbourne's own bay even on the best of days.

And I still had absolutely no idea where I was.

I followed the wall until I found a set of double doors that opened out into the yard and slipped underneath them. The outside air was cooler, but it was still far warmer here than in Melbourne. I slipped across the manicured lawn, then onto the sand. The sea rushed to greet me, its foamy fingers crashing upward, spraying my particles with salt water.

I studied the beach that stretched endlessly before me and suddenly recognized the long line of high-rise buildings that crowded the shore.

I was in Queensland—the Gold Coast, to be exact.

To have come this far meant those stones held some serious magic. Most transport spells—or at least the ones created by human witches and white sorcerers—were restricted when it came to distance. There were very few people with enough power capable of producing a spell that could take you from one state to another. Which meant that even if whoever the hell had made these stones wasn't involved with Lucian or the key quest, they were someone we needed to be very wary of.

I moved back through the greenhouse and into the house. As you'd expect of a property on such a prime piece of real estate, it was vast, bright, and expensive looking. The decor was minimal and modern, and this lower floor consisted mainly of a pool and barbecue area, as well as changing rooms and a bar. The entire first floor was devoted to a massive kitchen and living area, with panoramic folding glass doors opening onto a balcony that overlooked the beach. The second floor held all the bedrooms. There were no other standing stones that I could find, so maybe the ones in the greenhouse worked both as an entry and an exit point. The one we'd found underground certainly had.

The house was empty, and I could sense no other form of magic protecting it. Nor could I actually see any form of security system installed, which meant I could probably risk resuming my regular shape. I called to the Aedh once more, and the magic answered swiftly, sharply, sweeping me from energy to flesh in the blink of an eye before depositing me in an ungainly heap on the polished floorboards. Which was where I stayed, gulping down air, the pain in my head sharp enough to have tears rolling down my cheeks and my stomach jumping up my throat.

A heartbeat later, energy surged around me; then arms that were warm and familiar and oh so welcome wrapped around me and drew me close. As the side of my face pressed against Azriel's chest, I closed my eyes and listened to the steady beat of his heart, willing my own to match it. After a while, the rapid pace of my pulse began to slow, and the pain lessened.

He shifted his grip and held me at arm's length. "Are you all right?"

I took a deep breath and released it slowly. "Surprisingly, yes."

His gaze swept me, and his expression suggested he wasn't exactly believing that. No surprise, given he was connected to my chi and knew the truth. "Do you know where we are?"

I half smiled. "To paraphrase Dorothy: Toto, we're not in Kansas anymore."

"I'm bound to say that statement makes no sense."

"Do any of my statements ever make sense to you?" I brushed the solo tear tracking its way down my cheek with a somewhat shaky hand. I might have felt stronger changing to and from Aedh form, but the aftereffects still sucked. Big-time.

He rose and held out his hand. "On rare occasions, yes, they do."

I snorted softly and placed my fingers in his. He hauled me up gently, but the world did a brief three-sixty around me, and it was only his grip that kept me upright.

"Damn," I muttered, swallowing bile. "I really am going to have to eat something soon."

"I will refrain from saying I told you so."

"That's mighty big of you." I turned and studied the room. We were in what had to be the master bedroom, given it was twice the size of the other four. It was pin-neat, almost sterile, with little sign that anyone lived here. But someone surely had to—why else would the stones transport us here?

"I cannot say whether someone lives here or not," he said. "But there *is* magic in this place."

I raised my eyebrows. "Really? I didn't sense any when I was in Aedh form."

"That is because the magic has some form of sensory boundary around it. It is very subtle." He motioned toward the closet. "And comes from there."

I studied the double doorway somewhat dubiously, then pushed my feet into motion. The closet turned out to be another room—one as big as my bedroom and filled with enough designer shoes and clothes to make even Aunt Riley's heart sing. One side held feminine things, the other male, and in the middle stood several long, intricately carved Chinese sideboards. Now that we were close, the magic within them was easy enough to feel. It radiated from the drawers and cupboards in gentle waves, caressing my skin with an electricity that felt as dark and as dangerous as the stones in the greenhouse below.

I stopped and rubbed my arms. "Wonder what these things hold."

"The accoutrements of a dark sorcerer, from the feel of it. I would suggest you do not attempt to view them."

"There's not a chance in hell of me doing that." Even if part of me wanted to.

I swung away from the troubling source of magic, donned my gloves again, and went through the clothes, trying to find some clue as to the identity of their owners. Interestingly, all the male clothing—while exquisitely made—tended to be rather old-fashioned in design. If it weren't for the modern labels, it would have been easy to believe they belonged to a time when breeches and waistcoats were all the rage. In fact, they were the sort of clothes Jane Austen's men would have been perfectly at home in.

But again, there was nothing—not even a scrap of paper in pockets—to suggest that the clothes had ever been worn. It was as if we were dealing with a ghost.

But while a ghost could certainly haunt this place, one couldn't actually own it.

Frowning, I spun around and checked the other bedrooms. The result was, as I'd expected, more big fat zeros.

We headed downstairs. The kitchen was all shiny black and fitted out with silver appliances, and while the result was pretty spectacular, all I could envisage was the multitude of fingerprints and dust that would show unless you were vigilant about cleaning. Which whoever owned this place obviously was, because there wasn't a speck to be seen.

Thankful I hadn't ditched the gloves at the warehouse, I carefully opened the drawers and cupboards. All of them contained the usual kitchen paraphernalia, and all of them were as neat as the rest of the house.

"Whoever lives here doesn't seem to agree with your philosophy when it comes to storing things," Azriel commented.

I glanced at him as I moved over to the pantry. He stood in the middle of the oversized living area, arms crossed and expression wary. Like he expected something to jump out at us at any minute—and things certainly *had* during past investigations of places where we weren't supposed to be.

"And what philosophy would that be?" I said, opening the pantry door.

"To dump items wherever and worry about finding them again later."

I flashed him a grin over my shoulder. "Do my untidy tendencies bother you?"

"No. I just find them illogical."

"And now you sound like Spock. And I know that makes no sense because you have no idea who he is." I paused, my gaze falling on the small black organizer attached to the other side of the door. "Bingo."

He was beside me in an instant. "You've found something?"

"Bills." I plucked one out and opened it up.

My stomach dropped.

The person who owned this mansion was *no* stranger.

It was Lauren Macintyre—the dark sorceress who was Lucian's lover.

Chapter 4

"If you were looking for a connection between our dark sorcerer and Lucian," Azriel commented, "I think you just found it."

"But Lauren *isn't* the sorcerer we're looking for. Her magic felt different from the magic I sensed when that first key was stolen."

"And yet the cuneiform on all the stones—both the ones you discovered today and the one you and Jak discovered underground—bear the same markings and energy quality."

"Which suggests she's involved, not that she's the one we're looking for." I shoved the letter back, making sure it was in the exact same position. "Besides, it was a man I saw snatching the key, not a woman."

"You could have been mistaken. We were under extreme pressure at the time."

Extreme pressure was putting it mildly, given we'd been under attack from a horde of insane mutant shifters. "Yes, but I'm not mistaken. It *was* a man."

"There *are* male clothes upstairs. If Lauren is not the sorcerer we seek, then perhaps she lives with him."

That was certainly possible. "We need not only to find out more about her, but to keep an eye on her." I closed the pantry door. "Which means involving Stane again."

"This place has no security cameras that he can hack into."

"No, and that's an interesting point. Why would she own a massive place like this and have no obvious form of security?"

Did Lauren feel so secure about this location—or maybe even her own skills—that she felt no need for protection? Or was it, perhaps, that all her security was centered on the property's perimeter rather than within the actual house itself? It *would* make more sense to be aware of invaders long before they actually reached your door. And while I hadn't seen a security measure when I'd gone down to the beach, that didn't mean there wasn't one. Or that it wouldn't have reacted if I'd been in human form.

"Obviously, she has no desire for anyone to see what goes on in this house," Azriel said.

"Maybe it's not so much what goes on, but with whom."

That someone *wasn't* Lucian. The clothes upstairs hadn't been his size, nor, as far as I knew, his style.

For a change, Azriel made no comment on Lucian and simply said, "Did not Stane have a miniature camera device that proved useful once before?"

"He did." Said device had been made to resemble a bug, and we'd used it in an attempt to get information on a man we suspected of being not only a Razan, but perhaps involved with our sorcerer. Unfortunately, he, like many other of our leads, had turned out to be a dead end—in this case, literally. "I'm not sure if he managed to retrieve it, though."

"You can ask."

"True." I glanced at my watch and sighed. "But I'd better get back to work right now. I have to do Ilianna's shift, as she and Mirri are off celebrating their anniversary."

He raised an eyebrow as he took my hand and tugged me toward him. "An anniversary is something that should be celebrated?"

"Always." My gaze searched his. "I'm gathering reapers have no desire for such frivolity?"

"There is no need for it."

"Why not? I mean, it's not like you're incapable of emotion, and you do live in family units, so the concept of being with someone long term isn't an alien one."

"No." He hesitated. "Reapers do not view or feel emotions in the same manner as humans do. It is more about the harmony of energy than it is emotion."

"So a life mate—"

"Caomh," he corrected.

I made a face at him. "A *Caomh* is someone who is in perfect harmony with you energy-wise?"

"Yes. It is rare, which is why reapers tend to live in very large family units."

"Meaning parents, grandparents, etcetera?"

"Yes. Ready?"

I nodded. "So, what about your family? Do you have any brothers or sisters?"

The only answer I got was the surge of energy as he swept us from Lauren's mansion to the shadowed and minute-by-comparison confines of my office above the café. I blinked, caught my balance, then stepped back and said, "Well?"

"I have both. I do not see them."

Was that an edge to his voice? I frowned. "Why not?"

"I am a dark angel."

My confusion deepened. "So?"

He half shrugged and turned away, moving with easy grace to the sofa on the other side of the room. But red-tinged blue fire flickered down Valdis's sides—a sure sign Azriel was not as calm as he appeared. "Being a hunter is a punishment rather than a glory."

I moved around the desk and sat down. "But with the first gate down and the other two threatened, it's you guys who are holding everything together, not the supposedly more prestigious soul guides."

"They do not see it that way."

I stared at him for a moment, seeing the bitterness beneath the mask. "They don't, or you don't?"

A cool smile touched his lips. "Does it matter?"

"They're your family, Azriel—"

"And they're *not* important." This time there was no disguising the scathing edge, but I had an odd feeling that it was aimed just as much at himself as at me. "Nothing and no one else matters until the task that lies before us is completed."

I snorted softly and reached for the open bottle of Coke sitting on my desk. "And when this task is completed and you go back to hunting those who come through the dark portals, you still won't see them, will you?"

"Do you not have work you must do?"

Though his voice had lost the edge, there was a hard glint in his eyes and Valdis still flickered with angry fire. Frustration ran through me, but I resisted the urge to stoke the fire a little more and took a drink instead. He'd told me a whole lot more in those brief few seconds than he ever had about his reaper life, and while it was nowhere near enough to quench my desire to understand him more, I knew it was better to back away for the moment. Push too hard, and he'd make like a clamshell and not say anything else at all.

So I simply got back to work. It took me a couple of hours to get all the accounts done. Once I'd changed into clothes that weren't literally falling off me, I headed downstairs to help out with the wait-ressing. Tao was in the kitchen, but we were so damn busy that we barely had time to even smile at each other.

As it neared midnight—and the end of my shift—I counted the takings and secured the cash upstairs, then grabbed four glasses of ice and Coke and shouldered through the kitchen's double doors. The only person in the kitchen was our pot washer, Frank. Neither Tao nor Rachel, our other chef, was in sight, although the fridge door was open and the toe end of a brown work boot was visible. It had to be Rachel's—it was too small to be Tao's.

"Where's Tao?" I asked, handing Frank his drink.

The older man shrugged and wiped the sweat from his face with a brawny arm before accepting the glass with a smile of thanks. He was slightly simple, but he did a damn fine job and he seemed to enjoy it. At least he was reliable, unlike some of the kids we employed.

I swung around and headed for the fridge. "Hey, Rachel," I said, popping my head around the corner of the door. "There's a drink on the counter here for you. Where's Tao?"

"Outside I think, and thanks."

She didn't look up from her stocktaking, and I spun and headed out. The rear door was open, and the breeze was icy compared to the heat in the kitchen. I paused in the doorway, allowing my eyes to adjust to the darkness, but didn't immediately spot anyone.

I frowned. "Tao?"

There was a pause, then, "Here."

My gaze swung to the left, and even then it took me a minute to find him. He was hunkered down in the shadows of the Dumpster, his arms wrapped loosely around his knees.

"You okay?" I walked over and offered him one of the glasses. He smelled of sweat, grease, and ash. The latter had concern slithering through me.

"Thanks." He reached up and took it, but didn't lift his eyes. Didn't look at me.

"Tao, what's wrong?"

"Nothing." His voice was monotone. Clipped. "I'm fine."

"Then look at me." I squatted down in front of him and gently touched his chin. I might as well have touched a furnace, and I couldn't help the reflex to jerk my fingers back.

"Yeah," he said. "Nice, isn't it?"

"And the reason you're out here, I'm gathering." The fire elemental he'd consumed—the one he was locked in a constant battle with over control of his own body—didn't do too well in darkness and cold. Normally he'd just retreat to the freezer when the thing inside him started to threaten again, but with Rachel in there doing a stock take, the night air was the next best bet. I touched his chin again, ignoring the sting of heat as I forced him to look at me. His eyes—normally a rich, warm brown—were alien and fire filled. "Never turn away from me, Tao. You are not a monster, not now, not ever. Not to me, not to Ilianna, not to anyone that will ever matter."

He jerked out of my touch and snorted, the sound sharp with disbelief. "You say that now, but when the monster gains control, it'll be another damn story—"

"But it won't," I said sharply. "Because you're stronger than it is. So stop sitting there feeling so damn sorry for yourself and tell me about your date last night."

Just for a moment, I felt the flash of his anger—it rolled over me like the heated wind of a desert, drying my skin in an instant and sending little sparks dancing across my sweater. Then it dissipated, and he chuckled softly. "You really *do* like tempting the devil, don't you?"

"I have to deal with the devil in the form of Madeline Hunter on an almost daily basis, so maybe I've just become a little blasé about it." I sat down beside him, my shoulder touching his lightly. Although the heat was fierce, the tension within his body began to dissipate almost immediately. "And you avoid talking about your dates only when they go like crap. What happened?"

"Nothing. She was lovely, we had a good time, and we parted making plans for another date."

"So why all the doom and gloom?"

He sighed. "Because I'll have to break it off. She really *is* nice."

I frowned as I took a sip of drink. "I'm not understanding the logic of that statement."

"It's this." He waved a hand down the length of his body. "How can I commit to anyone for any amount of time when I have no idea just how long— if ever—it's going to take me to control this thing?"

I just about choked on my Coke. "Good grief, did you just admit to a connection? Is the lone wolf—the man who doesn't believe in long-term commitments— actually thinking he might have found the woman who could change that?"

He grimaced. "We went on *one* date—"

"And sometimes that's all it takes. You're a wolf, not a human or a monk."

He snorted. "I'm half wolf, and I'm certainly *not* a monk."

"Neat sidestep of the actual question, my friend."

He smiled. It was a somewhat pale reflection of his usual smile, but I was happy to see it nonetheless. "God, you're more tenacious than a dog with a bone. And yes, there was a connection."

"Then I can't see the harm in chasing it." I hesitated. "And it might just give you another reason to fight."

"Or another person I'm fearful of hurting."

"You won't." I nudged him gently. "I have faith in your strength, Tao."

He took a deep breath and released it slowly. "Yeah. And that scares the hell out of me, because you're seeing what I'm not feeling."

"Risa?"

I glanced up as Rachel appeared in the doorway. "What?"

"There's a gentleman here to see you."

"Business or personal?" I frowned as I glanced at my watch. It was after midnight, so it could hardly be business.

"He didn't say. Just said it was urgent." She shrugged, then added, "Tao, I may need help in a couple of minutes. A big group just came in from the Blue Moon wanting burgers."

"I'll just finish my drink and then I'll be in."

She nodded and disappeared. I climbed to my feet, then hesitated and looked down. "I can pull Danny off waiter duties to help Rachel if you'd like a few more minutes out here."

"It won't help much. I'll be fine." He squinted up

at me, expression half-mocking. "Isn't that what you're constantly telling me?"

It was a rebuke—a gentle one, but a rebuke nonetheless. I smiled, though it felt a little tight. "Yeah. And I'll keep saying it until you damn well believe it."

And with that, I left him. There was only so much I could say and do because, in the end, I couldn't help him win his war. He had to find the strength—and the desire—within himself to stop the elemental from taking over completely.

And, despite what I kept saying, part of me feared he wouldn't find either.

I walked back through the kitchen and into the café. The place was beginning to fill up again with wolves and a spattering of other non-humans, but we'd rolled into the next shift roster and there were plenty of people to deal with the rush. I couldn't see anyone obviously standing by themselves, so I poked my head back into the kitchen and said, "Where did you put him?"

"End booth, near the bathrooms," Rachel replied, without looking up.

"Thanks."

I headed down to the last booth, only to discover there was no one in it. But there was certainly someone standing in the shadows to the right of the booth. My gaze traveled up the long, lean length of him and clashed with his darkness.

This was no stranger. This was Markel Sanchez, one of the vampires who'd been ordered to not only follow me about astrally, but report my every move back to Hunter.

And as a Cazador, he was one of the most dangerous men I'd ever met.

I stopped abruptly. "Why are you here?"

"I am under orders, as you no doubt suspect." His voice held neither warmth nor inflection and yet somehow managed to be pleasant.

"So who's following me about on the gray fields right now?"

"Nick Krogan is currently on duty. Janice Myer shares the task at other times." He shrugged, the movement elegant. "It is my night off."

So they had female Cazadors? I guess there was no reason why they shouldn't, but it surprised me, for some reason. "And yet here you are."

"Because the wise in this world do not ignore the wishes of Madeline Hunter."

And yet I baited the bitch. What did that say about me? "Are you here to poke me into action or what?"

Amusement flickered through the darkness of his eyes and briefly warmed the coolness of his expression. "I am not here to poke. I merely deliver."

"Considering you're here under orders from Hunter, I'm rather hesitant to ask what, exactly, you're delivering."

The amusement was more pronounced, but he merely reached inside his rather classy-looking black trench coat and withdrew a small leather folder. With some trepidation, I took it and opened it up.

It was a badge. According to it, I was now an official investigator for the high vampire council. Talk about the shit-hole getting deeper.

I blew out a breath that did little to ease the tide of tension and shoved my shiny new credentials into the back pocket of my jeans. "Is that it?"

"For now, yes." He hesitated, his dark gaze flicking past me briefly. Then, more softly, he added, "Tread warily with Hunter on this one, Risa. She is ready to tear someone's throat out over this loss, and you are already close to pushing her past the limit."

I stared at him for a moment, then swallowed heavily. "Thanks for the warning."

"You are most welcome." A slight smile touched his lips, and just for a moment lent his austere features a surprising warmth. "I actually enjoy this duty. It makes a pleasant change from bloodshed, and you are certainly never boring."

I half smiled. "You obviously haven't been following me around for long enough, then."

"Perhaps not." He touched my shoulder lightly as he stepped past. "Be respectful. At least until this killer is caught."

"I will."

He nodded and walked away. I turned, watching him move through the crowd with ease, wondering how long he'd been a Cazador. He certainly wasn't the cold-blooded killing machine I'd grown up believing them to be—not on the surface, anyway. Of course, neither was Uncle Quinn, and he'd been a Cazador for centuries.

But that, I knew, was a rare feat. Most either died

on the job or were killed by the council after the endless killing sent them insane.

I headed back upstairs. Azriel still sat on the sofa, and I shook my head as I walked over to my desk to grab my coat, purse, and keys. "Don't you ever get bored, sitting there doing nothing?"

He raised an eyebrow. "Who said I was doing nothing?"

I glanced around. "Well, that's what it looks like from where I'm standing."

"Well, perhaps you should stand a little closer."

I grinned. "I keep trying. You keep pushing me away."

He rose and plucked the jacket from my grip, holding it out for me. "I did not mean in the physical sense."

I snorted softly as I shoved my arms into the sleeves. "Well, I can hardly get close to you mentally. The connection isn't two-way, remember?"

"I was not talking about either physical or mental connections."

I swung around, but he didn't move his hands, and his fingers trailed across my skin. His touch was warm, electric, and stirred to life the unsatisfied embers of desire once more. "What other connection is there?"

He hesitated. "For you and I, perhaps no other."

It was the "perhaps" portion of that statement that had me intrigued. "But reapers *do* have other choices?"

"Yes. It is the manner of our beings. This world of yours is filled with a vast array of energy harmonies, and it is a beautiful and wondrous thing to listen to."

"And rather noisy, I would have thought."

He smiled. "You learn to tune out the noisier melodies."

I arched an eyebrow. "You don't seem to have much luck tuning me out."

"No, but then, you're noisier than most. And more determined." His gaze lingered on mine for several heartbeats and, just for a moment, those bright depths showed a hunger as fierce as anything I was feeling. But it was gone just as quickly. He released his light grip and stepped away. "You're going to talk to the manager of Dark Soul now?"

I sighed in frustration, but there was little point in saying anything. He'd already stated that nothing would happen between us until I was stronger. "Yes. I'll drive, though. I feel like getting some air for a change."

He nodded. "I shall meet you there."

With that, he disappeared, making me wonder if he'd come closer to the edge than I'd presumed.

He didn't answer that particular thought, so I headed into the changing room, donned my leathers, then headed out to the secure underground parking lot where I kept my newly repaired Ducati.

Of course, she was no ordinary bike, but one of the first hydrogen-powered bikes to come onto the market. She was also the first thing I'd bought when RYT's finally began making a profit. And while she was nowhere near as efficient or as powerful as the current generation of hydrogen-fueled bikes, she was still sleek and sharp and comfortable, and that was enough for me.

I stashed my purse in the under-seat storage, then shoved on the helmet and sat down. The leather seat wrapped around my butt like a glove, and I couldn't help smiling as I fired her up. The vibration through the metal told me she'd come to life, although there was little other noise. Hydrogen bikes ran so silently that when they'd first become commercially viable, state laws had required manufacturers to add a fake engine noise device to warn people of their approach. I kicked up the stand and headed out. The night was cool and the streets relatively clear of traffic, enabling me to let loose. My grin just grew. Damn, I'd missed this.

Unfortunately, even though I'd taken the long way around, I reached Dark Soul far too soon. I reluctantly found parking up the road from it, then stored my helmet and walked back. Azriel appeared by my side as I neared the entrance.

"You should do that more often," he said softly.

"Do what?" It was said absently as I eyed the building in front of us. Dark Soul matched its name. It might not be a vampire-only hangout, but with blacked-out windows and smoke drifting out through the gothic metal gates guarding the doorway, it certainly gave off a dangerous vibe. Or maybe that was merely the haunting, ethereal melodies drifting from the shadowed interior.

"Ride your bike. It makes your soul glow."

I stopped abruptly and swung around to face

him. "Damn it, Azriel, you're going to have to stop doing that."

Confusion briefly crossed his features. "Stop what? *Complimenting* you?"

"Yes." I shoved my hands in my pockets and forced my feet onward again, feeling suddenly foolish.

He was beside me in an instant. "Why is this suddenly a problem?"

"Because," I muttered. "It just makes me want you more."

"Ah." Amusement laced his tones. "I see."

"No, I'm betting you don't."

"Then you would be wrong, Risa Jones."

I glanced up, saw that flare in his eyes again, and my breath caught briefly in my throat. Because it *wasn't* just need. Wasn't just desire. It was far deeper—far scarier—than that. Something that should not—could not—be, if only because we were two very different beings from two very different worlds. We might have made a decision to pursue this thing between us, but he was not of my world and never could be. What I'd just seen could *not* be anything more than an echo of my own emotions. It was an illusion—one that would turn to ash and totally destroy me once all this was over.

But maybe it was already far too late to start worrying about *that* happening.

I swallowed heavily. "Well, it wouldn't be the first time, would it?"

"No. And more than likely not the last."

Sadly, a truer statement had never been made.

The doorman opened the metal gates for us, and Azriel lightly cupped my elbow and guided me into the interior. It was, as the name suggested, a dark place, and it took a couple of seconds for my eyes to adjust. There was little noise in the room, even though it was full. Everyone's attention seemed to be trained on the stage at the far end of the room, their expressions one of rapture as they listened to the dark-skinned woman who played a pan flute. The music was haunting and beautiful and definitely not something you'd hear on the radio. I wasn't sure it was worthy of the rapture that seemed evident around us, but then, a pan flute, however nice the sound, wasn't really my cup of coffee.

The room itself was thin and narrow. A metal bar lined the left-hand side, and the scents emanating from it suggested it wasn't only booze being served, but synth blood. Maybe that was the reason behind the darkness—they didn't want to scare the human patrons with the knowledge of what they were serving vampires. It certainly wasn't illegal to serve synth blood, but it wasn't often done in places that catered to all races. Humans, vamps, and blood—even if only synthetic stuff—sometimes *weren't* a very good combination.

I made my way across to the bar. A small, thin vampire came up and gave me a pleasant smile. "What can I do for you?"

"I need to talk to the manager."

He raised a pale eyebrow, his gaze briefly skating down my length. Or what he could see of it, anyway, given the bar stood between us. Energy spun through the air, teasing the outer edges of my mind. He was trying to read me telepathically, but he didn't have a hope in hell, thanks to the superstrong nano microcells that had been inserted into my earlobe and heel. Nanowires—the predecessor of the microcells—were powered by body heat, but for the wires to be active, both ends had to be connected so that a circuit was formed. The microcells were also powered by body heat, but they were contradictory forces that didn't need a physical connection. Once fully activated, the push-pull of their interaction provided a shield that was ten times stronger than any wire yet created.

With them in place, no one was getting inside my head. Well, *almost* no one. Azriel certainly had no problems, and I suspected Lucian could read me more than he'd ever admitted.

And then there was Hunter, who always seemed to catch my thoughts at inopportune moments. Like when I was cursing her.

The energy died and he sniffed. It was a somewhat disdainful sound. "And who might I say is wanting her?"

"Risa Jones." I hesitated. "I'm here on orders of the vampire council."

"Really?" Amusement touched his mouth. "Just a moment, and I'll see if she's in."

"Tell her she'd better be, because she really *wouldn't* want a visit from Madeline Hunter right now."

The other eyebrow rose to meet the first, but he didn't say anything, just spun around and headed down the far end of the bar, disappearing through a rather solid-looking door.

I leaned back against the bar and studied the woman on the stage. "Do you think she might be our suspect?"

Azriel glanced at her, then shook his head. "She is a vampire. Whatever killed Hunter's friend was definitely something more."

"But the music she's playing seems almost hypnotic. I mean, look at them." I waved a hand around. "They can barely take their eyes off her."

"That is deliberate on her part. She feeds off them."

My gaze jumped sharply to his. "She's an *emo* vampire?"

"If that is a vampire that feeds off the life force of others, then yes."

"An emo feeds off emotion, not life force." I frowned at the woman. "Is anyone in danger?"

"I would suspect not. She appears to be taking only a small quantity from each—it amounts to little more than minutes from their lives."

"It shortens their *lives*?"

He raised an eyebrow, amusement lurking around the corners of his mouth. "Did I not just say that?"

"Apparently." I scrubbed a hand through my short hair. "Should we try to stop her?"

"That is not why we are here; nor is it your place to do so. If she takes it too far, the Directorate will deal with her."

"And will she? Take it too far, I mean?"

He studied her for a moment, his eyes narrowed.

"That possibility is there. It always is whenever a life depends on feeding from others."

"Huh." I glanced over my shoulder, saw the barman coming back, and turned around.

"You have a couple of minutes," he said. His tone held a mocking edge as he added, "Seems she'd prefer not to have Hunter after her."

"She's through that door?" I nodded toward the heavy wooden door.

"Yes." He picked up a tea towel and began polishing glasses, his expression one of disdain. Hunter's lackeys, it seemed, were not held in high regard in this place, even if the woman herself was feared.

I pushed open the heavy wooden door and stepped into a long, semidark corridor. Several doors led off it, all of them closed except the one down at the far end. Light flickered from within—some sort of computer screen, I thought, as I headed down. My footsteps echoed lightly, but no one came out to usher us into the room or greet us.

I paused at the doorway. The room was almost bare, with little more than a bank of security monitors and a large desk—complete with a light-screen monitor and keyboard—in the room. Behind the desk, in a chair that was larger than she was, sat a diminutive, dark-haired woman. She didn't bother looking up from whatever it was she was reading, merely waved a hand in a "come in" motion.

Given there were no seats on our side of the desk, I stopped in front of it and waited.

And waited.

She tests you, Azriel commented.

I gather that. My reply was grouchy. *Why is it that female vampires seem to be such bitches?*

Perhaps they feel the need to prove themselves more.

I snorted softly. *Or they just like being bitches.*

That is also possible. Perhaps you should flex a little muscle. Or would you prefer me to?

She's hardly likely to respect me more if I ask you to beat her up. By the same token, I doubted I'd actually have what it took to do that. I might be part were, but she was vampire. But then, I *did* have other talents I could call on—talents she *wouldn't* have seen before.

"You know," I said, keeping my voice conversational, "I came in here to ask a few polite questions about Wolfgang Schmidt, but if you'd rather do things the hard way, I'm more than happy to oblige."

She finally looked up, her expression mocking. "Am I supposed to cower in fear? Because, let's be honest here, a werewolf provides little threat to one such as I; nor does a man who wears the mask of death."

She sees you as a reaper?

Yes. To her, he added, "Then you are a fool."

"And certainly not a good judge of character." I raised a hand and called to the Aedh, then siphoned the surge of power into my raised fingertips. They went translucent in an instant, neither flesh nor Aedh, but somewhere in between. Her gaze went wide. I added, my voice still even, "Because, you see, I'm not *just* a werewolf. I'm someone who can reach into your chest, wrap my fingers around your heart, and rip it beating and bloody from your flesh."

She blinked, staring at my hand in awe and perhaps the tiniest touch of fear. And I have to admit, I *liked* seeing that, if only because I was getting a little sick of being on the wrong end of fear all the time.

Maybe it really *was* time for me to start flexing a little muscle.

"What are you?" she said after a moment.

"As I said, something more than a werewolf." I released the Aedh and let my hand return to full flesh. "Now, if you've finished with the games, tell me about Wolfgang Schmidt."

She shrugged. The fear—if indeed that was what I'd seen—was gone, but so, too, was her somewhat disdainful demeanor. "He's a regular, comes in two or three times a week."

"And he was in here last night?"

"Yes."

"With anyone?"

"No."

Obviously, she had every intention of answering what I asked and nothing more. "Then did he leave with anyone?"

"I can't say. I don't watch the movements of every single patron."

"Then why have the large bank of security monitors in the room?"

She smiled. "They are not trained on individuals. I simply like to be aware of what is going on in that room at all times."

A controlling bitch, in other words. Maybe I should have called Hunter instead of flexing a little Aedh muscle — the resulting fireworks might have been interesting.

"Then I want access to all the tapes from last night. Now."

"And you can prove you are actually from the council? Because I am not inclined to show those to any random stray off the street."

I ignored her jibe and tossed my badge onto her desk. She picked it up, briefly studied it, then handed it back. "Why do you wish to see the tapes?"

"Because Wolfgang Schmidt is dead. He was murdered last night after he left here."

"That is sad news indeed." It was hard to tell whether she actually meant it or not, because there was little emotion in either her voice or her expression. "You may view the tapes in the room opposite. I shall port them over to the screen there."

"Just the ones for the times he was here, not the entire night."

Another cool smile touched her lips. "Of course."

I spun and walked over to the other room. The lights came on as we entered, revealing another sparse room. At least there were two chairs here — one behind the desk and the other in front. I sat behind the desk, found the ported tapes on the screen, and hit PLAY. The quality wasn't top notch, but I guess it didn't have to be if the only reason she had the cameras was to source out trouble before it really started.

There was no sound, but the woman spotlighted on the stage seemed to hold the audience under the same sort of spell as tonight's woman. She had pale skin, black hair with an oddly jagged red streak in it, and coal-black eyes. She wasn't playing the pan flute, however, but some sort of short-necked lute. I hit FAST FORWARD and rolled through about an hour's worth of film before I spotted Wolfgang. He came in just after midnight, sat at one of the tables close to the stage, and watched the woman with the same sort of rapt attention as everyone else.

When the woman finished her set, she came down and sat with him. They chatted for another half hour or so; then the woman retreated—but not for long. She and Wolfgang left together.

We had a suspect.

I froze the screen on the woman's image, sent both Hunter and myself a copy of it, then switched off the computer and went back to see bitch-face.

"You were successful?" she said, without looking up.

"Who was the entertainer you had on last night? Wolfgang left with her."

"Her name was Di Shard. She wasn't one of our regulars, just someone brought in at the last minute."

"Have you got her contact details?"

"Yes." She reached into her desk and handed me a business card. *Classique Entertainers,* it said. *Specialist in art, chamber, and classical musicians.* She added, "Anything else?"

I hesitated. "If there is, we'll be back. Have a pleasant evening."

Her smile was as insincere as my words. "Oh, you, too."

I spun on my heel and got out of there. Once we were out in the cool air of the night, I drew in a deep breath and released it slowly. "I hate dealing with vampires. I know the world at large doesn't care about that, but I'm just putting it out there."

"You are right," a flat and all-too-familiar voice behind me said. "The world at large doesn't care. Nor do I."

I inwardly groaned, but somehow managed to fix a smile in place as I turned around. "And to what do I owe this pleasure? Or is it simply a matter of you not trusting me to do my job?"

Did Markel not warn you to be pleasant? Azriel commented. He was standing so close that Valdis's energy streamed over me, little flashes of fire that spoke of their readiness for action.

I am. It's not like I called her a bitch or anything.

Her dark eyes flashed. As usual, she'd caught the one thought I didn't want her to catch. One of these days I was going to learn.

Maybe.

"I was told you were here. I was close by, and thought I might get a report firsthand."

I grimaced. "There's not a lot to tell. Wolfgang left with Di Shard, last night's entertainment. I've already sent you her picture."

"Yes, and we're currently searching for all relevant details. Unfortunately, the entertainment agency that manages her maintains regular office hours, so we will be unable to talk to them until tomorrow."

How inconsiderate of them. "At least you can put an APB out on a woman matching her description or something."

"Hardly. She is mine to find and mine to kill."

There was death in her eyes. It might not be aimed specifically at me, but it would take only the slightest nudge and I'd be in her sights.

I had no intention of nudging.

"Then what do you want me to do? Until we talk to the agency or she kills again, the investigation has basically stalled."

"As I said, I have ordered a thorough search through both Directorate and council resources. We will uncover everything there is to uncover about this woman. In the meantime, you are to keep looking, as well."

"Of course." I said it politely, without inflection, yet still that darkness flashed. Sweat began to trickle down my spine, and my heart began to race. Never a good thing when standing in front of a vampire on the edge.

But all she said was, "Keep in touch."

I nodded. She shadowed, disappearing from my sight but not my senses. Only when the trail of her scent told me she had truly gone did I release my breath and turn around. "Will Hunter ever cross the line and become fodder for Valdis?"

"Hunter has crossed the line more than once, but Valdis will not taste her flesh unless she attempts to harm you."

"Damn. I was hoping you could bend *that* particular reaper ruling." It would be nice not to have to worry about the bitch, in any way, shape, or form.

A smile teased the corners of his mouth. "Trust me, I am most aggrieved by that particular ruling myself. Do you head home now?"

"Yeah. I'd better get some rest before I fall down dead or something." I rose on my toes and dropped a quick kiss on his lips. My own tingled in response, and it took a huge amount of willpower to step back. "I'll see you there."

He nodded and disappeared, though the heat lingering in the air told me he hadn't gone far. I walked back to my bike and rode through the almost empty streets, half wishing I could just keep following the road out into the darkness and the countryside, away from all the madness that had become part of my life of late. But that, unfortunately, wasn't an option.

Home was a square, two-story brick building situated in the heart of Richmond, and its somewhat bland gray exterior belied the beauty of its internal space. Ilianna, Tao, and I had purchased the old warehouse fresh from college and had renovated every inch of it—and were still regularly updating it with the latest and greatest technology.

After parking in the garage, I ran up the stairs to the thick alloy door that was both fire- and bullet-proof and looked into the little security scanner beside it. Red light swept across my eyes, and a second later the locks tumbled and the door slid silently open.

The huge industrial fans that dominated the

vaulted ceiling whirled lazily, gently stirring the aromatic air. The place was silent, and though the electrochromic windows weren't on blackout, there was little light coming in from the street.

"Lights on low," I said as I strode toward the kitchen. Soft mellow light flared through the darkness, gleaming off the exposed metal struts and lending the brick walls additional warmth. Tao had left the remains of last night's roast in the fridge, so I made myself a sandwich and a coffee and worked my way through both as I sorted through the stack of mail sitting on the kitchen table.

With that done, I had a quick shower, then headed for bed. I woke hours later with the sensation that something was wrong. For several minutes, I did nothing more than lie there, listening to the silence and wondering what the hell it was that I'd sensed. The apartment was silent, and there was little in the air to suggest that I was anything other than alone.

And yet the wrongness remained, scratching along the outer edges of my consciousness.

Frowning, I groped for my phone. No messages. Not that I'd really expected any. Tao would have finished his shift several hours ago and was no doubt chasing tail at one of the clubs, and Ilianna was with Mirri. If I rang either—especially given it was barely eight in the morning—I would not be popular.

"Perhaps it is nothing more than a premonition," Azriel said.

I twisted around. He stood at the window, his

hands behind his back, his stance that of soldier on guard. Valdis was silent, but her hilt, touched by a glimmer of sunlight, gleamed like a star.

"I can do without premonitions like that, thank you very much." I rose and padded across to where he stood. Tension rolled briefly across his shoulders, but he didn't otherwise acknowledge me. "Especially when they're that fucking vague."

My gaze dropped from the broadness of his shoulders to the stylized tattoos decorating his well-defined back. While the biggest of these was the Dušan, there were others. Some were recognizable—like a rose, or an eye with a comet's tail—while others appeared to be little more than random swirls. He'd told me once they were his tribal signature, although I had no idea what that really meant.

I raised a hand and ran my fingertips along the length of one of the swirls. The tattoo pulsed with dark fire, and tension rippled down the muscular length of his back.

"Azriel—"

"What you want is not wise, Risa."

"I don't care."

"I know." There was a hint of resignation in his voice, but he still refused to turn around.

I let my fingers trail on, tracing the outline of a comet. The tension in him grew. "Tell me," I said softly. "If you and I were both reapers, would you be standing there with your back to me right now?"

"No, I would not."

"Then don't do it now."

He sighed. "You do not understand the risk—"

"If assimilation is our fate, Azriel, then it will happen whether or not we make love."

"I was not talking about assimilation."

"Then what were you talking about?"

He didn't answer. He never did when it came to questions like that. I tried a different tack. "You once said that reapers make love by combining energies. Can we at least attempt something like that, if you're so set against physical lovemaking right now?"

"We could." He hesitated. "But I doubt it would be any wiser, and for even more reasons."

"Damn it, Azriel, just this once, why don't you forget reason? What the hell do you *want*?"

For a moment I thought he wasn't going to answer. Then he sighed and said, almost inaudibly, "You."

And with that, he turned around, took me in his arms, and kissed me fiercely.

Chapter 5

There was nothing sweet about this kiss, nothing soft, because it was filled with all the hunger of a man in desperate need. I wrapped my arms around his neck and returned it in kind, and for what seemed like ages, there was nothing but the kiss and the desire that exploded between us.

When he finally pulled back, his eyes burned with a hunger deeper than anything I'd ever seen before. "Just so you know, reapers do not engage in kisses like that."

"Well, they sure as hell *should*."

He smiled, then caught my hand and led me toward the bed. "I agree that there is something rather satisfying about flesh-on-flesh contact, be it lips or something more intimate."

"Something more intimate?" Amusement bubbled through me. "That's a polite way of putting it, I guess."

"I am nothing if not polite." He released my hand and sat cross-legged on the bed, then motioned for me to do the same. "Press your knees against mine."

"If a reaper's idea of sex doesn't involve more

touching than this," I commented, "I don't think I'm going to like it very much. Especially given I'm naked and you're not."

"Trust me, our state of dress will not matter." His smile creased the corners of his eyes and made my heart do a happy little dance. "And I am not entirely sure this will even work—although there is enough Aedh in you that it should—so behave."

"I am yours to command."

"If only." Though his voice was bland, it held a hint of sadness that tugged at something deep inside. "Because you are still flesh based, we will have to take this slowly. Are you ready?"

I smiled. "You should know me well enough by now to guess that answer."

"True." A smile briefly lifted the corners of his mouth; then his expression became serious again. "Close your eyes and concentrate on nothing more than your breathing."

"That hardly sounds like fun."

"Stop talking and concentrate if you want to do this." It was softly said, yet held a note of iron.

I shut up.

"Now," he continued. "Let go of the awareness of all that is around you, until there is no sound, no scent, just you and every intake of breath."

Meditate, in other words. I closed my eyes and concentrated on nothing more than breathing in and out. My heartbeat began to even out, and a sense of peace settled around me. As the minutes slid by, my breathing slowed further, until I was on the edge of an almost trancelike state.

"Feel," he said, picking up my hand and placing it on his chest. His skin was warm under my fingertips, his heart a steady, strong drum. "The rhythm of my breath. Breathe in as I breathe out."

My fingers rose with every movement of his chest, so even though I couldn't hear his breathing, it was easy enough to set mine on a separate course to his.

"Now, feel my breath on your lips," he continued softly. "Let it run across your tongue and into your body. Let it fill you, become you."

Warm air teased my mouth. My lips parted and I drew it in, filling my throat with his taste and my lungs with the scent of him, until all I could feel and all I could sense was the energy of his presence. In me, around me.

"Open your eyes."

I obeyed, and stepped into an ocean of blue. It was beautiful, that ocean, beautiful, but turbulent, and oh so powerful. My body began to tremble, not just with expectation and desire, but also fear. I was reaching for something I didn't understand, and it was far more dangerous than even Azriel thought. My throat tightened, and the rhythm of my breathing momentarily faltered. His fingers came to rest on my chest, his touch warm, electric.

"There is nothing to fear, Risa." His voice swirled around me, soft and hypnotic. "There is no darkness here. There is just us, two beings connected by flesh, connected by air, and connected by the essence of all that we are."

The fear ebbed away, and once again there was

only him. His energy, his being. Against my skin and in my mind. Burning bright, within and without, making me tremble, ache. Want.

"Imagine there is no flesh to separate us," he continued. "That there is only energy and desire. Call to them, Risa. Become them."

It was as if his words were some sort of trigger. Power surged, became a rush of fire that invaded every muscle, every cell, breaking them down and tearing them apart, until my flesh no longer existed and I was one with the air.

As was he.

He was bright and fierce, a being that glowed like the sun and who was as beautiful as the moon. He drew me toward him, wrapped himself around me, until the music of his being began to play through mine and mine through his. It was a dance, a caress, a tease. It was movement, heat, and desire. It was crazy and electric, a firestorm that ripped through every particle of my being. It was pleasure unlike anything I'd ever experienced or felt before, and it took me ever higher. Our beings continued to entwine, tighter and tighter, until there was no separation—no him, no me, just the music of the two of us combined. And oh, the song we made was beautiful, and powerful, and *right*. Still the dance went on, burning ever brighter, until it felt as if the threads of our beings would surely explode.

Then everything *did* explode, and I fell into a storm of electric, unimaginable bliss.

I'm not entirely sure when, exactly, I came back to flesh, but when I did it was to an awareness of utter exhaustion. My body trembled, sweat trickled down my spine, and my breath was quick, shallow pants, as if my body couldn't get air quickly enough. And yet I felt alive in a way that was indescribable.

"God," I murmured, when I finally could. "Is it always like that for you reapers?"

He brushed a thumb lightly across my lips and smiled. "No, not always."

There was a note that almost sounded like amazement in his voice. I opened my eyes and looked at him. He glowed with health and vitality, his skin golden and his blue eyes shining. "You recharged?"

"Yes." He hesitated. "I hadn't meant to, but the intensity of the moment got the better of me. Unfortunately, it is the reason you are now so weak."

I raised an eyebrow. "Do you see me complaining?"

He smiled, then leaned forward and kissed me tenderly. "No. However, you should rest now."

"But I don't want—"

He briefly pressed a finger against my lips to halt my protest. "For once in your life, just do what I ask without argument."

"In honor of that amazing experience, I'll obey. Just don't expect it to happen too often. Me obeying, that is."

"Oh, I won't." His voice was dry as he rose gracefully from the bed. "Sleep, Risa."

I did. And for longer than I'd expected, because it was late afternoon by the time I woke. I stretched, and suddenly realized I felt better than I had in days, if not weeks. I was refreshed, revitalized. Normal, almost.

Or as normal as someone like me could ever get.

"The recharging appears to have gone both ways," Azriel commented. "Which is good, but extremely unusual."

I glanced around. He'd returned to his post by the window, but this time his stance was relaxed and his skin gleamed warmly in the afternoon sunshine. "Meaning recharging for reapers is usually only one-way?"

"No, but you are not reaper; nor are you full Aedh. It should not have affected you as strongly as it did."

"Well, I'm not complaining about it, that's for sure." I sat upright in bed, but as I did, that nagging, niggling sense of wrongness returned. I frowned and reached for my phone a half second before it rang.

I glanced at the number and saw that it was Rachel. No doubt she was simply ringing to let me know someone hadn't turned up again. But one glance at the clock told me they were midshift, not at the beginning. It couldn't be that.

Something was very wrong. Of that I had no doubt.

I hit the RECEIVE button and said, throat dry, "Rachel, what's up?"

"It's Tao," she said. "He's disappeared."

Disappeared? *Oh fuck, please don't let it be the fire elemental. Please let it be something—anything—else.*

"When?" I asked. My throat was so dry with fear, it came out harsher than I'd intended.

"About an hour ago. He said he was hot and was going outside to cool down. Didn't think much of it, as he's been doing that a lot lately."

Because he was losing the battle. I rubbed a hand across suddenly stinging eyes. Damn it, I didn't need this on top of everything else. But then, it wasn't like Tao needed it, either, and it was my fault he was in this mess in the first place. If I hadn't included him and Ilianna—

You cannot beat yourself up over decisions others are ultimately responsible for, Azriel commented. *Tao had the choice. He chose to help, just as he chose to save Ilianna by consuming the elemental.*

If he weren't there, he wouldn't have had to make the decision.

And Ilianna would now be dead. You cannot have all things, Risa. Fate is not a generous woman at the best of times.

Yeah, I'm learning that. To Rachel, I said, "Did you try his phone?"

"I can't, because all his belongings are still upstairs. He didn't even change."

Damn. I closed my eyes for a moment and fought for calm. "Do you need me to get someone in?"

She hesitated. "Jacques is due in next shift— perhaps if you could get him to arrive a little earlier? We're not usually rushed until after six most Tuesday evenings."

"I'll do that. Let me know if Tao does show up again."

"I will."

She hung up. I called Jacques and asked him to start early, then threw the phone onto the bed and glanced at Azriel. "I don't suppose it's possible for you to locate Tao via his life force, is it?"

"That would depend very much on which life force is in control. If it is the elemental, then no."

"Well, at least we'd know for sure if the elemental has taken over."

Azriel nodded. "It may take me a few minutes. Do not leave the security of this place while I am gone."

"I won't."

He disappeared. I picked up the phone again and dialed Ilianna. "Hey, gorgeous," she said, expression cheerful and green eyes glowing with happiness. "How are you?"

I couldn't help smiling. "The celebrations obviously went well last night."

"Very well. I'm one contented mare right now. Not even the fact that I have to meet Carwyn again can spoil it."

Carwyn was the stallion her parents were trying to set her up with. According to Mirri, he was rather hot—in bed and out—but given Ilianna's preferences, she was either going to have to be honest with her parents or get stuck with a mate she didn't want.

"When is that happening?"

She grimaced. "Tomorrow night. I think it was supposed to be just him and me, but Mirri is coming along. She thinks we should be honest with him."

"It can't hurt, can it?" She couldn't help her sexual preferences, and the sooner Carwyn was aware of them, the better it would be for them all.

"He's a horse-shifter," she said dryly. "A *male* horse-shifter. They don't think straight when it comes to mares."

"I'm still siding with Mirri on this one."

"Traitor." The fierceness of her tone was more than a little diluted by the glint of amusement in her eyes. "To what do I owe the honor of this call?"

I hesitated, then said, "Tao's walked out of the café and can't be found. I don't supposed you've had any particular vibes were he's concerned?"

Ilianna wasn't only a powerful witch, but also a very strong clairvoyant—and a far more reliable one than I'd ever been.

"No, I haven't." She frowned, expression suddenly concerned. "Is it the fire elemental?"

"I think it could be. I know he was having trouble controlling it earlier."

"I'll do a locating spell and see if I can find him."

"Great." I hesitated. "Though if the elemental has taken over, will a locating spell even work?"

"I don't know." She bit her lip for a moment. "A locator spell works on the energy of the person, so with Tao's body chemistry constantly changing— flowing from flesh to elemental depending on which being has more control—it's going to be difficult to pin him down. But I can try."

"Let me know the minute you find anything. In the meantime, I'll rope in Stane and Jak."

"Why the hell would you involve *Jak*?" Her

voice held a note of disbelief. "It's not like Tao needs someone like him—someone only after a good story—on his case."

"Jak has his nose to the ground and can hunt stories in places neither of us would get near," I said. To say Ilianna had a hate-on for Jak was like saying night followed day—blindingly obvious.

"You be careful with him, Risa. The last thing you need in your life is another heartbreak."

"Trust me, Jak is getting nowhere near my heart." I gave her a lopsided grin. "Or my body."

She harrumphed. "I'll be in contact."

"Thanks."

I hung up, then scrolled through the contacts list until I found Jak—though truth be told I knew the number by heart—and rang him.

All I got was a recording telling me to leave a message. I did so, asking him to let me know if he heard about anything unusual dealing with fire, then tossed the phone back onto the bed and decided to grab a shower while I waited for Azriel to return.

He'd done so by the time I'd dressed, and one look at his expression told me everything I needed to know. I swore and thrust a hand through my damp hair. "Now what are we going to do?"

"There is nothing we can do—not until he regains his flesh form."

"And if he doesn't?"

He studied me for a moment, expression giving little away. "If he doesn't, you have a choice to make."

I stared at him, my stomach suddenly twisting itself into knots. "No."

"There may be no choice," he said, voice even but somehow relentless. "If the elemental has won the war, then Tao is already lost to you."

"No!" I clenched my fists against the anger—the useless, sick anger that was fueled part by fear and part by the knowledge that he was right—and added, "I will not give up on him."

While there was life, there was always hope.

Besides, I'd promised Tao I would do all that I could to help him win. Giving up at the first major hurdle was not doing *that*.

"Risa—"

I made a chopping motion with my hand. "I don't want to hear it, Azriel. I don't care what you say. I don't care what fate plans. I don't care about being sensible. I will not give up on my friend. Okay?"

He studied me for several seconds, then crossed his arms and turned back to the window. Every inch of his muscular back seemed to radiate displeasure.

"Okay."

"Glad we agree," I muttered. I grabbed my phone, then stalked out to the kitchen.

I wasn't feeling particularly hungry, but I wasn't about to fall into the trap of not eating. Not when I actually felt reasonably healthy for the first time in ages.

I made myself a coffee, then sat down and consumed a large bowl of Coco Pops complete with lashings of whole milk. Not the healthiest of meals, but a slight step up from the chocolate cake that had initially tempted me.

As I rinsed the bowl out, my phone rang, and the funeral march tone told me it was Hunter. I closed my eyes and, for all of three seconds, resisted the urge to answer it. But Markel's warning loomed large in the back of my mind. I swore softly, then did the sensible thing.

"There's been another murder," she said before I could even open my mouth to say hello.

Of course there was. I mean, why *wouldn't* fate just chuck more fuel into the bonfire of insanity that was my life at the moment? "Same MO?"

"Apparently. The report came in via Directorate channels, and it is not someone I know."

Thank god for *that*. The last thing we needed was for someone to be targeting Hunter's friends or lovers. She was close enough to the edge as it was. "I'm guessing you want me to check it out?"

"Yes. The address has been sent, so get there." Something flashed in her eyes. Something that was almost unholy. "Find this thing, Risa."

She hung up. The phone beeped as her message came in. I glanced at it, noting that this time, the murder had occurred in the more middle-class suburb of Caulfield.

Azriel appeared in the kitchen. "How do you wish to travel there?"

I hesitated. "As much as I'd love to go on my bike, I'm thinking that when Hunter said 'get there,' she meant immediately." If not sooner. I grabbed some gloves out of the cupboard under the sink, then stepped toward him. "Ready when you are, chief."

His arms came around me, wrapping me in warmth. "Hardly an appropriate name when you never listen to a word I say, let alone do what I say."

Though his tone was light, there was an edge that suggested there was more emotion behind the comment than he'd intended me to hear. I glanced up quickly, but his power surged, sweeping us from flesh to energy in a heartbeat before zipping us through the gray fields.

"Azriel—" I said, as we re-formed, but the rest of the sentence was cut off by a sudden and angry, "What the *fuck* are you doing here?"

And the shit just hit the fan, I thought, but plastered a smile on my face as I turned around. Uncle Rhoan stood in the doorway of the ultramodern brick and concrete two-story house, his red hair glowing in the last remnants of daylight and gray eyes glinting with anger. Obviously, Hunter had *not* given me priority over the Directorate this particular time.

"I was asked here," I said. "Believe me, I'm no happier about it than you are."

He eyed me for a moment, expression disbelieving. "Are you saying Jack *ordered* you here?"

"Yes, I am." And heaven help me if Jack didn't back *that* statement up.

If Rhoan detected the lie, he gave no indication of it. He came down the steps and strode toward me. I held my ground in the face of his fierceness, even though all I wanted to do was run.

"Why the fuck would he do that? You're *not* Directorate."

No, I was something far worse—Hunter's go-to girl when it came to all things hell related. And while Jack might be the senior vice president of the Directorate and the man who ran the guardian division, it was Hunter who held the reins of overall control. She also happened to be Jack's sister, and he was undoubtedly wise enough not to go against her wishes—not even when it came to something that would ultimately cause him grief. Uncle Rhoan had *not* been a happy camper last time I'd been called in to help the Directorate, even though that had been totally accidental. The lunatic he'd been hunting just happened to be the same one I'd come across on the astral plane, and the creepy bastard had subsequently decided he only wanted to play his games with me.

It was a game that had almost killed me.

"Look, ring *him* if you want to chew out someone. I'm here in an advisory role only."

Rhoan snorted. "Don't get me wrong, Ris, because you know I love you to death, but what the hell can you give a murder investigation that I and everyone else at the Directorate cannot?"

"Hell is *precisely* what I can give you," I replied, voice grim. Damn it, while I understood his anger stemmed from fear for my safety, it was fucking annoying to get chewed out over something I could *not* control. Not if I wanted to keep on enjoying my life, anyway. "Or rather, a working knowledge of what is—and isn't—coming through the gates now that one has been opened. And then there's Azriel."

Rhoan's gaze cut briefly to the man standing quietly at my back. "And whatever happened to the option of saying no? You're not employed by the Directorate. They can't force you to do anything you don't want to do."

Yeah, but Hunter *could*—not that *that* was something I could admit to. I took a deep breath and released it slowly as I racked my brain for an answer that wasn't going to get me yelled at too much more. In the end, I went with the truth—or as close to it as I was likely to get in this sort of situation.

"I agreed because if whatever—whoever—is committing these crimes *is* a denizen from hell, then it's my damn fault that it's out there."

He continued to glare at me but, after a few minutes, muttered something under his breath and thrust a hand through his short hair. "I hate that you're involved with the Directorate, however peripherally. They have a way of sucking you in deeper and deeper and never letting go. Neither Riley nor I want that sort of life for you."

"I don't want that sort of life for me, either." I gave him the best fake smile I could manage. "Trust me, you're welcome to the investigation. I'm just here to see what you might be dealing with."

His expression remained uncertain. "You're hiding something, Ris. I can smell it a mile off."

"Honestly, I'm not."

He snorted softly. "Yeah, trusting *that* statement, too. But for now, I'll let it drop. Come on."

He spun and headed back up the steps. I let out a silent sigh of relief and followed, putting on the protective booties and gloves as he identified me to the hovering crime-scene recorder.

The inside of the two-story home was as modern as its outside. Crisp white walls, shiny wooden floors, bright abstract art, and leather and chrome furnishings. This time the murder had taken place in an upstairs bedroom rather than in a living space, but as with the first victim, this man was fully dressed and apparently hadn't noticed the web being spun up his body.

Rhoan stopped at the end of the bed. I halted beside him, Azriel still a warm presence at my back. The man on the bed was a thin, graying individual who looked to be in his midsixties, and he was as modern in the way he dressed as he furnished his house. But the expression frozen onto his face was one of pleasure, and his stomach bore the two fist-sized slashes that had been evident on Wolfgang. I flared my nostrils, trying to find some hint of the odd alien musk that I'd smelled at the first murder scene, but either it had dissipated, or it was lost under the scent of all the crime men and women coming and going in the room.

"Did you get here first?" I asked, glancing at Rhoan.

"Yes." He met my gaze. "Why?"

"Did you smell an unusual aroma? It's similar to the musk of a shifter, but odder, if that makes sense."

"It was faint, but yes."

"What about at the first victim's?"

"Also present." His expression remained noncommittal, but the anger in him suddenly ramped up again. "How did you know about the scent when it's not evident now?"

"Because, uh—" My voice faltered, and I cleared my throat, resisting the urge to step away from the anger that would undoubtedly follow if I finished that sentence. I knew he would never hurt me, but that didn't make him any less scary at times like this.

"It is a smell common to many of the darker spirits who inhabit this world," Azriel cut in smoothly. "Especially those who are also capable of shape-shifting."

Oh, good reason, I said to Azriel. *Thanks.*

It is also the truth, he replied. His mental tones were still frosty.

I sighed. *And just how long are you planning to remain annoyed at me over something so trivial, Azriel?*

I do not know. For as long as it takes for you to regain common sense, perhaps.

You could be in for a long wait.

I am a reaper. Patience is part of our nature.

I snorted mentally. *Oh yeah, you've so totally proven that.*

As you've said to me often enough, sarcasm does not become you.

"I do get the feeling," Rhoan said, "that there's a whole conversation happening that I know nothing about."

I glanced at him. "I was just asking Azriel if he could tell whether we were dealing with a spirit or a demon."

"And the answer?" His tone suggested he wasn't believing *that* for a second, either.

"It's not a demon, but he can't confirm or deny the possibility of a spirit because they're of this world rather than the other and therefore not his field of expertise."

"Huh." He crossed his arms. "Anything else you can tell us?"

I frowned, my gaze drifting up the body. The silken web that encased the victim had been leashed to the bed end rather than the floor this time, but otherwise it looked almost identical. I opened my mouth to ask if they'd found a Dark Soul business card in one of his pockets, then remembered I wasn't supposed to know about that. Subterfuge, I thought, sucked.

"Is that wound on his stomach the only one?" I asked instead.

"Yes. And whatever was injected through those slashes liquefied every inch of his innards," Rhoan said. "There's nothing left but a hardened outer shell of skin."

So it was definitely the same MO. "What about the victim? Is he human?"

"He's a hawk-shifter. He's also a perp with a long line of break-and-enter convictions behind him."

I glanced at him sharply. "So this *isn't* his house?"

"It's not even his *suit*." Amusement briefly touched the corners of his eyes. "The actual owner is one Shamus O'Callagan, and he's overseas on business. Apparently, old Sam here has been putting his psychic talents to good use and keeping himself off the street by not only sourcing out temporary high-end accommodations, but taking over the owner's identity."

"He might still be alive if he'd been on the streets."

Rhoan raised his eyebrows. "Meaning you think our killer has a taste for the high life?"

Maybe not so much the high life, but possibly a taste for those who are psychically endowed. It couldn't be a coincidence that the first two victims were both gifted in that area. "How strong a psychic was he?"

"Strong enough to easily convince doubters he really *was* O'Callagan."

"From what I've been told, the first victim was a strong telepath."

"Given he was an old vampire, that goes without saying."

Not all vamps were strong telepaths. There were a few—*a very rare few*—who missed out on that particular gift. "Then being a strong psychic of some kind *could* be the link." I half shrugged. "Of course, he was also rich. Maybe our killer is going after the wealthy. Maybe their innards taste better than us more ordinary folk."

He snorted softly. "You're about as ordinary as a blue diamond."

I grinned. "I think that's the nicest thing you've said to me for ages."

"That's because you keep doing dumb things." He nodded toward the body. "Is there anything else you can tell us?"

I sighed. "No. Bit of a waste of time, wasn't it?"

"Maybe, but at least we now know we could be looking for a spirit; it'll give the witches in the Directorate's employ something to do on this one." He gave me a stern look. "You're not going to attempt to track this thing down, are you?"

"Not unless I'm forced to." I gave him a lopsided smile, then rose on my tiptoes and kissed his cheek. "Tell Riley I'll see her on Thursday for lunch."

"I'd advise not missing this one, or she'll be royally pissed."

"And that's never very pleasant for anyone," I said. "Tell Jack I'm sorry I couldn't be of more use."

He nodded. I turned and headed out. At the front door, I stripped off the protective booties and gloves, dumping them in the hazmat bin before walking down the front steps.

"Now what do you wish to do?" Azriel said, as I stopped near the front gate.

"Run away to a desert island somewhere with a mountain of chocolate and a refrigerator full of Coke." But running away wasn't going to solve anything. Not when I had a world to save, keys to find, and beings willing to kill those I loved if I didn't get my ass into gear sooner rather than later. I sighed. "But I guess we'd better go home and see if we can do anything to pinpoint the location of the next key."

"Home it is," he said, and had us there in a heartbeat.

I rang Hunter, but this time, she didn't answer. I left a message that our killer appeared to be going after men who were psychically strong and asked if I could grab a copy of the crime-scene report when it came through.

My phone rang the minute I hung up. "Ilianna," I said. "Please tell me you've found him."

"Unfortunately, no." Frustration and concern filled her voice and expression. "If he's out there, then I can't see him. God, I hope he's okay."

So did I. "Would it be worth trying location spells every hour or so?"

"If he's in a state of flux, yes. If the elemental has full control, then no. But I'll keep trying."

"Just don't tire yourself out too much. That's not going to help anyone."

"I won't. Let me know the minute you hear anything, won't you?"

"Absolutely."

I hung up, then stripped off my jacket and said, "Com-screen on," as I headed into the kitchen. A light screen flared above the small, dome-shaped computer unit I'd left sitting in the middle of the dining table a few days ago. Several seconds later, a laser-light keyboard appeared on the table surface near the unit. I grabbed another Coke from the fridge, as well as a wedge of the cake I'd resisted earlier, then sat down and said, "Show last search result."

More than twenty-five names immediately scrolled onto the screen. All were museums located within the golden triangle, with the biggest of them being Sovereign Hill, the open-air museum that re-created life of the goldfields during the mid-1800s. It was probably the most logical place to hide a dagger—which was what the second key had apparently been disguised as—and yet, for some reason, I had a nagging suspicion it wouldn't be there. But maybe that was due to little more than the fact that nothing else had been easy of late, so why the hell would the search for the second key be so straightforward and logical?

Besides, the clue my father gave mentioned "soil being stained by rebellion," and that *had* to refer to the Eureka Stockade—one of the biggest and bloodiest rebellions in Australian goldfields history. Given the stockade had happened on Bakery Hill in Ballarat, that removed more than half of the search results. I ran an eye down the list, then grimaced and sat back in the chair. "This is going to take forever."

"Though your father has been surprisingly patient thus far, I cannot see him waiting out eternity for the keys," Azriel said.

"Especially since I'm not immortal and haven't got an eternity to search for them." I ate some cake, then added, "Hell, for all we know, the bloody dagger isn't even *in* a museum, but rather some private weapons collection."

"Possibly." Azriel studied the screen for a moment, then said, "Logically, a dagger would not likely be found in either a pottery museum or a fine arts gallery, so that would erase at least half of those names from the list."

"True." I leaned forward and looked at the list again. "If logic *did* play any part in the placement of this thing, then it's more likely to be at either

Sovereign Hill, the Eureka Centre, or the Aviation Museum. And maybe—if it was disguised as some sort of artifact—maybe the Aboriginal Culture Centre."

"Four locations is not an overly large search area."

"No, but it would be better to visit them when they're open." If only because I needed to be in flesh form to feel the presence of the key, and I could hardly just pop in at this hour of night and start wandering around. Security would be on me before I got three steps. And while Stane could hack into their systems, he needed more than a few minutes' notice. I munched on the remainder of the cake, then said, "The real problem is not going to be finding the key. It'll be keeping the damn thing long enough to figure out what we're going to do with it."

"With the Aedh out of the equation—"

"It wasn't Lucian who stole the first key," I cut in, more than a little annoyed at his continuing insistence on blaming all of our bad luck on Lucian. He was undoubtedly responsible for *some* of it, granted, but definitely not all of it. "It was a dark sorcerer. A *male* dark sorcerer."

"Who might well be connected to both Lucian and his dark sorceress lover."

"He also might not. The point, however, is not who is involved with whom, but how do we stop them from grabbing the second key."

"Simple. We tell no one—"

I snorted softly. "Yeah. Except that my father, the Raziq, and probably Lucian all have varying degrees of access to my thoughts. Hard to keep a secret when your mind leaks like a sieve."

"And there is nothing we can do about *that*. However, your father is more than capable of creating wards powerful enough to keep the Raziq and possibly the dark sorcerer at bay. Perhaps the time has come to lean on his capabilities a little more."

I frowned. "Do you really think he's going to agree to make wards strong enough to keep the Raziq out when it will also keep him out?"

"He can easily add a back door for himself in any magic he creates."

Given my father was responsible for the wards that currently protected this building, as well as creating the Dušans, that was undoubtedly true. And yet something within me didn't want to depend on him for *anything*. I didn't trust him.

"You don't have to trust him," Azriel commented. "You just have to exploit his abilities. Besides, if you wish to keep both the Raziq and the sorcerer from the key, then there isn't anyone else who has the power required to create such magic."

I took a deep breath and released it slowly. "Then let's go talk to the bastard."

I pushed away from the table and walked back into my bedroom. I'd stashed the communication cube my father had given me in a shoe box at the back of my wardrobe, hoping against hope that I wouldn't have to use the thing again. I should have known better.

I dug it out, then walked across to the bed and opened the box up. The cube sat within. It was little more than a white stone roughly the size of a tennis ball. Its surface was slick—almost oily—looking, and ran with all the colors of the rainbow.

I picked it up somewhat gingerly. It was warm against my fingertips, the energy within it muted and unthreatening. Yet it had been created using Aedh magic, and it was activated by blood—my blood—and that gave it a certain edge of darkness that made me wary.

Or maybe that wariness simply stemmed from the fact that I didn't trust the man who'd made it.

And yet he'd also made the Dušan on my arm, and she'd saved my life twice now.

I contemplated the cube for several more seconds, then tossed it on the bed and sat cross-legged in front of it. I glanced up as Azriel appeared. "I don't suppose you could get me—"

"Done." He offered me the knife hilt first, then sat opposite me and drew Valdis, placing her across his knees. Blue fire ran the length of her bright blade, a sure sign she was ready for action.

Hopefully, she wouldn't be needed.

I drew a deep breath, then released it slowly. It didn't do a lot to calm the nerves. I pressed the point of the knife against a fingertip until a drop of blood appeared, then turned my finger upside down and let the blood drip onto the cube. As it hit, the rainbow swirl of colors stopped, and everything went still.

Then light burst from the stone and quickly encased me in a cylinder of glaring white. Azriel disappeared from sight, and Valdis's fierce blue flames were little more than a shadowed flicker.

"Father, are you out there?" My voice echoed slightly in the odd silence of the white void.

For several seconds, there was no reply; then his voice—a harsher, more masculine version of mine—said, "I'm here. Why are you using this cube?"

"You gave it to me to communicate. I'm communicating."

"So you have found the next key?"

"Not yet."

"Then why are you using this cube?"

Impatience—and perhaps a touch of anger—swirled through the whiteness around me. My stomach tightened. I'd felt my father's anger once before. I did *not* want a repeat of the bruises that had ensued.

And yet I couldn't quite help snapping, "Because if you want the damn keys, then you're going to have to do a bit more than provide indecipherable clues."

"I cannot give you what I do not have. The Raziq who hid the keys are dead. I cannot call them back from whatever hell they may have gone to, so I am at a loss as to the point of this request."

"The request isn't more information." Which he'd know if he was reading my mind. The fact that he obviously wasn't meant either he was some distance away or something else was going on. Aedh could usually read the minds of anyone nearby, and my father had implied he could read mine anytime he desired. "I want to know if you can create a ward or something like that to keep both the Raziq and the black sorcerer who stole the first key out of whatever building I happen to be searching. It would need to be reusable."

He was silent for a moment, then said, voice cool, "When would you need such an item?"

"As soon as possible. I don't want to start looking for the key before we have some means of protecting ourselves from outside forces."

And that outside force included him.

If he heard that particular thought, he thankfully didn't react to it. "It could be done. It would not, however, keep anything flesh based out."

"Meaning it won't keep the sorcerer out?" If that was the case, then it was pointless.

"It will keep the sorcerer out if he uses magic to transport in. I doubt I can make something quickly enough that would also stop him from using magic to transport out if he happened to arrive in flesh form."

I frowned. "Aren't they the same thing?"

"No, they are not. It is easy enough to bounce magic to prevent entry. It is harder to contain once in."

Ah. You learned something every day. "What about the Raziq?"

"The wards will be designed to react to the energy of their beings, so will restrict entry regardless of the form they take."

"Does that mean they will also restrict Lucian?"

"My *chráni* has basically been reduced to flesh form, so no. But the restrictions that apply to the sorcerer would also apply to him."

Meaning he could not use any of his lover's magic to transport in and snatch the keys from under our noses, but he could certainly walk right in. If he managed to get past Azriel, that was.

"So how long would it take for you to get something like that to me?"

He paused. "Perhaps a day. I will have a Razan deliver it to you."

"Thanks." It stuck in my craw to actually say that, but being polite didn't cost me anything, and it was certainly a better option than pissing him off in some way.

"Just ensure no one else gets this key, or I will *not* be pleased."

"I'll do my best."

The energy in the cylinder became so electric, the hairs on my arms stood on end. "I am *not* interested in your best. I just want that key."

You and everyone else. I rubbed my arms and didn't say anything. A heartbeat later, the white light died and I found myself blinking at the abrupt darkness.

"You were successful?" Azriel said, then raised a hand and lightly brushed the hair from my eyes.

I nodded. "He said whatever he creates will not restrict anyone in flesh form from entering, though, so we still could be attacked."

"It wasn't so much the attack that was the problem last time, but the fact that the sorcerer used it to divert our attention from his arrival."

"Well, he can still arrive, just not via magical means." I paused. "It also means Lucian will not be blocked."

"Trust me, it will be my great pleasure to deal with him if he *does* attempt to take the key from us."

I eyed in him for a moment, then said, "You're hoping he does, aren't you?"

"Yes." His reply was short, sharp. Angry.

"Because you want a reason to kill him."

"Yes."

"Why? Because of me? Because he was using me?"

He didn't reply, but he really didn't need to. I could feel the answer echoing deep inside of me. I reached out and placed a hand on his leg. His muscles tensed under my touch. "You cannot kill Lucian because of me, Azriel. I don't want that guilt on top of everything else."

"The guilt would *not* be yours—"

"If you break reaper rules to gain revenge for the way he's treated me, then that *is* my problem. We've broken enough rules lately, Azriel. Let's not top it with murder."

"There are some rules worth breaking." He sheathed Valdis and crossed his arms.

Talk about closing himself off, I thought with amusement. But before I could actually say anything, my phone rang. I bounced off the bed and ran into the living room to answer it.

"Risa? It's Jak," he said, rather unnecessarily

given his rather handsome face was crystal clear on the phone's screen. "You wanted to know if I'd heard anything unusual concerning fires?"

My heart began beating a whole lot faster. "Yeah, I did."

"Well, I might just have something. But it'll cost you."

I snorted. "I'm not giving you a story, Jak. Not on this one."

He grinned. It touched his eyes, warming the dark-chocolate depths and creating the usual havoc with my pulse rate. He might have caused me untold heartache in the past, but there was still a tiny part of me that remembered—and maybe even hungered for—the good times.

"Oh, I don't want a story." He paused, and the spark in his eyes grew. "I want a date."

"No."

"Fine. I'll talk to you later—"

"That's fucking blackmail, Jak."

"Yep." His voice was cheery. "I believe there's still something between us, Ris. You keep saying there isn't, but you lie, and we both know it. A date should sort it out one way or the other."

"Jak, I'm not getting into a relationship with you." Annoyance filled my voice. "Accept that and move on."

"I had, but then you went and kissed me, and it just reminded me of how good we'd been together."

I rubbed my forehead wearily. I hadn't actually kissed Jak—I'd kissed Azriel. At the time, he'd been wearing Jak's image, as we'd thought Jak might have been the target of a sniper. Those suspicions had turned out to be wrong, but I couldn't entirely regret it, because that kiss was the reason Azriel and I had finally ended up lovers. What I *did* regret was telling Azriel to give Jak full memories of what had happened that night—kiss included.

"Jak, just tell me what you've uncovered. It's important."

"Answer the question on the table, and I just might."

I opened my mouth to say, "For fuck's sake, one date, no sex," but what came out instead was a flat, "No."

Jak didn't immediately say anything, but I could see his surprise. Hell, *I* was surprised. And yet, weirdly, I also felt free. I may not have wanted him back in my life, but at least confronting him had finally freed me from the pain of our past.

I could move on.

At least until Azriel got around to shattering my barely healed heart again.

"Look," I continued. "I'm not denying there's still chemistry between us, but I have to wonder how much of it is just the pull of our wolf natures."

"This is more than *just* that—"

"Jak," I cut in, exasperated. "I'm with someone *else*. I don't care how much lust might flare between you and me—or anyone else for that matter—it's *not* going to happen. If you can't accept that and move on, well, then, good-bye. But I won't be blackmailed into something I don't want." Not this fucking time, anyway.

He stared at me for several seconds, then took a deep breath and released it slowly. "Okay."

"Okay, you accept what I said, or okay, you're out the door?"

He smiled. "The former. You still owe me a major story, my dear, and you're not getting rid of me until I get it."

I couldn't help a chuckle. He really *hadn't* changed. "Then cut the crap and tell me what you've got."

"I just hope your reaper appreciates what you're giving up," he said, amusement teasing his lips.

"Who said it was the reaper?"

He snorted. "Anyone with two eyes and half a brain. Don't try to kid a kidder."

"Jak—" I warned.

"Okay," he said, the amusement on his lips becoming an all-out grin. "There have been several weird fire-related reports popping up on the scanner over the last half hour."

"This is the scanner you haven't got because they're illegal?"

"Do you want to hear the news, or not?"

I smiled. "I'm listening."

"There's been reports of fires breaking out on freeway verges near Strathmore, Keilor East, Calder Park Raceway, and another of a grass fire near Diggers Rest."

"And?" I said, hoping there was more to the reports than just that. Spot fires weren't unusual, especially along freeway verges. Cigarettes being thrown out of car windows started too many fires in the summer and autumn months.

"And," he said, "all reports mention a figure seen fleeing the scene."

I closed my eyes. Here it comes, I thought. "Was there any description?"

"Just one," he said. "They all said the man was made of fire."

Chapter 6

Damn, damn, *damn*!

Of course, there was always a chance it *wasn't* Tao, but deep in my heart I knew it was a very remote one. While he wasn't the only fire starter in Victoria, they all had one thing in common—even though they *could* make their entire body flame, they never appeared to be *made* of flames. Their features were always visible underneath them. If the figure seen fleeing the string of fires *did* appear that way, then there could be only two reasons why: Either a witch had conjured a fresh elemental, or Tao's elemental was now in control of his body.

I rubbed my suddenly stinging eyes. "How long ago was the last report?"

"The Diggers Rest report came in about ten minutes ago." Jak paused. "Ris, what's going on?"

"Nothing that I can tell you about." I swung around, walked over to the light screen, and quickly brought up Google Maps. I typed "Diggers Rest" in the search area and waited for the screen to respond. "When did the first report come in?"

"About twenty minutes earlier."

Meaning it had taken him roughly twenty minutes to travel the twenty or so kilometers from Strathmore to Diggers Rest. At that rate, he'd be in Gisborne in ten minutes. I kept following the freeway up with my finger, but stopped when I hit Macedon. Oh, *shit*. The elemental was going *home*. Going back to where the witch had created the flames that had given birth to it. It *had* to be. What other reason could there be for it to be heading up to Macedon? Obviously, the witch fire was still alive, though how that could be after all this time I had no idea. That was a question Ilianna would have a better chance of answering than me.

"Thanks, Jak—"

"Don't you dare hang up on me without—"

I hung up, then swung around to face Azriel. "I have to get out there and find Tao before he creates too much more damage."

"You wish me to take you?"

I hesitated, then said, "No. I'll go in Aedh form. It'll be easier to spot him that way."

"Remember, I cannot follow you or help you until you retain flesh form."

I nodded, then grabbed my keys and gave Azriel a quick kiss. "Wish me luck."

"I wish you safety," he said. "Luck is not something either of us should depend on at this point of time."

"True."

Ilianna's wards were still active, which meant I couldn't actually change inside the apartment. I headed out to the street, making sure the apartment was locked and the alarm on, then gripped my phone and keys tightly and reached down for the power of the Aedh. It swept through me instantly, a force stronger than ever before, switching me from flesh to energy form in the blink of an eye.

An unpleasant tingle ran across my particles, a telltale sign that the wards were definitely working. I spun around and headed skyward, arrowing northwest, straight toward Macedon. There was no point in following the roads—not in this form, anyway.

I was going so fast, the streetlights were little more than vivid streaks. The wind buffeted my body, occasionally throwing me sideways, but I still made good time. Soon the lights of the civilization started giving way to longer patches of darkness as I moved from the city to the country. After a while, I found the Calder Freeway and started following it, simply because the elemental seemed to be. For several miles, there was nothing more than the occasional car zooming past; then, gradually, a deeper, richer glow began to show up on the horizon. It was slightly off the highway, walking through paddocks, flicking flames through the undergrowth and sparking more spot fires.

I sped up. The closer I got, the more certain I became that it was Tao. Or rather, the elemental. Fear slithered through me, but it was fear for my friend, not fear for me.

Soon a fiery form became visible. It was trunk shaped, with thick arms and legs and no head. It dripped fire as it moved, the molten globules sizzling as they hit the ground. The dark energy that

rolled off the creature crawled through my particles, making them quiver in discomfort.

This is Tao, I reminded myself fiercely. He
wouldn't hurt me. I had to trust that, if nothing else.

I flew downward, shifting shape as I neared the
ground. I landed on hands and knees and skidded
forward, skinning my palms and ripping the knees
out of my jeans. I cursed softly—more from the
pain of those injuries than the incapacitating pain
that usually followed such a shift—and forced myself upright. The abrupt movement had the world
doing a brief three-sixty around me, but I ignored it
and forced my feet forward. A heartbeat later, an
all-too-familiar heat ran across my skin.

"I have no sense of Tao within that creature," Azriel said, voice soft and holding little in the way of
emotion.

"You may not sense him, but he's still there
somewhere."

"If he attacks, you must defend yourself."

"No." I glanced at him. "And you won't defend
me, either."

Anger flickered through his eyes, even though
his expression was as remote as it had ever been. "It
is my duty to protect you from *all* danger. That in-
cludes threats from friends."

I stopped and swung around to fully face him. "If
you even go *near* Tao, I'll fucking attack you myself."

"Tao is *not* in control of that being," he all but
growled. The fury he was barely showing washed
through my mind, a whirlwind of heat that left me
singed. "And he *will* attack you."

"Maybe. But he won't kill me."

I had to believe that. *Had* to.

"I cannot stand here and watch—"

"You *will*," I cut in. "Promise me, Azriel."

"No."

"Damn it, I haven't asked *that* much of you. I'm asking this. Please, for me, stand back and let me deal with Tao."

He eyed me for a moment, then made a short, chopping motion with his hand. "Fine. I will not interfere unless I sense death is inevitable. I will *not* let you die. Anything more, I will not promise."

"Thank you."

I turned and walked toward the fiery form. Its steps were ponderous, as if its flaming trunklike legs were a weight it could barely lift. And yet, for all the appearance of slowness, it was covering a lot of distance fairly quickly.

The closer I got, the hotter it got. Heat rolled over me, furnacelike in its intensity. Sweat beaded across my brow and began to roll down my spine. But it wasn't all caused by heat. Some of it was definitely fear. No matter what I'd said to Azriel, no matter what I believed, I knew deep down that there was a very real possibility that this encounter would not end well for one of us.

Amaya's hissing began to fill the back of my thoughts. She wanted to kill, wanted to draw the life of the elemental into her steel and feed on its flesh.

I shuddered. *No way in hell, Amaya. This is a friend, not an enemy.*

Not, she replied. *Only way.*

I ignored her. I flexed my fingers, took a deep breath, and said, "Tao."

There was no response. The creature kept moving forward, its heavy steps making the ground quiver.

"Tao," I said, louder this time.

The creature paused, then slowly turned around. It didn't have a mouth or even a face, so, basically, it just stood there, dripping fire. I wondered what was going on within the creature, wondered if Tao had any awareness of what the elemental was doing and whether somewhere deep within the flames he still fought to regain control.

"You have to retake control, Tao. It's trying to return to the fire that created it. You can't let it." Because if it did, I'd never see my friend again. I was sure of that, if nothing else.

The creature twitched. Whether it was a response to my plea, I couldn't say. "Tao—"

The rest of the sentence was cut off as the creature raised a fist and punched. I swore and ducked, but not fast enough. The blow hit my shoulder rather than my face, melting my sweater and sending me sprawling backward.

Attack, Amaya screamed, her voice so strident, tears stung my eyes. *Touch you not.*

Damn it, no. I pushed to my feet, stripped off my still-smoldering sweater, and dumped it on the ground. The elemental had turned and was walking away.

I cursed and sprinted after it, looping around the left side of the creature until I was in front of it. "Damn it, Tao, listen to me—"

The creature swiped at me again. This time I was ready for it and ducked. The blow sailed over my head, but the heat of its flames was so fierce, it felt like my skin was burning. I backed away fast and kept out of fist range.

This *wasn't* working. Tao wasn't hearing me. Maybe he was gone. Maybe the creature was too strong . . . I briefly closed my eyes. *No*. Tao was still within that fiery form. I was sure of it. I just had to find a way to draw him back out. But how?

Last time the elemental had tried to take over, I'd physically dragged Tao into the freezer and doused him with ice—something that was impossible to do out here in the middle of nowhere.

But what if it had been as much the physical contact between us as the ice that had helped Tao get the elemental under control?

No, Azriel said, the same time as Amaya screamed, *Will kill.*

Fuck it, both of you. Stop telling me what I can't do and start offering suggestions.

Azriel's frustration rolled through my mind, as sharp as Amaya's hissing. *You can use Amaya as a shield.*

How?

Flames, she said. *I eat.*

That will kill him, Amaya.

No. Weaken.

Azriel?

She's right. It'll weaken him. He paused. *But it will also kill him if she goes too far.*

His mental tones suggested this might not be

such a bad thing. Anger rolled through me, but I ignored it. I had bigger battles to fight right now.

I stopped moving, drew my sword, and held her—point first—in front of me. Lilac flames began to roll down her sides, and her hissing became filled with anticipation.

Okay, Amaya, I said. *Do what you have to do to drain his energy. But don't kill him.*

Kill not. It was somewhat begrudgingly said.

Her flames leapt from her shadowed blade, then raced across to the elemental and ran up one tree-trunk leg. Her lilac fire contrasted sharply against the red and gold flames of the elemental as she ringed the creature's rotund belly. For several seconds nothing happened; then, as Amaya began to hum softly—almost contentedly—her steel began to vibrate and the flames around the creature's stomach suddenly seemed less incandescent.

The creature never stopped moving, however, and the closer it got, the hotter it got, until I stood in the middle of a firestorm that tore at my hair and burned my skin. Until I felt as much a creature of fire as the one who was now only feet away from Amaya's tip. And yet, for all that it burned, the creature's heat *didn't* destroy me, and this close, it should have. Whatever my sword was doing, it was working.

"Tao," I screamed, more out of fear than any real need to raise my voice above the roar of the flames that swept around me. "You *must* get control of the elemental again."

The creature growled—an ungodly sound that

came from somewhere out of its flaming middle—
and swiped at me. I didn't move—I didn't dare, lest
I break the contact Amaya had with the elemental—
but the blow never struck. It stopped inches from
my ear, the heat of it singeing hair but not actually
touching skin. The creature roared again, and this
time, it was a sound of frustration. The vibration in
Amaya's steel grew stronger, and fingers of dullness
were quickly spreading from the creature's belly to
the rest of its body.

If you're going to touch the elemental, do so now,
Azriel said, his voice barely hinting at the anger
and concern I could feel within him. *If Amaya
drinks too much more of the creature's power, she
will kill both the creature* and *Tao.*

Amaya, don't, I warned.

Fun, she grumbled. *You not.*

I snorted softly, then, as the creature roared and
took another swipe at me, raised my hand and
caught the flaming paw. This time, my skin *did* burn,
and I screamed.

*Risa! Do not expect me to stand here and see you
harmed—*

I can, I cut in fiercely. *And you will.*

Closing my eyes, I gritted my teeth against the
agony and the screams that pressed up my throat
and gripped the fiery paw harder. For several seconds, nothing happened, and I began to wonder if
Azriel was right. Maybe Tao *was* lost and I was
burning my hand for absolutely no reason. Then,
suddenly, my fingers were touching flesh rather
than heat. I opened my eyes. The flames were

receding—grudgingly, but retreating nevertheless—
from the point where my fingers clasped Tao's hand.
His fingers twitched, then convulsed around mine,
his grip fierce. It hurt like hell, but I didn't say anything, biting my lip and blinking back tears as the
flames continued to retreat, first up his arm and
then across his shoulders, revealing his head and
upper body.

Amaya, release him.

No; want.

Do it, I said. *Now!*

She hissed her displeasure, but her flames un-
furled from Tao's waist and dropped to the ground,
slinking back to her blade with some reluctance.

As the remaining flames flickered and died, Tao
opened his eyes and blinked. Then awareness
surged, and horror spread across his pale, thin face.

"Oh god, Ris," he said, voice hoarse and raw.
"What have I done?"

I quickly sheathed Amaya and tried not to think
about the agony radiating from my left hand—a
hard thing to do given it was so bad, all I wanted to
do was throw up. "Nothing that can't be—"

I cut the rest of the sentence off as he collapsed,
and I lunged forward to catch him. Azriel got there
before me. He slung Tao like a sack over his shoulder, then swung around to face me.

"Your hand—"

"I can heal it when I change to Aedh form," I
said, barely resisting the urge to cradle my hand
and weep like hell. "Let's just get Tao home and
worry about me later."

Azriel didn't look at all happy, but he merely nodded and disappeared from sight. I took a deep breath and glanced at my hand. *Bad* mistake. All I saw was a raw and swollen mess, and the pain— which had been bad enough up until that point— became overwhelming. A chill swept me, I began to shake, and my legs went from underneath me. But even as I hit the ground, my stomach rose, and I threw up.

Then Azriel was there, holding me, supporting me. The heat of his presence fanned through my body; a warmth and strength chased the weakness from my flesh and snatched the pain from my burned and blistered hand.

Eventually, I pulled away and glanced down. Though it was still red and tender, my hand was no longer blistered or weeping, and I could flex my fingers without pain. My gaze rose to Azriel's. "Thank you for healing me."

"I'm glad that I could." He brushed the sweaty strands of hair from my eyes, but despite the tenderness of his touch, there was anger in his expression. "You should not have endangered yourself that way, Risa. It could have ended very differently."

"But it didn't." I hesitated. "Where did you take him?"

"Home, as you wanted. I brought Ilianna in to tend to him." He placed a hand under my elbow and gently pulled me upright. "And we should go. The police are coming."

I glanced past him and saw the approaching red

and blue lights of the emergency vehicles. "At least no one got hurt."

"No one but you," he commented, as he wrapped his arm around my waist and swept us from flesh to energy form. He didn't immediately release me when we reappeared in the living room, simply continued to hold me close.

My gaze rose to his again, and there was an intensity, a ferocity, that had my heart doing an odd sort of dance. "What?" I said, almost breathlessly.

"Do not *ever* ask me to do something like that again," he said. "Because I will not."

Annoyance flared. I tried to step back, but his grip tightened around my waist, pressing me closer. "Damn it, Azriel. He's my friend—"

"And I mean nothing to you?" he cut in, his voice flat and even despite the fierceness that radiated from every inch of his being.

"You know that's—"

"What I *know*," he cut in again, "is that the link between us has evolved into something far stronger than a mere exchange of thoughts. I will not feel your agony like that again and *not* do anything about it."

My breath caught somewhere in my throat. "I'm sorry. I didn't know—"

"And wouldn't have cared if you had." His voice was grim. "I'm just giving you warning never to ask that of me again."

I took a deep breath and released it slowly. "Okay. But I also meant what I—"

"Oh, I am under no illusions where I stand when it come to your friends."

The edge of bitterness in his voice stung deep inside. "That's not fair, Azriel."

"And yet it is nevertheless true." He released me and stepped back. "Go tend to Tao."

"Azriel—"

He cut me off with a short, sharp motion. "You have what you wanted, Risa."

And with that, he disappeared, leaving me standing there feeling angry, confused, and oddly hurt.

"Risa?" Ilianna said.

I forced a smile and turned around. "How's Tao?"

"Unconscious." She hesitated. "Are you okay?"

"Couldn't be better. Is Tao going to be all right?"

"I don't know." Her expression was concerned. "What's going on between you and Azriel?"

"Nothing." And everything. "Is there anything I can do to help Tao?"

"The best thing you can do is get some sleep. You look like shit."

"Thanks."

"Seriously, I want you to get some rest. The last thing I need is to be looking after two of you. Especially given what a grouchy and unpleasant patient you can be."

I snorted softly. "I love you, too. Give me a yell if you need anything or he wakes, won't you?"

"I will."

I turned and headed for my bedroom.

"Ris?"

I paused and looked over my shoulder. "What?"

She hesitated. "Remember that Azriel isn't human. You can't expect him to react the way any human—or non-human, for that matter—would."

"I don't expect anything of him, Ilianna."

"Maybe that's the problem."

I snorted. "He's here for one reason only—the keys. He needs to secure them for his side, and he needs me to do it. No matter what I may or may not feel for him, that's the one truth that can never be ignored."

"But what if it's no longer the *only* truth?"

"It's the only truth that matters. In the end, he has his world, and I have mine, and as the saying goes, never the twain shall meet."

"Maybe you need to trust fate a little bit more. Or maybe you just need to enjoy what you currently have and not worry about the future."

How could I not worry about the future when the reality was I might not have one? "Fate is the one that got us into this mess, Ilianna. I'm not trusting her to get us out of it." I waved a hand. "I'll see you tomorrow."

With that, I went to bed and—surprisingly, given how much sleep I'd already had that day—slept.

A death march tone woke me. I groaned and rolled over onto my back, rubbing the sleep from my eyes and cursing the idiot on the phone for waking me. Then it twigged that the idiot was Hunter, and I lunged to answer it. But I hit the VOICE ONLY button—I had a feeling she wouldn't appreciate learning that I was still in bed.

"I haven't received the crime-scene report yet," I said, glancing at the clock. It was nine in the morning—no wonder my stomach was grumbling. What little I'd eaten yesterday, I'd thrown up last night. "So I really haven't got much more to report than what I've already said."

"I have no intention of discussing either your report or the Directorate's," she replied, voice snappish. Definitely not in a happy mood this morning.

But then, was she ever?

"So you're ringing me because . . . ?"

"Because another card was found in the pocket of the second victim—this one for the Blue Angels."

Which Rhoan would have no doubt already checked out. And I couldn't see the point in me doubling his work, especially given if he *had* found anything worthwhile, it would have been in his report. And *she*, subsequently, would now be hunting down the bitch behind the kills. All of which I wanted to say, but wisely refrained. "Is there any connection between the two clubs?"

"There is, actually. They both hired last-minute replacements from the same booking agency."

"I gather the Directorate has talked to the agency involved?"

"Yes." She hesitated. "And so have I."

Poor them. "And . . . ?"

"I told the agency owner to inform me of all last-minute requests for musicians," she snapped. "And he just did."

Hence the reason for the call. Wonderful. I

scrubbed a hand across my eyes and flicked the blankets off me. "I'm guessing you're not sending the Directorate to check her out."

"Rhoan hasn't your reaper, nor your ability to sense dark spirits."

The Directorate witches had the latter, if not the former. But again, I held the comment back. She didn't *want* the Directorate to find this killer—she wanted me to, so that she could then get her revenge. And what Hunter wanted, Hunter usually got.

Unfortunately.

I walked into the bathroom. Having a pee while talking on the phone wasn't something I usually did, but it was oddly appropriate when it came to Hunter—if only because I wished I could so easily flush her from my life.

"So where is the stand-in going to be playing tonight?"

"She'll be at the Hallowed Ground from midday today."

Which at least explained why Hunter wasn't going to interview the woman herself. She might be an extremely old vampire—and therefore able to stand far more sunshine than most—but the lunchtime hours were still as deadly to her as sunlight was to any of them. "Isn't it a little unusual for nightclubs to be open during the day?"

"Hallowed Ground has been around for a long time." She hesitated. "It is a haunt for those who might otherwise be alone during daylight restrictions."

Dread filled me. "Does that mean it's another blood whore club?" And if it was, why were they bothering to provide musical entertainment? It wasn't like the addicted vampires would care about anything other than getting their next fix.

"No," she said, voice cool but still holding an edge that sent chills down my spine. "Although it wouldn't matter if it was. You would still be going."

There was never any doubt about *that*. "I'll report back the minute I talk to her."

"If she *is* the one—report sooner."

Or else, her tone implied. I was suddenly grateful I'd had the foresight not to use the vid-phone. "Fine."

"Make sure you talk to the owner, not the manager. He is next to useless."

I frowned at the odd edge of amusement in her voice. There was something going on that I didn't understand. But I didn't bother questioning her because she had already hung up.

I tossed the phone onto the vanity, then had a quick shower. Once dressed, I headed into Tao's room. And noted, with some annoyance, that Azriel had yet to make his appearance. Apparently, when reapers were in a snit, they did it properly.

Ilianna was asleep on the chair next to Tao's bed, but started awake when I walked in. I grimaced. "Sorry. I didn't mean—"

She waved the apology away, then rubbed at her neck as she sat upright. "I've got to be up, anyway. I promised I'd ring Carwyn to confirm tonight's date."

I raised my eyebrows. "You're actually going?"

She frowned. "I told you I was."

"Yeah, but I figured last-minute nerves might step in and stop you."

She shook her head. "There's no avoiding it. Mirri's right." She hesitated. "Besides, he and I are destined to be, so I have to be honest with him."

"Destined?"

She wrinkled her nose. "It's just something I saw a long time ago."

I frowned. "Just because you foresaw this union happening doesn't mean you should let it override your own feelings for Mirri—"

She smiled. "It won't. You should know me better than that."

"Then why all this 'destined to be' shit? How much pressure is your dad putting on you?"

"Lots, but I can understand his reasons—a union with Carwyn has financial advantages for both families."

"So what? What you and Mirri have is more important than anything else."

"We may be in love, but we are also mares. It is a fact of life that mares end up in the herd of a stallion, whether we like it or not."

"Well, that sucks."

"Yeah, totally." She gave me a somewhat wan smile. "Trust me, I've done my best to avoid the whole situation, but the reality is, I have little choice. If I reject Carwyn, it'll be some other stallion—and maybe someone far less understanding and patient than he seems to be."

I sat on the arm of the chair and gave her a quick hug. "I'm sure you *will* work something out."

"And hopefully that something will be artificial insemination," she muttered. "I am *not* going to bed with the man if I can at all avoid it."

"So why not suggest that? What have you got to lose?"

She snorted. "Um, have I mentioned he's a stallion?"

"I'm sure even stallions are sometimes capable of thinking with their brain rather than their dicks."

"I wouldn't be betting on that," Tao muttered, his voice hoarse but nevertheless music to my ears. He opened bloodshot eyes and glared at us. "And don't you two know it's not polite to be talking about sex when a man is trying to get some sleep?"

I grinned. "A werewolf complaining about people talking about sex. I think the world just ended."

"I think it did for a while there." He closed his eyes and scrubbed a hand across his bristly jaw. "I'm sorry—"

Ilianna caught his free hand and squeezed it lightly. "Don't be sorry. Just be damn sure it doesn't happen again."

"And how the *fuck* am I supposed to do that?" His voice was a rich mix of anger, frustration, and fear. "This damn thing inside me is strong—"

"And so are you," she snapped back. "Or you would be, if you damn well stopped feeling so sorry for yourself and started taking the offense."

He glared at her. "It's not like I'm fucking sitting back, issuing the elemental an open invitation—"

"Isn't it?" she snapped. "Then why the hell aren't you looking after yourself? Why aren't you eating? You were told at the Brindle that you must keep strong both physically *and* mentally if you wanted to keep this thing contained."

"I'm trying—"

"But not fucking hard enough. You have to get serious about it, Tao, or this thing *will* win."

He snorted. "So you've seen that? Then what the hell is the point?"

"The point," she said, jumping to her feet and clenching her fists, "is that nothing is set in stone just yet, and I don't want you lost for eternity to flame. So, damn it, fight!"

My breath caught at the anger and desperation in her voice. Whatever she'd foreseen had been *bad*, and fear again stepped through me. I half reached out to her, but Tao beat me to it. He sat up abruptly, caught her hands, and tugged her into a hug that was as fierce as his expression was alarmed.

"I'm sorry," he whispered. "I promise, I'll try harder."

"You fucking better." She returned his hug for a moment, then pulled back and punched his shoulder. "Now I'm going to prepare you the world's biggest steak sandwich, and you will consume every fucking inch of it."

"Promise."

"Good." She turned, gave me a weak smile, then headed out.

I waited until she'd left, then met Tao's gaze. "How did the elemental get loose?"

He half shrugged. "One minute I was heading outside to cool down; the next I'm in some random field staring at you and realizing just how close I'd come to cindering my best friend."

"But you didn't." I dropped down into the seat, then raised my hand. "See, not even the smallest of blisters to show for my ordeal."

He eyed my fingers for a moment, then said, "I could hear you, you know, but I couldn't do anything. Not until you caught my hand and drew me out."

So I'd been right—touch *was* the key to breaking the elemental's control. "I knew you wouldn't hurt me, Tao."

"But I did, and we both know it." He took a deep, somewhat unsteady breath and released it slowly. "I think I'll remember your scream for the rest of my life. And it's because of that, more than anything, that I'll fight this thing." His gaze met mine. "It hates you, Ris. A witch created it to kill you, and the minute you spoke to it out there in the field, that's all it wanted to do."

"What it wanted was to return to the fire that created it."

"Primarily, yes. But if it regains control again, don't confront it. Because next time, I may not be able to stop it."

"Then, as Ilianna so politely put it, make sure there *isn't* a next time." I rose to my feet, then leaned over and dropped a kiss on his cheek. "Get better. I have to go hunt a dark spirit."

"Hunter's still on your case, huh?"

"Yeah. You rest up, and maybe I'll regale you with the whole sordid tale when I get back."

"I'll look forward to it."

I wouldn't—if only because in order to tell a story about hunting a dark spirit, I'd actually have to *do* it. I headed out to the kitchen. The smell of frying steak filled the air, and I took a deep breath, savoring the delicious aroma. My stomach rumbled happily. "Don't suppose you're cooking one of those for me?"

She glanced pointedly at the two waiting plates of buttered toast. "I'm vegetarian, remember?"

I grinned as I plopped my butt on the kitchen counter. "Hey, you're going on a date with a stallion tonight, so miracles can definitely happen."

She snorted. "Not twice in one day, they won't." She studied me for a minute. "Did you sort out your shit with Azriel?"

"No, because he isn't around."

"He's always around, and you know it."

"That's not the point."

"Then what is? The fact that you're scared of your own feelings?"

"Ilianna, stop, okay?"

She sighed. "Between you and Tao, I'm going to end up gray before my time."

I frowned. "Why? What have you seen?"

She hesitated. "Nothing."

"Yeah, like that sounded *so* convincing." I studied her for a minute. "So what, exactly, did you see in Tao's future?"

"Nothing. Nothing but flames." She stared at me,

and all I saw was her fear. "I think we're going to lose him, Ris."

No, we're fucking not. I forced a smile. "As I've said before, fate is a bitch who enjoys her games. She's just as likely to do the opposite of what you fear."

"God, I hope you're right." She poked the steak with a stiffened finger, then picked it up on a fork, slapped it onto a piece of toast, and handed it to me. "What are you up to today?"

"I've got to check out a few museums, and then I'm off hunting a dark spirit."

Ilianna's eyebrows rose. "Museums? You?"

I waved a hand. "Don't worry. I'm not on a culture kick or anything. We're looking for the next key."

"Do you want help?"

"No." Especially given what had happened last time I'd found one of the keys. I was already in danger of losing Tao. I wasn't about to risk losing Ilianna as well. I slapped the second piece of toast over the steak, then grabbed the sandwich one-handed and got off the counter. "If I don't see you before tonight, enjoy your date."

She snorted. "The only way that'll happen is if I get totally plastered first. And I've promised Mirri I wouldn't."

"Tell her she's a spoilsport."

"Oh, I have, trust me."

Grinning, I walked across to the dining table to transfer the search results from the computer to my phone, then walked into my bedroom to grab a coat and my purse.

Once I'd finished my sandwich, I stood in the middle of my room and said, "So, are you going to make an appearance, or is this snit going to continue?"

"As Ilianna has already noted," he said, voice even, "I am never very far away."

I swung around. He stood several feet away from me, his arms crossed and his expression back to its usual noncommittal self. "Then why couldn't I sense you?"

"Because I didn't allow it."

I frowned. "If you've always had the ability to stop me from sensing you, why haven't you?"

"Because I haven't always been able to."

I blinked. Definitely *not* the answer I'd been expecting. "Then why have you suddenly gained the ability?"

"For the same reason you are catching more of my thoughts and emotions than I might otherwise wish. The closer our link becomes, the more it opens some . . . abilities and closes down others."

"Meaning it's a two-way street?"

"Possibly."

Meaning yes. I briefly wondered just what it meant for me other than more insight into his thoughts and feelings, but I knew him well enough by now to know he was never going to tell me *that* sort of information. "And you can't stop it from happening?"

"No." He regarded me steadily for a moment. "We are going in search of the next key?"

"Yes. As scary as Hunter is, she has nothing on

the Raziq. If I don't start actively trying to find the keys, they just might stop threatening and start *doing*."

And Tao and Ilianna would be their first targets; of that I had no doubt.

A chill ran through me, although I wasn't entirely sure whether it was the thought of my friends coming under attack from the Raziq, or a premonition of trouble of another kind headed their way. Fast.

"How do you wish to travel to Ballarat?"

I hesitated, very tempted to ride the Ducati there and tell him where to shove it until he got over the moodiness, but I really didn't have the luxury of time. Not if that premonition was to be believed.

"You can take me, if you'd like."

Amusement briefly touched his lips, and there was something close to mischief shining in the blue of his eyes. "Oh, I *would* like."

I raised an eyebrow. "If I didn't know you better, reaper, I'd think not only was *that* a double entendre, but you were flirting."

"Reapers don't flirt." He stepped close and wrapped an arm around my waist. His body was warm against mine, his touch tender and yet oddly possessive. "It is merely a truth I cannot deny."

I rose up on my toes and said, my lips so close to his that I could almost taste him, "So you're saying that you want me?"

"From the very first moment that I saw you," he murmured; then his lips met mine and he kissed me fiercely and very thoroughly as his energy rose and swept us through the gray fields to the chill of Ballarat. Not that I actually felt, in any way, cold. Such a thing wasn't possible when Azriel's arms were still around me.

"God, get a room, will you?" a woman muttered as she walked past us.

I laughed softly and stepped back. His hand slipped from my waist, and my hormones mourned the loss. "Where are we?"

"At the Aboriginal Culture Centre."

I turned around. The building was modern in style, all concrete and glass, and painted in colors that reminded me of the outback—reds, gold, pinks, and browns. I frowned. "This really doesn't look like a museum."

"That is something we cannot be sure of until we go inside."

"True." I half shrugged and headed for the entrance, paying the fee for both of us but refusing the guided tour. It was interesting to look around, but there was nothing in this place for us.

"Well," I said, once we were back out. "*That* was a waste of time."

"At least there is one less option on the list." He pressed warm fingers against my spine, gently guiding me away from the cultural center. "What do you wish to do now?"

I pulled out my phone and glanced at my list. "Let's try the Aviation Museum. That's probably the next least likely."

"Done." He wrapped his arms around my waist again and took us there. The museum, it turned out, was a big tin shed.

"It is also not open," he commented

It certainly looked that way. The huge sliding doors that ran almost the entire length of the building were closed, and the tarmac forecourt was empty. I grabbed my phone, brought up the files I'd transferred, and checked the opening time. "What sort of museum is open only on weekends and public holidays?"

"This one, obviously."

There was amusement in his voice. I smiled and lightly nudged him with my elbow. "That was a rhetorical question, not one that wanted an answer."

I scanned the outside of the building. Though I couldn't see any physical guards, there were plenty of cameras on the outside and no doubt plenty of security measures on the inside. "I might just take Aedh form and have a quick look around."

"If the second key *is* in there, you will not sense it in Aedh form."

"I know, but at least we'll know if the place has any sort of military weapons on display."

"Presuming it *is* a military dagger."

"Yeah." Given the cryptic nature of the clues, who actually knew?

I called to the Aedh, and she swept through me in an instant. In energy form, I made my way through the fence, across the tarmac, and through the small gap underneath the massive doors. The shed was huge and filled to the brim with all sorts of old-looking airplanes—some single wing, some double wing, some with propellers and others without. I didn't know much about planes overall, but I had a feeling this collection was pretty impressive. There were also engines, various machine parts, and tools. But nothing that resembled an actual dagger. I turned around and headed out.

"Nothing?" Azriel said, as I became flesh again.

"Not as far as I can tell." I rubbed my arms against the chill in the air. "I guess we should try the Eureka Centre next. If the dagger isn't there, then we're left with Sovereign Hill being the most likely location."

"And yet you do not think it is there."

"No, but I've been known to be wrong before."

"I think it best I not say anything about *that* particular point."

I grinned and wrapped my arms loosely around his neck. "Wise man."

He smiled as his hand came around my waist again, but he didn't say anything, just swept us across to the Eureka Centre. Which was also closed—for renovations, this time.

"Well, shit," I said, staring at the sign on the door.

"Which leaves us with Sovereign Hill, I believe."

"And that's too big to check right now." I briefly glanced at my watch. "We've got only an hour and a half before we have to be at Hallowed Ground."

"Then what do you wish to do?"

I hesitated and stared up at the huge blue flag with its famous five eight-point stars that formed a cross in the middle of it. Though it was now a symbol of democracy and protest, it had originally been designed as a flag of war, and it was that symbol that spoke to me now. In very many ways I was in the middle of a war myself and, like the men who had fought under her on this very hill, my war was one I suspected could not be won. Not by me, anyway.

I pushed the rather gloomy thought away and swung around to look at Ballarat. "I don't know. Maybe we should wander down to the Visitors Center, on the off chance there's something the search missed."

"You wish to walk?"

I hesitated, then nodded and headed down the hill. He fell in step beside me, his arm brushing against mine and sending little slithers of desire skittering through me. It was, I thought with amusement, an almost normal moment in a life that had become insane.

With a little help from Google Maps, we found the Visitors Center and headed inside. It was, as was usual with these sorts of places, filled to the brim with information and souvenirs as well as local food and clothing. The thick jackets, I noted with amusement, seemed to be particularly popular today.

I walked across to the wall of information about local events, and almost immediately a brochure caught my eye. I picked it up and showed Azriel. "Well, looky here—an Arms and Militaria Exhibition."

"That is the one place we are certain to find military daggers. Whether it is the *right* place is another question."

"And one we won't answer until we go see it." I

flicked the brochure around. "It doesn't open until tomorrow and runs until Sunday. At least that gives us plenty of time to check it out."

He nodded. "And plenty of time for your father to come up with a way of keeping the sorcerer and the Raziq out."

"Yeah." I tucked the brochure into my pocket and glanced at the time. "I guess we can head to Hallowed Ground. Maybe we'll get lucky and she'll start her set early."

"Luck has not been particularly favorable to us as yet," Azriel commented, as he caught my hand and drew me closer. There was something in the way he looked at me that had my pulse racing. "And I can think of other, more pleasurable ways to fill in our time."

A smile teased my lips. "Can you, now? And what about the snit you were in not so long ago?"

"Would you rather talk yet again about the reasons for the snit?" he said, voice soft as he slid an arm around my waist. "Or perhaps explore the possibilities of a rather quaint human expression that goes something along the lines of makeup sex being the best kind?"

"Hard choice," I murmured, pressing myself against the warm, hard planes of his body. "But I've never really had the chance to test that expression out."

"Then perhaps we should."

"What, here?" I raised an eyebrow and glanced around the Visitors Center. "I might have werewolf blood in me, but I'm not that much of an exhibitionist."

He smiled and touched my cheek gently. "I meant in your bed."

"Perfect—"

His energy swept around me even before I could finish my sentence.

And I have to say, that old saying was right. Makeup sex *was* the best kind.

Needless to say, we did not arrive at Hallowed Ground on time. In fact, we were a good twenty minutes late. The club was situated on the corner of Wellington Parade and Simpson Street, not far away from what most Melbournians considered hallowed ground—the Melbourne Cricket Ground. The club was situated in a rather unusual two-story, redbrick building that had an old-fashioned concrete turret on one corner and small sash windows at regularly spaced intervals. The entrance was nondescript, and it would have been easy to pass by and think it was nothing more than an apartment entrance. Certainly, the small, discreet sign above the door did little to give it away.

Azriel opened the white-painted wood and glass door and ushered me inside. Darkness greeted me, and it took a moment for my eyes to adjust. The room was midsized, with a bar to the right and a stage at the back of the room. A thin woman with an oddly ragged red streak running through the middle of her dark hair was spotlighted on the stage. She was playing some sort of lute, and the music was strange and yet somehow evocative. There were more than a dozen people sitting at the various tables scattered throughout the room, and most of them had their eyes closed, listening with something close to rapture in their expressions.

I walked across to one of the tables sitting in the deeper shadows of the room and pulled out the chair. "Is she a dark spirit?"

Azriel hesitated, studying her as he sat down next to me. "It is difficult to tell. She has some sort of shield around her."

I frowned. "Meaning you can't break past it?"

"I could, but then she would sense that I am here. Spirits may not be the normal prey of dark angels, but they generally will not take a chance and remain in our presence if they sense us."

I studied her for a moment, noting her long, thin fingers and sharply pointed fingernails. Handy for plucking lute strings ... or slicing stomach flesh, I thought, and shivered.

"Why would she have a shield up if she wasn't up to no good?"

"She is sitting in a room filled with vampires, many of whom are not above using their telepathic powers to seduce or influence the thoughts of others. It is natural she would have some means to protect herself from such events."

That *did* make sense. I continued to frown at the woman on the stage. There was something about her that made my nerves crawl, but maybe that was nothing more than my desire for this hunt to be easy.

"She'll have to take a break soon. We can interview her when she does." I leaned back in my chair and glanced at Azriel. He was little more than shadow in this darkness, but his eyes shone brightly—almost as brightly as his sword. "Why is Valdis reacting? Amaya's not."

Can, she said.

No. The last thing I wanted was her hissing like a banshee in my brain.

Banshee not. Her tone was a trifle huffy. Maybe she'd been taking lessons from Azriel.

"I had good reason for the huffiness," he replied evenly. "And I thought we'd moved past that."

My eyebrows rose. "You *heard* her?"

He nodded. "Through you. And a banshee is a spirit; she's a demon."

Better, Amaya grouched.

I snorted. "Tell me, do all demon swords have such attitude?"

He smiled. "The attitude of the sword very much depends on the attitude of the owner."

"So you're saying I'm a sweet-tempered, silver-tongued woman?"

He caught my hand in his, drew it to his lips, and kissed it. "Would I dare say anything else?"

"Usually, yes."

"Then maybe I am merely in an exceptionally good mood."

"Good sweaty sex will do that to you every time," I replied, voice wry.

His smile grew, touching the corners of his eyes and making my heart do several little happy skips. "Then perhaps I should get in a snit more often."

I laughed. The sound seemed to echo softly

through the darkness, and the woman on the stage turned to look at us. Though she didn't move, there was an almost imperceptible tightening in her shoulder and arm muscles.

"She knows what I am." Azriel squeezed my hand, then released me. "Get ready to move. I believe she's about to finish her set."

The woman on the stage finished the song she was playing, then rose and bowed to the audience. They didn't immediately respond, but as the spotlight died and she walked from the stage, it was as if a spell had been released and they all began to clap—some conservatively, some not.

I rose and wove my way through the tables, planning to cut the woman off before she could slip backstage. She was moving deceptively fast, however, and slipped through the curtains and disappeared from sight. I swore softly and ran forward, flipping the curtains aside and following the sound of her retreating steps down a dark corridor. Somewhere up ahead, a door opened and closed. I slowed.

Valdis's blue fire flickered across the walls, highlighting the peeling paint and dusty cobwebs. I shivered, not wanting to think about webs when I was chasing a woman whose alternate form could well be the world's biggest spider.

"I cannot sense her presence in the room ahead," Azriel said.

"Does that mean she's escaped us? Or is it simply a matter of the shield continuing to block you?"

"It could be either."

Meaning the only way we were going to find out

was to enter that damn room. I flexed my fingers and opened the door. Nothing immediately jumped out at me, but the room was pitch-black and my reluctance to enter grew.

I reached to the left and brushed my hand down the wall, looking for the light switch. Something skittered across my fingertips, and I yelped and jumped backward—straight into Azriel. He grabbed my arms and steadied me.

"It was only a small spider," he said.

I snorted. "I don't care if it's big or small; they're all spiders and they all deserve to die."

"Spiders are generally harmless creatures."

He reached past me. A second later, I heard the light switch being flicked up and down. No light came on, so the bulb was obviously blown.

"Can I remind you that this is Australia? We have some of the deadliest spiders known to man."

"That does not alter the fact that the one that touched you didn't actually harm you."

"That *isn't* the point." I stared at the darkness a moment longer, then drew Amaya and took a wary step. Lilac flame flared down her sides, providing enough light to view the immediate area. The room was small and furnished sparsely. There was a dressing table with an office chair in front of it, as well as a small sofa and a minibar fridge. I stepped farther inside and swung Amaya around. There was nothing and no one else in the room. Our musician *had* fled.

"Well, I guess that points to her—" Something dropped onto the back of my neck, and I swiped at it irritably. "What the hell?"

Something else dropped, but this time it raced under the collar of my shirt and down my spine. I yelped and flung myself backward at the wall, hoping to squash the hell out of whatever it was.

"Risa, I think we'd better get you out of here."

I gulped, my heart in my mouth and fear twisting my stomach. "Why?"

But I knew why even as I asked the question. There were more than just a couple of spiders in this room. I raised Amaya and looked up.

The entire ceiling was alive and moving.

Chapter 7

I opened my mouth to scream, but before I could, the whole damn lot dropped down, covering both the floor *and* me in a mass of tiny black bodies.

Horror filled me, and for a moment I couldn't move, frozen to the spot and praying like hell that this was nothing more than a nightmare. Then thousands of tiny fangs began to dig into my flesh, and I screamed and jumped and swung Amaya around wildly, swatting at the creatures I could barely even see.

Azriel pulled me into his arms, then swept us away. We reappeared in my bathroom, but it wasn't enough. I could still feel the fangs. I raced under the shower, throwing off my clothes and stomping on the black bodies that fell like rain around me. Despite the heat of the water, I was shivering like crazy, and my skin crawled with the sensation of movement.

"Are there any left?" I asked, spinning around almost wildly, trying to spot the creepy little bastards.

"No." Azriel caught my arm and made me stop. "They're gone. It's okay."

I shuddered. "It still feels like they're on me."

"No." He hesitated. "But we should go back—"

"There is no way in *hell* I'm going back into that room."

"If you'd let me finish a sentence occasionally," he said, voice a mix of amusement and annoyance, "I was going to suggest you talk to the manager while I investigate the room to see if the woman left anything behind in her haste to escape."

"Oh." I gulped down some air in an attempt to calm my still-racing pulse. "That I can do. Just wait until I get dressed."

He handed me a towel. "I was not intending otherwise."

I raised my eyebrows. "If I didn't know you better, reaper, I'd suggest there was an almost propitiatory note in your voice when you said that."

"Then you would be wrong."

"Really?"

"Yes."

"So if I started shagging Lucian again, you wouldn't care?"

He gave me a look. One that suggested I was being silly. I grinned.

"There is a *vast* difference between not caring about who sees your outer layer and whether you're with Lucian."

"So, Lucian aside, you wouldn't care if I found myself another lover?"

He crossed his arms, his expression giving little away. But tiny flickers of annoyance danced both along Valdis's sides and through the outer reaches of my mind, a sure sign that he was not as calm as he appeared. "That is not your intention, so why bring it up?"

"Because it's sometimes amusing to see your very human reactions." I rose on my toes and kissed him. "And now I'll get dressed."

"And I would like to point out that the workings of your mind are sometimes incomprehensible."

"Does that mean I sometimes make sense?" I brushed past him, dumped the wet towel down the laundry chute, then headed for my wardrobe.

His gaze followed me, a caress that sent a tingly warmth skittering all the way down to my toes. It was certainly a more welcome sensation than the tiny tickles of thousands of spidery feet.

"Occasionally. *Very* occasionally."

I grinned again. "Just think how boring your life would be without me."

"I do." He hesitated. "Possibly more than is wise."

I shot him a glance. "So you're actually going to miss me when this assignment is over and you leave?"

He hesitated again, and my amusement died. Hesitation was *not* what I'd expected. Not now. Not after all that had happened between us. And yet, as Ilianna had so rightly pointed out, the future was not something I should be worrying about right now. But, at the same time, how could I not when it came to him and me? Because I didn't *want* him to leave. Not now, not ever.

Yet that was the *one* thing that was never in doubt.

I ignored the ache that accompanied the thought and quickly waved a hand. "Sorry. Dumb question. Forget it."

I turned and grabbed the nearest clothing item. It turned out to be a short jean skirt that was more suited to summer than the chill of a day like today, but what the hell. I teamed it with a thick cashmere sweater that hugged me in all the right places, then wondered who I was trying to impress. Azriel certainly couldn't care one way or another what I was wearing.

Once I'd pulled on tall leather boots, brushed my hair, and grabbed my handbag, I turned around and gave him a bright smile. "Okay, let's go."

"Risa—"

I cut him off with a sharp motion. "Don't worry about it, Azriel."

"I can hardly *not* worry about it when you are." He caught my hand and drew me toward him. But he didn't kiss me, didn't do any of those things that a human—or non-human—male might have done. Instead, he said, "The future is in a vast state of disarray right now. No one, not even those of us whose duty it is to know the future of everyone who lives on this plane, can guess at where this quest might lead."

My gaze searched his. "Meaning death is becoming more and more likely?"

He shrugged and gently brushed a stray strand of damp hair from my eyes. "It has always been a possibility."

"And yet you got angry when I said my death might be a good thing."

"Because there is a huge difference between taking one's own life and a death that has been foretold. I would not like to see you end up as one of the lost ones."

"Trust me, it's not like I'd want that, either." Yet I couldn't shake the notion that *that* possibility was still on the table. I sighed. "As I said, let's forget it. We need to go talk to the people at Hallowed Ground before bitch-face rings and blasts me."

"Her time will come," he said. "Have no fear of that."

"Then I hope I'm still around to see it."

"I suspect that even if you are *not* instrumental in the event, you will at least be there," he said. "And no, I will not say more."

"Damn you—"

"I was and am," he said grimly; then his energy swept through us, zipping us across to the Hallowed Ground in no time at all.

He dropped me in front of the place, then disappeared again before I could question him. I cursed him softly and headed inside the club. Though there was no entertainer onstage, the club had lost none of its patrons. But I guess that wasn't surprising given it was barely one thirty and most of them were vampires. I walked across to the bar and showed the man idly polishing glasses my badge. "I need to talk to someone about the fill-in entertainer you hired today."

The bartender—a balding, pot-bellied vampire who smelled of an odd mix of garlic and alcohol—shrugged. "I'm afraid I can't help you, love. Not my line of work, that, and I don't talk to the entertainers much."

"Not even briefly?"

"No."

A non-chatty bartender was not what I needed right now. "What about the owner?"

"He's not here."

"Then who hired the replacement?"

"That would be Harry, the manager." Amusement lit his brown eyes. "But you didn't ask for the manager, now, did you?"

"I think it could have been taken as a given, seeing I asked to talk to whoever was in charge," I said, barely holding back the annoyance in my voice.

"Ah, but you see, if there's one thing I've learned over my many years of working in non-human establishments, it's that you should never take anything as a given or anyone at face value."

"Which isn't bad advice in general." I hesitated, remembering Hunter's warning, then gave a mental shrug. If she wanted answers, then I had to question the people who were here, whether she liked it or not. "Can I speak to Harry, then?"

"Sure. He's in the office down past the end of the bar."

"Thanks."

He nodded, and his gaze followed me, burning a hole in the middle of my spine as I headed down. I had a feeling that it would be a bad mistake to think he was as meek and as mild as he appeared.

The office door was open, and the vampire inside—a man with ebony skin and dark hair—

looked up before I could knock. His eyes were an almost incandescent green that glowed brightly against his skin.

"You wanted to see me?"

Obviously, the bartender had psychically warned his boss of my presence. "I did."

He waved a hand toward the somewhat scruffy leather chair on the other side of his desk. "About what?"

I sat down. "The fill-in entertainer you hired today."

He snorted. "I can tell you one thing: She won't be coming back. She did a runner well before her set was finished." He studied me for a second, something close to amusement in his eyes. "Seems someone scared her off."

And I had a feeling he knew it was me. "Unfortunate, given I need to speak to her."

I showed him my badge, and his eyebrows rose. "So we *are* hiring werewolves these days."

"Well, no, just me. You could say I'm special."

"Could I, now?" He leaned back in his chair and studied me for several seconds before adding, "And did they give you the nano microcells you're wearing?"

The amusement I'd glimpsed in his eyes was definitely evident in his voice, and I had to wonder what the hell was going on. "No, they are a means of self-preservation."

"Do they keep Hunter out?"

I hadn't felt him attempting to read my mind, but then, with the best telepaths, you didn't. "Mostly." I shrugged. "Probably as much as it has kept you out."

He smiled. "I can read only the occasional surface thought."

"As can she, and usually the worst possible ones."

His smile grew as he leaned forward and offered me his hand. "Harry Stanford, at your service."

His grip was firm, but not overpowering. A vampire who was confident in his own strength and who saw no need to display it — unlike Hunter.

I studied him for several seconds, mulling over our brief conversation, then said, a little hesitantly, "Are you, by chance, on the high council yourself?"

"And where would you get that idea, young lady?"

"It's a guess."

"Then it is a good one." He picked up a pen and began to tap the table lightly.

Unease slithered through me, and my pulse rate began to skip—never a good thing when cornered in a small room with a vampire.

"And, uh, were you on the side of those who thought I could be of use to the council, or one of the ones who thought it would be better for all concerned if I were killed?"

"Neither. I could not see the sense in killing you before we'd explored and discussed all possible outcomes." A half smile touched his lips. "And I would never, under any circumstance, side with Hunter."

"Oh." Great. He hated Hunter, and I was here under her orders.

"Never fear," he said, almost jovially. "There is no point in killing the messenger when it is the master I would rather see dead."

"If you *did* attempt to harm her," Azriel said, voice flat but nevertheless deadly. He rested a hand on my left shoulder as he reappeared beside me. "You would be dead before you even left your chair."

"Ah, the reaper himself. I was wondering when you'd turn up."

"I am never far away."

"Indeed." He studied the two of us for a moment, then said, "You do realize, don't you, that Hunter has no intention of ever letting you off her leash? Her plans for you are vast, and the keys play only a minor part of that."

The keys were hardly a minor part when the earth risked being overrun either by the denizens of hell or unhappy souls unable to move on. "I got that impression. But, for the moment, I need her. Or rather, I need her resources."

His snort was disparaging. "What, to find your mother's murderer? Do you honestly think she has any intention of allowing that? Or that she even cares, now that she has what she wants? You, in her pocket?"

My unease grew. Why the hell was he saying all this? I had no damn idea—but one thing was for sure. It couldn't be for any *good* reason. "There are Cazadors working—"

"There was one. He found no clues, just as the Directorate found no clues. Your mother's killer might as well be a ghost, for all the evidence he left behind."

I flexed my fingers, trying to relax, but it didn't help much. "I agreed to help her if she helped me. I cannot back out of that arrangement."

Yet, I added silently.

"Not unless you have the help of someone strong enough to rival her."

And there it was, I thought. The twist in the tale fate just loved applying to make my life even more interesting.

My smile was grim. "I may not know much about the inside workings of the high council, but I do know that if you thought yourself her match, you could challenge her anytime you wanted."

"I could, but that would be playing by the rules. She doesn't, so I see no reason for me to do so."

Wonderful. Another schemer. Just what I needed in my life right now. "If you're so powerful, how come you're the daytime manager of a club like this?" I hesitated, then added rather hastily, "No offense meant."

He waved a hand—an elegant gesture that nevertheless managed to highlight the muscular nature of his arms. "It amuses me to work here."

And it had the advantage of keeping him out of Hunter's eye, I suspected. Just as I suspected that *this* man was the reason for her warning about talking to anyone but the owner.

"Why are you saying all this to me?" I asked, a little hesitantly. "Aren't you afraid I'll tell Hunter?

Or that she'll pick the conversation out of my thoughts?"

"Do I fear the former? No." He leaned forward and crossed his arms on the desk. "As to the latter, she is welcome to whatever remnants she can retrieve past those nano cells. She knows I plot, just as I know she plots. It is a game we have played for a very long time."

"Well, it's not one *I* want to be in the middle of."

"And yet here you are, right in the middle."

"Uh, no. I'm working for Hunter on a case, nothing more, nothing less."

"Hunter intends to use you *and* the keys to become overlord of the council."

"And you don't?"

He smiled. It was quite a pleasant smile compared to Hunter's, but that didn't mean he wasn't as cold-blooded and calculating as she was.

"No, actually, I don't. I just believe that the council—and the world in general—would not only be better off if the gate situation remained as it is, but a hugely nicer place to live in without her polluting presence."

A sentiment I could totally agree with—and I had to wonder if he was choosing his words to match whatever thoughts he might be catching.

"I see no point in falsehoods," he commented, thereby confirming that he was, indeed, catching some of my thoughts. "Especially when Hunter herself is my greatest asset when it comes to convincing others she must go."

Something else I could agree with. "Look, I'm really *not* interested in either your plans or Hunter's. I just want to do what I have to do to get free."

"Which you will not do without assistance."

I couldn't help smiling. "Don't take this the wrong way, but I very much suspect asking for your help would simply mean jumping from the frying pan into the fire."

"Oh, I am far more honorable than Hunter. And I, at least, am sane."

"If she's insane, then she's doing a good job of hiding it." I didn't like her. I didn't trust her. But she would hardly be head of the Directorate *and* a high-ranking member of the high vamp council if she was off her rocker. The vamps, at the very least, would not have stood for it.

"Oh, trust me, she long ago mastered the art of hiding what she truly is."

"And you, of course, are a paragon of honesty."

He conceded that point with a regal incline of his head and a half smile. "Well, you know where to find me if you change your mind. And I very much suspect you will."

"Don't swear off drinking blood until that happens," I said, "because you might well starve."

Amusement crinkled the corners of his brown eyes. "I'm tempted to ask if you'd like to bet on that, but I suspect you are not the betting kind."

"Not on stuff like this." I crossed my legs, and his gaze briefly dropped. It was only then I remembered I was wearing a short skirt. I cleared my throat softly, drawing his gaze upward again. "Can we get back to the reason I'm here now?"

"Indeed we can." He leaned back in the chair again, his expression still amused. "What do you wish to know about our Ms. Jodie Summer?"

"For a start, have you used her before?"

"No. Whenever we need to cover a shift, we simply ring the agency."

"And that agency is Classique?"

"Yes." He reached to the left of his desk, picked up a business card, and handed it to me. It was the same card I'd gotten from the manager at the other venue. I flipped the card over, but there was nothing written on the back. "Have you got a contact there? I might have to talk to them."

"Either James Parred or Catherine Moore should be able to help you. I've dealt with both."

"Thanks." I tucked the card into my handbag. "Is there anything you can tell me about Ms. Summer? Did you notice anything unusual about her?"

"Aside from the fact she was neither human, shifter, nor vampire, you mean?"

I half smiled. "Yeah, besides that."

"No, because she had some sort of shield operating that I could not slip past." He hesitated. "It was neither a nano shield such as the one you wear, nor one of magic."

My eyebrows rose. "Meaning you have working knowledge of magic?"

"Those of us who have been around a very long

time do tend to become proficient in all manner of things."

Not just magic, then. And it did make me wonder what else Hunter had become proficient in. Beside killing and being a coldhearted bitch, that was.

He chuckled softly. "It *is* a wonder you're still alive if you're having those sorts of thoughts around Hunter. She can be somewhat highly strung when it comes to those who disrespect her."

"Yeah, noticed that," I muttered, then got back to the business at hand. "So there's nothing else you can tell me?"

"I'm afraid not."

Meaning I was at another dead end. Hunter was not going to be pleased. I hesitated, then said, "I don't suppose you could pull a picture of Ms. Summer from your security cameras?"

"If you give us a couple of minutes, Jonathan will have a printout waiting for you at the bar."

"Thanks." I rose. "You've been most helpful."

"But not as helpful as I could be," he said, expression back to being amused. He opened a drawer and drew out another business card. It was a simple card—black background and white writing—and said *Harold Stanford, manager, Hallowed Ground*, with a cell phone number underneath. "Just in case you change your mind."

I accepted it somewhat reluctantly. "I won't, you know."

He shrugged. "It never hurts to have an escape option, Ms. Jones. That is all I am offering."

"Thanks for your time." I tucked the card in the side pocket of my handbag and headed out. Once I'd collected the printout of our suspect, I walked back outside.

"Well, that was fun," I said, making a beeline for the 7-Eleven several doors down from the club. I needed a Coke and chocolate fix to calm my still-quivering nerves.

Azriel fell in step beside me. "*Interesting* is more the term I would use."

I glanced at him sharply. "You believed his bullshit?"

"I believe he intends to oust Hunter from the council. I also believe he desires your help to do it."

A chime rang cheerfully as I entered the 7-Eleven. "That doesn't mean I should trust him."

"I never said you should. But it is certainly worthwhile keeping his offer in the back of your mind. Especially since I will not be around once the keys are found."

Him not being around was something I did *not* want to think about. "I can hardly keep it in the *front* of my mind, given Hunter's predisposition for picking up all the wrong types of thoughts."

"She will be well aware that you have talked to Stanford."

"Yeah, but I'm not going to rub her nose in it." I plucked a can of Coke from the refrigerator, but there wasn't a whole lot of choice when it came to smaller chocolate bars. After a couple of seconds' deliberation, I grabbed a Mars bar, then paid for them both at the self-service scanners. "And I'm certainly not going to mention the fact that he made me a counteroffer."

"If they are longtime foes, then she will guess what he will or will not have done."

"You know, I really don't want to be talking about Hunter right now."

"Then what do you wish to talk about?" He opened the door and ushered me outside, one hand pressed lightly against my spine.

"Nothing. How about we just walk down to the gardens so I can eat my chocolate and enjoy the quiet?"

"You? Requesting silence? A rare moment indeed."

I snorted and nudged him with an elbow. "No smart remarks from the peanut gallery, thanks."

"And what, precisely, is a peanut gallery?"

I rolled my eyes. "Just escort me down to the park before I die of caffeine withdrawal."

His nod was decidedly regal; then he offered me his arm and said, "As you wish."

I slipped my arm through his and we walked down to the park, where I found a bench seat near the fountain and had my snack, listening to the dance of water and the songs of the birds in the trees. It was, I thought, another one of those rather pleasant—almost ordinary—moments to treasure in a life gone crazy.

Unfortunately, it didn't last. Just as I tossed the empty Coke can into the nearby bin, my phone rang. I dug it out of my handbag and hit the vid-phone's ANSWER button.

"Stane," I said. "How'd the date go?"

"Ah, the date," he said, a somewhat bemused expression on his face. "You could say it wasn't what I expected."

"Meaning it was worse, or better?"

"Better is something of an understatement."

I smiled. "So your mother wasn't so far off the mark when she arranged this blind date?"

"Nope. Holly Green is not only pretty, but she's a *gamer*." He sighed. "I think I'm in love."

"You haven't invited her around to your place yet. She might yet be a clean freak."

"No one who is a gamer can be a clean freak. The two are totally incompatible."

My grin grew. The lone wolf had been snagged, and *bad*. "I take it you'll be seeing her again—sans mothers this time?"

"Oh, hell *yeah*."

I laughed. "Is that the only reason you're ringing? To boast about your hot date?"

"Uh, no." He composed himself, his expression becoming a touch more serious. "Got a hit on that storage locker. Someone just came out of it."

"Who?"

"I don't know yet. I'm running a scan, but nothing has come up yet." He disappeared briefly as he scooted from one screen to another. "I just sent you a picture. It's a woman, so it might be Genevieve Sands."

"How long ago did she actually leave?"

He hesitated. "Just going out through a side door now."

"Let me know the minute anyone else enters or exits. And thanks, Stane."

"No probs."

As I hung up, my phone chimed, telling me a message had been received. I pulled up the pic, then glanced at Azriel. "You want to take us there?"

He nodded and did so, depositing us again in the side parking lot near all the shrubs. I swung around, but didn't immediately see anyone matching the image on the phone. Then I spotted the tail end of a white overcoat disappearing around the Hoddle Street corner and raced after her.

As I ran into Hoddle Street, I spotted her. Like the woman in the photo, she was tall and thin, with short dark hair and a long, almost manly walk. She also was twenty yards away and heading briskly for a taxi.

"Miss Sands?" I had to yell to be heard over the roar of passing traffic. "Can I talk to you?"

Thankfully, she paused and looked over her shoulder, a frown marring her pale, lightly lined features. I'd expected Genevieve Sands to be a much older woman, for some reason, but she looked to be in her midforties, if that. "Do I know you?"

I slowed to a walk, dug my badge out of my handbag, and showed it just long enough for her to see the badge but not read the finer print that said I was vamp council rather than anything more official.

"I need to ask you a couple of questions."

She frowned, her amber gaze skating my length briefly before rising to mine. I had the feeling that I'd been found wanting—and it oddly reminded me of Lauren Macintyre's initial response to my presence.

"In regard to what?" She looked down the length of her long, Roman nose at me, her voice cool and collected.

I hesitated. "John Nadler."

She turned fully around, her handbag clasped in front of her like a shield and her expression puzzled. "Who?"

"John Nadler, a businessman who recently died." I stopped in front of her and forced a smile. "I believe you're one of his three beneficiaries."

She blinked. "In what way?"

"As in, he's dead and you've been named in his will."

"Why on earth would I be named in the will of a man I don't know?"

"I don't know." I frowned. If she was putting on an act, then it was a good one. And yet there was something about her, an energy radiating off her that had the hackles rising at the back of my neck. "You haven't been contacted by his lawyers?"

"Not that I'm aware of." She hesitated. "But I've been out of town on business for a few weeks. It is possible that their communication is being held at the post office along with my other mail."

Which was a perfectly legitimate excuse, so why didn't I believe it?

"Is that why you're using one of the storage units here? Because you've been away?"

She frowned. "What on earth has my renting a storage unit here got to do with being the beneficiary of a man I don't know?"

"Please, Ms. Sands, just answer the question."

She huffed somewhat haughtily, then said, "I've been renting the unit for several months now. My house is quite small and I needed somewhere secure to stock several valuable items."

I pulled my phone out and pretended to look up some notes. "And is your unit G-18?"

"Yes." She frowned. "I'm really not seeing the connection here."

"It's in regard to the ongoing investigation into Nadler's death," I said. "We believe there might be some connection to your unit. Would it be possible for us to have a look at it?"

"No, it would not. Not without a warrant." She paused, looking me up and down. "Produce one, and I'll be more than happy to comply."

"That will take a few hours. It really would—"

"I do not care about what is easy or not," she cut in coldly. "The law is the law, young lady, and I will not be railroaded into doing anything that might not be advantageous to myself."

"I'm not implying that you're in any way involved—"

"Then what are you implying?"

"As I said, I'm merely trying to tie up some loose ends."

"Well, this is one end that will remain loose until you get the proper paperwork, and not before."

Okay, then. I forced another smile. "If you happen to remember just where you know John Nadler from, could you perhaps give me a call?"

"That I can do." She took out an old-fashioned notebook and pen, then looked at me pointedly. "Number?"

I gave her my cell phone number, then added, "I'm sorry to have delayed you so long, Ms. Sands."

She nodded, tucked her notebook back into her bag, then turned and strode to the still-waiting taxi.

"What do you think?" I asked, as she climbed into the cab and slammed the door.

"I could not read her."

I glanced at him, surprised. "That seems to be happening an awful lot these days."

He shrugged. "There *are* humans we cannot read."

"You said it was rare."

"It is. We just seem to be coming across more of them than usual."

"So she *is* human?"

"Yes." He glanced at me. "Why?"

"Because there was something about her that didn't feel right."

"Well, given she was exiting a storage locker containing a sorceress's transport gate, it is very possible she is either in league with said sorceress, or the sorceress herself."

"It can't be the latter." I watched the taxi's

blinker come on as it readied to pull away from the curb.

"Why not?"

"Because she didn't have the same build as Lauren Macintyre."

"I cannot see—"

"Face-shifters can change only their *facial* shape, not their bodies."

"That does not mean there cannot be those who *are* able to do a full-body shift."

"If there is, I've never heard of them." As the taxi pulled into the traffic, I added, "I'm going to follow her."

"Be careful."

"That goes without saying."

"But given your somewhat reckless nature, it bears repeating."

"If I had the time, I'd be offended by that statement."

"It can hardly offend when it is the truth."

"Only as you see it. Meet you back home." I dropped a quick kiss on his lips, then slung my handbag over my shoulder and called to the Aedh. She came in a rush, and within a heartbeat I was trailing after the taxi.

We followed Hoddle Street, went under the Swan Street rail overpass, then followed Punt Road for several miles until the taxi turned left into Greville Road and stopped at a redbrick and concrete house that looked totally alien among all the more traditional terraces.

I waited until Genevieve had stepped inside and

slipped in after her. A quick look around her house didn't reveal anything out of the ordinary. It was neat and obviously well lived in, with plenty of clothes in the wardrobe and little dust on the furniture. I briefly wondered how long she'd been away, because surely if it had been any length of time, there would have been dust. And if she'd had the time to dust, why wouldn't she have collected her mail?

She dumped her coat and bag on her bed, checked her answering machine, then headed into the bathroom. I waited until she'd filled her bath and climbed in before I gave up and retreated.

"Anything?" Azriel grabbed my arm as I reappeared in my bedroom, steadying me.

I shook my head, gulping down air as dizziness swept me and my stomach briefly rose. But this time, there was no my-head-is-going-to-explode pain accompanying the shift back to flesh form, and though my legs felt weak, they didn't collapse underneath me. Although no doubt Azriel's grip had something to do with that.

He guided me across to the bed and sat me down. He plucked the phone from my fingers, dropped it lightly on the bed, then squatted in front of me and clasped my hands between his. Warmth began to flow through me, gently chasing away the remaining weakness.

"What did she do?"

"Nothing. She just went home and had a bath." I grimaced. "I don't know. Maybe I'm just jumping at shadows, but she still feels wrong to me."

"Perhaps our next step should be uncovering whether there are shifters capable of full transformation."

"Yeah." I took a deep, somewhat shuddery breath, then pulled my hands from his and picked up my phone. "Uncle Rhoan," I said, and watched the psychedelic swirls run across the screen as the call was connected.

"Ris," he said, after a couple of moments. "What can I do for you?"

"Got a weird question for you—are there such things as face-shifters who are capable of transforming their whole bodies?"

He frowned. "Well, I've never come across one, but I can't see why there wouldn't be. They're probably rarer than hens' teeth, though."

"Would something like that be registered on a birth certificate?"

"I doubt it. Even face-shifters are registered only as shifters—and only if they come from a known line of shifters. If it's an out-of-the-blue occurrence, or they're the product of a human-shifter mating, then probably not." He hesitated. "Why?"

"I was just following a woman who reminded me of someone else, but she looked nothing like her."

"Could she be a sister or a relation?"

"We can't uncover much about her, let alone anything about her family. She may exist, but there's not a whole lot of paperwork to prove it."

"So you're thinking a fake ID?"

"Maybe." I scratched my nose. "I don't know."

He studied me for a moment, gray eyes narrowed. "I hope this woman has nothing to do with our two spiderwebbed victims."

"Not a thing. It's key related."

"Huh. Well, the best I can do is run a search for you, but I doubt anything will come up."

And I doubted whether a search done by Directorate resources would bring up anything more than one done by Stane, but I guessed it couldn't hurt. "The woman's name is Genevieve Sands. She lives at sixty-five Greville Road, Prahran."

"Posh address."

"Posh woman." I hesitated. "Speaking of the other deaths—"

"No, Risa."

"Damn it, I'm just curious—"

"And you know what *that* did to the cat," he said with a smile. "You've got enough on your plate. Don't go stealing my work as well."

I half laughed. "You're welcome to your work. I'm just curious as to whether you'd uncovered anything interesting—"

"If I did, I wouldn't be telling you. Talk to you later, Ris."

"With some interesting information on Sands, hopefully," I said, and hung up. I tossed the phone back on the bed and sighed. "Another dead end."

"Possibly not. Despite her assertions to the contrary, she must know who Nadler is, because she would not be named heir otherwise, true?"

"Well, maybe. You occasionally see reports of strangers or even animals being gifted money in wills."

"But it is unlikely to be the case here."

"Very unlikely."

"And we also know she must have some acquaintance with Lauren Macintyre, as that transport portal ultimately leads to her place."

"Actually, it leads to the house Lucian's Razan are staying in. There's another portal that goes to Lauren's from there."

"Lucian's Razan?"

The edge in his voice had me frowning. "What, you didn't pick that information up from my thoughts?"

"No, I did not."

"Oh." I hesitated. "Why the hell not?"

He waved the question away. "The Razan?"

"There was only one there, but his name is Mark Jackson, and he was the one we knocked unconscious in the tunnel."

"Why are you so sure he is Lucian's Razan?"

"Because there's no one else he could belong to."

"Your father—"

"Would not be dealing with a dark sorcerer. I might not be sure of much, but I'm pretty sure of that." I shrugged. "Lucian was his *chráni*, and you said yourself that they often shared the same markings as their masters."

"It would be interesting to uncover whether—if Jackson *is* the Aedh's *chráni*—he was a recent creation or one that was created before his power was ripped from him by the Razan."

I frowned. "What difference would it make?"

"If before, then not much. If the latter"—he

paused, something close to hatred glimmering briefly in his eyes—"then he has thoroughly concealed his true self and is far more powerful—and dangerous—than I suspected."

"Meaning he *could* take on his energy form?"

He hesitated. "No. There is no doubt he has been trapped in flesh form for eons. But it *is* possible he could not only take on partial form, but have all his other powers available as well."

I frowned. "What sort of powers would we be talking about?"

"The ability to use magic, for a start. The Raziq are proficient in its use—they have to be, as masters of the gates."

"I thought the priests were the masters?"

"And the Razan were once priests. Lucian, as your father's *chrání*, is very likely to be magically strong. Your father would not have taken him otherwise."

Meaning Lucian had never had to enlist Lauren's help to spell me—he could have done it all himself. I frowned. "So why did he get Lauren to make that cube? Why wouldn't he have made it himself?"

"Because he would have wanted to belay any suspicions. *His* magic would feel very different from that of his mistress."

"But I've never felt any of his magic."

"And perhaps never would. As I said, he would be extremely strong and—I suspect—very adept at hiding it after all those years on this plane."

I blew out a breath. "I really was fooled by him, wasn't I?"

"But not for as long as he might have desired."

"Thankfully," I muttered, then jumped as my phone rang. The tone told me it was Hunter, and I groaned. "Like I need to speak to her right now."

"Talking on the phone is preferable to talking in person, is it not?"

"There is that." I hit the ANSWER button and said, "I had nothing to report, which is why I didn't report."

Her voice was cool and disbelieving. "So the woman wasn't there?"

"No, she was there, but she did a runner on us. We chased her to her dressing room, but she escaped and left lots of little friends behind to play with us."

And the memory of it had my skin crawling all over again.

Amusement briefly touched Hunter's lips. "Spiders, I'm guessing?"

"Lots of them, as I said."

"How quaint that you're afraid of something so small."

"We all have an Achilles' heel. Spiders just happen to be mine."

Something glimmered in her eyes. Something that could have been humor but felt like something far darker. "Oh, you have more than just spiders, my dear."

I found myself clenching the phone so tight, I was in danger of cracking the case. "What weakens can also give you strength. You might want to remember that sometime."

"My, my," she murmured. "Aren't we all aggressive this afternoon? I wonder why."

I took a deep breath and released it slowly. "Talking to uncooperative vampires tends to do that to me."

"I gather you mean those who run Hallowed Ground rather than myself?"

"Of course." I kept my voice flat, without inflection. To have done anything else would have been dangerous. "I didn't learn much, but I did get a picture of our suspect."

"So she *is* the one we're after?"

"Hard to tell, because she was using some sort of shield that stopped Azriel sensing what she was. But given she had a boatload of spiders sitting in her dressing room, I think it likely."

"So she left nothing behind other than the spiders?"

"No." I hesitated. "But she's killed two nights in a row, so I'd bet she'll attempt to do so again tonight."

"More than likely." Hunter studied me, a deeper darkness creeping into her eyes. "I believe you talked to Stanford, despite my warning not to."

I shivered, wondering how she'd known. The bartender, perhaps? Then I remembered—I had a damn Cazador following me around, reporting every little move back to her. "I had no choice. The owner wasn't there and the bartender didn't know anything."

Hunter snorted. "Bartenders know *everything*."

"Well, this one wasn't talking." At least not to

me. "The only way to get any information was to talk to Stanford."

"And did he have anything interesting to say beyond his lack of knowledge about his fill-in entertainer?"

I hesitated. Stanford might be planning to oust Hunter, but he could also be doing nothing more than stirring the pot. Hell, for all I knew, he'd picked up the phone and talked to Hunter the minute I was out the door. Which meant that no matter what I said, it wasn't going to make her happy.

Although I could hardly lie, given the Cazador.

"Nothing worth listening to," I said eventually.

Amusement touched her lips. "I'm glad to hear it."

I bet she was. Couldn't have her pet joining the opposition, after all—not before she'd done what was expected of her, anyway.

"He did give me his contacts at the entertainment agency. I thought I might go talk to them, unless you'd prefer—"

"If I wanted to get deeply involved in this case, I would have," she said. "Report back to me if you uncover anything else."

And with that, she hung up.

"Hunter was her charming self, I see," Azriel murmured.

I laughed, as he'd no doubt intended. "Yeah, she was."

He caught my hand and rose, dragging me upright with him. "Tao is about to call for you."

"Why?"

"I believe he is hungry." He gave me a somewhat

stern look. "And you should be eating something, too."

"Yes, Mom," I murmured, as I brushed past him.

"Hey, Ris?" Tao called, just as I neared his bedroom door. "You out there?"

I poked my head around the door. "I am. What can I do for you?"

"Ilianna threatened to make the old boy go limp for the next three months if I got out of bed for anything more than a pee," he said, expression amused. "But she hasn't come back from her shopping expedition, and I'm absolutely starving."

"So get up and get something. She's not going to know."

He snorted. "Maybe, but I enjoy sex too much to risk it."

I grinned. "What would you like?"

"Anything that involves lots of meat."

"Steak, eggs, and chips?"

"Perfect." He grinned. "And I'll have a beer while I'm waiting."

I raised an eyebrow. "Did Ilianna really make that threat? Because you seem to be milking it a little here."

"Hell yeah." He grinned. "Having you run around waiting on me hand and foot isn't something that happens every day. Gotta make the most of it."

I snorted softly and headed into the kitchen. Half an hour later, I dished up two plates and walked back into his room.

"That," he said, practically drooling as he accepted the plate, "smells divine."

"Then eat up." I sat down on the chair beside his bed and followed my own advice. I was about half-way through my meal when my phone rang again. This time the tone said it was Stane.

I cursed softly. "I swear, people are intent on not letting me eat today."

"So ignore it," Tao said sagely. "It's not like you can't ring him back."

Azriel appeared by the chair and offered me the phone. "It could relate to the storage unit."

"Yeah." I accepted the phone and hit the ANSWER button. "Stane, what's up?"

"Genevieve Sands just got out of a taxi in front of that storage place again."

I glanced at Azriel. "Maybe we spooked her."

"Could be."

"I think we should go see what she's doing." To Stane, I added, "I discovered her address today. Do you think it'll help you dig up any other information about her?"

"Worth a try."

I gave him the address, then added, "And while I'm thinking about it, have you still got that bug we used at the nightclub?"

"Certainly do. I wasn't about to let that baby go—do you know how hard those things are to get?"

Given they were black market, I'd imagine very hard, and very expensive. "What's the range of the thing?"

"Fairly extensive. Why?"

"So if I were to place it in an apartment up on the Gold Coast, you'd be able to pick up its signal?"

"No, but if you were willing to fork out the cost of hiring a buddy of mine, I could get him to pick up the signal and bounce it down to me."

"Done. Can we pick it up later, after we've checked out the storage unit?"

"You can, but I won't have everything in place by then. And I'm not sure if Fitz will have the necessary relay stuff on hand."

"Do what you can."

"I will."

"Thanks." I hung up and shoved my plate toward Tao. "You want to finish any of that?"

He snagged the rest of the steak and gave me a thumbs-up. I took the rest out to the kitchen and dumped it in the trash, then grabbed my bag and coat and turned to Azriel. "Let's go."

We reappeared in the side parking lot again. The evening air was cold enough for my breath to fog, so I pulled my coat on as I walked toward the entrance.

But I'd barely taken half a dozen steps when the building exploded in a gigantic ball of flame.

Chapter 8

The force of the blast knocked me off my feet and sent me tumbling. I landed in an ungainly heap near the shrubs that lined the parking lot, with bricks, metal, and wood thudding all around me. I didn't move, just squeezed my eyes shut, threw my hands over my head, and prayed like hell that I wasn't hit. Then Azriel landed on top of me, knocking out whatever breath I'd had left.

But the minute his body covered mine, the debris stopped falling—not just on us, but around us. And it became quiet. Whisper quiet. I frowned and opened my eyes. We were surrounded by a halo of blue fire.

"What the *hell*?"

"Valdis shields us." His warm breath tickled my ear. "She formed it the minute the building exploded."

"Is that why you're lying on top of me?"

"Yes. It was easier than transporting us both out of here—especially given you would only want to come back." He hesitated, then added, with a hint of a smile in his voice, "Of course, this way I also get to touch you more fully, and that is not entirely unpleasant."

I snorted. "You're beginning to sound like a regular male, and that's scary."

"Right now, I feel like a regular male."

Laughter bubbled through me. "Well, I *was* going to be polite and not mention that bar you have—"

"I meant," he cut in, the amusement in his voice deeper this time, "that I was feeling protective. You, Risa Jones, have what I believe is called a dirty mind."

"Hey, I'm *not* the one manning up."

"*That* is a function of *this* body I have no real control over." Valdis's shield flickered and died, but he didn't immediately move. "Are you all right?"

I opened my mouth to say yes, but the word never came out. With the shield gone, the noise hit, and it was *horrendous*. But the creak and groan of a dying building wasn't the worst of it. It was the screams of those trapped and injured that were the hardest to take.

"Oh god, Azriel, we have to help—"

"We cannot," he said, voice firm. "It is too dangerous to go in there just yet."

I bucked my body, trying to get him off me, but I might as well have tried to shift a brick wall. "Damn it. I can't just lie here—"

"You can, and you will," he said. "It is not within your ability to save those people."

"But it *is* within your ability."

"No."

"Azriel—"

"*No.*" This time there was an edge of anger in his voice. "I am not here to alter the hand fate has dealt to any of those people inside."

"Not unless it had something to do with the keys, which this *does*."

"Only peripherally. I have no justification for interfering in either the life or the death of those within that building."

"What about Genevieve Sands? She might be connected to both the dark sorcerer *and* the keys, so why can't you at least go in there to see if she survived?"

"Look at the building, Risa. Do you really think it possible she could be alive?"

I twisted around and my gaze widened. Flames leapt high from either end, but it was the middle of the building—in the area that had held Lauren Macintyre's storage unit—that had taken the brunt of the explosion. It was *completely* destroyed. There was nothing left but the charred remnants of brick walls and the twisted remains of metal. There is no way in hell anyone in that area could have survived.

"There's no guarantee she was actually *in* there at the time of the explosion. She might have set it all up and then used the stones to escape." That was what I would have done if I'd been in her somewhat ugly shoes. "We need to go check the Razans' place and see if she's there."

Azriel's expression went back to being noncommittal. "You cannot go in Aedh form, as they will sense you."

I met his gaze. "You could go."

He hesitated. "I prefer not to leave you—"

"Who's going to attack me here? The Raziq are

waiting for my father's appearance, Hunter still has use for me, and anyone else I can cope with."

"Given you do have the unfortunate habit of attracting danger, that is no comfort."

I smiled. "It's going to take you a couple of minutes, if that, to check. What trouble could I get into in that amount of time?"

"Plenty, I suspect." He rose, his movements fluid and graceful, and offered me a hand. "Do not go into that building."

"I won't." Not in human form, anyway.

"Risa—"

"Stop being such a worrywart and go before she escapes us again."

He did. I brushed the dirt and grit from my hands and clothes as I studied the blackened, broken building. There was little sound coming from the building now—little in the way of human sound, anyway—but the flames were intense, a caress of heat that would burn my skin if I got any closer. But I had to get closer, no matter what Azriel said. Though the approaching wail of the emergency vehicles was barely audible over the fierce burn of the fire, they were little more than a couple of minutes away. If I wanted to check if anything in that locker had survived the blast, I'd better do it now, before officialdom descended and perhaps destroyed whatever evidence still survived.

My gaze went to the front of the building. Fire licked along the roof, but much of the front office still seemed to be standing. Which meant that Maggie, the cheerful receptionist who'd been working there yesterday, might still be alive.

And I couldn't escape the sudden notion that I needed to check—not only to save her life if that were possible, but for the sake of our mission.

My clairvoyance sure picked the oddest times to kick in.

A good-sized crowd had gathered across the other side of the road, but few of them were looking in my direction. I called to the Aedh and she rushed through me, changing my form in an instant.

Heat and dust whispered through my particles as I moved closer to the building, an unpleasant combination that made me want to scratch even though I had no flesh. I slipped through the ugly hole blown in the side of the building and made my way above the debris that had once been a corridor. The storage units on either side were little more than skeletal remnants, with boxes and god knows what else hanging out of them like the innards of a gutted body.

But the wall between the storage section and the office area was still basically intact, and though it was barely visible through the smoke and flames, hope rose.

The door into the office area hung limply from one hinge, tilted inward by the force of the explosion. Flames licked the doorframe and slipped fiery tentacles along the inside ceiling. I went through, mentally wincing as the flames danced through my energy form. It felt like red-hot fingers were being shoved inside me.

The office itself hadn't escaped damage, despite the buffer of the standing wall. Furniture was strewn everywhere, paper and glass littered the floor, and the front windows were smashed and were held in place only by the thick mesh grills covering them. The air was a morass of dust, smoke, and heat.

I spun around, searching for any sign of life, but couldn't immediately see anything. The desk where the receptionist had been sitting had tipped over sideways and was now covered by part of the ceiling. There was no sign of life. But, by the same token, there was no evidence of blood or broken body parts.

Then what sounded like a groan came from under the debris of the desk. I swore mentally and shifted back to flesh. The air was so damn hot that it felt like I'd fallen into an oven set on high, and the thick, heavy smoke swirled around me, stinging my eyes and catching in my throat, making me cough.

"Maggie?" I had to shout to be heard above all the noise. "Where are you?"

No answer came, but after a moment, I heard another groan. It was definitely coming from underneath the desk area.

I began grabbing bits of plaster and rubbish from the pile covering the desk and tossed them to one side. Another explosion ripped through the building, and the walls around me shuddered. I ducked instinctively, scraping my thigh along a jagged piece of wood as dust and bricks fell around me. The remnants of plaster still clinging to the ceiling began to crack alarmingly; it wouldn't take much to bring the rest of it down.

I swore and drew Amaya. *Don't cut or burn the woman's flesh.*

Will not, she replied.

Fire ignited along her blade, the lilac flames bright in the smoky darkness. I used her steel to hack apart the larger chunks of wood, plaster, and metal that lay between me and the receptionist, kicking the smaller bits aside as Amaya's flames consumed everything else.

From somewhere under the mess came another groan.

"Maggie? Can you hear me?" I shoved Amaya's tip under a long piece of wood, then thrust it up and back.

There was a pause, then a weak, "Here. Help."

Something shimmered in the smoky shadows near the door. I tensed, my fingers tightening around Amaya, then realized it was a reaper. She wore the image of an elderly woman and had a kind face and sorrowful blue eyes.

"You can't have her," I said fiercely. "She's not going to die."

"That is neither your decision nor mine," the reaper replied softly.

I blinked. None of them had ever talked to me before. None of them except Azriel, anyway.

"That is because you have never spoken directly to any of us before now," she said, her expression somewhat amused.

"I had no real reason to before now," I muttered.

I grabbed another chunk of wood and threw it away.

A flash of familiar heat across my skin told me Azriel had also appeared. "I thought you weren't coming in here in flesh form," he said.

"Yeah, well, you knew it was a lie, so why sound so aggrieved now?" I shoved another piece of wood out of the way. "You could help, you know."

"I cannot interfere in this one's life or death, Risa, and you know that."

"Damn it. I'm *not* asking you to interfere. I'm just asking you to help me remove some of the rubbish on top of her."

"I cannot."

"Well, fuck you *both*, then!" I raised Amaya and brought her down hard. Her blade hit the desk and, with a resounding crack, split it in two. As her lilac flames began eating into the wood, I raised a foot and kicked half of the desk with all the force I could muster. It tumbled up and back, revealing the bloody and bruised torso of the young receptionist.

I squatted beside her and gently brushed the hair from her eyes. "Maggie? Can you hear me?"

She nodded, though she didn't open her eyes, and the movement was so weak it might have been imagination on my part.

My gaze slid down her length. Her hips and legs were trapped under the remains of the desk, and the blood I hadn't seen earlier was there. Everywhere. I bit my lip, then added, "I'm going to get you out of here, okay?"

Her eyes fluttered open. She blinked, and just for

a moment, confusion briefly outshone the pain in her eyes. "You. Changed again."

I frowned, not sure what she meant. Not even sure if she was seeing me. "Your legs are trapped under the desk, Maggie. I'm going to free you, but it could hurt. Okay?"

She swallowed, then nodded and closed her eyes again. I rose, stepped over her, then, as quickly but as gently as I could, grabbed the edge of the desk and flung it up and over her. She screamed. The sound cut through me, as sharp as a knife, then abruptly stopped.

The reaper stepped forward.

"No," I said. "Please, don't."

"Her decision is made. Her soul moves on." The elderly reaper's voice was filled with gentle understanding. "There is nothing you can do for her now."

"Damn it, no," I said, and looked down. A soft shimmer rolled over the receptionist's body; then her soul pulled free. She looked at peace, happy almost. I closed my eyes, not wanting to see her spirit take the reaper's hand and move on.

Not wanting to acknowledge my failure to yet again save someone.

Another explosion ripped through the building. Above, the ceiling cracked and plaster began to fall, the pieces small at first, then getting gradually larger as the cracks grew and joined.

I swore and called to the Aedh, changing form just as the remainder of the ceiling crashed down. It would have crushed me if I'd still been standing there. As it was, dust and debris plumed through my particles, making me feel as if every inch was coated in grime.

I headed back into the hellhole that the main storage area had become, quickly winding my way through the remnants of the corridor until I found Genevieve's storage locker. Or rather, where it once had been, because this area was definitely ground zero. There was very little left here, nothing but a few blackened, twisted metal remains. I turned around, trying to find the middle of the unit where the stones had stood. What I found instead was the remnant of a leg—though it was little more than crisped strips of skin and meat hanging from a cracked and blackened femur. I looked around for the rest of the body, but couldn't see anything. Why just that section of whoever's body it was had survived was anyone's guess.

There was little evidence left of the stones, which no doubt had been the intention of the blast. Genevieve Sands obviously didn't want to risk me investigating this locker. It's just too bad for her that I already *had*—something she would have known if she'd accessed the site's security system. For once it seemed that fate had played us a better hand than the bad guys.

I checked the rest of the storage units in the hope that someone else might have survived, but the effort was futile. All I found were bodies. There was nothing else I could do, so I turned around and headed home. Once there, I stripped off and showered, although the dust was so ingrained, I had a sneaking suspicion I'd be rubbing it out of my skin for the next week.

Once I'd finger combed my hair, I headed out to find Azriel. He was back in his usual spot.

"What is it about you and windows?" I grabbed some socks out of the nearby dresser and plopped down on the bed to pull them on.

He shrugged. "It is, quite literally, a window to a small section of your world. It is endlessly interesting watching what goes on."

"Meaning your world is boring?"

"My world is one of rules and duty. It is not so much boring as that nothing ever changes."

"I can't imagine the life of a Mijai would be too boring."

"The life of a hunter-killer is exciting for only the first couple of millennia."

I stared at him for a moment, not quite sure I'd heard him right. "Millennia?"

He glanced at me, amusement briefly touching his eyes. "I am young in Mijai terms."

"But ancient in mine."

His eyebrows rose. "And this is a problem?"

"No, just surprising, that's all." I pulled the last sock on, then reached for my boots. "Did you find Genevieve at the Razans' place?"

"No, she had already moved on."

"To the place on the Gold Coast?"

"I checked both there and her house in Prahran. She was at neither."

"Damn." I thrust a hand through my hair and

wondered if that meant she were dead, or if she were merely being cautious.

"That is a question that cannot be answered until she turns up either alive or dead."

Very true. We had no idea how involved Genevieve Sands might be with either the magic or the key quest, and it was certainly more than possible that she *was* dead—but I was betting on the former rather than the latter. Something about the grim remains I'd seen just seemed a little too convenient. "So what do we do now?"

"Given we can do nothing on our own quest until tomorrow, perhaps we should concentrate on Hunter's."

"I guess." I glanced at the clock. It was just after four, so there was still plenty of time to head on over to the entertainment agency and talk to either James Parred or Catherine Moore, the two contacts Stanford had given us for the agency. "I might go over to the agency on my bike. My head still feels achy after all the shifting to and from Aedh form."

"That you have shifted so much and have not suffered the consequences suggests you are becoming more adept at the process."

"Or it's a result of whatever Malin did to me."

He hesitated. "Yes."

I snorted softly. "You're determined not to give me any information about that, are you?"

"You know I cannot. Your dealings with your father are dangerous enough as they are."

"Just because I understand your reasons doesn't mean I'm not frustrated by them." I gathered my phone and ID, then walked to the wardrobe to get my leather bike gear. "I'll meet you at the front of Classique Entertainers."

He nodded and disappeared. I headed down to the garage, gearing up in my leathers before I hopped on the Ducati and drove out.

Of course, going anywhere near the city approaching peak hour always added far too much time to the journey, so it was close to 4:45 by the time I got to Port Melbourne.

The agency was located in an area that was all concrete warehouses and office buildings. I found parking under one of the trees lining the center strip, then pulled off my gloves and helmet, shoved them into the under-seat storage, and headed across the road to Classique. It was situated in a building that was basically a glass-fronted concrete box, though the colorfully painted wooden strips lining the upper half of the building on either side of the windows at least gave it a bit of personality that was sadly lacking in its neighbors.

Azriel joined me as I walked toward the steps. "Would not a disguise be useful at this point, given that your uncle would not be pleased to discover you're investigating these crimes?"

I stopped cold. "Shit, yes. Thanks for reminding me." I did a quick look around, scanning the nearby building to see if there was anyone staring out the window. There didn't appear to be, so I imaged myself with a long, thin face, with freckles over a somewhat large hooked nose, and spiky red hair. Once the shifting magic had done its work, I glanced at Azriel. "Well?"

"Definitely *not* an improvement," he said, barely managing to restrain his smile.

I laughed. "What about you? There may be cameras inside, and we can't risk Uncle Rhoan recognizing you any more than we can me."

"Both human and electronic eyes will see a leather-clad, hairy-faced individual of impressive proportions."

"Hopefully not too impressive—we don't want to scare them."

"Impressive proportions toned down, then."

I grinned, loving his growing sense of humor more and more, and all but bounced up the steps. I pushed open the bright red metal doors, then stepped inside. The reception area was as modern as the outside of the building, with glass and bright colors being a central theme. The seated woman did something of a double take as we walked in. Her eyebrows rose slightly, but all she said was, "Can I help you?"

I dug my ID out of my pocket and showed it to her. "I need to talk to either James Parred or Catherine Moore about an entertainer they booked for Hallowed Ground this afternoon."

She studied the badge for a moment, then frowned. "An investigator for the high council? What the hell is that?"

She had good eyes, because I'd deliberately kept the badge some distance from her.

"It means I work for the vampire high council."

I kept my voice in the lower tonal ranges. There was a security camera in the corner, and while it was focused on the door, I had no idea if it was sound capable or not. The last thing I needed was Uncle Rhoan raiding their system and hearing me.

"So, not Directorate?"

"No." I hesitated. "I take it they have been here, though?"

"Yes. Yesterday." She frowned. "So are you a cop or what?"

I gave her what I hoped was a reassuring smile. "I lean more toward being a private investigator than something as official as a cop."

"Meaning you don't have the same sort of powers?"

"No." And I could see where this was leading—me being shown the door. I glanced at Azriel. *Don't suppose you can apply a little reaper charm, could you? I know you're not supposed to, but we need to get this case moving so we can concentrate on our own.*

He raised an eyebrow, but he gave the woman a full-wattage smile and said, "We tend to be the intermediaries between the council and the Directorate. We're used when the council does not wish a more official investigation."

"But they *are* involved with whatever you are here to ask about, aren't they?"

A woman immune to your wily ways, I said, amused. *How amazing is that?*

I suspect the reason is all the hair. She does not find it attractive, apparently.

Amusement bubbled through me, although I

could certainly sympathize. Lots of hair wasn't on my must-have list when it came to men, either. *Can you give her a little push into accepting us?*

Only if it was key related, which this is not.

I mentally sighed, then said, "Look, we just have a couple of quick questions, but if you think either James Parred or Catherine Moore would prefer to speak directly to the guardians, that can be arranged."

She bit the bottom of her lip, her expression uncertain, then made her decision and picked up the phone. "James, there are some investigators from the vampire council here who wish to speak to you about Ms. Summer."

"Another bloody complaint, no doubt," he replied, voice clearly audible even from where I stood. As was his annoyance. "Send them in."

The woman hung up and motioned to the vibrant yellow door at the far end of the desk. "Through there, green door on your left."

"Thanks."

We followed her directions, and a balding, middle-aged man rose from his chair and gave a welcoming—if somewhat tense—smile. "James Parred, at your service."

I shook his offered hand. "Annie Logan and Bear Brown," I said, grabbing at the first names that came to mind.

He glanced at Azriel, amusement briefly touching his lips. "Bear?"

"It is more a nickname," Azriel replied, giving me a "must-you?" sort of look.

"Well, it's certainly appropriate, if you don't

mind me saying." He waved a hand toward the seats, then sat back down himself. "What do you wish to know about Ms. Summer?"

"We went to Hallowed Ground to talk to her this afternoon, but she disappeared—"

"Yeah, damn annoying, that was," he cut in. "She did me out of a booking fee and annoyed a good customer."

"Have you been in contact with her? Do you know why she ran?"

He shook his head. "I tried calling her, but she's not answering her phone."

"And have you had any problems like this with her before?"

"Like this? No."

"But you have had problems?"

He hesitated. "Earlier this week we were having problems contacting her, but she called yesterday and said her phone had been on the blink." He grimaced. "Obviously, it still is."

Either that, or the shape-shifting spirit behind these kills had decided to abandon the Summer identity. And that, in turn, meant we were dealing with a spirit with more intelligence than I'd thought them capable of. Although why I'd thought them incapable of logical thought, I couldn't say. Maybe I'd just figured dark spirits were all about the need to kill and little else.

"What about Di Shard?"

He blinked. "What about her?"

"Well, have you had a similar problem with her recently?"

"She was out of contact for a couple of days, but it wasn't a problem because we didn't actually have her booked for anything." He shrugged.

"Have you been in contact with her recently?"

"She called this morning to ask if there were any bookings."

"And were there?"

"Nothing last moment. But I did have to remind her about her regular midnight booking at the Falcon Club, which was a little odd."

Meaning if our dark spirit *had* taken over the identities of both Summer and Shard, the Falcon Club was most likely her next hunting ground. "Have you got a picture of the two women?"

"Sure."

He rifled through the paperwork on his desk and handed me two photos. Both women were tall, with thin features and dark hair. Other than the fact one had pale skin, the other dark, they could have been mistaken for sisters.

I glanced up at Parred. "Until recently, how reliable were they?"

"Very." He grimaced. "Reliability and quality performances are necessary assets in this business. Without it, you don't survive that long."

"I don't suppose you could give me their addresses?"

He frowned. "No, I'm sorry, but information like that is private. I couldn't hand it over without a warrant."

"What about a cell phone number? It's urgent that I speak with both women."

His frown deepened. "I'm not sure—"

"It's only a cell phone number," I said, using my most persuasive voice. "It's not like I can use it to track down their addresses or anything."

He snorted. "The Directorate could."

"The Directorate could have just pulled their driver's license details and gotten the information from there."

I could have, too—or rather, Stane could have. But I needed to take all the right steps to satisfy Hunter, and that had to include talking to the people who employed the two women.

He studied me for several seconds, then half shrugged. "I guess it won't hurt."

He leaned forward, pulled an old wireless keyboard out from under his desk, and began typing. I glanced at Azriel. *Don't suppose you could take a sneaky look over his shoulder without him noticing?*

I could. His tone was amused.

I smiled. *Then would you?*

Of course.

He appeared behind Parred. *Shard lives in flat one, ten Martin Street, St. Kilda, and*—he hesitated, waiting as Parred did some more typing—*Sands lives in flat eleven, one twenty Newman Street, Kensington.*

He reappeared on the seat beside me just as Parred grabbed a piece of paper and scrawled two phone numbers onto it. "Here," he said, sliding the paper across to me. "The first is for Shard, the second for Sands. Hope you have better luck contacting them than I have of late."

"Thanks for your help."

"Anytime."

We headed out. Once safely across the street and well out of earshot, I pulled out my phone and gave both women a call. Neither one answered. No surprise there, I guess. Especially when it was more than likely that both women were either incapacitated or dead.

I shoved my phone away and glanced at Azriel. "We'll try Di Shard first. She's slightly closer."

"I will meet you there."

He disappeared. I called to the shifting magic and made my face my own again, then pulled on the helmet and climbed onto the Ducati.

The trip across to St. Kilda was hell, thanks to the traffic, and by the time I got to Martin Street, I was more than a little pissed off and totally wishing I'd simply come here via Aedh form.

I cruised slowly past the apartment building, then parked around the corner, stored my helmet, and walked back. Ten Martin Street was a modern glass and concrete building that looked like a series of receding boxes, each layer sitting farther back, giving that "box" more of a courtyard than the one below it. The top layer apparently had enough room for a large outdoor umbrella to be set up.

I glanced at Azriel as he appeared beside me. "Can you sense anything inside?"

"There is life in the first two apartments; nothing in the other two."

"Are there any bodies?"

"If death occurred some time ago, as you suspect, I would not sense it. A soul's resonance does not last beyond a few days in this world, unless they become one of the lost ones."

"So if Shard is dead in there, this death was meant to be?"

"Yes."

I studied the building a minute longer, but I was only delaying the inevitable. "Right. Let's go."

I wrapped my fingers around my keys and phone and called to the Aedh. Once I'd changed form, I moved across the road, hesitating briefly to study the names on the intercom before slipping through the small gap between the door and the floor. Flat one, according to the directory, was up on the first floor. Shard's flat was the only one on that floor. I went in.

At first glance, there didn't seem to be anything wrong. The place was tidy, but not overly so. There was a small stack of mail sitting—unopened—on a glass side table near the door, dishes draining on the sink in the kitchen, and laundry sitting in the basket in the small laundry room. There was nothing that immediately jumped up and screamed "problem." Not until I went into the bedroom, anyway.

Because the entire room had become one gigantic web. Even though I was little more than particles, it seemed to cling to me, making me feel itchy and sending horror coursing through me. I backed away faster than I'd ever done before—in either form—and returned to the relative safety of the doorway.

I hadn't noticed any motion sensors in the flat, so

I shifted back to flesh form. Dizziness swept me, and I had to grab the doorframe to steady myself—but the pain that slithered through me was next to nothing when compared to the state I was usually in after a shift. I might not know what Malin had done to me, but if this lack of pain was one of the side effects, then I couldn't entirely be sorry about it.

The cobweb hung from one side of the room to the other, the gossamer strands shining like gilded silver in the evening light filtering in through the bedroom window. Little white pods hung in various corners, but all of them were split open and empty of contents. I couldn't be sorry about that, considering what they'd probably held was spiders. Lots and lots of baby black spiders. Goose bumps fled across my skin, and I rubbed my arms, trying without succeeding to warm the chill from them. Even Azriel reforming behind me couldn't do anything about that.

Di Shard lay on the bed. Or what remained of her did, anyway. Like the two male victims we'd seen, she was wrapped in spiderweb and her skin was like parchment—brittle and almost translucent. The only difference was, she didn't have just two slashes in her abdomen. Instead, her body was littered with little cuts. Tiny cuts. As if they'd been made by the fangs of thousands of little black spiders.

Another shiver ran through me. I could only hope she'd been dead when they'd begun consuming her.

"Well," I said eventually, "this really doesn't tell us much."

"Other than the fact that she has been dead for

at least a week." His hand rested lightly on my hip, the touch comforting rather than sexual.

My gaze swept the room again, but there wasn't much to find in the way of clues. "Why would she be consuming the men herself, but leave the women for her young?"

"She would probably need to keep her own strength up if she is in a breeding phase."

"Any idea how long that phase is likely to be?"

"No. As I have said before, I normally do not hunt spirits." He half shrugged, a movement I felt rather than saw. "But her actions so far suggest she is not working purely from instinct, but rather from intelligence."

I glanced up at him. "Meaning not all dark spirits are capable of logic?"

"There are levels of spirits, just as there are levels of demons. This one is obviously one of the higher ones."

"So the Rakshasa we hunted would be have been considered a higher-level spirit?"

"Yes. Although perhaps not as high as the spirit we seek here, because she could not ignore the call of the ghosts."

"Does that mean she won't be hunting tonight? I mean, she knows we're looking for her after this afternoon's events."

"Yes, but remember, she is also in breeding mode. That is an imperative not even intelligence can ignore." His grip tightened on my hip, and the tension suddenly evident in his touch echoed through my being. "We should go. Someone comes."

"Who?"

He hesitated, then said, "Directorate. Your uncle."

I swore softly, called to the Aedh, and hoped like hell that I hadn't been in human form long enough for my scent to linger in the air. And thanked whatever gods that happened to be listening that I'd parked my bike around the corner rather than directly opposite the apartment as I'd first planned.

I swept out as Uncle Rhoan walked in. He hesitated, as if he'd sensed me, but I just kept going. Hanging around to see if he actually *had* would not have been a bright idea.

"What do you wish to do now?" Azriel said, the minute I re-formed beside the Ducati.

I grabbed my helmet and shoved it on. "Go home and make mad, passionate love to you."

Amusement touched his lips, and desire flared briefly around me, bathing my skin with its warmth.

"That is something I would not find unpleasant." His voice was even despite the desire that pulsed between us. "I suspect, however, you merely tease."

"You suspect right. We need to check out Summer's place before my uncle beats us to it." Hell, for all I knew, he already *had*. Maybe there was a cleanup team there right now, photographing, cataloging, and pulling apart any clues that might be left. I had no doubt that Summer had suffered the same fate as Shard.

I flipped the helmet's visor down. "I'll see you there."

He nodded and disappeared. I booted up the

bike and headed across town. Thankfully, peak hour had eased now that night was setting in, and it was definitely more pleasant to be on the Ducati. At least I could weave my way through the traffic without having to worry about some impatient motorist suddenly swinging into my lane.

One twenty Newman Street turned out to be one of those modern, split-level town houses that had been popular with the upwardly mobile about fifty years ago. This one was showing its age more than most, the redbrick darkening with grime and the concrete portions showing remnants of past graffiti attacks. Still, it was in better shape than some of its neighbors, which looked to have been abandoned for many years—decidedly odd given how close to the city Kensington was. At the very least, a developer should have stepped in and purchased the land because it would have been worth a fortune if developed properly.

And maybe I was thinking about *that* sort of nonsense rather than contemplating what might be waiting inside.

I glanced around. There weren't any Directorate cars about, and nobody seemed to be watching, so I shifted shape and silently made my way into the town house. Summer's place, like Shard's, looked lived in—there was an empty dinner plate sitting on the coffee table, a mug with a tea bag sitting ready near the kettle in the kitchen, and clothes in the dryer, ready to be pulled out. For all intents and purposes, it looked as if someone were living here. And maybe they were. Maybe this was where our dark spirit had made her lair. Which meant that maybe this was where all those tiny spiders were living ... My gaze jumped to the ceiling, but it was free of movement or threat. There wasn't even a spiderweb decorating any of the corners.

Which didn't mean there weren't any in the bedroom.

The bedroom door was closed, and there was no way in hell I was going to slip underneath it until I knew for sure what waited on the other side. I shifted back to flesh form, then flexed my fingers and made my feet move forward. As I gripped the door handle, I closed my eyes and sent a brief prayer to whatever gods might be listening that there wouldn't be anything untoward waiting beyond this door.

But, as usual, they had the IGNORE button pressed when it came to me.

What lay inside wasn't only the biggest damn spiderweb I'd ever seen, but a goddamn army of little black crawly things.

I jumped back, a squeak of fear escaping my lips, and hit Azriel so hard that I actually forced him back a step before his hands gripped my arms and he steadied us both.

"Her nest," he said, rather unnecessarily. "But I suspect it is not her only one."

I swallowed heavily, my gaze on the ceiling and all the critters up there. There was no way in *hell* I was getting any closer to that room. They didn't appear to have noticed me, and I had no inclination to change that situation. "What makes you say that?"

"These spiders are larger than the ones who attacked us and therefore more likely to be older."

That a dark spirit was capable of having more than one cache of babies was something I did *not* want to think about. I forced my gaze from the creepy-crawlies and studied the body on the bed—although to call it a body was something of a misnomer. The other victims we'd seen might have been little more than preserved skin, but there wasn't even *that* much left of Summer. Just some dark hair on the pillow and a few bits of what looked like nails and bone remnants.

A shudder ran through me. Azriel rubbed my arms, but the heat of his touch did little to combat the chill.

"Why would she have more than one lot of babies?" I asked. "And if she does, why the hell aren't we overrun with spiderlike dark spirits here on earth?"

"I would suggest the reason is because they're cannibalistic."

"What?"

"Look at the carpet. It is littered with carcasses."

He was right. It was. In fact, the remnants of little black bodies were so thick that the gray carpet looked like patchwork. "So she kills the victims to feed her young, but when the young get old enough, they feed on one another? How does that make sense?"

"It would ensure only the strongest of them survive. It is not unusual behavior."

"Maybe in your world, but not in mine," I muttered. I knew that there were some animal species where the young *did* eat one another, but only if there wasn't another food source, and it was generally rare.

"Children are not as common in my world as yours and therefore somewhat revered." His voice held a hint of censure. "We certainly would *not* allow them to harm one another in *any* way."

Which wasn't what I meant and he knew it. But I let it slide and glanced up at him. "I thought reapers lived in big family groups?"

"We do."

"Then why would children be rare? Do you suffer the same sort of problem that has killed off most of the Aedh?"

"No. Aedh breed only when their death is imminent, which kept their numbers stable for millennia. No one can say what changed, but we think the Raziq had a lot to do with it."

That raised my eyebrows. "They killed off their own kind?"

"They believe in their cause and would certainly be capable of wiping out all opposition. In this case, that would mean those who tended and believed in the current viability of the gates."

"All of which doesn't explain why reapers don't breed willy-nilly."

He hesitated. "It is a combination of our long life spans and the fact that our recharge partners aren't always our Caomhs."

"Can you have both?"

"Rarely. And if a reaper only ever finds his recharge companion, he will not be blessed with children."

"And have you any children?" I asked, curious and perhaps a little . . . afraid. Because if he had children, that would mean he'd met his Caomh, which in turn meant there was never any hope for us.

Not that there ever really was.

His expression closed over. "I am not the Aedh, Risa. I do not want or need multiple partners. If I had a Caomh waiting in the fields for me, I would not be with you."

Summarily—though gently—chastised, I pulled my gaze from his and stepped back onto safer ground. "So what do you suggest we do about these spiders? Do we leave them, keep watch on the apartment, or what?"

"You do not wish to call your uncle?"

I hesitated. "How likely are the spiders to attack anyone who enters that room?"

"Very. Their hunger stings the air."

"So why aren't they attacking us?"

"Because we have not entered their lair."

And I had no fucking intention of doing so. "Can they be destroyed by something like pest spray, guns, or even fire?"

"Not ordinary fire. Though they wear flesh, they are spirit in design. Witches would more than likely be capable of destroying them, but not someone like your uncle."

Which meant I either had to ring Rhoan and warn him—and get the shit blasted out of me for interfering in his case again—or get rid of the damn things myself. Great. Just fucking great.

Can kill, Amaya said with an eagerness that had me shaking my head. *Will enjoy.*

No doubt. I glanced up at Azriel again, and he nodded a confirmation. "It will not draw our dark spirit to us, though. She obviously does not look after her young any more than the initial feeding."

"So how come we were attacked at the club? She wouldn't have had time to lay her eggs, let alone for the things to hatch. She was only the fill-in entertainer."

"She may have been carrying some young on her. Do not some spiders do that?"

"None that I want to meet," I replied, with another shudder. I drew Amaya and held her in front of me. Lilac fire raced down her sides, and her eagerness ran through the back of my mind. "Go for it."

She did. Fire exploded from her tip and spread out in a deadly wash that consumed all that stood in front of it without actually burning the walls or ceiling. The fire alarms went off regardless, but their strident ringing was almost lost to the roar of Amaya's flames. The thick web shriveled against the onslaught of heat, dripping in silver globules onto the carpet. The spiders tried to flee, attacking one another as they scrambled to seek refuge from the flames. Only there was no refuge—Amaya devoured everything. Web, spiders, furniture. Even Summer's few remains fell victim to her hunger.

Soon there was nothing left. Nothing but scorched

plaster and melted carpet. Amaya's flames retreated back to the steel, and her roar became little
more than a contented hum. If she'd been a cat, I
suspected she would have been purring. Loudly.

I sheathed her, then rubbed my arms. It didn't do
a lot against the chill still invading my limbs. "Would
she have felt the death of her young?"

"I do not know enough about her kind to say for
sure, but it is a possibility."

"Meaning she might not turn up for her perfor-
mance tonight."

"If she has more young to feed, she might have
no choice."

"Meaning it would be helpful if we knew more
about the breeding habits of the Jorōgumo—if
that's what this thing is." I bit my bottom lip for a
moment. "I wonder if the Brindle witches can tell
us anything about them."

"Given they are the keepers of all witch knowledge, it is more than likely they could."

"Then that's where we'll go next." My phone
rang, the abrupt noise making me jump. I took a
calming breath, then hit the ANSWER button and
said, "Mirri, what can I do for you?"

"You haven't heard from Ilianna, have you?"

I frowned. "No. I thought she was supposed to be
meeting you. Didn't you have that date with Carwyn tonight?"

"That's the thing—she hasn't turned up."

My heart began to beat a whole lot faster. "What
do you mean? Has she backed out again?"

"No. At least, I don't think so. She was pretty determined to hash everything out with Carwyn tonight." She paused, and even through the phone's tiny screen, her worry was evident. "Risa, I think something has happened to her."

Chapter 9

For a second I swear my heart stopped. Just thinking that something had happened to Ilianna made my stomach churn so badly, it felt like I was about to vomit. Damn it. I *couldn't* lose Ilianna. Not when there was a very real possibility we would lose Tao.

Panic surged, thick with fear, but I somehow reined it in and said, "Have you tried calling her?"

"Of course—"

"What about Tao? Or her parents?"

"Yes and yes. No one's heard from her, Risa. She's just gone. Completely and utterly disappeared."

No, I thought, swallowing heavily against the bile rising up my throat. She hadn't disappeared. She *was* somewhere. It was just somewhere Mirri couldn't find.

"What about the hospitals?" As much as I hoped she hadn't been hurt, it was always a possibility, and certainly one we had to consider before we pressed the panic button too far.

"Also checked. Nothing."

At least that was *something*. I took a quivering

breath and released it slowly. "I'll find her, Mirri." I hesitated. "What about Carwyn?"

"He's here with me at the restaurant. He's got a friend in the police force he's going to hit up for any information that might come through official lines."

If it came through police sources, then it wouldn't be good. But Mirri knew that just as well as I did. "I've got to go across to the Brindle, so I'll talk to Ilianna's mom. Maybe she can scry for her or something."

"It's worth a shot." There were tears in Mirri's dark eyes. "You don't think something bad has happened to her, do you?"

"No." I gave her a reassuring smile and hoped it didn't look as forced as it felt. "I'm sure it's just something dumb—like her phone running out of charge and her car breaking down."

A tremulous half smile touched her lips. "She does have a habit of letting her phone run out of charge."

"Yeah, she does." But rarely to complete emptiness. "We'll find her, Mirri. I promise you."

"Let me know the minute you hear or find anything."

"I will."

She hung up. I pocketed my phone, then glanced at Azriel. "I don't suppose you could do a sweep and see if you could find her."

"I'll try." He studied me for a moment. "What do you plan to do?"

"Go to the Brindle, as I said. I vaguely remember

Ilianna saying her mom was on night shift this week, so I can kill two birds with one stone." My stomach tightened as the words left my mouth. Damn it, she *wasn't* dead. I'd know. Surely to *god* I'd know. I hesitated, then added, voice a little hoarse, "If she *were* dead, would you know?"

"No." He hesitated. "But I could find out if you wish."

"That would be good. Thanks."

He nodded and disappeared. I took another of those calming breaths that did jack all to calm, then called to the Aedh and got the hell out of there. I left the Ducati where she was—right then, I didn't particularly care if Rhoan saw it or not. All that mattered was getting to the Brindle and talking to Ilianna's mom. If anything *had* happened to her, surely she'd be the one person who *would* know.

I zoomed through the night with all the speed I could muster, reaching the Brindle in record time. I shifted shape, splatted with my usual inelegance onto the carefully manicured lawn in front of the building, then thrust to my feet and pulled the remnants of my clothes into some semblance of order as I ran for the front steps.

The Brindle was a white, four-story building that had once been a part of the Old Treasury complex. It had been built in the Victorian era and was both beautiful and grand in design. It wasn't until you neared the steps and felt a tingling caress of energy against your skin that you realized this place was very different from its brethren. It was the home of all witch knowledge, and it was protected by a veil of power so strong that it snatched away the breath of those who were sensitive to these things. I'd never considered myself overly sensitive to magic, but I'd always been aware of it. This time, though, the feeling was weirdly different. It wasn't just awareness — it felt like the power of this place was alive. Fingers of energy crawled across my skin, its touch sharp, electric. It made my flesh itch — crawl — and almost felt as if it were testing me. The Brindle didn't suffer evil to enter, but it had never troubled me in any way before.

So why the change? Did it have anything to do with the key quest or what the Raziq had done to me?

Possibly. And yet Kiandra — who was the head witch at the Brindle — had told me that as powerful as the magic around the Brindle was, it could not stop the Aedh from entering. Logically, therefore, it shouldn't be able to stop me. But then, I wasn't full Aedh. I was both flesh *and* energy.

That will change, an inner voice whispered darkly.

I shivered, but thrust the odd premonition out of my mind and took the steps two at a time. The huge — almost medieval-looking — wood and wrought-iron doors had been closed for the night, so I walked to the left side of the massive entrance and pulled the discreet cord. Deep inside the building, a bell chimed. I waited, and after a few minutes, footsteps approached. One door opened, revealing a brown-haired, slender, tunic-clad figure. It wasn't someone I'd met before.

"I'm sorry, but we're closed for the night." Her voice was soft, gentle. Raised voices were rarely used in this place of power.

"I know, but I need to speak to Custodian Zaira, please." I hesitated. "It's urgent."

"I'm not sure that she's here—"

"Then check," I cut in. Then, at the flash of annoyance that crossed her face, added, "Please. Tell her it's Risa Jones, and it really *is* important."

Her gaze swept me assessingly; then she nodded and closed the door. I listened to the retreat of her footsteps and wondered whether she was simply walking away or doing what I asked. After a few minutes, I heard her talking. Misplaced mistrust, I thought, and gave myself a mental slap. After a few minutes, she returned and opened the door, wider this time.

"Zaira has agreed to see you. Please, come in."

"Thank you."

I stepped through the doorway. The foyer wasn't exactly inviting, even in the daylight, but at night, its sheer size seemed to weigh on the shadows, so that they almost appeared to loom over me. It was a weird sensation—almost as if the walls themselves were standing in judgment of not only me, but all those who walked past.

I very much suspected I would be found severely wanting. At least at the moment.

"This way," the woman said softly.

She led the way down the long hall. The energy of this place was so strong that every step was accompanied by a spray of golden sparks. The old-fashioned electric sconces threw just enough light to ensure we didn't run into the walls, but they did little to otherwise lift the shadows.

The young witch led me into the visitors' waiting room, told me to wait, then went through the door behind the small desk and closed it firmly behind her. I knew from previous visits that you didn't get past this area without either a witch escort or special dispensation from Kiandra, but I was a little surprised at being held here this time. I'd have thought Ilianna's mom would have been here given I'd mentioned it was urgent.

That she wasn't probably meant we were all panicking over nothing.

No, that dratted inner voice whispered, *you're not.*

I crossed my arms and began to pace. Several minutes crawled by, ratcheting up my tension and frustration. When footsteps echoed in the hall outside, I swung around and all but ran out—and almost collided with Ilianna's mom in the process. Only quick reactions on *her* part kept us both upright.

"Risa," she said, her soft tones holding a hint of surprise and perhaps amusement. "This is not a place where speed is required."

I took a deep breath and tried to calm down. "I know, and I'm sorry."

She nodded. Ilianna had inherited her palomino coloring and her shifting abilities from her dad, as Zaira was human. But Ilianna had the same powerful green eyes as her mom and right now they'd narrowed considerably. "What can I help you with?"

"Two things." I hesitated, but there was no easy

Keri Arthur

way to say it, so I just came straight out with it. "First off, we think something has happened to Ilianna."

Zaira frowned. "Mirri called earlier looking for her, but I didn't get the impression that she was in any way worried."

Then Mirri was better at containing her concern than I was. "I know. But Ilianna hasn't turned up for her date with Carwyn, and we can't get her on the phone."

The older woman smiled, although there was a slight edge of tension emanating from her now. "Well, given she isn't too pleased about our matchmaking efforts, her standing him up again is *not* entirely surprising."

I was shaking my head before she'd even finished. "Not this time. Mirri said she was determined to talk to him about the match."

"Talk him out of it, you mean," she said. But the tension in her ratcheted up several more notches. She studied me for a moment, then abruptly turned and walked away.

"Come along, child," she said over her shoulder, when I didn't immediately follow.

I hurriedly caught up. "I was hoping you could do a scrying or location spell for her."

"A location spell won't work." She opened a door and walked into another dark hall. "She learned to divert such spells at a very early age."

There was an odd mix of annoyance and pride in her voice. I half smiled. "How young?"

She hesitated. "She was twelve. Even at that age it was evident she was very gifted."

"So why wasn't she ever asked to become a custodian?"

Our footsteps beat a sharp tattoo against the marble floor, and the sound echoed in the hushed shadows that surrounded us. I half wondered if we'd wake anyone up. I knew from past experience that there were at least two dozen witches staying here at any one time, some of them permanent residents like Kiandra, and some, like Ilianna's mother, here only when rostered on for duty.

Zaira turned left at the end of the hall and started up some stairs. Lights flickered on as we approached, then went dark once we'd passed, and there wasn't a sensor to be seen.

Zaira gave me a quick but nevertheless shrewd glance over her shoulder. "She did begin training as a custodian, but her tenure was brief."

I knew that. I also knew she'd seen something that scared the hell out of her. "She has mentioned that, but she's never said why she left."

"No, she would not." We entered another hall. For a moment I thought that was the end of the conversation, but she surprised me by adding, "This place, and all the wisdom it holds, is not only protected by magic, but sometimes by steel and bloodshed. Ilianna witnessed a latter event and was too young to understand the necessity."

"She's not too young now."

"No." There was a smile in her voice. "But she *is*

incredibly stubborn. I fear she will not come back to us until Kiandra leaves."

Meaning Kiandra was the one who had done the bloodshed, obviously. Still, it was odd. Ilianna wasn't the squeamish type; nor was she illogical. And she was certainly more than capable of understanding the necessity to sometimes use force to protect what was, basically, the spiritual home of witches here in Australia. There *had* to be more to the story.

"So what did she see?"

"That, I'm afraid, I cannot tell you."

I guess I had to be thankful she'd told me as much as she had, although it was certainly frustrating to pick up a little more knowledge and yet know there was a whole lot more to uncover.

We continued on down the darkened hall. This was an area I'd never been through before and, if it had been day rather than night, I might have slowed and had a good look around. As it was, I could barely see anything more than the darkly stained wood panels that lined the hall.

"What was your other reason for coming here?" Zaira asked.

It took me a moment to remember. "Oh. Yeah. Do you know anything about Jorõgumos?"

She frowned. "I am by no means an expert, but I *can* tell you they are particularly nasty spirits."

"That," I said grimly, "they are."

She shot me a glance. "Meaning there's one active here in Melbourne?"

"Maybe. Anything you can tell us about them would be helpful."

She grimaced. "They're often called whore spiders, and for good reason. When they come into season, they take on the form of beautiful women and lure their chosen victims by playing magical Biwas, which is a type of Japanese lute. Once their prey is ensnared, the Jorōgumos bind them in order to either devour them or feed them to their young, depending on where the particular Jorōgumo is in her breeding cycle."

Which was an exact description of what was happening. This thing *was* a Jorōgumo. "Do you know how many kills they need per breeding cycle?"

"Up to half a dozen." She shrugged. "Depends on the size and age of the Jorōgumo."

Meaning this spider spirit wasn't finished hunting yet. "I don't suppose you know an easy way to find this one."

"No. But they rarely stray from established hunting patterns. Work that out, and you should be able to ascertain where she will attack next."

In other words we were already on the right track. Zaira opened a door about midway down and flicked on a light. As had been the case in the hall, warm light spread across the room but barely lifted the shadows.

We were in a small, sweet-smelling office that was basically furnished. An old wooden desk dominated the center of the room, and with it was a leather chair that had seen better days. Shelves lined all the walls and were overflowing with books of every size and color. The weight of them had many of the shelves bowing, and the smell . . . I drew in a deep breath and sighed in appreciation. There was nothing quite like the scent of old books, even when it was almost overwhelmed by the richer scents of lavender and rose.

Zaira sat down at her desk, pulled open a drawer, then carefully lifted a silk-covered ball onto her desk. This wasn't any old ball, but one of power. I could feel the energy radiating off it even from where I stood in the doorway.

"I'll attempt a scrying," she said. "But there's no guarantee it'll work. As I've said, she learned long ago to block my efforts of tracking her."

I crossed my arms and leaned a shoulder against the doorframe. "I just want to know if she's okay. I know I may be panicking over nothing, but—"

"But you are your mother's daughter and, in many respects, even more powerful. I would never ignore your premonitions, however slight, and neither should you."

Surprise rippled through me. More powerful than my mother? That was unlikely, because her talents had been sharpened and honed in a madman's laboratory. While I was more than adept at using my psychic skills, I'd certainly never honed them—something that *had* frustrated the hell out of Mom.

But all I'd ever wanted was a normal life—or as normal as it could ever be given who my mother was and how wealthy we were—and in many respects, my psychic abilities had stood in the way of that desire. I *had* learned to control and use the skills that being half Aedh endowed, simply because Uncle Quinn had always stressed the danger of doing otherwise. I might be stubborn, but I wasn't a fool.

But it was moments like this, when I was standing here in Zaira's office, having to rely on her for information, that I wished I'd listened to Mom.

Zaira unwrapped the crystal and placed her hands on either side of the ball. Light flickered deep in its heart and sent sprays of silver cascading around the walls. Zaira took a deep breath, released it slowly, then closed her eyes and placed her palms on either side of the crystal. Her breathing grew deeper and, after several minutes, the crystal became cloudy and the silver cascade muted.

I watched, wondering what she was seeing and whether it involved Ilianna. Mom had sometimes used a crystal ball when trying to contact the dead for her clients, but it was never her favorite method. She preferred séances, simply because a physical connection with the living relative made communication with the dead easier. For her, it was also less taxing and more accurate.

But Zaira was witch trained. She would be able to do far more with a crystal ball than Mom could ever have imagined.

Time seemed to slow to a crawl, and tension curled through me. I hating waiting, hated not knowing what, if anything, was happening. The only reason I didn't start pacing was the knowledge that it would more than likely disrupt Zaira's scrying.

But eventually she sighed and removed her hands from the crystal. The cloudiness eased immediately and the swirling silver light returned.

Zaira leaned back in her chair and rubbed her forehead wearily. "Well, the good news is that she's not dead."

That was at least something, though it didn't exactly ease the tension still curling through me.

"But?" I said, because there very obviously was one.

"But I can get no feel for her. Something is blocking my ability to pin down her essence, and I cannot tell whether that something is her own magic or something else."

I frowned. "What else could there be?"

She shrugged. "All magic can be blocked, whether by magical means or physical."

"Physical? How do you block magic physically?"

"Certain elements—white ash and iron, for instance—are immune to magic and therefore can be either used as a weapon or shield against it." She wrapped the silk covering around the ball and placed it carefully back in her drawer. "Whatever is being used, I'm afraid I can't get past it."

"Damn."

"Indeed." She rose. "And it might just mean, despite her assertions to the contrary, she had last-minute qualms about meeting Carwyn. Which would be unfortunate, because she would not find a better match herself."

It was a point Ilianna had finally acknowledged—if only to me—but it didn't change the fact that she'd rather remain in a relationship with just Mirri than join Carwyn's herd and risk the dynamic between them changing. I couldn't actually say that to Zaira, though, given she didn't even know her daughter was gay.

"I know she doesn't want to be forced into a herd, but I doubt she'd back away at the last minute. Not without informing Carwyn, at the very least. She has better manners than that."

Zaira smiled as she walked around the desk. "That she has."

She motioned me into the hall, then walked beside me as we made our way back down to the foyer.

"You'll call me the minute you find her?" she said as she unlocked the front door.

"Yes, of course." I touched her arm in reassurance. "And I'm sorry to have worried you over what will probably turn out to be nothing."

"When it comes to the safety of my daughters, I would rather be worried over nothing than something." She placed her hand briefly over mine and lightly squeezed. "Be careful. I might not have found Ilianna, but I did sense the shadows that surround you. There are people in your life who are more dangerous than you know."

Which wasn't something she needed to tell me. I forced a smile. "Thanks. I will be."

I headed out. The night air was cool after the warmth of the Brindle's halls, the gentle breeze like ice. I zipped up my jacket as I ran down the stairs. Azriel reappeared in front of me, forcing me to stop on the bottom step.

"I could not find her," he said. "But she is alive. Her death is not slated for this time."

"Just because she's not meant to die now doesn't mean she won't. Accidents happen." Nevertheless, relief slithered through me. If both Zaira and Azriel were saying she was alive, then surely to god she was. But that didn't mean she couldn't die. That she wasn't in trouble. "Damn it, something *is* wrong, I can feel it."

"Then what do you wish to do next?"

"There's nothing we really *can* do." I bit my lip for a moment, then said, "Maybe Stane can locate her through the GPS in her car."

"And if she is not in her car?"

"Then maybe via her phone." I half shrugged. "It's the only option I have left."

"Then we will try it."

He held out a hand. I placed my fingers in his and allowed him to tug me into his embrace. For a second, he did nothing more than hold me, surrounding me in his warmth and silently offering me the comfort I so desperately needed. Then his energy surged and we swept through the gray fields to Stane's.

He jumped and swore a blue streak when we reformed in the middle of his living room.

"Don't *ever* do that to me again," he said, leaning back in his chair and holding his hand rather dramatically over his heart. "I don't think I could survive the shock a second time."

"You are not slated for death until you are old

and gray," Azriel commented. "So do not fear the strength of your heart."

Stane gave him a somewhat dubious glance. "I'm not entirely sure whether to be comforted by that statement or not." He glanced at me. "I'm gathering something dramatic has happened?"

"Yeah. Ilianna's gone missing." I sat in one of the spare chairs and scooted it across to his "bridge" of computer screens. "I need you to hack into either her car's GPS signal or locate her via her phone."

He gave me the sort of look a father might give a child that was being exceptionally dumb. "And have you tried using Latitude?"

"Um, no?" Mainly because I was of the opinion that if my friends wanted to find me, they could damn well ring and ask me.

He sighed. "Did I not tell you all to sign up for it some time ago?"

"Yes, but—"

"No buts. I told you, it's the easiest way ever invented to uncover where your buddies might be hiding, and it doesn't even require GPS." He swung around, swiped one of the screens across to Google, and logged in. A map of Melbourne appeared, dotted with arrowed face pics. He leaned forward a little, studying all the names, then grinned.

"Here you go," he said, enlarging the screen. "She's at South Bank."

Which wasn't that enlightening given how big the place was. Although, if I remembered right, Carwyn had booked a table at Harvest Time—did this mean she *was* headed there? That she was okay, despite being incommunicado? "Where in South Bank?"

He frowned, zoomed the screen in a little more, then said, "According to this, she's at Wilson's Parking, just off Freshwater Place." He glanced up at me. "It's the riverside quay area, if you don't know it."

"I don't, but we'll find it." I jumped up and dropped a kiss on his unshaven and definitely scratchy cheek. "Thank you."

"No probs. Just give me some warning next time you decide to drop by." He gave Azriel another dubious look. "Despite what your friend here says, my heart really *can't* take surprises like that."

I grinned. "I'll send some more champers to make up for it."

He snorted. "I haven't got the last lot yet."

"You will."

"And I'll need it if you keep popping into existence willy-nilly. Now, go find Ilianna so I can get back to my gaming."

"Done."

I stepped into Azriel's arms and he whisked us out of there. We reappeared on the center strip that divided the two lanes of Freshwater Place, the eight-story parking garage in front of us and the remaining wall of an old brick warehouse behind us. Several cars zoomed past, briefly spotlighting us before sweeping on.

I grabbed Azriel's hand and ran across the road. "Can you sense her?" I asked, as we headed into the garage via the exit lane.

"No." His fingers squeezed mine lightly. "But that does not mean she is not here."

Didn't mean she was, either. I ignored the fear that rose with the thought and hurried on. The garage had eight levels, and we found Ilianna's car on the seventh.

She wasn't in it.

I swore vehemently and punched the roof of her Jeep hard enough to actually dent it.

"There are security cameras dotted around this place," Azriel commented. "I would suggest you avoid such outbursts unless you wish company."

I flexed my fingers, somehow managed to control the somewhat insane desire to continue to take my frustration out on Ilianna's car, and peered in through the windows instead. And there, sitting on the front seat, were not only her phone, but her purse and coat as well.

Ilianna might have left her phone behind if it had gone dead, but she sure as hell wouldn't have left her purse.

Something *had* happened to her.

"Damn it!" I all but exploded. "What the *hell* is going on?"

"I don't know—"

"Neither do I," I cut in, voice bitter. I leaned back against the car and closed my eyes. "This day has just gone from bad to fucking worse. Maybe we should just quit while we're ahead."

"A sentiment I would agree with, except for the fact that Hunter, at the very least, would not be pleased by such an event."

As if on cue, my phone rang. And the tone told me it was Hunter.

"The bitch obviously has her phone linked to my thoughts," I muttered, but nevertheless dug it out of my pocket and hit the ANSWER button. "No, I haven't found her yet. I haven't found anyone fucking yet."

Amusement touched her lips, though it did little to lift the shadows from her bright eyes. "I take it the day has not been a good one for you."

"No. Ilianna has gone missing." I paused. "I don't suppose you'd know anything about that, would you?"

She arched an eyebrow. "And why would I bother with such an endeavor?"

"Well, you did make less-than-veiled threats against my friends if I didn't do what you want."

"Ah yes, I remember." Her amusement grew. "But given you are doing as I desire, there is no need for such action as yet, is there, now?"

Her reply was almost purred. If I could have reached down the phone and strangled the bitch, I would have.

"I guess not." It was said through somewhat clenched teeth. "But the fact of the matter is that I'm not having much luck tracking down the Jorõgumo."

"But you found two of her nests. Or was the burned-out bedroom not your handiwork?"

I mentally swore and rubbed my forehead wearily. I was starting to get one hell of a headache, and I suspected it wouldn't go away in a hurry. Not unless I drowned it under several gallons of alcohol,

and that wasn't particularly practical right now—
even if it sounded like the best idea I'd had for ages.

"What did Rhoan say in his report?"

"That something or someone destroyed what appeared to be a nest of spiders in one Ms. Summers's
bedroom."

And how had he come to that conclusion given
that Amaya's flames had consumed just about everything? And why hadn't I received a phone call de-
manding to know why the hell I was even anywhere
near the place given my promise not to investigate?
He surely wouldn't have missed the fact that the
Ducati was parked right outside. *If* she was still parked
outside, that was. Knowing my uncle, he'd probably
ordered her confiscated, just to teach me a lesson.

"I burned the bastards because I didn't think
anyone would want a friggin' nest of Jorōgumos remaining in existence," I said, with a touch more annoyance than was probably wise. Just because she
seemed to be amused didn't mean she actually was.
"They were too young to be in any form other than
spider, so it was unlikely the Directorate witches
would have gotten any information out of them."

"And what about the mama spider?"

"Well, she's supposed to be performing at some-
place called the Falcon Club at midnight, but I don't
like our chances of catching her there."

The amusement faded. Rapidly. "And why
would that be?"

*Because I burned her babies and it's more than
likely she sensed it.* But I wasn't about to actually

say that. My life might not be fun at the moment, but I sure as hell wasn't ready to see it end just yet.

"Because we're not dealing with a dumb spirit here. She spotted me at Hallowed Ground and did a runner. She knows we're after her."

"Not even a spirit can deny the urge of a mother to feed her young," Hunter commented. "She didn't kill this afternoon, so if she still has young to feed, she will be forced to do so either tonight or tomorrow."

Undoubtedly. "So do you want me to go to the Falcon Club, or would you rather?" I kept my fingers crossed for the latter, because the last thing I really felt like right now was traipsing off to another bloody club.

As usual, it was a forlorn hope.

"I have no desire to be involved in the grunt work of investigating. That is what underlings are for."

A smile touched her lips, but it was in no way a nice smile. Just for a moment, I thought about Harry Stanford's offer and was tempted. *Seriously* tempted.

But only briefly. However desperate I might be feeling, I wasn't insane, and there was no way in hell I was going to cross the line and go up against Hunter.

"Just remember to contact me once you have found her," she continued, in that same sweet, do-it-or-I'll-kill-you voice. "Because I very much intend to do to her what she did to Wolfgang."

Consume her? Not just her blood, but her intestines, guts, and brain? Surely to god that wasn't possible for a vampire to do—blood yes, but not the innards as well? And yet if any vampire *could* be capable of it, then it would be Hunter.

Somehow, I managed to keep the horror out of my voice as I said, "You'll be the first person I call."

"I had best be the only call you make where this case is concerned."

I'd meant the comment sarcastically—it wasn't like I could call anyone else, anyway. But I didn't bother replying. I just hung up, shoved the phone away, and glanced at my watch. "Well, it's nine o'clock. Given I can't do anything else to find Ilianna, and I have no intention of going to that damn club earlier than I have to, we've got only one option left."

"And that is?" Azriel said, the slightest hint of a smile breaking his otherwise bland expression.

"We go home and make mad, crazy love to each other. Let's grab a moment of utter normality before the shit hits the fan completely."

Because a storm *was* coming. I could feel it. And I had a bad, bad suspicion I might not survive it.

Azriel caught my hand and tugged me into his arms. "While I am alive, you will remain so. I promise you that, if nothing else."

I melted into his embrace and listened to the strong, steady beat of his heart. "If death is my fate, even you cannot change that."

He didn't answer, and my stomach dropped. I looked up quickly and caught the flash of . . . something dark—perhaps even a little guilt—in his eyes. Then it was gone, and all that remained was tenderness.

"Can you?" I asked, frowning.

"That is a question I hope I will never be forced to answer," he said. Which wasn't exactly an answer, but I knew him well enough now to understand it was all I was about to get. "Now, about this business of mad, crazy lovemaking. I'm not sure I understand the concept."

I smiled. "Then take me home and I'll show you."

He did, and I did.

And it was glorious.

Chapter 10

The Falcon Club was decidedly seedy. The air was thick with the scents of cigars, alcohol, and unwashed flesh, and it was packed with people—mainly men, but there was a good smattering of women here as well, most of whom were scantily dressed and very obviously working the room. Sex, I suspected, could be found here for a price.

My nose twitched at the unpleasant aromas surrounding me, but I ignored them the best I could, grabbed a drink from the bar, then wound my way through the shabby tables, choosing one in the thicker shadows near the bathrooms. It was far enough away from the bar—and most of the patrons—that the air was almost breathable and had the added bonus of affording a good view of the small stage situated to the left of the bar.

I sat down and nursed the icy glass of beer between my palms. This club obviously wasn't one of your more upmarket ones, so it was a little surprising that they'd employed someone like Di Shard to provide their entertainment. Given the state of this place—and the less-than-dapper look of its customers—a stripper would probably have been more appropriate. Or, at the very least, a rock band—although given the club's close proximity to homes, noise regulations would probably have stopped that.

I took a drink of beer and briefly caught the eye of a tall, somewhat hairy individual several tables over. He reminded me somewhat of the visage Azriel had said he'd adopted when we'd visited Classique, and I couldn't help smiling. The bear-shifter—he couldn't really be anything else looking like that—obviously took my smile as a go-ahead signal, because he rose, hitched up his trousers, and began wandering over. He was little more than four feet away when he abruptly turned and headed off toward the bar.

I just about choked on my drink. *And here I was thinking you couldn't interfere with the thoughts or actions of others unless it involved the key search in some way.*

Given the direction of that man's thoughts, you should be thankful I did turn him away.

I grinned at the annoyance in his mental tones. *And what if I'd wanted to be mauled by a hairy bear type?*

You have far better taste than that.

The amusement bubbling through me got stronger. *That wasn't what you were saying when I was with Lucian.*

The Aedh's attraction was magic enhanced.

And the fact that he was also a fantastic lover had absolutely nothing *to do with it.* That comment was greeted by stony silence. I somehow controlled my amusement and switched to safer subjects. *No sign of our spider-spirit yet?*

We'd decided that—given the Jorōgumo's sudden retreat last time we'd tried to confront her—it might be wiser if Azriel remained outside, in the vague hope that out of sight would mean out of sensory range. I could hide my features easily enough—and was, in fact, now green-eyed, brown-haired, and definitely not anything you'd label pretty—so it was unlikely she'd even recognize me, let alone sense I was anything more than just another non-human. Spirits, Azriel had assured me, weren't often attuned to the Aedh. Amaya's presence on my back was another matter entirely, but given I wasn't about to go anywhere without having her close at hand, it was a risk we had to take.

No sign of her, he said. *But she is unlikely to arrive early given she is aware that we hunt her.*

Which makes me wonder if she'll even turn up. I mean, if she's as smart as you said, she'd be stupid to come here.

But, as Hunter noted, sometimes maternal demands overrun common sense.

I took another sip of beer. It was, despite the grimy air of the place, surprisingly good. A couple walked past me, the man radiating lust and grinning with expectation. The woman's expression was rather world-weary. Just another mark for her, I thought, as they made their way into the bathroom. I grimaced at the thought. If the bathrooms were as grimy as the rest of this place, it sure as hell wouldn't have been *my* first choice for a rendezvous. Even the lane behind this joint would have been cleaner.

Trying to tune their noise out, I said, *If she merely wishes to feed her young, why wouldn't she just snatch someone off the street?*

Perhaps she requires more in a victim than just mere flesh and blood. Her male victims were strong psychically, remember. And she consumed them, not her young.

Meaning maybe I should do a quick reconnoiter and see if I can sense any psychically strong targets in the room.

You do not need to subject yourself to the less-than-savory nature of those in the club. His mental tones held a note that I would have sworn was proprietary had it been anyone else. *There are four such people in the room.*

Who?

As I am not in the room, I cannot say precisely. I merely sense the vibrations of their souls.

Which isn't much good given the room is packed. Our task would be easier if we knew who to keep an eye on. I downed my drink in several gulps and rose. *I'll take the long way to the bar and see what I can uncover.*

If you wish. His tone suggested he didn't think it was necessary, and I couldn't help grinning all over again. My reaper might have accused me of being jealous over his flirting with other women on more than one occasion, but it really was beginning to sound like he was suffering from the same affliction. And I couldn't help but be happy about that, if only because it suggested that I wasn't imagining the caring I sometimes sensed in him.

Of course, taking the long way to the bar did mean walking past a lot of very merry men, many of whom seemed to think a female rump in close proximity really *did* need a pinch, if not a good fondle. It irked the hell out of me, but I kept my temper in check and a smile on my face and was rewarded by finding all four psychics. Two had parked themselves at the bar, one was sitting with a dark-haired woman near the front door, and the last one leaned casually against the wall opposite the bar, sipping his beer and idly surveying the crowd.

His gaze met mine briefly, and a frisson of recognition raced through me. Not because I knew him, but because I knew the *type*.

If he wasn't Directorate, I'd eat my damn hat. If I'd been wearing a hat, that was.

At least his gaze slid past me and continued on. My inner devil was tempted to go over and chat him up, not only because he was one of the few half-decent-looking guys in the room, but because it would have been interesting to see if I could tease any information out of him.

But we were both here to catch a killer, and *that* sort of behavior wasn't something either of us needed. Besides, it wasn't like I needed another man in my life, however briefly I might flirt with the idea.

I made my way back to my table, but had barely sat down when Azriel said, *She's here.*

Where?

Just entering the club via a rear door. He paused. *She can sense me.*

I swore softly and pushed up from the table so quickly that I half spilled my beer. *Meaning she's running again?*

No. I retreated fast, and she remains.

I sighed in relief. *Keep your distance, then. With the Directorate here, we can't do anything until she picks out a victim and leaves with him.*

The guardian will follow her, just as we plan to.

Yeah, but we can knock out his car or even him. Though it would undoubtedly be easier to do the former rather than the latter. He might be a shifter rather than a vampire, but he was still a guardian and therefore dangerous.

I sat back down and took a sip of beer. I had only half of it left, but I wasn't going to walk over to the bar to get another one. Given our target had entered the building, it was better if I remained where I was.

After a few more minutes, a tall, thin man walked onto the stage and lightly tapped the microphone to get everyone's attention. Unfortunately for him, just about everyone but me ignored him.

"I'm afraid tonight's entertainment has been canceled. The lively Di Shard called in sick at the last moment, and we weren't able to get a replacement."

The news was greeted by general indifference, but it had me frowning. *Azriel, has she left again or is she still here?*

She's there. I cannot pinpoint her location pre-cisely because doing so means moving closer and increases the chances of her sensing me again.

So why the hell would the manager announce she was unavailable?

I cannot say.

Neither could I, and it was damn worrying. And it wasn't like I needed anything else to worry about given the whole key situation and now Ilianna's dis-appearance.

I searched for the four psychics again and spotted all but the guardian. I saw him a couple of seconds later as he jumped onto the stage and followed the manager into the back room. He was obviously in-tending to question the man—something I really would have liked to have done but now couldn't. The guardian might not have recognized me, but he'd know I was wolf. The last thing I needed was him reporting a werewolf working for the vamp council questioning the manager. Rhoan could put two and two together as easily as the next man.

My gaze swept the room again, but I didn't see anything that spiked the internal radar. Then a tall, somewhat slender woman pulled away from the deeper shadows to the left of the stage—in fact, it looked almost as if she was *re-forming* from them. And maybe she was.

She was tall, brown-haired, and had a faint red stripe running along her center part. She didn't physically resemble either Shard or Summer—except for that stripe—but then, that was no surprise given she was able to take on different forms. And she would, because she knew she was being chased.

I wrapped my hands around my almost empty glass and tried not to be overly obvious about watching her. She looked around the room for several minutes; then her gaze centered on one of the shifters standing near the bar. She strolled toward him and trailed her fingers along the nape of his neck as she sat on the vacant barstool beside him. He jumped as if he'd just been stung, and maybe he *had*. She was a spider after all.

They began to chat and were soon as animated as old friends. She wasn't overly obvious with her flirting, just went with encouraging smiles and the occasional casual touch. But the psychic energy radiating off her was strong enough that I could feel it from here—and it felt *hungry*.

I shivered. In the back of my mind, Amaya began humming, the soft sound filled with expectation. *This one is not for you, I'm afraid.*

It hunts, she replied, somewhat testily. *Should kill.*

Oh, she will be killed, just not by us.

Task mine.

Not this time.

I swear she swore—although if she *had*, it was in a language I couldn't understand. Did demons even have their own language?

Of course, Azriel commented, his tone amused. *All sentient beings do.*

I guess I just didn't expect it from a demon in a sword.

Remember, before she was in the sword, she was

a very powerful demon causing a great deal of havoc.

Havoc good, she commented. *Should cause more.*

I snorted. *Bloodthirsty little beast, aren't you?*

She preened. I shook my head, then tensed as the shifter and the Jorōgumo rose in unison. My gaze swept the club, but I didn't see any sign of the guardian. Maybe he'd left after talking to the manager.

Not entirely, Azriel said. *He's outside, watching the entrance.*

Damn. I should have guessed a guardian wouldn't abandon his post so easily. Or that we'd be *that* lucky. *We need to take him out.*

The shifter and the spider-spirit didn't head for the front door, however, but rather turned and walked, arm in arm, in my direction. I swore softly, but kept my head down and sipped the remains of my beer.

Awareness crawled across my skin. The closer she got, the worse it got, until it felt like thousands of tiny black feet were skittering all over me. My grip on the glass became so fierce, my knuckles went white—how it didn't shatter, I had no idea.

They walked past, whispering like lovers. I resisted the urge to jump up and follow them, forcing myself to remain still and listen to their retreating footsteps. They didn't go into the bathroom as I'd half expected, but rather through the rear fire exit.

I thrust to my feet and followed them, catching the door with my fingertips before it closed again.

The alarm, I noted, had been disconnected—and had been for a while, if the state of the wires was anything to go by. Obviously, the Jorõgumo and her lover were not the first to make a retreat out the rear door.

I cautiously peered out. The two of them were halfway down the small lane that ran the length of the row of buildings in this block. I waited until they'd neared the main street, then slipped out, stopping the door from slamming closed before moving—as stealthily as I could—down the lane. The minute the two of them turned left and were out of my sight, I quickened my pace but didn't run. Even a drunk shifter had damn good hearing. While he might not connect my footsteps with them being followed, he might just mention it. I couldn't risk the Jorõgumo fleeing again.

Where are they going? I asked.

They have stopped near a car. Azriel paused. *The guardian is on the move as well.*

Shit. He must have put either movement sensors or temporary cameras in the lane. My gaze swept the shadows around me, but I couldn't spot either of them. Of course, he very obviously wouldn't have put them anywhere that they *could* be easily seen.

If there were damn cameras, though, it might lead to trouble for me. A brown-haired woman following the Jorõgumo and her next victim might not make *this* guardian suspicious, but it certainly would prick Uncle Rhoan's internal radar.

Where is he?

He's just turned left into the street you move toward.

Great. Unless I wanted him following the Jorõgumo and perhaps interfering with Hunter's desire for revenge, I had to take him out. I looked around for some sort of weapon, but there wasn't anything particularly handy lying about. But there was some sort of industrial Dumpster near the far end of the lane. I spun, ran back, and climbed in. After a few seconds of fishing around the stinking refuse and building rubbish, I found something usable—an old chair leg about one foot long.

I jumped out of the Dumpster, brushed off the worst of the gunk clinging to my jeans, then shoved a hand in my purse and wrapped my fingers around my phone and keys as I called to the Aedh. The magic transformed me in an instant, and I scooted down the lane. Now I just had to hope that the guardian wasn't sensitive to energy forces.

I paused at the junction of the lane and the street and glanced left. The shifter and the Jorõgumo were about one street down, getting into a pale blue Toyota. I swore mentally and spun left, searching the shadows flowing across the footpath for the guardian.

He was moving with surprising speed for someone who wasn't a vampire, and something silver glinted in his fist. Tracker, I thought. That was the last thing I needed.

I flowed past him, then spun around and moved up behind him. How the hell was I going to knock him out? Total re-formation was out of the question, especially given my less-than-stellar re-formation technique. Which left me with the option of doing a partial one—something I *had* done when in flesh form, but never from Aedh. Or on the move.

I snuck closer, then called to the Aedh. This time, I controlled the surge of power, channeling its fury, containing its strength, focusing it on just the arm that held the old chair leg. Making both real and solid.

The guardian must have sensed something was happening because he suddenly spun, but I'd already let loose with the chair leg. It smashed against the side of his head with a heavy crack, and he dropped like a ton of bricks. Guilt flickered through me. I hoped like hell he wasn't hurt too badly, but it wasn't like I could stop and check.

I drew my arm back to Aedh form and raced down the street just as the shifter's car pulled away from his parking spot.

He drove fast, obviously eager to get home, and I had to wonder what the hell I'd do if he got pulled over by the cops. I couldn't keep attacking law enforcement officers—especially given few cops traveled alone these days, and all of them had onboard cameras in their cars.

But he wasn't pulled over, and eventually he stopped in front of a small weatherboard home that looked as unkempt as the shifter. Obviously, it was just the psychic power our dark spirit was attracted to rather than the sort that came with success and wealth.

He climbed out of the car, ran around the rear of it, and opened the Jorōgumo's door, ushering her out and taking her arm as he escorted her through the front gate and up the steps. I waited until they'd gone inside, then re-formed. Once I'd picked myself up off the pavement and sorted out my clothing, I grabbed the phone and rang Hunter.

She answered almost immediately. "I do hope it's good news, Risa dear," she drawled. "I am not in the mood for the other sort."

"I'm standing outside of an old weatherboard house. The Jorōgumo is inside, about to feast on another victim."

Something dark, dangerous, and very, very hungry flashed in her eyes. "Give me the address immediately."

I did. "What do you want us to do? Wait here or leave?"

"What I want you to do is go in and pen the bitch. As much as I do not care about the shifter himself, Jack has insisted I not risk more lives than necessary in my quest for revenge."

Meaning Jack actually held some sway over her actions? Somehow, I suspected *that* would be the case only if his requests meshed with her own desires.

"I have no idea how the hell I'd pen—"

"I don't care how you do it; just do it," she cut in. "I will not be pleased to arrive and find her gone."

A displeased Hunter was *not* someone I wanted to face. "Fine," I muttered, and hung up.

Heat swirled through me, warm and familiar as Azriel appeared beside me.

"Is it safe for you to re-form?" I leaned my shoulder against his to steal more of his warmth. The night air hadn't gotten any warmer, that was for sure.

"I am as far away now as I was back at the club, so I would presume so."

"How the hell are we going to cage her?"

"Not we," he said grimly. "You. The minute I get nearer, she will run."

"Oh, fabulous." I rubbed my arms, but it didn't do a whole lot against the sudden sense of dread. "What do you suggest?"

"Amaya should be capable of containing her long enough for me to get in there and help complete the task."

"She's capable of consuming her, too," I muttered. My sword's response to this was what sounded like a wicked chuckle.

"Yes. You will have to be firm with her."

Easier said than done. "When the Jorōgumo appeared in the club, she seemed to merge from the shadows—can she actually do that?"

"Most spirits who can take on flesh can just as easily dissolve. You will have to be quick to capture her."

"And hope like hell she doesn't decide to attack rather than run."

"If she attacks, I *will* be there."

If she flung little black babies at me, him arriving quickly was *not* going to help. "So, wish me luck."

"I wish you speed and strength," he said. "As I

have noted before, it is not wise to rely on luck in this sort of situation."

I guess not. I drew Amaya and gripped her fiercely. *Okay, we are going to cage her, not consume her; you got that, Amaya?*

Fun not.

I don't care.

She muttered for several seconds, the words indecipherable but their meaning clear. Happy not, as she would say. Then she said, *Can nibble?*

Not even a little taste. She is Hunter's meal, not yours.

Eat Hunter, she muttered.

That, I replied grimly, *might yet be an option in the future.*

She perked up no end at this and began humming happily. I took a deep breath, released it slowly, and wished the nerves and the tension would just fuck off. They didn't, however, so I just called to the Aedh once again and carefully made my way inside the house.

To hear music rather than the sound of lovemaking.

I inched forward, following the haunting, melodious sound, and found the shifter and the Jorōgumo in the living room. He was sitting on a chair, his jacket dumped on the floor and his shirt undone to the waist. His eyes were closed, and his expression was one of bliss. I couldn't actually see why—the music, while different, wasn't exactly a sound that would put me into raptures. But then, my tastes tended to run to pop and rock rather than more classical stuff.

Besides, his state didn't really have a whole lot to do with the actual music, but rather the lute it came from. Zaira had said the instrument was magic, and the room was thick with it.

The Jorōgumo knelt at his feet, her head bent and her dark hair cascading over what looked to be a small, odd-shaped lute. She plucked the strings with nails that were long and glistened with silver—silver that fell onto the wood floor and spun up and around the shifter's sneakered feet.

Her web.

The music spelled him, distracted him, while she spun her cocoon around him.

Remember, I said to Amaya, although I wasn't entirely sure she could hear me when we were both little more than energy particles. *No consuming. Just containment.*

With that, I called forth the Aedh and reformed—but only enough to give Amaya room to do her stuff. There was no way in *hell* I was about to risk baby spiders being thrown at me.

The minute Amaya formed, she flung fire at the Jorōgumo, but the spider woman reacted with lightning speed, throwing herself sideways and out from under the range of the flames. They chased her, eagerly crawling across the floor toward her, but already she was dissolving, her face and torso becoming little more than wisps that trailed behind the rest of her body as she continued to run from Amaya's flames.

"Fuck," I said, and regained full form. "Amaya, grab her legs!"

A rope of fire lashed out instantly, whipping around what remained of the Jorõgumo's limbs. She screamed and stumbled, crashing to the floor and finding form again.

Only her form was spider rather than human this time, and she was big and black, with skin that writhed and pulsated. I did *not* want to know what was causing that movement. I really didn't.

The Jorõgumo lunged at me, her fangs bared and as thick as my arm. I yelped and jumped backward, but my calves clipped the edge of the coffee table and I tipped ass over the top of it. I landed awkwardly, but had barely rolled onto my back when Amaya screamed a warning. I looked up to see a hairy black leg coming straight at me. I swore, swung my sword, and steel met flesh with a clang that sounded oddly like a death knell. Not mine, I hoped. Amaya's screaming was fierce as her steel bit deep into one of the fleshier parts of the Jorõgumo's leg, and blood flew. As did little black objects.

It was my worst fear come to life. There were baby spiders *under* her skin.

Somehow I kept a lid on the utter horror that crawled through me and rolled out from under her leg.

"Azriel!" I screamed, wrenching Amaya free as I jumped upright. "I need some damn help here!"

Already here.

His mind voice was sharp, distracted, and I risked a glance across the other side of the room as I con-

tinued to back away from the Jorōgumo. A second
creature had appeared, only this one was made up
of thousands of little tiny bodies that writhed and
moved and hissed and yet acted as one deadly enemy. Azriel attacked the mass with Valdis's steel
and flame, moving so fast, he was little more than a
blur. But for every part of the mass they destroyed,
others just crawled in and resumed the attack.

Fuck, fuck, *fuck*!

Mom Jorōgumo lunged at me again, liquid dripping from her fangs. I ducked away from her attack
and smashed Amaya across her fangs. One went flying but the other remained. Liquid splashed across
my clothes, stinking to high heaven and stinging
where it hit flesh. Hoping like crazy the stuff had to
be injected to actually work, I batted away another
attack, then leapt high, twisted in midair, and came
down on the middle part of her body, right behind
her eyes. Amaya screamed again, the sound echoing across the room as well as in my head.

Don't kill, I ordered her fiercely. *Just blind and bind.*

Then I swung her with all the strength I had. Her
steel bit into the bitch's eyes just as the Jorōgumo
flung herself at the wall. We hit hard, and breath
whooshed from my body. Not satisfied with merely
winding me, the Jorōgumo hissed and writhed, and
I fell, ending up on the floor underneath her. One
foot scraped my leg, cutting deep, and a scream
rolled up my throat. I bit down on it and crawled
out from underneath her, barely avoiding several
strikes of fang and leg. A hand grabbed me and
dragged me upright.

"Amaya!" Azriel said. "Flame and ensnare. *Now!*"

My sword responded instantly, and twin lances of flames rolled out from the swords, shooting across the writhing creature's body, spreading out in vibrant fingers, weaving in and out of each other, joining the rope of flames that still encased two of the Jorōgumo's legs, until it had formed a net that encased the spider-spirit's entire body.

She didn't stop writhing and screaming, but she was trapped and not going anywhere.

I collapsed back against the wall and closed my eyes in relief. My head was pounding, and my leg was bleeding, I was aching all over from my encounter with the wall, but hey, I was alive and the spider *wasn't* dead. As outcomes went, it wasn't all that bad.

"I guess the fact you have only one injury *is* something to be grateful for," Azriel agreed, voice wry. "However, it would have been nice if you could have remained wound free for a change."

"Tell *that* to the bad guys who keep attacking me." I opened my eyes. Azriel stood several feet away, his body covered with tiny wounds that gave his skin a bloody glint. Concern rolled through me. "Are you all right?"

He nodded. "I am energy, remember."

"But you're wearing flesh." I pushed away from the wall, took two steps, and gently ran my fingertips across the worst of the wounds on his arm. "If the babies were as venomous as their mom—"

"I will burn off their venom the minute I return to energy form." He gave me a sweet, somewhat lopsided smile. "But I appreciate the concern."

"Hey, I don't want to lose you over something dumb like getting bitten by a damn spider."

"That is not something I would be overly pleased with, either."

Amaya's steel began to vibrate in my hand, and I glanced down with a frown. Both swords were still blazing, but Amaya's flames were beginning to pulse. It was almost as if her strength was faltering.

"It is," Azriel commented. "Which means she's now drawing on your strength to help hold her share of the net."

"Why can't she hold it herself?"

Strength not right, she muttered, the surliness in her mental tones suggesting she was very put out by the fact.

"She's young in demon terms," Azriel commented. "She will get stronger with both age and your continuing merger."

Merger. Not something I really wanted to be doing with a demon spirit with a hankering for bloodshed, but I guess that option had gone out the window the minute I'd taken her steel and stabbed her into my flesh.

And, if I was being at all honest, for all my wariness about owning a demon sword, I really wouldn't want to be without her now. Having her so readily at hand had saved my ass more than once.

"I hope Hunter gets here quickly, then." I paused. "Or can you and Valdis hold the Jorõgumo yourselves?"

"We can kill her, but containing her as we are takes more strength and generally requires two swords." He grimaced. "They were never designed for this."

I guess they weren't—and they were doing it now only because Hunter wanted bloody revenge.

"Speaking of Hunter, she approaches the front door."

"Meaning we now have the problem of getting her *into* the house." As a vampire, she had to abide by the old "invite only" rule.

"Can she not telepathically order such an invite?" Azriel said.

"No. It has to be freely given."

The doorbell rang. I shot a look down the hall and saw her silhouette through the glass panes. "Now what do we do?"

"I would suggest you get the door open, Risa dearest," Hunter replied, proving the keenness of her hearing yet again. "Otherwise I will not be pleased."

"Kinda hard to do when the owner is unconscious." But I walked over and booted the cobwebbed heel of his shoes. "Hey, wake up."

He didn't flinch. I tried again, harder this time. Still nothing. "Can you wake him?" I said, glancing at Azriel.

"I shouldn't, but given the growing precariousness of the situation—" He paused, his expression one of concentration. After a moment, the shifter groaned and rubbed his eyes. Then he saw us.

"What the fuck?" He jerked upright abruptly. "Who the hell are you two? And what the *fuck* is *that*?"

"That," I said grimly, "is the woman you brought home."

"No fucking way."

"Look, I don't particularly care if you believe me or not," I said, voice tart. "The fact is you have the mother of all spiders in your living room and you were almost her dinner. Now, be a good chap and go invite Director Hunter into your house so she can deal with the beast."

He blinked. "The director? As in, the Directorate?"

"Yes," I said, and mentally ordered the man to just go. It wouldn't have done any good, of course, even if I *had* been telepathic, because of the whole "freely given" restriction.

But if he *didn't* hurry, things were going to get bad pretty quickly. The throbbing in Amaya's steel was stronger, as was my damn headache. And I didn't even want to think about the amount of blood I was losing, but my socks were beginning to feel rather wet.

"If this spider escapes the power net," I continued, "we'll all be damn dinner. So please, just go open the door."

He looked from me to the spider, then to Azriel, and rose—and just about fell flat on his face again. I'd forgotten about the web wrapping his feet and lower legs.

"Fucking hell, it *was* trying to eat me!" His voice held edges of both anger and hysteria.

"But it didn't!" I cut in harshly. "Just hop down

the damn hall and open the door. We can't hold this bitch much longer." I paused. "We'll explain everything later."

He gave me a "you'd better" look, then hopped in a rather ungainly fashion down the hall and opened the front door. Two seconds later, Hunter was striding toward us. There was little emotion on her face, but her pupils had expanded to the point where there was little green left and the sheer depth of hunger that radiated off her stole my breath and had my gut churning. This was Hunter as I'd hoped I'd never see her—eager for her revenge, ravenous for the blood of her enemy.

Thank god I had Azriel with me.

I glanced back down the hall. The shifter was still standing by the open door, but his expression was slack.

"His expression is as empty as his mind," she said, her low voice vibrating with anticipation. "Do you think I desire a witness to what I am about to do?"

I swallowed heavily. "We're witnesses."

She turned her black gaze on me, and I took an involuntary step back.

"Yes," she murmured, voice silky. "But I have nothing to fear from you; do I, Risa dear?"

I felt like a rabbit caught in the spotlight, only this particular one shone with a dark, dark light and promised a bloody, brutal death.

"Your threats grow tedious, Hunter." Azriel's voice held little inflection and no doubt for good reason. It wouldn't take much to set her off. "And you are here for the Jorõgumo, remember."

"Yes."

Hunter's gaze returned to the caged spider, and the energy radiating off her suddenly spiked. Only it wasn't aimed at any of us, but rather the Jorõgumo herself. Her form began to flicker, change, shrink, until what stood before us was once again a woman.

A woman who looked suddenly scared.

Just for a fraction of a second, I almost felt sorry for her. Then I remembered what she was and what she'd done. The death Hunter was about to give her was surely quicker than the one she'd given any of her victims.

"Lower the force of your flames and allow me access," Hunter said.

Chills raced across my skin. There was nothing human behind those words.

Lower Amaya's flames so they leash just her legs, Azriel said.

I echoed his words to my sword, and she obeyed. *Hurry must,* she said. *Weak growing for both.*

Yes, it was. I bit my lip and tried to ignore the fact that my head felt like it was about to explode.

Amaya's flames followed Valdis's down the Jorõgumo's body until they encased just the lower half of her legs. The spider-spirit didn't move. I suspected the energy radiating off Hunter had a whole lot to do with that.

"For the crime of killing four, you are sentenced to death," Hunter said, stepping so close to the Jorõgumo that she was practically in her face. "But for the crime of killing one of those four, you are sentenced to death by *me*."

And with that, she attacked.

But she didn't just sink her teeth into the Jorõgumo's neck and drink her blood. She rendered her apart and consumed everything.

Absolutely everything.

Even her soul.

Chapter 11

It was sheer survival mode that kept me rooted to the spot and watching, even though every instinct in my body was screaming to get the hell out of there—to get away from the monster that was consuming one of its own kind.

Hunter might not be a Jorōgumo, but given what I was witnessing, it was impossible to think of her as just another vampire—however powerful and old she was.

Normal vampires didn't consume flesh and bone and brain matter. Normal vampires didn't drink souls.

How I didn't lose the entire contents of my stomach, I'll never know.

Unbidden, Harry Stanford's words came back into my mind. *Oh, trust me, she long ago mastered the art of hiding what she truly is.*

I guess the question that needed answering now was, what sort of monster had she become?

Unfortunately, it wasn't a question I could exactly ask anyone in the know. I had a more than vague suspicion questioning Hunter herself would not be a good idea, and the only other people I could approach who might have some clue were

Uncle Quinn and Harry Stanford himself. Both were out of the question, for very different reasons.

So I swallowed the bile backing up in my throat, kept my knees locked, and ignored the ever-increasing shuddering in both Amaya's steel and my body. And found myself looking anywhere but at the scene in front of me.

But it seemed to take far too long for the Jorōgumo to meet her end.

My knees and Amaya's flames gave out at the exact same time. I hit the floor with a grunt and drew in shuddery breaths, my head swimming and my body on fire.

A heartbeat later, Azriel knelt in front of me, his concern radiating through me like the wash of a warm summer breeze. He pressed his hand against the wound, my blood oozing up through his fingers as energy radiated from the epicenter of his touch. It flushed strength through my shaking muscles as it began to heal my leg, and, after a few seconds, I felt decidedly better.

My gaze met his. In the depths of his differently colored eyes, barely leashed fury burned.

If she but gives me the tiniest of excuses, he said, mind voice flat and in many ways scarier than even Hunter herself, *she will be dead.*

She won't. I lightly brushed some spider goo from his cheek. His skin was far cooler than usual, and concern sharpened anew. *Will you please shift into energy form and burn away the venom?*

Your wound is not fully healed, and I am in no danger as yet—

I don't care about my wound—

A continuing problem with you, he cut in. There was both amusement and frustration in his mental tones.

I smiled. *I'm okay, so just humor me and heal yourself, will you?*

If you insist.

He disappeared, leaving me once again staring at the scene in front of me. There actually wasn't that much to see anymore. All that remained of the spider woman were the bits I'd sliced off—some leg pieces, her fang, and one of the spinnerets. Everything else—all the gore and other body parts—had been consumed.

Hunter turned and our gazes met. I froze again, pinned by the awful darkness of her eyes, and for a moment feared that I was about to become her second victim. Then she blinked, and the darkness retreated.

But the air still burned with the wrongness of her being. Worse still, blood and flesh covered the lower part of her face and dripped from her chin, and her shirt was soaked with gore.

My stomach once again threatened to rebel, but I had a feeling vomiting all over her no-longer-shiny shoes would be a sign of weakness I could *not* afford. I just wished I could control my pulse rate as easily, because right now it was through the roof.

"So," she said, "have you got anything to say?"

Her voice was cool, unthreatening, but my skin crawled. "Absolutely nothing."

She smiled, revealing razor-sharp, blood-stained canines. "Wise choice."

I swallowed heavily and wished like hell I could take back the words that now bound me to this woman. But breaking our deal was an option I'd never really had, no matter how much I might have flirted with the idea. Yet I had no doubt *those* flirtations were the reason behind her revealing her true nature here today. She'd wanted to show me just what would happen to Ilianna and Tao if I ever stepped out of line.

It was my desperate need for revenge that had led them into this woman's sights, and I hated myself for that.

But what was done was done, and regretting the path I'd chosen in a desperate moment of pain and anger didn't help anyone, particularly them.

I licked dry lips and said, "Are you going to call in the Directorate, or do you want me to?"

"Oh, there's no need for them to be advised of events here." There was cold amusement in her voice. "The Jorōgumo is dead and I will erase the shifter's memory. I'm afraid this is destined to become just another of the Directorate's cold case files."

And how many of those files, I wondered, were cold because of Hunter's intervention?

"Then I can go?" I tried not to sound overly eager, but failed dismally, if the gleam in her eyes was anything to go by.

"You may. Just remember, I want to be advised if

you do find the next gate key at that gun exhibition later today."

"Given you have Cazadors following me about like trained puppies, that goes without saying," I snapped, and regretted it almost instantly.

That darkness flared in her eyes again. My breath froze in my throat, and I took an involuntary step back. Even that one small movement had her half baring her teeth, and it wasn't only Amaya who began screaming inside my head. I was at full voice, too.

Then Azriel appeared in front of me, providing a physical barrier against the wash of hunger and darkness coming from Hunter and allowing me to breathe normally again—although the fury and tension rolling off both him and his sword wasn't any less breathtaking.

"Do it," he said softly. "I will enjoy watching your soul be escorted through the gates of hell."

For a moment, she didn't move. Didn't even blink. Then she smiled—still all teeth—and said, "Oh, I will give you your chance, reaper, but not now. Not yet. There is still much to be achieved."

Yeah, first high council domination, next the world. Azriel reached back and caught my hand, squeezing it in either reassurance or in warning. Then his energy surged around us, tearing us apart swiftly, but he didn't take his gaze off Hunter until the gray fields were around us.

"What the *fuck*," I said, as we reappeared in the secure surrounds of my bedroom, "has she become?"

"I cannot say." He turned around, but didn't immediately release my hand. "I suspect the only people who would know are the two people you've already noted."

Stanford and Uncle Quinn. I rubbed my free hand across my eyes wearily. "What the hell are we going to do, Azriel? Stanford is right about one thing—whatever she is, she's *not* sane."

"Actually, I would suggest the opposite. However, she is a being without emotion, someone whose soul lost contact with all that is humanity a very long time ago. She is incapable now of seeing beyond her own needs, desires, and plans."

I frowned. "You can't say she's without feeling given she had us chasing the Jorōgumo for revenge."

"That did not come from either the heart or the soul, but rather a far darker place. Someone took something of hers, and she could not let the matter slip unchallenged."

"So if I ever *did*?"

His smile was somewhat wry. "You challenge her every time you speak to her."

I grimaced. "I meant seriously challenged. As in, agree to work with Stanford."

"Then you'd better hope I am still around to defend you."

Fear swirled through me. I knew I wasn't any sort of match for Hunter, even with Amaya at my back, but still, hearing Azriel basically confirm it was as scary as hell.

"Well, it's not actually something I'm planning, however much I'd like to see the bitch dead."

"Which is the first sensible statement you've made for quite a while."

"I am capable of sensible on occasion." I rose up on my toes and quickly kissed him. "I'm going for a shower. If you want to be useful, you could make me something to eat."

His eyebrows rose. "I am not adept at human domestic duties."

"Now, *that*," I said, voice wry, "is a comment echoed by men the world over. All you need to do is slap some of the lamb that's in the fridge between a couple slices of bread, squeeze on some tomato sauce, and I'll be one happy lady."

"That I can manage." He raised my hand, kissed my fingertips, then disappeared.

I checked my phone to see if Ilianna—or anyone else for that matter—had called, then headed into the shower. By the time I'd dried my hair, dressed in comfortable jeans and an old sweater, Azriel had set the dining room table with not only a sandwich, but a glass of Coke and a steaming mug of coffee.

"You know," I said, as he pulled out a chair and seated me. "You might just become a keeper if you carry on like this."

He didn't immediately answer, but when he did, his voice was oddly formal. "And would you wish that, if the situation were different?"

I paused, the sandwich halfway to my mouth, and met his gaze. "If the situation were different, if we weren't who we were, and the option was there, yes, I would like that very much."

He nodded, and it oddly felt as if an agreement

had been reached. I frowned, wondering what exactly that might have been, but his expression—or lack thereof—very much suggested he wasn't about to elaborate.

"Because there is nothing to elaborate," he said softly. "What happens next lies in the hand of the fates."

I swallowed against a suddenly dry throat and tried to ignore the tiny slivers of both hope and fear that began coursing through me. "Meaning there *could* be some way we could explore this thing further?"

While that possibility scared the hell out of me, I couldn't help the leap of excitement at the thought of being able to explore whether what was between us had the strength to blossom into something real *and* permanent.

But all he said was, "That is for the fates to decide."

"Then the answer is probably no, because fate and I have not been on friendly terms of late."

He didn't reply, and there was little to be read in his expression. I bit into my sandwich and had to bite back a groan of sheer pleasure. Besides sex and a cold glass of Coke, the best thing in life had to be a fabulous lamb sandwich.

My phone rang just as I finished my meal. The tone told me it was Jak, and my heart began to beat a whole lot faster. Something was wrong. I was certain of it even before I answered the damn thing. I pushed up from the table and ran across to my handbag, fishing around for several seconds before I found my phone.

"Jak," I said, my heart seeming to beat somewhere high in my throat. "What's up?"

"I need to talk to you. Urgently."

Despite his words, he neither looked nor sounded worried. In fact, he looked rather distracted.

I frowned. "What about?"

"Can't say on the phone, but you'll want to hear it, believe me."

I bit my lip, frustrated with both his reticence to answer the damn question—although *that* was something I should have gotten used to, seeing as everyone was doing it of late—and that inner voice that kept insisting something was wrong. But was it clairvoyance, or the simple knowledge that every time the phone rang, the shit got deeper? "Where?"

"At Larry's, in Brunswick."

It wasn't a place I knew, but then, that was what Google was for. "When?"

He paused. "Ten minutes."

"Shit, Jak, you're not giving me much time to get—"

I cut the rest of my sentence off as my damn phone beeped, then shut down. The stupid battery was dead.

I swore softly, threw it down, then stalked across to the computer and Googled Larry's in Brunswick. It was situated on Hope Street, not far down from Sydney Road.

I grabbed my keys, then glanced at Azriel. "I'll meet you there."

"You do not wish me to take you?"

I hesitated. That niggly sense of wrongness was

still present, but I wasn't really sure whether it was related to Jak, or the still-missing Ilianna. I bit my bottom lip, weighing options, then said, "Can you go to Stane's first and ask him to keep an eye on police reports, just in case something comes through about Ilianna?"

He frowned. "Why not ring him? He does not appreciate me suddenly appearing on his premises."

No, he didn't, but he wasn't about to keel over in shock from it, either, according to Azriel, and he should know. Besides, I needed information on Ilianna, and Stane was probably our best method of getting it—and it was stupid of me not to have asked him when I was there earlier. "My phone is dead, and I don't want to waste time going there myself. And I'm only meeting Jak. He's not a threat."

"Perhaps not, but given your own sense of unease—"

"Look," I said, impatience edging my voice—which wasn't really fair given he was only trying to keep me safe. But there was safe and there was mollycoddling, and this had the feeling of the latter. "It'll take you all of three seconds to get to Stane's and less than that to ask him to scan the police frequencies. I can hardly get myself into too much trouble in that short time."

Surely even *I* wasn't that clever.

He studied me, clearly unhappy, then nodded abruptly and disappeared. I headed out the front door, locked up, then called to the Aedh. A sliver of pain ran through my head, but I wasn't entirely sure whether it was a warning that I was pushing my limits again—despite the energy Azriel had given me—or the mere fact that I was too close to the wards that prevented the Raziq from entering our home. But if pain and pushing my limits found Ilianna, then I really didn't care—though I had no idea why I thought Ilianna might be the reason behind Jak's sudden demand for a meet. Maybe it was nothing more than stupid hope.

I zoomed through the streets, the bright lights little more than a blur underneath me. Larry's, it turned out, was an old, somewhat rambling warehouse structure that had obviously been no more successful as a bar than it had as a warehouse. I reformed and pulled the somewhat holey remains of my sweater together, my gaze sweeping the grimy, blue-painted building dubiously. I couldn't imagine any good reasons for Ilianna being in a place like this, and I sure as hell did not want to think about bad reasons. But maybe this *wasn't* about her—after all, it was Jak who'd collected the information that had led us to the standing stone gateway under the run-down warehouse near Stane's. Maybe he'd found another one.

I walked across the road, every sense I had attuned to the old building. Nothing stirred, and I couldn't see or hear anyone near. The night air was cool and whispered through the holes in my clothes, chilling my skin and causing goose bumps. Or maybe they were simply the result of growing unease.

"Jak?" I kept my voice soft. If he was here, he'd hear.

"Inside." His voice was as hushed as mine, but oddly lacking warmth.

Unease growing, I grasped the door handle and wrenched it open. Unfortunately, I used more force than necessary and it crashed back, trapping my hand between the door handle and the wall. I bit back my yelp and shook my fingers, my gaze searching the dark room as I eased inside. I couldn't see anything, couldn't hear anything.

"Where are you?"

"Here."

He sounded closer, but no warmer. Trepidation prickled across my skin, and my footsteps slowed even further. "Where the hell are the lights?"

"Can't risk them."

"Why?"

"Get in here, and you'll see."

Impatience threaded his distant tones, and just for an instant, he sounded like his old self. Maybe I was just being paranoid.

Maybe I should just wait for Azriel . . .

Damn it, *no*. I couldn't keep relying on him to keep me safe. Sooner or later, he would leave, but I was stuck with Hunter long term. If I wanted to survive *her* post-Azriel, then I had better *not* start jumping at shadows the minute he wasn't at my back.

Still, it was with a whole lot of trepidation that I continued to move into the darkness. "Jak, I can't see a goddamn thing in here. Can't you at least use the flashlight app on your phone?"

I'd certainly be using mine if the damn thing hadn't decided to die on me.

"No." He paused. "Take three steps to your right, then five to the left. Watch the table—"

I crashed into said table and bit back another curse. "Warning me a little earlier might have been handy."

"Sorry."

There was little amusement in his voice, and again I frowned. This whole thing felt decidedly off . . .

"Almost there," he added. "Just one more step."

I hesitated, then cursed myself for doing so. Jak wouldn't harm me. Bed me—given half a chance—yes, but not harm. Not only did he need me to get his story, but he was well aware just how thick and fast trouble in the form of Uncle Rhoan would hit him if he in any way caused me damage—physical or emotional.

I took that step.

Realized almost instantly it was the wrong thing to do when something grabbed me and held me.

But that something wasn't flesh and blood but rather magic. I had one moment to wonder what the hell—who the hell—had me this time and even less time to fear; then thought was torn away and I knew no more.

Waking was a slow process and felt rather like the tedious climb to awareness that often accompanied a heavy alcohol binge. Thanks to our faster metabolic rate, it was harder for werewolves to get drunk than humans, but it *was* certainly possible if you applied yourself well enough. I had on several occasions, generally when I'd stupidly embarked on a drinking contest with Liana and Ronan, Riley's two eldest. But at least I'd had the pleasurable buzz of consuming all that alcohol first. There was none of that joy here, just the sick queasiness and thick head that generally hit after consumption had well and truly finished.

For several minutes, I did nothing more than simply lie there, willing my head to stop pounding even as I wondered where the hell I was.

But as awareness of my surroundings grew stronger, I discovered that not only was I in a bed *and* naked, but I was spread-eagle, with my hands and feet tied.

What the *hell* was going on?

My first thought—naturally enough—was that I'd been raped, but I had no sense of violation. It didn't feel like anyone had abused me in any way other than tying me. My body *did* ache, but I suspected it was more a residue of whatever magic had knocked me out rather than someone having forced themself on me.

Of course, no one ever *had*, so how could I be so certain that it *hadn't* happened? God, the way I was tied certainly suggested that even if it *hadn't* happened, it was very much in the cards. It was a thought that should have frightened me, but all it actually did was make me mad. Werewolves had a free and easy attitude when it came to sex, but force was an entirely different matter—and one that was *not* dealt with lightly. Fortunately, it was something that rarely happened among werewolves. But then, rape was rarely about sex and all about either gaining power over—or causing degradation to—another person.

Who the hell would wish either of those on me?

Even as the thought hit, the answer came. Lucian.

Touch not, Amaya said, her sharp voice cutting like razor blades through my brain. *Tried.*

Lucian?

Him, she spat. *Tried to slice it off. Missed.*

I blinked. As statements went, *that* was pretty dramatic, and it was one that had just a touch of amusement vibrating through me. At least I'd had a defender when I was unconscious.

It was just a damn shame that she'd missed.

I very much wanted to open my eyes and see where the hell I was, but caution prevailed. Until I had some sense of what was going on around me, it was better that Lucian thought I was still unconscious.

There was little in the way of movement or sound—other than the nearby rumble of traffic—to indicate there was anyone close, but the air was thick with the scent of dust and mold and age. Wherever we were, it wasn't Lucian's apartment. But he was here. His scent—lemongrass, suede, and musky, powerful male—was a strong undercurrent to the other scents.

So why wasn't Azriel here, ripping Lucian's head off his fucking shoulders?

Can't, Amaya muttered. *Blocked.*

She had to mean magically, because there were few physical forces that could actually stop him.

So did those same restrictions apply to me becoming Aedh? I quickly reached for the magic. The pounding in my head sharpened dramatically—suggesting that part of me *was* trying to respond—but I remained as I was. In flesh and bound.

And *that* was a little frightening. We'd guessed Lucian had been capable of magic, but I hadn't thought it possible that he could create a spell powerful enough to either bind an Aedh to human form or stop the movement of a reaper. And if he could do *that*, then he probably knew how to kill them, too. It made me suddenly glad that Azriel wasn't here.

Besides, I wanted the pleasure of killing the bastard myself.

Not self, Amaya said, her background noise ramping up a notch. *Me include.*

Trust me, you'll be included.

The hissing changed to a happy humming. I still wasn't entirely sure whether that was an improvement.

I pulled on the ropes binding me to test their strength. There was no give and no sign that they'd break easily. No surprise there, I guess. Lucian was well aware of what I could and couldn't do.

Just as, I suddenly realized, he was well aware that my friends were very much my Achilles' heel.

God, was *he* the reason for Ilianna's disappearance?

I hoped like hell he wasn't, but the dread that filled me suggested otherwise.

I opened my eyes. The ceiling was wood and heavily stained and draped with cobwebs that hung in long, dusty strings. The walls to the left and the right had been semidemolished, but there was little to see in the rooms beyond except rubble.

The bed itself was wide and would have been comfortable if not for the ropes holding me so tightly. They snaked from my wrists and my ankles over each corner of the bed and were, I presumed, anchored somehow to the floor.

I lifted my head to see if I could spot anything else. There were industrial-looking windows running the length of the wall in front of me, but they were all covered with black plastic. Wouldn't want the neighbors seeing what he was up to, after all.

Why the hell was I even here? Why hadn't I been rescued? Azriel might not be able to get into this place, but he'd have to know I was here. Why hadn't he called for help from Riley, Quinn, or even Tao?

I had absolutely no idea, and given it was a question that couldn't immediately be answered, I turned my attention back to the ropes. They were thick, coarse, and tight, and my wrists were red but not yet bleeding. I yanked on the left one as hard as I could, but the only thing I managed to do was rub my wrist raw. The fucking rope didn't give.

Amaya, any chance that you can cut the damn things?

She didn't answer, but half a second later, her energy began to burn through my flesh. Slowly but surely, she moved from her position near my spine to the right side of my body, then into my shoulder. It was a weird sensation, and even weirder to see the broader end of her blade and her hilt find substance and stick out of my shoulder. Her sharp tip appeared near my wrist, and a second later, that arm was free.

She repeated the process with my left arm. This time, the Dušan twisted around to watch, though it kept its tail firmly wrapped around the bracelet of leaves inked into my skin. Of course, it was no more a tat than the Dušan was—it was one of Ilianna's charms that the Dušan had made a permanent part of me. Just how she'd done it, nobody knew. The Dušans weren't supposed to be active on this plane, but for some reason no one could explain, mine was.

The minute both wrists were free, I sat upright and reached for Amaya.

But in that moment, I realized I was no longer alone.

"Make no further move to free yourself, my dear," Lucian said, "because I really *would* hate to shoot you."

His familiar tones flowed over my skin like a warm summer breeze and made me hunger for the touch of his clever fingers. It was a reaction that annoyed the fuck out of me, if only because I knew my response couldn't entirely be blamed on the spell he'd placed on me. Some of it was simple, old-fashioned lust.

He stood in the wide, unfinished doorway, an image of golden perfection, holding a gun. He was tall, muscular, and, if I was being at all honest, a perfectly formed piece of manhood. Lucian's faults were internal rather than external, emotional rather than physical. *His* wishes, *his* desires were all that mattered to him. The wants and needs of others were of little relevance, even if he sometimes offered others utter bliss. He'd certainly offered it to me often enough, but he'd also magically bound me to ensure I kept coming back to him. He might have wanted my body, but he'd also wanted the knowledge of not just what was happening with the key search, but also my father and the Raziq. Lucian hated them with a passion and depth that was as fierce as it was frightening.

And the only way he could completely keep track of both their movements and mine was to read my mind when we fucked.

"What the hell are you doing, Lucian?" My voice was amazingly calm given the anger that surged through me. "Have you got a death wish or something?"

"The reaper may want to kill me," he said with a half shrug. "But he will not overstep the rules to justify his own petty desires."

"That's where you're wrong." My fingers twitched against Amaya's hilt, and it took every ounce of willpower not to aim her steel at his black heart and release her. But he wasn't a fool, and that meant I couldn't be. Not until I knew the full length and breadth of whatever he had planned. "By kidnapping me, you've given him carte blanche to break the rules where *you're* concerned."

"Then he is most welcome to try to kill me. But I doubt that he will."

His confidence was as irritating as it was unnerving. "What do you want, Lucian?"

"What I have always wanted." His low tones were laced with amusement and slid across my skin like silk. "I want to fuck you senseless."

I shivered—a reaction that was a weird mix of loathing and desire. "And suck me dry information-wise."

"Well, yes, that *is* a luscious side benefit." He grinned. "You cannot deny that our time together was mutually satisfactory."

I snorted. Side benefit, my ass. If anything *had* been a side benefit, then it was the sex. And yeah, it had been great, but the truth of the matter was, I was just another cog in the many wheels he had spinning.

"And you were so damn sure of your prowess in bed that you had to place a spell on me to ensure I came back."

Something flickered in his eyes. Something that was dark and ultimately dangerous. It was a quick reminder that for all the time I'd spent fucking this man, I didn't really know him.

"Let's not kid ourselves, Risa." His voice was as soft as his expression was dark. "It was not just the spell that kept you coming back, but your own insatiable desire. And we both know if I were to touch you now, you would beg me for more."

"If you tried touching me, the only thing you'd feel is Amaya's steel." I paused, then added somewhat cattily, "Oh, that's right, you've already *had* a close encounter of the ugly kind with her."

He laughed. It was a short and sharp sound, but held little of the anger and frustration I could sense within him. "Yes. I wasn't aware that demon swords were capable of thought or action when the bearer was out of it. To discover the sharp end of a sword literally sticking out of your cunt was something of a surprise."

Thank you, thank you, thank you, I said silently to my sword.

Kill him to thank.

I have to admit, it was a very tempting thought. But until I knew whether he was at all involved with Ilianna's disappearance, my hands were still as tied as my feet.

"So you kidnapped me just to fuck me?"

"Oh, I didn't intend to just fuck you, my dear." Amusement played about his mouth, but there was something decidedly dark in the green depths.

"Then what the hell *did* you intend?"

"What I intended," he drawled, "was to seed you with my child."

Chapter 12

For a moment I simply stared at him, wondering if he'd gone absolutely bonkers in the brief time we'd been apart. He'd been in this world long enough to know it was law that all werewolves—even those of us who were half-breeds—had to be chipped at puberty to prevent conception. The government still seemed to think—despite centuries of evidence to the contrary—that just because we fucked like rabbits, we'd breed like them, too.

"Well, you wouldn't have had much luck with that," I bit back. "Even without Amaya's well-placed intervention, I'm chipped. If you took it out, it would still take several cycles for me to conceive."

He smiled. It held a very nasty edge. "Yes, but you are no longer what you were. You have been remade by the Raziq."

My stomach flip-flopped, but I didn't let the sudden surge of fear show. "Meaning what?"

"That you are fully fertile, for one thing." His gaze slid down my body, and despite the distaste that rolled through me, I nevertheless reacted as strongly as I ever had. My hormones, I thought in frustration, needed to be bitch slapped. "It is such a shame your sword intervened, but in truth, I am not so annoyed. I do prefer my partners awake and willing."

A statement that had trepidation crawling through me all over again. But what was more interesting was the fact that he'd intended to breed. Aedh felt that imperative only when their life was coming to an end. Of course, thanks to an Aedh's long life span, that end could be many years away. Hell, my father was still going strong, more's the pity.

"I'd love to say I'm sorry to have disappointed you, but I'm not. Now, why don't you just put that fucking gun down and release me. You're not going to get what you want from me—no baby, no fucking keys, no revenge—"

"Oh," he cut in, his expression altogether too confident for my liking. "That's where you are very, *very* wrong."

Again that sick, fearful feeling began to rise up my throat. My fingers tightened against Amaya's hilt, but I didn't draw her free from my flesh and throw her at the bastard's heart. But I wanted to. Oh, how I wanted to.

"What do you mean?" The edge in my voice was fear and anger combined.

"Simply that I have combined my need for offspring with my desire for revenge on all those who have made me less than I am."

That feeling of dread ramped up several notches. My throat was so restricted, I could barely even say, "How?"

But I knew.

And he knew I knew. That was very evident by the amused glitter in his bright eyes. "Ilianna."

My reaction was instant. Without thought. In one smooth movement, I drew Amaya free, swept her across the ropes binding my ankles, then lunged at him. But he was even faster than me. He jumped back and fired the gun. The shot tore through my hand, blowing apart two fingers before it hit Amaya's hilt and ricocheted into the nearby wall. Pain and blood surged, but all I felt was anger. My anger, Amaya's anger, and the utter need to just rid the world of the man who might well have destroyed my best friend. I attacked him, Amaya raised high above my head and screaming for blood.

Just for a moment, surprise flitted across his features; then he retreated from my onslaught and held up the gun.

"Know that I will shoot you again if I need to," he said. "And know, too, that if I die, so will Ilianna."

That stopped me. Even Amaya muted her screams. "What do you mean?"

"Just that." He paused, but the tension in his body suggested he was very much ready to react the minute I so much as twitched. "If I do not contact the people holding your friend every hour, they will kill her."

"You *bastard*."

Amusement flitted across his features. "All Aedh are bastards, dear Risa, because we seed and leave. We are not prey to the emotions and needs that wreck so many human lives."

And were poorer for it. "But to rape Ilianna—"

"There was *no* rape," he cut in, sounding oddly annoyed. "An Aedh's kiss always ensures that their chosen breeder is more than willing."

"Ilianna is *gay*. You would have had to force a kiss, if nothing else."

Though anger kept the worst of the pain at bay, I was bleeding all over the place and would be in very serious trouble if I didn't do something about it soon. Yet I remained still. To do anything else would not have been wise right now.

"Well, yes, but we both know I was not her first male lover."

No, because Ilianna *had* experimented when she was young. After the attack on her sister had left her incapable of conceiving, her parents' desire for grandchildren had fallen solely onto Ilianna's shoulders. The weight of their expectations had all but forced her to least *try* to have a relationship with a male. But she could no more change her orientation than the moon could rise during the day.

"That doesn't alter the reality that you forced yourself on her. Whether the magic made her willing or not doesn't matter in the end." And I would kill him for it. If not now, then later.

I shifted Amaya to my left hand and tried to ignore the warm slickness covering her hilt. The pain was getting stronger, a monster ready to consume. I clenched what remained of my fingers on my shattered hand, but it did little to stem the tide of blood.

He made a "who cares" motion with his free hand. "It has been done. She will bear my child, no matter what happens to me. The decision *you* have to make is whether *she* actually gets to live or die."

"And why the hell would you impregnate her if all you intended to do is kill her?"

"Come now, let's not play dumb, Risa. She is captive to your good behavior. And, of course, she is not the only one I have seeded." His smile was all arrogance. "The Raziq may have stolen many things from me, but they did not take my potency."

I wished they fucking *had*. "So does your dark sorceress know she's about to become a mom?"

"You always did catch on to the inconsequential things faster than most," he murmured, looking amused. "But no, she does not. It is not necessary. Besides, she has not entirely upheld her part of our agreement, so I see no problem in not entirely upholding mine."

"That's a decidedly risky game to play when dealing with a sorceress as powerful as Lauren Macintyre." But maybe she'd kill him and save the rest of us the trouble.

"Yes, but there is also great pleasure to be found in playing such games."

I resisted the urge to glance at his body and see for myself just how much delight he was taking in this game. "So what's next?"

"Why, you find the keys; then we both go to retrieve them, of course."

"Of course." Dizziness swept me. I licked my lips and tried to ignore the trembling that was beginning to hit my muscles. "But what the hell are you going to do with them once you get them, Lucian?

It's not like you can get onto the gray fields anymore."

Again that dark and dangerous energy flashed through him. "Perhaps, but I can use them as a bargaining chip with the Raziq."

"If you think they'll agree to restore you to full Aedh in exchange for the keys, you're not playing with a full deck."

"They will have no choice."

I snorted. "They tortured you once for information on the keys. What makes you think they won't do it again?"

"Because I will have them placed where even the Raziq can't get them—hell itself."

I stared at him. He was insane. He had to be to even think *that* was a logical solution. "I'm sure the inhabitants of hell are going to be as happy as all get-out when they discover what they've been handed."

"I am not so foolish as to simply hide them," he growled. "They will be guarded by the most powerful demons in hell."

"And suddenly Lauren's presence in your life makes sense."

"Everything I do, I do for a reason, Risa." He nodded down at my hand. "You'd better do something about that. I need you fit and able to find the keys later today."

"So much for being able to read my mind only during sex," I spat. "Is everything that comes out of your mouth a fabrication?"

"Only when it suits me." His smile was lazy and

arrogant. "That, however, was not a total lie. The only time I *can* generally read you is during sex—it just doesn't have to be between you and me."

My stomach clenched, and I came so close to throwing up that the bitter taste of bile filled the back of my throat. *Every* time I'd had sex with Azriel, *he'd* been reading me. God, was there no end to this man's depravity?

"I'm going to fucking kill you. You know that, don't you?"

He laughed softly. "Keep believing that if it makes you feel better, Risa. However, you are no more capable of doing that than I am of sprouting wings—and not even the banshee you hold in your hand will alter that one fact."

Banshee not, Amaya growled. *Throw. Will gladly eat.*

Not until we find Ilianna. To Lucian, I said, "You always were an arrogant sod. I just didn't think you were stupid."

"I guess only time will prove which of us is right." He shrugged, the movement casual and elegant. "Now, as I suggested before, you'd best heal that hand."

I glanced down. Blood streamed from what remained of my fingers, and the ever-enlarging pool underneath them shimmered softly in the semilit darkness. And just like that, the anger gave way and the pain hit. My legs started trembling, and my head began spinning so badly, it was all I could do to remain standing.

I wasn't even sure I could heal a wound this bad,

but if I didn't try soon, then I'd be unconscious and in his power again. *If he moves near me,* I ordered Amaya, *slice him up. Just don't kill him.*

Pleasure.

I closed my eyes and called to the Aedh. It came in a trickle rather than a rush, a sure sign the magic that had prevented me from changing in the bedroom still held some sway out here. Either that or I was simply reaching the limits of my strength. And in the end, the result was pretty much the same.

I grabbed at that trickle fiercely, forced it down into my arm, imagined my fingers and hand fading into energy. I felt the burn of power roll down the muscles, and an instant later, the ever-growing throb of pain was gone as my lower arm and hand became particles rather than flesh.

The trembling in my body grew stronger, and my control began to slip. I bit my lip, called up the Aedh again, and imagined fingers that were healed and whole. But this time, the energy was little more than a weak wash.

Then my knees went out from under me and I hit the concrete. Hard. I bit back a yelp and, with some trepidation, opened my eyes. I had four whole fingers back on my hand, but they were still a bloody—and very painful—mess. But the bleeding had at least slowed to little more than a trickle.

I met Lucian's gaze again. "Now what?"

His gaze slid insolently down my body and my stomach clenched. *He not touch,* Amaya warned. *Will slice.*

Her fierce readiness to defend my honor was infinitely gratifying, but I had no doubt that having sex with him would be the ultimate price for setting Ilianna free. He didn't want just *any* offspring, no matter how much he'd loaded the bases with Ilianna and Lauren. He wanted *our* offspring. Wanted a child that was as close to full Aedh as someone like him was ever likely to get.

And if that was the price of freeing Ilianna, then it was one I would pay, however much I—and my sword—might hate it.

"What do you think is next?"

The desire radiating off him was so fierce and strong, it hit like a summer storm. My body trembled under its force, and my nipples puckered, reactions that only increased the strength of the storm.

"If I knew, I wouldn't have asked." I continued to meet his gaze steadily, even though my heart was beating a million miles an hour and my throat was dry.

A smile played about his lips. "You lie, Risa Jones."

I didn't reply, because there was very little I could say or do at this point. If sex was what he now intended, then it would happen, no matter what. And if I killed him, as I ached to, it would be Ilianna who paid. I was the reason she'd been kidnapped, raped, and impregnated, and that was guilt enough. I couldn't bear the weight of her death as well.

He took several steps toward me, then stopped. "Get up."

I rose slowly and somewhat unsteadily. Lust continued to roll off him in waves, and tiny beads of perspiration began to dot my skin. My damn nipples were so hard, they ached and, as much as I hated it, I couldn't entirely ignore the desire that slithered through me. And while most of it was undoubtedly the spell he'd placed on me, some of it was not.

I might hate him, but I also wanted him.

But I'd be damned if I admitted it.

Our gazes clashed for several more nerve-racking minutes; then he raised a hand, pressed a fingertip between my breasts, and pushed me backward. Amaya's screams echoed in my head, and I ordered her to shut up and *not* cut.

My back hit the wall, the wood rough and grimy against my skin. He kept me pinned, not moving, not saying anything, just watching me with that smug, insolent expression I was beginning to hate.

Then he stepped back.

For a moment, hope leapt, but the amusement touching his lips soon killed that.

"Undress me," he ordered. "Slowly."

I flexed my fingers, battling anger and the urge to do as Amaya desired, then raised my hands and unbuttoned his shirt. When the last button came undone, I placed my hands on his skin and slid them upward, over the taut muscles of his stomach and chest and then under the shirt. As it slipped to floor, I ran my hands back down his body and played with the waist of his pants.

His warm breath fanned across my skin, its tempo one of expectation. Mine was no better, despite my loathing of the situation. My gaze rose to his. Desire burned in those green depths, but so, too, did warning.

I unfastened his pants. His cock strained against the restriction of his silk boxers, thick and hard and ready for action. I hooked my fingers into the waist of both and slid them down his legs. He stepped out, then pressed a hand against my head, keeping me down.

"Suck me."

I did as he bid, sucking and licking and teasing until the salty taste of come began to fill my mouth.

Abruptly, he tangled his fingers in my hair and yanked me upright. He spun me around so that I faced the wall, then pulled my head backward, kissing me fiercely as he entered me from behind. What followed was animalistic and hard, and, despite my loathing of both him and the situation, felt good. But I did *not* give voice to my pleasure. There wasn't much I could keep to myself given the situation, but I refused to give him *that*.

He came with a shout that was as fierce as it was triumphant, pumping hard as he emptied himself inside me. I closed my eyes, my body still trembling with unfulfilled desire, his fluids dribbling down my thighs and hate in my heart.

He withdrew, turned me around, and kissed me fiercely again. But just as quickly, he pulled away.

"Respond like you mean it, dear Risa, or I will not make the call that is keeping your friend alive."

"You can't keep either of us forever, Lucian," I said, my voice edged with the anger I was barely keeping leashed. I could almost taste his death, and god, it tasted *sweet*. "Sooner or later, this will have to end."

"Oh, it will." He bent, picked me up in his arms, then spun and walked back to the bedroom. "But the military exhibition does not open until ten, and that gives me five hours to fuck you senseless."

He threw me onto the bed, but didn't immediately join me. "By the time you leave here, you will be carrying my child. And *that* will be the greatest revenge I could ever have on your reaper."

My *flesh-and-blood* reaper. If he could bleed, if he could gain human emotions when in flesh too long, why then would he not also be fertile? If the Raziq *had* taken the chip out, then it was more than possible that I was *already* pregnant.

God, wouldn't that be the perfect twist? If I had to be pregnant, then I would much rather the father be someone I actually cared about than someone I intended to kill.

Of course, given fate's apparent desire to crap all over my life, it was *not* a likely outcome, but my heart still sang at the thought.

And it was a hope that got me through the hours that ensued.

I woke to the scent of mold, dust, and age. Similar scents, yet different from what I'd woken to before. Disoriented, I rolled onto my back, feeling the rough edges of wood rather than the silk of sheets. My eyes were heavy and my head was booming, and that "drank too much" sensation was well and truly back.

He'd obviously transported me magically rather than just letting me go. I couldn't remember his doing it, but then, I hadn't *actually* been around for the last few hours of our encounter. I might not have done much astral travel, but I'd learned enough to get the hell out of my body. Lucian either hadn't noticed or hadn't cared. He might have paid lip service to wanting me to be an eager, vocal participant, but in the end all he'd wanted was a body to impregnate.

And I wasn't entirely sure what I'd do if I *was* pregnant, especially since there was just as much chance of it being Azriel's as Lucian's.

God, please, let it be Azriel's.

A desperate plea that in itself suggested the psychic part of me already knew my fate in *that* regard.

I opened my eyes. Daylight drifted in from the grimy windows to my right, highlighting a mess of upturned tables, broken chairs, and graffiti-littered walls. It had to be Larry's, and I wondered if Jak had ever been here. Lucian was much more than we'd *ever* suspected, and maybe magic wasn't the only thing he'd become adept at. Maybe he could imitate voices, as well. Right now, I wouldn't put anything past him.

I pushed into a sitting position. The first thing I saw was the ring of black stones that surrounded me. But they weren't just any old stones; they were wards. I raised a hand and carefully touched one. Color swirled through its dark heart, but it didn't react in any other way. Their presence, however, might explain why Azriel—or anyone else, for that matter—hadn't come to my rescue. Warding stones were generally used to keep things either out or in, but I knew they could also be used to confuse. Maybe no one had rescued me simply because they'd been unable to pin down my location.

I carefully flicked the nearest stone out of sequence. It rattled noisily across the old floorboards, the sound almost thunderous in the hush holding the building captive. A heartbeat later, energy burned across my skin and Azriel was in front of me, pulling me into a hug as fierce and as desperate as any I'd ever experienced.

I melted into him, enjoying the security and warmth of his embrace. "I'm okay," I said eventually. My words were muffled against his chest, but I wasn't about to move. Not yet. Not until the trembling that was as much utter relief as it was weakness stopped. "I wasn't there for most of it."

"The Aedh's death will be slow and very painful." Azriel's voice was flat but filled with such fury, it momentarily stole my breath. "And I will savor every single moment of it."

"But not until we find Ilianna."

"He cannot get away—"

"You will *not* kill him." I pulled away from him, my gaze searching his. Saw the anger, the pain, and knew it was all for me. It warmed me just as much as it worried me. "Far worse can and has been done to me, Azriel. Ilianna is a hostage against my good behavior, and until we can find her, then Lucian has to live."

He said something in his own language, the

words soft but vehement. It didn't take much imagination to know he was swearing. "You can*not* seriously think we should allow him in on the search for the keys. That is taking things too far."

Things had already gone too far, and it was too late to stop it all now. "I am, and he will." I gave him a lopsided smile. "At the very least, it means we can keep an eye on him."

"I would much rather keep a sword on him, if it's all the same to you." He tugged me close again and wrapped his arms around me. It felt like heaven. "Let's get you home."

If I was in his arms, then I *was* home, but I didn't give that particular thought voice. His energy swept around me, and in no time we'd zipped through the fields and were re-forming in the middle of my bedroom. I stepped back and glanced at the clock on my side table. It was just after ten.

"I'll have a shower and clean up; then we can go see if the key is at the exhibition."

"And if we find it?"

I shrugged. "I guess what happens next depends on what sort of security they have in place."

He studied me for a moment, then said, "What of the Aedh?"

"He's going to meet us there at eleven thirty."

"So we should try to get there sooner—"

"No," I cut in. "Remember Ilianna."

He swore again. I smiled, dropped a quick kiss on his lips, and said, "I know. Trust me, I know."

"I bet you do *not*."

He caught my broken hand and gently ran his

fingers over the mangled remnants of mine. Energy flowed from his touch, renewing my reserves even as my fingers began to heal. Or rather, heal as much as they were ever going to. But I could bend them, use them, and the scars—which were red and fierce-looking right now—would eventually fade. I'd been lucky, and I knew it. If not for the fact I was half Aedh, I would have lost them.

He raised my fingers to his lips, brushing a sweet kiss across them, then said, "Go. I will prepare you something to eat."

He disappeared, and I headed for the shower. For the longest time, I did nothing more than stand under the water, letting the heat wash the ache from my bruised body and the scents of lust and Lucian from my skin. I wished it could similarly wash the niggling sense of violation from my mind, but there was nothing in this world that could do that except time.

I ran my fingers across my belly and wondered if I did indeed carry the beginnings of life deep inside. Wondered how I would feel if it turned out to be Lucian's rather than Azriel's.

Another two questions only time could answer.

I took a somewhat shuddery breath, then got the hell out of the shower and dressed. Worrying over events far in the future was not particularly the best way to spend my time at the moment. Not when I had keys to not only find but, hopefully, this time, keep. How we were going to do that given the whole Lucian situation, I had no idea, but one thing was certain. The bastard might think he held all the cards, but there was always, *always*, a way out. You just had to look hard enough.

And perhaps be willing to pay the ultimate price.

But that price would *not* be Ilianna's death. That was the one place I would *not* go.

Azriel, it seemed, had been picking up cooking tips from somewhere, because this time he'd produced the world's biggest steak and some steamed veggies.

I sat down and tucked in with gusto. Once I'd demolished everything on my plate, I grabbed my Coke, sat back, and asked the one question that had been quietly bugging me. "Why weren't you able to rescue me?"

"Because, as you have already guessed, he used magic to not only snatch you, but to disguise your whereabouts."

"And Jak?"

"Unharmed." His voice was as neutral as his expression. "I will admit to a somewhat angry response to his part in your abduction, but I controlled it the minute I realized he was an unwilling participant."

"Meaning you beat him up, then healed him?"

"Something like that." He returned my gaze evenly. "He does not now remember the event."

Meaning the event, as he put it, had been pretty bad. "I told you Jak wouldn't willingly betray me, Azriel."

"He has before, so that is an illogical statement."

Perhaps it was, but I nevertheless believed it. "What, exactly, did Lucian do to him?"

"Nothing more than luring him to the warehouse with the promise of a story, then capturing his mind."

Which was why Jak hadn't really sounded himself. They had been Lucian's words, not Jak's. I drank some Coke, enjoying the fuzzy goodness for several seconds before saying, "We need to find Ilianna. Until she's free, we're stuck doing whatever Lucian wants us to do."

"I would suspect that he has her position well hidden by his magic."

I frowned. "Does it take much magic to do that sort of thing?"

He shrugged, the movement brief but somehow elegant. "I am not knowledgeable when it comes to magic, but I would suspect so."

"So perhaps what we need is someone who is not only knowledgeable in all matters magic, but who is able to detect such things."

"Ilianna's mother."

I nodded and thrust upward. "We need to go see—"

I cut the rest of the sentence off as a phone rang. It wasn't my phone—I hadn't yet gotten around to charging the damn thing—but rather a phone coming from Tao's room. It was answered after a few seconds, but that didn't do much to ease the tension suddenly running through me.

I knew who was making that call. Knew why.

After a few minutes, Tao stumbled out, looking somewhat disheveled and far from awake. "It's Mirri," he said, thrusting the phone at me. "She's not making sense. Is Ilianna missing or something?"

"Yes." I grabbed the phone and said, "It's okay, Mirri. I know what's happened to her, and she's okay."

"Oh, thank god." Tears filled her bright eyes. "I was so afraid something bad had happened to her. Where is she? Why hasn't she contacted me?"

Something bad *had* happened, but I wasn't about to tell her that. At the same time, I couldn't *not* tell her what was going on. I hesitated, then said, "I'm afraid she's being held hostage against my good behavior. She hasn't been hurt, and won't be, as long as I do everything her kidnapper says."

"Oh, *fuck*."

That, ten times over, I thought grimly. "I think we've worked out a way to free her, Mirri—"

The phone was snatched from her hand, and suddenly I was staring at a man with piercing, light blue eyes, pale skin, and silver-white hair. Albino, I thought, and then realized this was probably Carwyn.

"I want in on any rescue attempt," he said, voice deep and fierce.

"I doubt that Ilianna would—"

"I may not yet be her mate," he cut in. "But I will be. Whoever did this to her must pay."

And *that* was both the stallion *and* the man speaking, I thought grimly. And yet I couldn't do everything. If I were to have any hope of prizing Ilianna away from Lucian's clutches, then it would have to be when Lucian was otherwise distracted.

"We've got to find her first," I said; then, when he opened his mouth to obviously argue, I quickly added, "The minute we do, we'll ring you."

"I'll be standing by."

"Great." I hung up and handed the phone back to Tao, who was looking decidedly more awake.

"Ilianna's really missing?"

"Lucian's snatched her and hidden her location through magic. I'm about to go over to the Brindle to see if her mom can find her."

"What can I—"

"No," I cut in. "Time is of the essence. We'll come back here the minute we uncover anything."

"To echo Carwyn's words, I'll be standing by." He half turned, then clicked his fingers and added, "Oh, a parcel was delivered for you an hour ago. I dropped it on the coffee table so you'd see it coming in, which you obviously haven't."

No, because I hadn't come in the regular way, but rather via the Azriel express. I walked across to pick up the small white box. It wasn't particularly heavy, and the writing was my father's. This *had* to be the wards he promised. Heart beating a whole lot faster, I glanced up at Tao and said, "Thanks."

He frowned. "It's not one of *those* parcels, is it? Because you're suddenly looking a whole lot paler."

"It is, but it's something I've asked for this time." I forced a smile. "Hopefully, it's something that'll keep the hordes at bay while we grab the next key."

"Shame it couldn't also keep Lucian at bay," he muttered.

"A sword would," Azriel commented, voice as

flat as his expression. "And I know two that would gladly cooperate."

"He does make an excellent point," Tao said, then held up his hands as I opened my mouth. "Yes, I know. We can't do anything until Ilianna is safe. But that doesn't stop either of us from wishing the worst on the bastard, does it?"

"You can't wish anything worse on him than *I* am, trust me."

I couldn't stop the bitterness in my voice, and Tao's gaze narrowed. "Is there something else going on you're not telling me about?"

"No." He didn't look convinced, but then, I guess he *had* known me a long time. "I'll call you when we find anything."

"You'd better."

I turned to Azriel. He caught my hand unasked, drew me to him, and whisked us through the fields to the Brindle. I handed him the box, suspecting the Brindle would *not* react kindly to Aedh magic being taken into its midst, then ran up the steps and into the foyer. A geyser of golden sparks followed me as I ran through the shadows.

A gray-clad woman appeared. "Please, there is no need for haste—"

"There's *every* need," I bit back, but I nevertheless slowed. "I urgently need to see Custodian Zaira."

"I do not think—"

"Risa, what draws you here in such a state?" The familiar voice was as soft as the shadows around us and just as powerful.

I glanced past the gray-clad young woman and watched the willowy figure approach. Kiandra wasn't only the woman charge of the Brindle, but one of the most powerful witches I'd ever met. "I need to speak to Zaira urgently."

"As Indara was no doubt about to tell you, Zaira is not on duty today." She stopped several feet away and studied me. The power so evident in her gray eyes, was breathtaking. "Is this about Ilianna?"

"Yes. She's been kidnapped, and we suspect magic is being used to stop anyone from finding her."

"And you wish us to find her by tracking the magic itself?"

"Yes. I have no idea if it's possible—"

"It is." She tilted her head, and just for an instant it felt like she was seeing into my mind, reading all my hopes and fears. Judging me. My breath caught somewhere in my throat, and I found myself hoping I came up to scratch. After a moment, she added, "This way."

Once again I was led through the Brindle's quiet, shadowed halls and into yet another area I'd never been before. This one felt and looked far older than the other areas I'd visited, and power seemed to ooze off the walls. It was almost as if the centuries of spell making had infused the old stones with a magic all of their own.

We made our way through the dimly lit corridors, each one getting progressively smaller and darker, and eventually stepped into a room that appeared little more than an antechamber. The air was rich with such a riot of scents that my nose twitched and

I didn't even bother trying to sort them all out. There was power here, too, and the force of it made my skin itch and tingle.

"Wait here," Kiandra murmured, waving an elegant hand toward the two small chairs that were positioned on either side of the doorway. "You are not an initiate and therefore cannot follow me into the next room. I will see what magic there is to be found."

"It won't feel like human magic," I said. "Because it isn't."

She didn't ask what type of magic it could be, but then, given she appeared to know all about my key quest and the forces that fought for control of both me *and* them, maybe she didn't need to.

Without further comment, she turned and walked into the next room. The door closed behind her with a heavy *click*, leaving me alone in the silent shadows. I sat for all of three seconds, then got up and began to pace. I couldn't help it. So much of what we could do next depended on the information Kiandra did—or didn't—find for us.

It seemed to take forever. I didn't have my watch or phone, but I guess the reality was closer to ten minutes. I spun around as the door opened and she reappeared, a slight haze of smoke and magic accompanying her as she walked toward me. Her expression gave little away, so it was with some trepidation that I asked, "Did you find her?"

She stopped and clasped her hands in front of her. Her expression held an odd sort of excitement. "Ilianna is with child?"

I closed my eyes for a moment and swore internally. If Kiandra knew, then Ilianna's mother would more than likely find out sooner rather than later. Given her desire to see Ilianna join Carwyn's herd, I wasn't entirely sure how'd she react. Or, indeed, how Carwyn would.

"It's more than possible. The man who holds her is an Aedh—"

"And her child will be as you are: born of two worlds, powerful in magic, and gifted with foresight."

I frowned. "I'm not—"

"Just because you do not acknowledge such things does not mean they do not exist or that you are not capable." She paused, her gray eyes glowing molten silver with the shadows that held the room hostage. There was more than just power in her gaze now. There was excitement. "The old ritual site on Mount Macedon would not have acknowledged you in the manner that it did if it were not so."

The site had acknowledged me? When? Then I remembered the odd sense of watchfulness and the feeling that the trees themselves were sentient. Remembered that I'd been able to become Aedh when the magic of that place barred all such beings entry.

"Ilianna may not choose to keep—"

"She will," Kiandra said, with a certainty I couldn't help but believe. "Because she knows, as I know, that this child has been a long time coming, and a long time needed."

I frowned. "I don't understand—"

"No," Kiandra agreed. "But Ilianna does. There are many reasons she ran from us. What she witnessed when young was the excuse but not the truth."

I rubbed my forehead wearily. Fate, it seemed, had been brewing her plans for us all for a very long time. "Look, right now, all I want to do is rescue her. Did you find her?"

"Yes. And you were right—great magic holds her."

"Meaning we won't get past it?"

"Meaning that neither you nor your dark defender will. It is aimed at energy beings rather than mere flesh and blood."

"So Tao and Carwyn would get past it?"

"I suspect so." She hesitated. "There are beings within who guard her, but I could gain no true sense of them. They may or may not be human."

"Well, neither are Tao and Carwyn, and both are pretty pissed off right now."

She nodded. "It may be enough. Just tell them not to go in all guns blazing, because that will have dire consequences."

For Ilianna, I thought, not for them. I swallowed and nodded. "I'll pass on the message."

She nodded. "She is being held in an abandoned warehouse in Link Court, Brooklyn. The magic lies within the building, not along the perimeter."

"Meaning they'd need to be wary of other security measures?"

"Yes." She moved past me and led the way back through the warren of shadowed, powerful corridors. When we neared the front door, she stopped and lightly touched my shoulder. "Be careful, Risa Jones. There are more games being played than you realize."

My smile was almost a grimace. "Tell me something I don't know."

"There are two people in your life who are in reality one, and their deception goes deeper than you think."

I blinked. "What do you mean?"

She half shrugged. "What I see is not always clear. But I would suspect that a shape-shifter of some kind has entered your life."

"There is—he stole the first key. It's tracking the bastard that is proving the problem."

"Then perhaps you should start looking closer to home."

I frowned. "Are you saying it's a friend?"

She hesitated. "Acquaintance, perhaps. As I said, these things are not always clear."

Then I wished she hadn't mentioned it, because now I'd be looking at everyone suspiciously and suspecting the worse. But I forced a smile and said, "Thanks. I'll keep an eye out."

She nodded and, with one eloquent gesture, ushered me out of the building. But I was aware of her gaze as I ran down the steps, and it made my back itch. She knew more than what she'd said; of that much I was sure.

Azriel appeared near the bottom step. "You were successful?"

"Yes. Now we just need to plot our next move."

"Back to your apartment, then."

"No. I need to go see Aunt Riley. She's the expert in this sort of stuff. As much as I hate to do it, I think I need to bring her in rather than risk using only Tao and Carwyn."

"And once again, you do something thoroughly sensible. There is hope for you yet, I think."

I grinned. "Don't say that too loud. Wouldn't want the word getting around and spoiling my reputation."

"Your secret is safe with me." He wrapped his arms around my waist, dropped a kiss on my nose, then zapped us across to my aunt's.

To say our sudden appearance in the middle of her living room was something of a surprise would be the understatement of the year. I waited until she stopped swearing, then dropped a kiss on her cheek. "And good morning to you, too."

"Well, it was a good morning until you scared the life out of me *and* made me spill my coffee." Amusement teased her mouth and lit her gray eyes as she walked into the open kitchen area and grabbed a cloth. She tossed it to me, then added, "Seeing as I have to make a fresh cup, do you want one?"

"No, I haven't the time." I bent and wiped up the spillage. "I'm actually here for help."

"I'm gathering it's not key related, given your determination *not* to involve any of us in that search." Her voice was wry. "Which, by the way, is neither warranted nor necessary. We have faced far worse in our lifetimes than rogue Aedh."

"Which is precisely *why* I don't want you involved." And she *knew* that. "But this is related. Sort of."

"Go on."

She crossed her arms and regarded me steadily. A rock I could always depend on, no matter what, I thought with a half smile.

"Lucian has kidnapped Ilianna and is holding her hostage against my good behavior at a warehouse in Link Court, Brooklyn. According to the Brindle witches, she's protected by magic that will allow neither Aedh nor reaper entry."

"Then I'm surprised Lucian is still alive. In a similar situation, I would have killed the bastard."

"A sentiment I totally agree with," Azriel said.

I gave him a look over my shoulder, but he merely raised an eyebrow at me.

"Then why isn't he dead?" Riley said. "It would solve the problem of being forced to do what you do not wish to."

"If he doesn't report in every hour, the men holding her have orders to kill her."

"Ah."

"Also, I do not think those men are human."

She shrugged. "Non-human I can deal with."

"Yeah, but these are non-human *and* Razan."

"Meaning the fight will be infinitely more exciting." She grinned and cracked her knuckles. "I haven't had a good fight in quite a while."

"That is because you're *supposed* to be settling down to a quiet life." Uncle Quinn's gently lilting tones seemed to come out of the air itself. "And you *were* intending to call me in on this, weren't you?"

He re-formed next to Riley, his expression a mix of love and amusement. Like me, he was half Aedh, and was, in fact, the man who had taught me all of my skills.

"Of course," she replied, a smile on her lips and her eyes sparkling. "I wouldn't want you to miss out on the excitement."

Quinn rolled his eyes and glanced at me. "What do we face?"

"Magic, electronic security, and more than likely Raziq." I hesitated. "Tao and Carwyn—Ilianna's potential mate—want in on the action."

Quinn frowned. "Given we face an unknown number of combatants, I don't think it wise to involve anyone who isn't fight trained."

"Maybe, but the magic is aimed at those who are energy or half-energy beings, so it'll prevent you from getting in." I switched my gaze to Riley. "I know you're one of the best, but I don't want you going in there alone. I couldn't stand to see you hurt." Or worse. I didn't say it, but it hovered in the air, regardless.

"I won't be alone. I have a twin, remember, and he loves a fight even more than I do." She smiled, walked over to gather me in her arms, and hugged me fiercely. "It'll be all right, Risa," she added softly. "It always is."

Tears stung my eyes, and I blinked them away rapidly. And wished, with all my heart, that I could believe her. But deep down I knew it *wasn't* going to be all right, that it was never going to be all right. All right had long ago passed me by, and I was sliding faster and faster into the darkness that my mother had foreseen wrapped around me all those years ago.

"What we need," Quinn said, "is eyes on the situation. Once we know what we face, we can plan our attack."

"Stane can hook into all the security cams in the area—"

"So can the Directorate," Riley said. "And it'll be easier and faster. I'll get Rhoan on it immediately."

I frowned. "I'm not sure it's a good idea—"

She waved my objection away as she picked up her phone. "Jack owes me more than one favor. Besides, if this goes sideways, it's better that the Directorate be involved."

Please, God, don't let it go sideways. I licked my lips, then nodded. As Riley made the call, I glanced at Quinn. "I'm meeting Lucian at eleven thirty. I know that doesn't leave much time to plan anything, but I can delay him for at least an hour."

He said, "The longer you can delay, the better it will be. We'll ring—"

"You can't. My phone is dead and I left it home."

"Then I will shoot you a telepathic message when we've freed her."

"But I'm wearing nano microcells—"

"Which have not the capacity to stop me, no more than they could Riley." Quinn glanced at her as she got off the phone. "All set?"

"Rhoan is gearing up surveillance as we speak, and Jack has approved full Directorate participation." Her gaze met mine. "He said he owed you a favor. Care to explain that?"

I kept my expression—and thoughts—carefully neutral. "I was asked for advice on some demon-related killings Rhoan's investigating. Couldn't do a whole lot to help, though."

"Hmm." Her expression suggested she very much *didn't* believe my reply, even though it was the truth as far as it went. "We're not going to need your friends, so tell Tao and Carwyn to cool their jets. We'll contact them the minute we can."

If they are not going to help free Ilianna, perhaps we should bring them in on the key—

No, I said, before he could finish. *Definitely not.*

Risa, I do not trust the Aedh, and it might be wiser—

I won't risk my friends again, Azriel. I've already done enough damage to them. Out loud, I said, "You'll let me know the minute you have her? And you'll both be careful?"

"We will, on both counts." Quinn glanced at his watch. "If you were planning to scout the area before you met Lucian, you had better hurry. It's almost eleven now."

We left.

But not without a prayer to the fates and whatever gods were listening that everything went as planned and everyone got out alive.

And that included me and Azriel.

Because the shit, I suspected, was about to hit the fan big-time.

Chapter 13

The Arms and Militaria Exhibition was being held in a beautiful redbrick building that had once been a post office. It sat on one corner of a street that was a mix of old architecture and more modern—but infinitely uglier—concrete buildings, a grand old lady that time had not diminished.

The street itself wasn't crowded, although the parking lot across from the old post office was full, and I doubted they were all here for the nearby florist or the computer shop.

A roundabout was situated at the right end of the old building, but to the left there was a small metal gate and a green covered pathway that led—presumably—around to the back. Handy, given I had to set up the ward somewhere it wouldn't be noticed—presuming it *was* a ward in the box my father had sent, and not something else.

"Whatever lies in the box," Azriel said, "it certainly involves some form of magic. It crawls over my skin."

I frowned. "Why would it have that reaction? It's supposed to keep the Aedh out, not you."

Azriel's smile was tight, without humor. "Your

father does not want me in possession of the keys any more than he does anyone else."

I rubbed my head wearily. "You know, I hadn't even *thought* of that possibility."

He shrugged. "It is better to have us all locked out than none of us."

"You can bet my father won't be locked out. Or the Razan." Not to mention the dark sorcerer. I doubted *he* was going to miss out on the action, given his success stealing the first key.

And then there was Lucian, the joker in the mix.

My gaze dropped to the box Azriel still held. "Should we use it, then?"

"Yes." He handed it to me. "I can patrol the perimeter and cut any off who attempt to breach the wards."

"What about my father?"

"Your father can't gain flesh form, so even if he has created a back door in the ward's magic, he still needs you to actually find and retrieve the key."

"He needs me to find it," I said darkly. "But he has Razan to retrieve it."

"And if any *do* get past me, the Aedh will be beside you to stop them."

I gave him a surprised look. "I can't believe you just said that."

"I would rather Tao be in there beside you, but it is an inescapable truth that the Aedh wants the keys for himself. He *will* fight anyone who gets in his way." He regarded me steadily. "Do not turn your back on him."

Definitely not. The bastard was just as likely to

fuck me as kill me. I glanced down at the box in my
hand, then took a deep breath and, with slightly
shaking fingers, opened it. Inside were four small
stones in varying shades of gray and a note. I tucked
the box under my arm and opened the note.

Place these wards on each corner of the building,
it said. *Activate them in sequence, light to dark, with
a drop of your blood.*

Losing more blood, even if it was only a couple
of drops, wasn't exactly what I needed right now.
Especially to activate damn wards. Still, if it kept
the hordes out, then I guessed it was worth it.

I rolled the stones out onto my hand. They felt
extraordinarily light and yet oddly warm. I couldn't
sense any magic in them, but my skin still crawled
at their touch. I forced my fingers closed around
them, then glanced up at the building again. Placing stones on three sides of the building would be
easy enough, but the last side was right on the intersection corner, with only a small strip of pavement between it and the roundabout. Placing a stone
there, however close to the building, was risking it
either being kicked away or picked up by some curious kid. Not that there were actually kids in the
street at the moment, but knowing my luck, they'd
flood the place the minute I started activating the
wards.

"What about the roof?" Azriel said. "He did not
define that the corners had to be the base of the
building."

I glanced up. The roof was tiled and not particularly steep, but it was very visible from all parts of

the street. If I got up there, I'd attract all sorts of unwanted attention.

"Then you must risk the last stone at the corner."

I guess I did. I took another deep breath that did next to nothing to release the tension in me, then said, "Let's get this done before Lucian turns up."

I walked across the road, glanced up and down the footpath to see if anyone was paying undue attention to us, then pushed through the old wrought-iron gate and quickly headed around the corner. Ivy and shrubs crawled all over the fence lining one side of the path, which would have been the perfect place to hide a stone except for the fact they had to be on the corner of the building. I found a crack in the concrete that was as close as I was ever going to get and wedged the lightest-colored stone into it. "Blood," I said suddenly. "Amaya won't cut me, will she?"

"She is incapable of doing so, even if requested." He drew Valdis and held her point down, near my leg. Her steel flickered with an odd purple fire. It was almost as if she were displeased. "She is."

I raised an eyebrow. "Why is that?"

His hesitation was brief, but nevertheless there. "Because of the connection we have formed."

I studied him for a moment, sensing that was the truth as far as it went, but knowing there was a whole lot more to it than that—and that he wasn't about to explain it. I lightly pressed a fingertip against Valdis's point. Blood welled. I let it drop onto the ward. In an instant it was gone, sucked into the stone itself. Dark, bloody light flickered deeply in its heart, then stilled. But it was not inert. It was waiting.

I shivered, then stood and walked to the next corner. This time I wedged the ward into the strip of garden bed that ran the length of the rear of the building. When I dropped blood onto it, that dark, bloody light began to beat very slowly.

They were coming to life.

I repeated the process with the third stone, and this time the magic was tangible. It crawled across my skin, a force waiting for completion.

I jumped over the rear fence and walked up to the final corner. There was absolutely nowhere to safely put the ward. It was pavement right up to the edge of the building, and there were no cracks in either the concrete or the bricks.

"Then let me make one." Azriel pressed Valdis's sharp tip against the lowest visible brick near the corner of the building. Her flames flared briefly and, in seconds, there was a small, thumb-sized hole large enough to securely hold the last ward.

"Perfect." I squeezed my finger to get a final drop of blood, put it on the stone, then hurriedly dropped it in place.

The energy that crawled across my skin expanded in a rush, sweeping out and up, creating a wall of power that was invisible, but not entirely silent. It reminded me of the crackle and hum often heard when standing under high-voltage power lines. It would certainly be a warning to those who were sensitive to such things that something major now protected this building.

I rose and met Azriel's gaze. "Are you sure the wards will keep you out?"

In answer, he raised his hand and held it close to the wall. Little bolts of lightning shot toward his fingertips, a warning of what was to come if he pressed closer.

He lowered his hand. "The Aedh is here."

"The bastard is early." I flexed my fingers against the sudden urge to grab Amaya and thrust her sharp point into Lucian's dark heart, then forced a smile and walked around the corner.

He waited in the middle of the three arches that made up the main entrance into the building. "Lucian," I said, voice somehow very neutral. "How pleasant to see you."

Amusement touched his lips. "And said with such sincerity, too. Just as well you're a restaurateur rather than an actress, my girl."

"I'm not *your* anything." I stopped several feet away and crossed my arms. "It's seven bucks an adult to get into the exhibition. You can pay."

"My pleasure." But his gaze wasn't on me; it was on Azriel. "And it was, many times."

The anger that exploded from Azriel was so strong, it actually forced me forward a step. How he managed to rein it in, to *not* attack Lucian, I had no idea. But he did.

He didn't say anything, either. Maybe he simply couldn't, lest it break the wall of control.

"Lucian, cut the shit and just get inside," I growled. "We're here to find the key, remember?"

"So we are," he murmured. "But it is infinitely

satisfying to know that I have succeeded where *he* has failed."

"I wouldn't be so certain of that," I bit back, then pushed him up the stairs. Just for a moment, darkness flared in his eyes, yet another reminder that the man I'd spent so much time with was *not* the person he truly was.

I followed him up the steps and into the shadowed confines of the building's foyer. Old bank-teller-type windows lined one wall, and it was behind several of these that tickets could be purchased.

"I see your father has done his bit to make this place safe," Lucian said, smiling at the woman as he paid the entrance fees.

"It's just unfortunate he was unable to keep the likes of *you* out."

Lucian chuckled softly, handed me a ticket, then grandly ushered me forward. "After you, my sweet."

"You can stick the politeness where the sun don't shine," I muttered, then handed the ticket to the collector at the main door and went in.

The next room was vast and had obviously once been the main mail sorting area. There were three rows of exhibits here and, at the rear, a sign stating there were more up the stairs. There were also about a dozen people wandering around and a guard for each of the aisles.

I scanned the room for security cameras and saw four—one on each corner. Between them and the glass covering the majority of the display tables, there was little chance of snatching the key inconspicuously—if it was here, that was.

I made my way to the first aisle and slowly walked through, lingering near each table for several seconds to see if I got any reaction to the items within. This aisle seemed to be a mix of pistols and swords, but none of them set off the internal radar. I walked on.

It was a slow process and one that was utterly nerve-racking. Not just because I needed the key, but because of the rising expectations of the man who followed so closely behind me. Of course, the growing sense that the shit was about to hit the fan didn't help all that much, either. By the time I reached the end of the last aisle, I was so wound up, I was shaking.

I flexed my fingers again, trying to relax. A hard thing to do, given the tension radiating through me and around me. Tension that was mine, Lucian's, *and* Azriel's, all combining to make a stomach-churning mix. How I was managing to *not* throw up was a miracle.

"There are more exhibits upstairs." Lucian wrapped his fingers around my upper arm and propelled me forward.

I wrenched my arm free, but bit back the anger and somehow managed to say, almost civilly, "I'm well aware of that. There's no need to manhandle."

He glanced at me, the amusement playing about his lips at odds with the cool distance in his eyes. "You and I both know that you are not averse to a little force now and again, no matter how much you might say otherwise. This morning's efforts are a case in point."

Which explained the bruises I couldn't remember getting. God, how had I ever been fooled by this man?

Because he hid behind magic and years of pretending to be what he never was, Azriel said.

You weren't fooled.

No, but then, there were other reasons for that. He paused. *Be wary. The Raziq approach.*

Concern shot through me. *How many? God, don't fight them—*

I will do what I must, he said, in a tone that suggested he wasn't about to listen to reason no matter what I said. *You worry about finding the key. Let me do what I am here to do.*

I grabbed the banister and began climbing the stairs. *You're here to keep me safe and find the keys. Getting dead isn't a part of that.*

I have no plans in that direction.

It isn't your *plans I worry about.*

Ah, but you should, Risa, he said, his mental tones soft and almost wistful.

I frowned. *Azriel, I really don't need to be worried about your motives on top of everything else, so quit it.*

I wasn't talking about motives, he said, then, in more normal tones, added, *But as you say, this is not the time. Razan have arrived.*

Fear shot through me. *What about the Raziq? And how many Razan?*

I reached the top of the stairs and hesitated. The floor plan was a mirror image of the one below, but there were more people up here. My gaze swept the walls. Another four cameras. I wondered if anyone was watching them, or if they merely recorded events for viewing later if something went wrong.

Because something was most *certainly* about to go wrong. Just not in the way they suspected.

The Raziq keep their distance and wait. There are six Razan. Azriel hesitated. *They do not feel right.*

Oh, great. *Meaning?*

They have been infected with magic.

My stomach twisted a few more knots. *You mean like the ones who attacked us when we lost the first key?*

The same. His mind voice was grim. *I will stop them, but it will attract attention. It is also possible they are little more than a diversion. Stay wary.*

"I suspect your mind is not on what you are supposed to be finding," Lucian murmured, cupping my elbow and propelling me toward the row of long rifles. "Wouldn't be bitching to the reaper, would you?"

"What would it matter to you if I was?" I snapped, and yanked my arm free again. "But as it happens, he was informing me that Razan have arrived. Wouldn't be yours, would they?"

His expression darkened. Meaning he *wasn't* overly excited by this news and, warped or not, it cheered me up no end. I mean, anything that pissed *him* off had to be a good thing, if only marginally, right?

"I do not have enough magic left to create Razan," he said. "So if they come, they are not mine."

"But has your dark sorceress got enough magic to create them? Or something similar to them?"

He shot me a glance, his expression unreadable. "What makes you think that?"

"Call it an educated guess. You're the one who said you don't do anything without reason. Perhaps your apparent lack of magic strength—by Aedh standards, I'm guessing, not human—is the real reason you're making out with a very powerful sorceress. I bet she could create all manner of magic with a little help from you."

"Perhaps," he said. "But those Razan are not here under my orders."

"Yeah, but maybe they're here under *hers*."

He didn't answer that particular accusation, meaning I'd hit the nail on the head. And if she was behind the creation of the twisted Razan who'd run interference when the first key was stolen—and who were here now—then maybe she was more involved than we'd thought. After all, there *had* been male clothes in her Gold Coast apartment. Maybe Lucian was being played just as much as he was playing us.

"Just find that key," he growled.

"It may not even be here," I reminded him. "And don't stand so fucking close."

"Or you'll do what?" he mocked. "Let's not forget who holds all the cards here."

"Not *all* the cards," I retorted. "You still need me to find the damn keys, and standing so close, radiating tension all over me, is interfering with that."

He stepped back, but only a pace or two. Still, it gave me not only breathing room, but room enough to draw Amaya if I needed to.

From downstairs came a shout, then the sound of fighting. I knew Azriel was involved, but I resisted the urge to reach out to him. Distractions were the last thing he needed.

I walked on, scanning the displayed weapons, finding nothing, sensing nothing. Then, as I reached the end of the aisle, energy slithered across my skin—a caress so light, it barely brushed the hairs on my arm. But the Dušan stirred in my flesh and my gaze swept the remaining aisle. It was in one of them, somewhere.

"You've found something?" Lucian said, excitement in his voice.

"Not exactly." I hesitated as another wash of energy ran over my skin, but this one was stronger and darker. "There's something wrong."

"Aside from the hullabaloo your reaper is causing downstairs, you mean?"

"Yes." My gaze swept the room. There were still a dozen men up here, and none of them seemed overly interested in what was going on downstairs. In fact, they appeared to be deliberately *ignoring* it. Even the guards. Unease stirred. "It just doesn't feel right."

"The wards your father so kindly created have stopped the Raziq. Your reaper is taking care of the Razan. There is nothing and no one else here to worry about, Risa."

He was wrong. Totally wrong. But I guessed he knew that. Guessed whatever or whoever I was sensing were either his people or his magic, or those belonging to his dark sorceress.

I forced myself to keep moving and tried to catch the elusive sensation that would lead me to the next key. The awareness of danger grew until it was a pulse beating in tune with my heart. My skin itched and sweat began to trickle down my spine, and all I could smell was fear. It was thick and rich and it was all mine.

I walked down the next aisle, drawn by the growing pull of power. The Dušan's movements grew stronger, and she appeared to be moving from the left to the right. Knowing that the last time she'd done this, she'd actually been hinting at the key's location, I walked to the end of this aisle and into the next one.

And stopped abruptly. The key was here.

But every sense I had screamed that pinning down its exact location was *not* a good thing to do right now.

"You've found it." It was a statement, not a question, and again suggested that Lucian had not been altogether truthful when he'd said he couldn't read my thoughts. Like *that* was a surprise.

"It's there somewhere." I pointed to the largest of the three remaining display cases.

But the words were barely out of my mouth when the shit hit. The dozen strangers in the room turned as one, and for the first time I saw their faces. They *weren't* just men. They were the half-human, half-animal beings that had attacked us the first time.

Fuck.

Lucian yanked me backward and drew a long

knife from god knows where. Its sides gleamed with an unearthly fire that matched the glow in his eyes. "You will *not* take it from me this time," he growled.

And with that, he attacked. Three of the shifters met his charge head-on. The remainder flowed around him and came straight at me.

I swore, drew Amaya, and fell back. Her anger filled me, but it did little to shore up my courage. I knew what these fucking things could do, and I knew that against so many I stood little chance.

I swung my sword, slashing right and left, Amaya's blade little more than a blur as she cut through the air and flesh with equal efficiency. Blood and body parts flew, and my arms shuddered with every strike, but nothing seemed to halt the creatures' onslaught. They didn't feel pain, didn't even acknowledge limb loss, never hesitated for one moment in their mad charge. Their eyes were filled with the desire to kill, to rent and tear and taste blood, and yet, oddly, they didn't. They attacked, but it was nine against one, and even with Amaya in my hands, the odds *should* have been overwhelming. But while they kept forcing me back, they hadn't yet done any serious damage.

And maybe that was the whole point. Distraction, *not* destruction.

The key, I thought, and desperately jumped sideways, trying to see past the wall of twisted flesh. A dark figure stood near the display cabinet, sweeping everything within it into a large rucksack.

"No," I screamed, but was hit by one of the shifters and sent tumbling backward, over the guardrail.

I hit one of the display cases below with a resounding crash and for a moment saw stars. Every breath hurt, and pain slithered down my back and right leg. Then twisted flesh replaced the spinning stars, and I threw myself sideways, off the broken display case and onto the floor.

"Hey, what the hell do you think—" someone shouted, but the sound was cut off abruptly as one of the shifters leapt at him.

There was a gargled cry and somewhere a woman started screaming, but I barely had time to scramble to my feet before the rest of the shifters were on me. I slashed Amaya across the face of one, sending bits of flesh and blood flying, then spun and stabbed upward, hitting another square in the chest. Amaya screamed as her flames leapt from steel to flesh, eating into him even as she sucked his life into her steel.

I shuddered at her voraciousness, then pulled her free and ran as hard as I could for the stairs. The remaining shifters came after me, snapping and snarling at my heels. Fingers snagged my foot on the third step and brought me down. I twisted and booted the shifter in the face with my free foot. His head snapped back under the force of the blow, and he snarled, revealing a bloody mouth and broken canines. But he didn't let go. I swore and swept Amaya from left to right. Her steel bit into the shifter's neck and she screamed in pleasure as she severed arteries and sprayed blood all over us both. I bit back bile and scrambled to my feet, only to be brought down again by another shifter. Teeth tore into my arm, and I screamed as he worried at my flesh like a dog with a bone. I hit him with my free hand, clawing at his eyes, trying to force him to release me. His teeth were biting deeper and deeper, and my fingers were beginning to lose strength. Amaya was stuck like glue, but it was her doing, not mine. I gouged my fingers deeper, until one of his eyeballs popped. He snarled and his grip on my arm momentarily lessened. I pulled free, clenched my bloody fist around Amaya's hilt, and hit him, as hard as I could. His head snapped backward and he went tumbling back down the stairs, knocking down several others in the process. But they were only down, not out, and already others were leaping over them and coming at me. I spun and raced up the rest of the stairs.

And saw Lucian thrust his arm into the middle of a shifter's chest and literally blow him apart.

I stopped cold.

Watched the bloody body parts fall as if in slow motion. Saw in the way they fell an echo of my mother's death.

And knew, with absolute cold certainty, that it had been Lucian who'd killed my mother.

Chapter 14

My mind went dead.

For several seconds I couldn't move, couldn't think, couldn't do anything. I just stood there, horror filling every part of me, as the man who had fooled me in more ways than I'd ever imagined stepped over the broken remnants of the body and turned around. He didn't see me, didn't even look in my direction. He just raised the knife and ran at the darkly shadowed person still stuffing weapons into the rucksack.

The thief swore; the voice was male, not female. Not Lauren, then, some distant, still-aware part of me registered. Then magic surged and the cloaked stranger disappeared. Lucian screamed his fury, and it was that sound, more than anything, that unfroze my lips and got my mind working again. Suddenly, I became aware of the footsteps behind me and Amaya's screams. I swung, lashing out as hard and as fast as I could, slicing across the chest of the nearest shifter. As blood flew, I twisted and lashed out with a booted foot, knocking the second into the first and sending them both back down the stairs. Then I turned and ran straight at Lucian.

He saw me. He was always going to see me, given the noise Amaya was making. He made a mocking half bow, then threw something to the floor. Power surged, and he began to disappear. No fucking way, I thought, and threw myself at him. I hit him at the precise moment the energy reached its peak, and the power tore through us both, disintegrating flesh and body and bone in a manner very similar to the Aedh shift. It swept us into a void that lasted for several seconds; then the power surged again, and suddenly we were skin, rather than energy, and tumbling to the ground in a tangled mess.

Ground, not floor, not concrete. Wherever the hell we were, it *wasn't* back at his apartment, as I'd half expected.

He threw me off, then scrambled to his feet. "What the fuck are you playing—"

I didn't give him a chance to finish. I just attacked. Amaya was little more than a blur of my hands, and her steel spat flames that sprayed all around us. Lucian swore and parried every blow with his long knife, retreating slowly but surely, his expression intent but not unduly worried.

When energy surged around me, I realized why. By reacting without thinking, I'd very neatly stepped into his trap.

He lowered his weapon and shook his head, his expression somewhat bemused. "This cage was not meant for you, but I'm damn glad I set it up, all the same."

I slammed Amaya against the wall of power that surrounded me. Spidery veins of red spread for several inches from the impact point, then faded away, and Amaya hissed in fury.

Break can, she said. *Time needed.*

"That cage was designed to hold a sorcerer," Lucian said, amusement in his voice. "Neither you nor your sword have the power to break it."

"Why did you do it, Lucian?" I growled, hitting the wall again. This time, I left Amaya against it. She hissed and spat, her steel throbbing as she sucked at the power of the cage. "Just tell me that."

He frowned and held his hands wide, as if pleading his innocence. For the first time it actually registered that we were underground. Both the walls and ceiling that soared high above us were stone, and the air was thick with the scents of moisture and damp earth.

"I didn't steal the key, Risa. Indeed, I was hoping to trap the thief in the cage that now surrounds you."

"I'm not talking about the fucking key, Lucian, and you *know* it."

His frown deepened. For half a second I honestly believed he had no idea what I was talking about; then I remembered what a consummate actor he was. What a liar he was.

"Trust me—"

Never again. "I'm talking about my mother. You *killed* her."

"Ah." His voice was soft. "That."

Rage exploded, and I leapt at him without thinking. The cage bowed under the force of my impact but it didn't break, and I was flung backward, landing in an inelegant heap on the floor.

"*That,*" I hissed. "That's all you've got to say about my mother's *murder.*"

He shrugged. "She died well, with great grace, if that is of any consequence."

"But you killed her."

Amusement touched his lips. "Yes, I believe we've already established that fact."

"But *why*?" The word was torn from me. "What the hell did my mother ever do to you?"

"Nothing, of course. But without her presence, without her advice, you were infinitely more alone and vulnerable."

So he'd killed her merely to make me more accepting of his advances?

"You *bastard.*" Bastard, bastard, *soon-to-be-dead fucking bastard.*

"Another fact we have already established." His amusement was stronger this time. "It's not as if I have taken her from you for all eternity, Risa, so please cut the dramatics. You and she will meet again on another plane."

"*That* is beside the point!"

"No, it is not, because I could have done otherwise."

A chill went through me. "What do you mean?"

He smiled, but this time, there was nothing pleasant or amused about it. "I may be one of the fallen, but I still retain my power over souls. I could have stopped her from moving on, if I'd so desired. You should be grateful that I left you the chance to meet her again in another lifetime."

"Grateful? *Grateful?*"

He tsked. "Enough with the dramatics, Risa. It is time to concentrate on things we *can* still do something about. Like retrieving the key."

Amaya, I hope you're going to get that fucking wall down soon.

Trying, she growled. *Patience must.*

Coming from my sword, *that* was almost amusing. I rolled my shoulders, trying to ease the tension. It didn't do much, but I suspected little would. Not until the Aedh in front of me was in bits all over the floor.

"So are you intending to enlighten me on who stole the damn thing? Because it's very obvious you know them and are maybe even working with them."

"*Working* is not quite the right term to use," he replied. "Let's just say we have a somewhat fluid agreement."

I snorted. "Meaning you're both doing your utmost to stab the other in the back."

"It does add a degree of excitement to the proceedings," he said, voice droll. "Much like fucking you, really."

I snorted. "Only in that you're betraying us both."

"And fucking you both."

I blinked. "The person who took the key was a man—"

"So? As I have said before, it is pleasure that matters, not source."

"So you're fooling around with *two* dark sorcerers?" I asked incredulously.

"Perhaps," he replied. "Perhaps not. I am hardly likely to give you such information, my dear, when I still need cards to play if I am to survive this encounter."

"And we both know you're *not* going to survive; otherwise you wouldn't have been such a busy little beaver trying to impregnate any woman you could get your grubby little paws on."

"*That* was merely a precaution." He glanced at his watch, and I suddenly remembered Ilianna.

Fuck, fuck, *fuck*! Had she been rescued, or had the whole thing gone ass up?

"A precaution?" I bit back, relief filling me when he didn't immediately dig out his phone. We obviously still had some time left before he needed to make his next call. "Another lie. Aedh breed only when their death is imminent."

"As your father only bred?" He shook his head. "Like him, I have a few years left before I am forced to leave this world permanently."

Amaya's steel was getting heavier in my hand, her hissing more strident in my mind. I hoped that meant the wall was weakening rather than her.

"Is the person who stole all the weapons out of that display case," I growled, "the same person who stole the first key?"

He considered me for a moment, expression a mix of amusement and condescension. "It was."

"And is that person a dark sorcerer who is also a shape-shifter?"

God, it felt like we were playing twenty questions. But this wasn't a game, and I had to get as much information out of him as I could while I was still trapped, because there *wasn't* going to be any talking once I was free. Not by me, anyway.

Amaya, on the other hand, was a whole different story.

"I believe that might also be correct." The amusement got stronger. "You will never guess their identity, Risa, but you are most welcome to try for as long as you like. However, it will not get us that key back."

"Is it even possible to get the key back, given what happened to the first one?"

"The difference that time and this," he said, "is that it wasn't only the key stolen, but rather a whole bunch of weapons in which the key is just one. Our thief has not the capability to find it himself and will need our help."

Relief slipped through me. We may have momentarily lost the key, but it still was within the realms of possibility that it could be retrieved. That was something, at least.

"Our help, or yours? You can sense the key when you're close, can't you?"

"Yes, but I need you to pin down its location. Which is why I suggest an agreement would be in order—"

I snorted. "The only agreement you're going to get from me is one at the end of a sword."

He tsked again. "Now, let's not forget Ilianna here. I would hate to have to kill her after all the effort I've put into snatching and seeding her."

Amaya—

Close, she growled. *Close.*

"What sort of agreement?" I spat. "And why the hell would you even expect me to believe you'd actually uphold your end of it?"

"I don't expect trust," he said. "But I do expect that you'll remember I hold your friend's life in my hands and that you'll control not only your own need to kill me, but that of your reaper's."

"In exchange for what?" I spat.

"In exchange for the key, of course. What else matters?"

Indeed, what else did? For him, my father, the Raziq, and even Azriel, there *was* nothing else. And if Lucian thought I could control the actions of *any* of them, then he was seriously insane.

"I can speak only for myself and Azriel, but we both know there are other players in the mix who want the key just as much as you."

Ready soon, Amaya said.

Anger—and the need to kill, to rent and tear—surged, and I could almost taste his death on my tongue. And I knew that *this* time, it wasn't Amaya's need, but my own. I wanted his blood on my hands, wanted to feel his life slipping away, wanted to watch the realization of defeat dawn in his eyes.

"With the keys in my possession, neither your father nor the Raziq will be a problem," he said. "Because they will not move against me until they are sure of the keys' location."

I pushed to my feet but made no other move to give away my readiness to react the minute I got the all clear from both Amaya and Uncle Quinn. *God, please, let him contact me soon.*

"You're overconfident, Lucian, and that's never a good thing."

"I have lived many lives in this world in that state, and I have always surpassed my own expectations." He glanced at his watch again. "And now, I believe, a phone call is required."

Amaya!

Through, she screamed back. *Attack!*

At the same time, Uncle Quinn's lilting tones said, *We have her. She's safe and well.*

As Lucian dug his phone out of his pocket, I launched myself. There was a brief flare of magic, a moment of resistance, and then I was free and running. He looked up and swore, the phone smashing to the stone floor as he brought his sword up. Steel clashed with steel, and Amaya screamed, the sound one of fury.

Magic, she screamed. *Burns*.

I guess it was no surprise that Lucian had a weapon prepared against Amaya, given he was well aware I never went anywhere without her.

I pivoted and lashed out with a booted foot, hitting him square in the chest and forcing him backward. He laughed—laughed!—then brought the long knife down. I jumped back but not fast enough, and the knife slashed through my boot and into flesh. The warmth of blood began to flood my boot, but I ignored it, ducked under another blow, then thrust upward with Amaya. He twisted out of her way, but not fast enough, and her sharp steel skated along his ribs, instantly drawing blood.

More, she screamed, her noise within my head and without.

Lucian's eyebrows rose. "It talks?"

"Yeah," I bit back, "and *she's* eager to drink in your death."

He avoided another blow, then lashed out with a clenched fist. I ducked but not fast enough. It skimmed my chin and rattled teeth, and I almost missed his follow-up. I jumped over the sweep of his legs, then raised my sword and brought her down hard. He twisted, so rather than splitting his head open as I'd intended, it hit his shoulder. A shudder ran through her steel; then blood sprayed and his arm was swinging uselessly from the few remaining bits of flesh and tendons that Amaya hadn't severed.

And just like that, all his amusement was gone.

What remained was anger. Anger that was deep and dark and utterly, *utterly* inhuman.

"For that, you will wish you were dead."

"You can't kill me," I retorted. "You can't find the fucking keys without me, remember."

"I never said I would kill you," he replied softly. "I merely said you will *wish* for it."

And with that, he attacked, a whirlwind of power and speed and sheer, bloody force. I weaved and dodged and blocked, using every skill, every instinct. Amaya was a blur in my hands, her flames sparking off every stone and her fury stinging the air itself.

But as fast as I was, as fast as *she* was, he was faster. He was also bigger and heavier, and his reach was twice that of mine.

It was inevitable that some of his blows would get through my defenses; one slashed my hip, another my thigh, but I was still upright, still mobile, after several minutes of heavy fighting. And he was hampered by his useless left arm and was now bleeding from wounds on his chest and legs. It enraged him further, as I'd hoped it would. I needed him reacting, *not* thinking. It was only through blind rage—his, not mine—that I truly had any hope of winning.

He came at me again, a blurring mass of muscle and sheer bloody anger. I spun and kicked. Lucian sucked in his gut, and my blow missed. Not so his knife. It sliced across my foot and sheared the end off my boot. Only quick reactions on my part stopped my toes from joining it on the stone. But it was the same foot that had previously encountered his blade, and without the boot to restrict it, blood began to flow more readily and pain surged.

I jumped back, limping now.

He laughed, the sound a weird mix of anger and amusement. "The first of many, dear Risa."

"I'm glad you're enjoying yourself, Lucian," I said, catching the edge of his blade with Amaya, holding it still as her flames leapt from her steel to his and she screamed blue murder. Nothing happened. The knife didn't melt. Amaya's flames died even as I added, "Because as an aunt of mine has been known to say, a condemned man should always enjoy his last meal."

He merely laughed and attacked. Again and again. I dodged, attacking him when opportunities arose, taking more and more hits but unable to find a way through his defenses. In the end, I knew there was only one way I was going to get the upper hand.

Do what must, Amaya said.

Do what must, I repeated grimly, then lowered her steel and stepped into his next blow. His blade punched into the middle of my stomach and right out the other side. As his fist came to a rest against my skin, I swung Amaya low and hard. Her blade reverberated as she hit flesh, but then she was cutting, sawing, burning her way through his legs. He barely had time to open his mouth when he dropped, dragging his long knife from my stomach as his body went one way and his legs the other.

I swung Amaya again, removed his good arm, then dropped to my knees and pressed one hand over my stomach, vainly trying to stop the flow of blood and gore as I stared at the man I had all but beaten.

His expression was one of utter amazement. There was no pain, no sense of loss, just sheer disbelief I'd done what I'd done.

Kill! Amaya screamed. *Finish!*

Not you. Me.

And with that, I released her, and with my now free hand, I dragged myself forward.

"You killed my mother," I said softly. "You raped

my friend; you worked with a dark sorceress to steal the keys and threatened the safety of this world. You betrayed me in more ways imaginable, and for all those crimes, you must die."

And with that, I dredged up the last of my reserves, called to the Aedh, and forced it into my arm. Then I shoved my fist into his chest and blew him apart.

Just has he'd blown my mother apart.

Chapter 15

It was over. I'd done what I'd sworn to do—found my mother's killer and dealt with him. Without help, on my own.

There should have been a sense of victory. Should have been a sense of relief. There wasn't.

There was only an odd numbness.

It was almost as if I'd given all there was to give and there was nothing—absolutely nothing—left inside of me. I raised my re-formed, bloody hand and, as if from a great distance, watched the bits of flesh and blood dribble toward my elbow.

Then, without warning, my stomach heaved and I threw up. The pain hit seconds later, and I was shaking and crying and wanting nothing more than to just let it all go. The pain, the horror, the guilt, and the expectations of others, just let it all wash away and become someone else's problem.

Can't, Amaya said sharply. *Finished not.*

Isn't it? I wondered. I closed my eyes and fought the wash of weakness in my body, and yet I could not deny the allure of ending it all here and now. Why not let fate take whatever course she'd decided to take and no longer fight it?

Everyone would be better off without me. *Everyone*. No one could hold them hostage against my behavior; no one could kidnap and rape them, and—perhaps best of all—there would be no one to find the remaining keys and threaten the very safety of the world.

That alone was worth one life.

That alone was certainly worth *my* life.

Everyone not safe, Amaya said. *I not. The life within not.*

A life that might well be Lucian's. God, he'd murdered my mother—how on *earth* was I to survive looking at his child every day and being reminded of his deed? How was that fair to the child? Or to me?

I couldn't. I wouldn't.

The death I'd seen so long ago wasn't the truth. I wasn't going to die in an automotive accident. I was going to die here, underground, all alone except for a nagging sword.

My arms collapsed underneath me, and I fell face-first onto the stone. For several minutes I simply lay there, my breathing becoming more and more labored and my life leaking out through various wounds in not-so-slow rivers.

And wondered, just for an instant, where Azriel was.

Magic, Amaya spat. *Stops.*

It was a shame. I wouldn't have minded seeing him just one more time ...

No, Amaya screamed. *Go not!*

Must, I replied, the roar in my mind going stronger. *It's too late.*

Not! she bit back; then she was in my hand. Power exploded around us, through us, merging steel and flesh with equal ferocity. It was a storm that tore my core apart, fiber by fiber, then pieced me back together, all within a matter of heartbeats.

Then it was no longer me, but *we.*

Die not, she said with fierce determination. *Live must.*

And with that, she forced my limbs into action, and I found myself crawling, slowly, painfully, past all the bloody, broken remnants of flesh toward two standing stones I hadn't even realized existed. Only they weren't just standing stones, but ancient, cuneiform-marked ones. Another gateway.

She kept me crawling, even though every movement had more blood pouring out and the pain was so intense I could barely even breathe. Energy washed across my skin, fierce and dark, but something was wrong with my eyesight because I could no longer see the stones, let alone tell whether they were active.

Not go! Stay!

I can't—

She wasn't listening. She never did, I guess. That surge of energy grew closer and closer even as my mind seemed to drift farther and farther away. It tore through me like a summer storm, sharp and electric, breaking me apart, then sweeping me away. I have no idea where it deposited me. I was no longer capable of caring.

My world was one of darkness and peace, and I smiled. *Yes,* I thought, *I'm ready.*

And not even Amaya's howls of protest could stop me from stepping free of my soul.

Light flared all around me, light that was warm and golden and peaceful. The figure of a woman appeared, her face glowing and serene. I smiled, unsurprised that the image the reaper who'd come to escort me onward had chosen to wear was the countenance of my mother. Of everyone I knew, she was the one person I trusted utterly.

Though Azriel had come pretty close.

As my thoughts turned to him, the light around me seemed to dim. No, I thought with determination. I *was* ready to move on.

The reaper wearing my mother's face smiled and offered me her hand. I hesitated and, just for a moment, thought of Tao and Ilianna, Riley and Quinn, Rhoan and his partner, Liander, and everyone else I was leaving behind. They would undoubtedly mourn my loss, but by my leaving, they could no longer be hurt by the madness that surrounded me.

And this was my chance, perhaps my only chance, to be with my mother again. I wanted that. More than anything, I wanted to see her, be with her, one more time.

I closed my eyes briefly, took a deep breath, then stepped forward.

It was then that Azriel appeared and blocked my path to the reaper.

What on earth are you doing? The words seemed to echo across the golden light, and an odd hush fell around us.

I'm sorry, Risa, but this cannot happen.

It is my time—

Yes, it is, but that does not mean I can let you go.

It is better for everyone—

Not everyone, he said and with such ferocity the very world around us quivered under its force. *Definitely not everyone.*

Then he reached out, grabbed my arm, and yanked me forward.

Not into death.

Into life.

I have no idea how long it took me to wake. I know I fought it for a very long time, desperate to snatch back what had been taken. Desperate to find that reaper again and move on, to be with my mother and far away from the pain and the hurt and the guilt and the never-ending expectations of others.

But that was an option that was not mine to take. Not now.

When I finally did open my eyes, it was to discover I wasn't alone. I guess that was no surprise. I did have people who cared for me, even if a tiny part of me actually resented that fact right now. If I'd moved on, as fate had destined me to, then I would not once again be responsible for their safety.

You are not responsible for our safety, Risa. We are more than capable of taking care of ourselves.

The voice wasn't Azriel's. It was Aunt Riley's.

I turned my head and looked at her. She was standing at the end of my hospital bed, her arms crossed and her expression severe. "You, my girl, will stop wishing yourself dead and start celebrating the fact you were given a second chance."

"I wasn't given anything," I retorted. "It was *forced* onto me."

"Running away, however you intended to do it, is never the answer—trust me on that."

"It would have been a hell of a lot easier than remaining here and being forced—"

I cut the words off before I could reveal a little too much, and she narrowed her eyes. "Being forced to do what?"

"The bidding of the fucking Raziq and my father and god knows who else. Ilianna was kidnapped because of me. Tao fights for control of his own body because of me. My mother is dead because of me—"

She sucked in her breath. "How did Dia get into this?"

Tears stung my eyes, and all that anger suddenly just washed away. "It was Lucian who killed her."

"And he's dead?"

"Well and truly."

"Good." She moved up the side of the bed, then sat and gathered my hand in hers. "I know it feels right now that death would be the easier option, but trust me, it isn't."

"But the keys—"

"We can sort out the key problem together," she said. "But you cannot allow yourself to fall into the trap of death. There are those in this world who can recall spirits and force them to do their bidding. What makes you think they will not do that to you?"

"Because they need me in flesh form to find—"

"So they've told you," she cut in, "but are you certain it's the truth?"

No, I wasn't. I took a deep, shuddering breath and released it slowly. "Life," I said softly, "sucks."

She laughed and bent over to drop a kiss on my forehead. "Yeah, it often does. But I'm so glad you decided to stay with us. I couldn't bear to lose you so soon after losing your mother."

If she'd wanted me in tears, then she'd damn well succeeded. She smiled and brushed them away with a gentle finger. "I couldn't be more proud of you if you were one of my own. You know that, don't you?"

I knew. In her eyes, she'd always had six children, not five. Dia might have given birth to me, but Riley had nevertheless adopted me. And I loved her almost as much as I loved my own mother. Which was why I couldn't let—

She pressed her fingers against my lips. "Enough with the self-sacrificing behavior. You can and will have our help, whether you like it or not. Now," she added, brisk and businesslike, "Ilianna is waiting out in the hall, desperate to see you, but she's under strict orders from the nurses and from me *not* to be more than a few minutes. Okay?"

"Okay."

She went out. Two seconds later, Ilianna appeared. I smiled, utterly relieved to see her safe and sound, but there was tension in me, too. I was ultimately responsible for what had happened to her, after all.

But when my gaze rose to hers, all I saw was complete and utter acceptance of all that had happened. There was no hate, no bitterness, not even regret or reproach. Just acceptance.

And I found myself wishing I could find even *half* of her serenity. Those damn tears welled again. "God, Ilianna—"

"Ris, it's okay," she said. "This event was foretold a long time ago, and even though I *had* thought it would be Carwyn's child I'd bear, I can't regret what happened. Not knowing what I do of her fate."

"But he forced you—"

"He used magic, yes, and it wasn't pleasant, but neither was it life-ending. I hate him, but I can't hate the result."

Which made me all the more ashamed, because I *could*. I didn't want to bear Lucian's child. No ifs, buts, or maybes.

But could I abort the child? Could I do that, when there was also a slim chance that the child was Azriel's?

That was a question I just couldn't answer.

I caught Ilianna's hand and squeezed it lightly. "Where's Tao? And Carwyn? Last time I saw them, they were both all fired up to ride to your rescue."

She smiled. "Well, right now they're both more than a little pissed at missing all the action. I believe Carwyn had pictured himself coming to my rescue and sweeping me off my feet in the process."

"Oh, I have no doubt about that." I hesitated. "Does he know what happened?"

"Not yet. But I'll tell him soon."

"How will that affect things?"

"It won't. He's after the merger with my family more than just me." She shrugged, expression unconcerned. But then, it wasn't like it was a love match. She had that in Mirri. "Stallions never take kindly to the offspring of others, but he won't hurt the child, and she'll be allowed to remain in his herd until grown."

"I guess that's something."

"That's everything. At least everything that matters." She smiled. "Tao said he'd visit tonight, seeing your aunt is adamant you get no more than one visitor at a time, lest it weaken you."

"She can be rather fierce about these things," I said with a smile.

"Too right she can," the woman in question said. "Ilianna, time's up. You can visit her tomorrow. Right now, she needs to rest."

Ilianna dropped a kiss on my cheek, then, with a promise to be back, left.

And that, basically, was the pattern of the next four days. Visitors in between bouts of resting, but no sign of the one person I really wanted to see.

Azriel.

It was deliberate on his part; of that I had no doubt. He'd crossed a line, with me and with death, and there would be a price to pay. Whether by me, or by him, or by us both, I had no idea.

On the fifth day, the doctors declared my werewolf heritage had worked another goddamn miracle and that I was fit enough to go home. *That* was music to my ears.

I rang Ilianna and arranged for her to pick me up, then climbed out of bed and took a shower. I was clean, dressed, and ready to get the hell away from the hospital and the awareness of death that continuously washed over me, thanks to the presence of the sick and the dying, when a different kind of awareness hit.

Azriel had finally decided to show up.

He appeared on the other side of the room, his arms crossed and his stance easy. And, as usual, his expression gave nothing away. He was holding his emotions—and his thoughts—very much in check.

I studied him for a moment, then said, "What did you do?"

"You know what I did," he replied, voice even. "I made you live."

I snorted softly. "Okay, let me rephrase that. *How* did you do that?"

He hesitated. "By leashing our energy beings together."

Fear curled through me. A fear unlike anything I'd ever experienced before. "You leashed our beings? As in, forever bound together?"

"Yes."

"So if you die, I die?"

"If I die, you take my place."

I stared at him. Did that mean . . . ? "No, that's not possible. I'm a flesh-and-blood being. I can never be what you are."

"You were never *just* flesh and blood, Risa. You were born half Aedh and became more so after what Marin did. When I snatched you from fate's pathway, I altered not only your destiny, but your very being."

No, no, *no*! How was something like that possible? How could I be born one thing and be made, on death, into another?

"What if *I* die? What if I decide to kill myself rather than become something I never wanted to be?"

Something flickered through his eyes. Anger, fear, hurt. I wasn't entirely sure. "You would not kill yourself."

"But what if I *did*?" I all but shouted.

"Then you would still become what I am—a dark angel."

I just stared at him. I couldn't do anything else. I was stunned. Broken. Betrayed. Again.

"Damn it, Azriel, *why*?"

"You know why."

"The mission. The key." I swung away, not wanting to look at him, not wanting him to see the hurt. It was always the *damn* key. Always about the damn mission.

"It *wasn't* about the damn mission or the key!" The sharp denial was accompanied by an explosion of anger that rolled my senses and just about fried my mind. "And if you'd listen to your heart *and* your body, you'd know it!"

I closed my eyes. Listen to my body, he said. Which implied he knew not only that I was pregnant but that the child was his.

So he'd saved what was rare and precious in his world. Not me. Never me.

"Damn it, Risa, that's not—"

"Isn't it?" I cut in and scrubbed a hand across suddenly aching eyes. I wouldn't cry. I *wouldn't*. "I listened to my heart, Azriel. I let you in. And you repaid that trust by taking away everything from me—"

"I haven't—"

"You took my *future*, Azriel! When I die, I won't move on. I won't be reborn." Wouldn't ever meet Mom again. "How can you stand there and say you *haven't* taken everything away?"

He didn't say anything. Didn't deny anything.

I closed my eyes and leaned my forehead against the windowpane. "I can't do this anymore, Azriel."

"Do what?"

Just for a moment, I swear there was fear in his voice. But that had to be imagination. Reapers didn't do fear. Didn't do emotions. Not the way I wanted emotions, anyway.

"You. Me. I can't do it. I don't want you near me. I don't want you in my life. I don't want you following me around anymore."

"Risa, that's not possible without—"

I swung around, my fists clenched against the sudden explosion of anger. "I don't *care* what is or isn't possible. I just want you out of my life!"

He stared at me for several minutes, his expression stony. Not even Valdis was emoting. "If you take this step, if you force me to go, I may not be allowed to come back."

"And I should be sad about that?" I spit out.

"Besides, it's not like you *won't* know what's going on. Not with the chi link—"

"That link was cut when you stepped onto death's plane."

"So why are you still able to read all my thoughts and emotions?"

"Why do you *think* I can, Risa?"

"Goddamn it," I said, my voice rising again. "If I knew, I wouldn't be asking!"

"Wouldn't you?" he said, bitterness edging his tones.

Leaving me none the wiser. But then, nothing was ever easy, nothing was ever straight, when it came to my reaper.

"No more, Azriel. I just—" I shrugged. "I can't. I won't."

He made a short, sharp motion with his hand. "So be it, then."

He winked out of sight, and I closed my eyes against the instinctive need to call him back and tell him I didn't mean it, that it was just anger and fear talking.

But I didn't.

Because it wasn't. Not entirely.

One thing, he said, his mind voice cool and distant as it flowed through my thoughts. *Rephael.*

What?

It is my name. If you ever need me, for whatever reason, say it. Wherever I am, whatever I am doing, I will hear.

And with that, he was gone, leaving me wondering if I'd just made the biggest goddamn mistake of my entire life.

Fuck it, no!

I *would* stand on my own feet and get on with whatever life I had left. I *would* sort out the mess that was the keys and Hunter and the Raziq the best I could, and I *would* goddamn survive in the process.

But the very first thing I needed to do was get drunk. Absolutely, mind-numbingly drunk.

Because before I could do anything else, the first thing I needed to do was *forget*.

If only for a day or so.

Don't miss our special preview of

Darkness Splintered

the next book in Keri Arthur's
fantastic Dark Angels series.

I woke up naked and in a strange bed.

For several minutes I did nothing more than breathe in the gently feminine—but totally unfamiliar—scents in the room, trying to figure out how, exactly, I'd gotten here.

And where the hell "here" was.

My brain was decidedly fuzzy on any sort of detail, however, and that could mean only that my mission to consume enough alcohol to erase all thought and blot out emotion had actually succeeded. And *that* surprised the hell out of me.

Thanks to our fast metabolic rate, werewolves generally find it difficult to go on a bender. I might be only half were, but I usually hold my alcohol fairly well and really *hadn't* expected to get anywhere near drunk. I certainly hadn't expected to be able to forget—if for only a few hours—the anger and the pain.

Pain that came from both the worst kind of betrayal and my own subsequent actions.

My eyes stung, but this time no tears fell. Maybe because I had very little in the way of tears left. Or maybe it was simply the fact that, somewhere in the alcohol-induced haze of the last few days, I'd finally come to accept what had happened to me.

Although it wasn't like I had any other choice.

If I *had*, then I would have died. *Should* have died. But Azriel, the reaper who'd been my follower, my guard, and my lover, had forced me to live and, in doing so, had taken away the very essence of what I was.

Because in forcing me to live, he not only ensured that my soul could never be reborn, but he'd made me what he was.

A dark angel.

The next time I died, I would not move on and be reborn into another life here on earth. I would join him on the gray fields—the unseen lands that divided this world from the next—and become a guard on the gates to heaven and hell. And that meant I would never see my late mother again. Not in any future lifetime that might have been mine, because he'd stolen all that away from me.

What made it all that much worse was the knowledge that he'd saved me not because he loved me, but because he needed me to find the lost keys to the gates.

And because I might be carrying his child.

The stinging in my eyes was *nothing* compared to the pain in my heart. I curled up in the bed and hugged my knees tightly to my chest, but it did little to stop the tidal wave of grief washing over me.

If he'd said, just the once, that I mattered more than any quest or key—or even the child we might have created—then perhaps the bitterness and anger would not have been so deep, and I wouldn't have banished him from my side. But he hadn't, and I had.

And now all I could do was try to figure out what had actually happened in the days that had followed his departure, and move on.

Because despite what he'd done, my task in *this* world had not changed. I still had keys to find, and I very much doubted whether the patience of either my father or the Raziq—the Aedh who'd jointly created the damn keys with my father before he'd stolen and then lost them—would hold for much longer.

Hell, it was surprising that one or both of them hadn't already appeared to slap me around in an effort to uncover what the hell had gone wrong *this* time.

But maybe they had no idea that I'd actually found the second key. After all, this time it had been stolen not only from under my nose, but *before* I'd managed to pinpoint its exact location. Which meant the thief—the same dark sorcerer who'd stolen the first key, and who'd permanently opened the first gateway to hell—wouldn't know which of the many military weapons he'd stolen was the second gate key in disguise. Thanks to the fact that my father's blood had been used in the creation of the three keys, only one of his blood could find them.

And I *would* find them. Without my reaper. Without my protector.

A sob rose up my throat, but I forced it back down. *Enough with the self-pity,* I told myself fiercely. *Enough with the wallowing. Get over it and move on.*

But that was easier said than done when my entire world had been turned upside down.

I scrubbed a hand across gritty eyes, then flipped the sheets off my face and finally looked around the room. It definitely wasn't a place I knew, and I very much doubted it was a hotel room. There were too many florals—the wallpaper, the bedding, and the cushions that had been thrown haphazardly on the floor all bore variations of a rose theme—and the furniture, though obviously expensive, had a well-used look about it. There was a window to my left, and the sunshine that peeked around the edges of the heavy pink curtains suggested it was close to midday.

Curious to see where I was, I got out of bed and walked over to the window. My movements were a little unsteady, but I suspected the cause was more a lack of food than any residual effect of my drinking binge. Alcohol cleared from a werewolf's system extremely fast, which was why it was so damn hard for us to get drunk. And *that* was definitely a good thing if I *was* pregnant, because it meant my desperate attempt to forget wouldn't have done any harm to my child.

I drew one curtain aside and looked out. In the yard below, a dozen or so chickens scratched around a pretty cottage garden. To the left of the garden were several outbuildings—one obviously an old stable, the other a large machinery shed—but to the right there was nothing but rolling hills that led up to a thick forest of gum trees.

It definitely *wasn't* somewhere familiar.

Frowning, I let the curtain fall back into place

and turned, my gaze sweeping the small room again. My clothes were stacked in a neat pile on the Georgian-style armchair, and flung over the back of it was a fluffy white dressing gown. Set on the nearby mahogany dressing table was a white towel, as well as bathroom necessities. Whoever owned this place at least didn't intend to keep me naked or unwashed. Whether they intended me other sorts of harm was another matter entirely.

Not.

The familiar, somewhat harsh tone ran through my mind and relief slithered through me. I might be without my reaper, but I still had my sword, so I wasn't entirely without protection. Amaya—the name of the demon trapped within the sword—was as alert and as ready for action as ever. The sword itself was shadow wreathed and invisible, so the only time anyone was truly aware of her presence was when I slid her dark blade into their flesh. Although she *did* have a tendency to be vocal about her need to kill, so she certainly could be heard on occasion— generally when she was about to kill someone.

What do you mean, not? I walked over to the Georgian chair and started dressing. Like the room itself, my clothes had a very slight floral scent, al- though this time it was lavender rather than rose, which was definitely easier on my nose.

Harm not, she replied. *Foe not.*

Which didn't mean whoever owned this place was a friend, but my sword had saved my butt more than once recently and I was beginning to trust her judgment.

Should, she muttered. *Stupid not.*

I grinned, not entirely sure whether she meant she wasn't stupid or that I'd be stupid not to trust her. I sat down on the chair to pull on my socks and boots, then headed for the door. It wasn't locked—another indicator that whoever had me didn't mean any harm—but I nevertheless peered out cautiously.

The hall beyond was thankfully free of the rose scent that had pervaded my room, and it was long, with at least a dozen doors leading off it. To the left, at the far end, was a wide window that poured sunshine into the space, lending the pale green walls warmth and richness. To the right lay a staircase. There were voices coming from the floor below, feminine voices, though I didn't immediately recognize them.

I hesitated, then mentally slapped myself for doing so and headed toward the stairs. My footsteps echoed on the wooden boards, and the rhythmic rise and fall of voices briefly stopped.

I'd barely reached the landing when quick steps approached the staircase from below. I paused on the top step and watched through the balusters. After a moment, a familiar figure strode into view and relief shot through me.

"Ilianna," I said. "Where the hell am I?"

She paused and looked up, a smile touching the corners of her green eyes. Ilianna was a shifter, and her human form echoed the palomino coloring of her horse form, meaning she had a thick mane of pale hair and dark golden skin. She was also a powerful witch, and one of the few people outside my adopted family I trusted implicitly. Tao, our flat-mate; Mirri, Ilianna's partner; and Stane, Tao's cousin, were the others.

"We're at Sable's winter retreat," she said. "And it's about time you woke up. I was beginning to think you intended to sleep the rest of your life away."

Sable was Mirri's mom. I'd met her only once, but I'd seen her often enough on TV. The woman was a cooking phenomenon, with two top-rated cooking shows behind her and a slew of books on herbs and healing still among the country's best-sellers. Mirri's dad, Kade, had worked with my aunt Riley years ago, but had unfortunately been killed in action when Mirri was little more than a baby. It had been Sable who had looked after his herd and kept them all together when he'd died.

"After the events of the last week or so, sleeping the rest of my life away certainly has its appeal." I couldn't help the grim edge in my voice. "Why the hell are we at Mirri's mom's rather than at home?"

"Because we figured a change of scenery might get you out of your funk. You coming down for lunch?"

"Funk" was definitely the *polite* description of what I'd been through the last few days. "Lunch would be good," I said, even as my stomach rumbled rather loudly.

Ilianna's eyebrows rose at the noise. I grinned and walked down the rest of the stairs, only to be enveloped in a hug so fierce I swear she was trying to squeeze the last drop of air from my lungs.

"God," she whispered. "It's good to have you back."

I blinked back the sting of tears and returned her hug. "I'm sorry, Ilianna. I didn't mean to worry you. I just—"

"Needed to cut loose a little," she finished for me. "I understand. More than anyone else ever could."

It was gently said, but nevertheless a reminder that I wasn't the only one who'd been played and abused. Guilt swirled through me and I pulled back, my gaze searching hers.

"Are you—"

"Yes," she said, interrupting before I could finish. "As I said in the hospital, my pregnancy was meant to be, even if the method of conception was both unforeseen *and* unwelcome. But we are *not* discussing me and my pregnancy right now."

I half smiled. No, we were discussing me and mine. "I've a feeling I'm about to be told off."

"Not told off. Just . . . warned."

Tension rolled through me. "About what?"

She hesitated. "While I understand your need to cut loose after everything that has happened recently, others do not, and they are looking for you. Specifically one person. And she's not someone any of us should piss off."

"Hunter." I practically spat the word.

Madeline Hunter was the head of the Directorate, a top-ranking member of the high vampire council, and a monster clothed in vampire skin. She was also, unfortunately, my boss, thanks to an agreement I'd made the day I'd scattered my mother's ashes.

Of course, that agreement technically no longer

stood, because I, not Hunter, had been the one to find and kill the man who'd murdered my mother. That man had been my Aedh lover, Lucian, who had managed to fool me in more ways than I was willing to think about. He'd not only been responsible for my mother's murder, but he'd also been involved in the theft of the keys.

And, as a parting gift, he'd kidnapped and impregnated Ilianna, and had tried to do the same to me.

I still wasn't sure that he hadn't succeeded, despite Azriel's statement that the child I apparently carried was his.

Ilianna grimaced. "Yeah. Tao's fobbed her off a couple of times now, but she's getting pretty scary."

Scary was a normal state for Hunter, but I certainly didn't want to piss her off any more than necessary. Not after what I'd seen her do to the dark spirit who'd murdered her lover.

Still, it was decidedly odd that she didn't know where I was. "Why would she be hassling Tao, or anyone else for that matter? She knows *exactly* what I'm doing every single minute of the day, thanks to the fucking Cazadors."

Cazadors were the high vampire council's kill squad, and they'd been following me about astrally for weeks, reporting my every move back to Hunter.

"In this case, she doesn't, because they *can't* follow you here." Ilianna tucked her arm through mine and escorted me down the hall.

I raised an eyebrow. "You've *spelled* the place?"

She nodded. "Mom found a spell that automatically redirects astral travelers every time they approach the spell's defined area."

Just astral travelers, not Aedh, I guessed. Which was logical given that the only spell we had to keep the Aedh out was the one we were using around our home, and that had originated from my father. Which meant my father and the Raziq could get to me here. I shivered and tried to ignore the premonition that I'd be confronting both far sooner than I wanted.

Still, some protection was better than nothing, and at least we could plan our next move without the Cazadors passing every little detail onto Hunter. "There wouldn't happen to be a mobile version of that spell, would there?"

"Unfortunately, no."

Of course not. Why on earth would fate throw me a lifeline like that? "Then I guess I'd better give the bitch a call ASAP."

And pray like hell she didn't have another job for me. I really didn't need to be chasing after escapees from hell right now—especially, I thought bleakly, when chasing hell-kind was all I had to look forward to in the long centuries after my death.

Besides, I needed to find the sorcerer and snatch the second key back. While he might not know which one of the items he'd stolen it was, there was nothing stopping him from taking them all to hell's gate and testing them out one by one.

And while my father and the Raziq had been relatively patient so far when it came to my lack of progress on the key front, I doubted that would last

They'd already threatened to destroy those I loved if I didn't find the keys. I wouldn't put it past any of them to actually kill someone close to me just to prove how serious they were.

As if tearing *me* apart to place the tracker in my heart hadn't already proved that.

"Calling her should definitely be a high priority," Ilianna agreed. "But come and eat first. You look like death warmed up."

No surprise there, given I nearly had been. "So what's stopping Hunter or the Cazadors from *physically* finding us?"

"She probably could, given enough time. While the spell is designed to confuse astral senses, they'd still have a general idea of location."

"But all she has to do is hack into my phone—"

"Which was left at home," Ilianna interrupted. "Along with anything else that could be used to track you. We're not that dumb."

No, they weren't. And Hunter was undoubtedly hassling Tao simply because she couldn't get to anyone else. Even *she* had more sense than to contact Aunt Riley. I might not be related to Riley by blood, but she and her pack were the only family I had left. They would not have reacted nicely to the news that Hunter was after me.

"Knowing Hunter as well as I now do, I'm surprised she hasn't done more than merely threaten him."

Hell, she probably considered a spot of bloody torture a good way to start the day. Although, given that Tao was rapidly losing the battle with the fire elemental he'd consumed, maybe I should've been hoping the bitch *did* attempt to torture him. Crispy-fried Hunter was a sight I wouldn't have minded seeing.

"She's given him until tonight to find you, so there's time. You need to regain some strength before you run off to confront that psycho bitch."

"Ain't that the truth," I muttered. "Especially now that I have to do it alone."

Ilianna hesitated, then said quietly, "Look, I don't know what actually went on between you and Azriel, but—"

Something twisted deep inside me. Pain rose, a knife-sharp wave that threatened to engulf me. *No,* I reminded myself fiercely, *you can't go there.* Not just yet. Not so soon after waking. I needed at least *some* time by myself to mull over the implications of my actions.

"Ilianna," I said, when I could, "leave it alone."

"But he wouldn't have left you—"

"He did, because he had no choice. I banished him." *How* I'd actually managed that, I had no idea. I mean, he was a reaper, a Mijai, and my telling him to leave me alone had never worked before. So why the change?

"Why the hell would you do that? Damn it, Ris, you need—"

"Ilianna," I warned, the edge deeper in my voice this time.

She drew in a breath, then released it slowly. "When you want to talk about it, I'll be here. But just remember one thing—he's not human. He's energy, not flesh, and he doesn't operate on the same emotional or intellectual levels as we do. But whatever he did, he did for a reason. A *good* reason. And no matter how absolute or final his actions may seem to you, it may not be a truth in his world."

"The truth," I replied, bitterness in my voice, "is that the keys were always first and foremost to him."

And I wanted more than that. Wanted him to feel about me the way I felt about him. But was love an emotion reapers were even capable of?

I blinked at the thought. I *loved* him. Not just cared for him, but *loved* him. How or when it had happened, I had no idea. It wasn't like love and I were on familiar terms. Quite the opposite really, given the only other man I'd loved had been Jak — the werewolf reporter who was one of the people we'd pulled in to help with our key search — and that had turned out to be a complete and utter disaster.

Maybe love and I just weren't meant to be.

Ilianna said, "I would not be so — "

"Ilianna," I warned yet again.

She sighed, then pushed open the door and ushered me through. The twin scents of curry and baking bread hit, making my mouth water and my stomach rumble even louder than before.

The room itself was a kitchen bigger than our entire apartment. The country-style cabinets wrapped around three of the four walls, providing massive amounts of storage and preparation space, and there were six ovens and four stovetops. A huge wooden table that could seat at least thirty people dominated the middle of the room, and it was at this that Sable, Mirri, and two other women sat.

They glanced around as we entered. Sable smiled and rose. In both human and horse form she was a stunningly beautiful woman, with black skin and brown eyes that missed very little. Mirri, a mahogany bay when in horse form, had taken after her dad.

"Risa, I'm so glad you've recovered." Sable kissed both my cheeks, then stood back and examined me somewhat critically. "Although you do need some condition on you. You, my girl, are entirely too thin."

I smiled. "Werewolves tend to be on the lean side."

"Not this lean, I'll wager. The ladies and I are just about to go out, but there's a curry in the oven and the bread should be done in about five minutes."

"Thank you—"

She cut me off with a wave of her hand. "Ilianna is family, and her family is my family. So please, don't be thanking me for something we'd do for anyone in the herd."

I smiled. At least Mirri's mom had accepted her relationship with Ilianna. The same couldn't be said of Ilianna's parents—although I personally thought they *would* come round if they actually knew about it. But Ilianna refused to even tell them she was gay.

Sable collected her coat and bag from the back of one of the chairs, and then she and the two women retreated out the sliding glass door.

I raised an eyebrow and glanced at Mirri. "That felt like a deliberate retreat."

Mirri grabbed a couple of tea towels and rose. "I told them you and Ilianna needed some alone time for a war council when you woke up."

"War council? Sorry, but whatever I do next—"

"You're *not* doing alone." Ilianna grabbed some plates from a nearby cupboard and began setting the table for the three of us. "Azriel may be gone, but Tao and I are still here. And we're a part of this now, Risa, whether you like it or not."

I didn't like it. Not at all. She and Tao had been through enough because of me and this damn quest. I wasn't about to put them through anything else. But I also knew that tone of voice. It was no use arguing—not that that ever stopped me from trying.

"The first thing I have to do is find the damn sorcerer who stole the key, and that's not something I want you involved with. It's too dangerous, Ilianna."

"Maybe," Ilianna said, giving me a somewhat severe look. "But the Brindle is more than capable of taking care of a dark sorcerer. There aren't that many in Melbourne, you know, and they'd be aware of all of them."

The Brindle was the home of all witch knowledge, both ancient and new. Ilianna's mom was one of the custodians there, and Ilianna was powerful enough to have become one—and in fact had started the training when she was younger. She'd walked away for reasons she refused to discuss, but if the predictions of the head witch, Kiandra, were to be believed, not only would Ilianna one day finish that training, but her daughter would save the Brindle.

"Yeah," I said, "but given Lucian was probably working with him, he'll know about my connection to both you and the Brindle." I grimaced, then added, "I'd bet my ass he's taken steps to ensure you—and they—can't find him."

"But it would take *major* magic to achieve something like that, and that in itself can also be traced."

Undoubtedly. But it still meant dragging more people into the search, and I really didn't want to do that unless absolutely necessary. It was just too damn dangerous.

"It's an option." I sat down. "But it wouldn't be my first."

Ilianna placed the hot bread on the table. "Why not? There's no easier way to find a sorcerer than to trace his magic."

"A normal sorcerer, perhaps. But this one has been working with an Aedh, and has probably acquired much of his knowledge." Which was another reason to be glad Lucian was dead. At least the bastard couldn't pass anything else on to our ever-elusive sorcerer. "Besides, our best option right now is to go through Lucian's things and see if he left any clues behind."

Mirri snorted as she began dishing out the huge chunks of curried vegetables—which wasn't normally a favorite of mine, but it smelled incredible. "Forgive me for stating the obvious, but you've been on a bender for three days. That would have given our sorcerer plenty of time to go through Lucian's things and ditch whatever evidence there might have been."